CARVER

CARVER

High Mountain Tragedy

C. H. FOERTMEYER

Writers Club Press
San Jose New York Lincoln Shanghai

Carver
High Mountain Tragedy

Writers Club Press
an imprint of iUniverse, Inc.

For information address:
iUniverse, Inc.
5220 S. 16th St., Suite 200
Lincoln, NE 68512
www.iuniverse.com

This is a work of fiction. All events, locations, institutions, themes, persons, characters and plot are completely fictional. Any resemblance to places or persons living or deceased, are of the invention of the author.

ISBN: 0-595-21686-2

Printed in the United States of America

For Jennifer—For her inspiration—

Grade school and high school are merely stopping off places in our lives. No matter how cruel you may be treated, remember that there is a whole life awaiting you beyond your current experience.

Contents

Foreword

In regard to the location of this novel, it exists only in the mind of this author. Hopefully, the reader will find Carver, Oriel Peak, and Blind Valley as intriguing as I do.

To go in search of these wondrous places would be to search in vain, but perhaps, somewhere out in the Rocky Mountains there may be places similar in description and mystique. The valley described as Karl and Alicia's private valley, does indeed exist, in New Mexico. It is an oasis, of sorts, in the Doña Ana Mountains of Doña Ana County. It has been over twenty–eight years since I've been there, so I'm not sure I could ever find it again, but it is there, for you to search out, if you so desire.

As to the characters in *Carver*, they are also the creation of the author, but children like Wiley and Kevin live everywhere among us. Normal kids whose lives have been turned into a nightmare by the insensitivity and cruelty of their classmates. Be aware of them and try to help them understand that with the passing of time, they will be accepted, and even cherished by their peers.

C. H. Foertmeyer

CHAPTER 1

"Spider"—Kevin Reynolds had grown up with this name and had grown used to it, or had he?

Kevin was born, Kevin Wilson Reynolds on December 23, 1951 in the small mountain town of Carver, Montana. Kevin's birth came at a time when parents of young and infant children had one major concern, polio, often referred to as infantile paralysis, and it had parents all over the country scared to death.

The disease had been declared an epidemic yet the odds of contracting it were only one in five thousand. This was enough however, to send families from coast to coast scurrying to the mountains or deserts or anywhere else they thought they might escape the scourge.

The Reynolds family was not overly concerned with this epidemic because they were already in the mountains away from the big cities and their blight. They lived in God's Country and felt relatively isolated from the problems, which beset the flatlanders in the cities below. This all changed for them in December of 1954 when their precious Kevin was diagnosed with polio.

Kevin's parents, Buck and Nancy, were terrified for Kevin, picturing him spending his life in a wheelchair or in braces. And then, of course, there was the guilt. How could this happen? They were isolated up here in Carver! But then Nan would remind Buck that he had taken Kevin to Liddelman with him on business several times.

Buck would shrug and accept the blame saying, "I know, I probably shouldn't have done that," and Nancy would hug him in a consoling embrace and think to herself that her shopping trips to Bennett were just as likely to have been the cause. *Had she really needed to go to Bennett?*

But Kevin was a trooper and came through the disease well, with very little physical damage. It wasn't until Kevin started school that the effects of the disease would become apparent to him.

The most noticeable effect of his childhood disease was his lack of normal locomotion. When he was forced to run, which he did with great reluctance, he had quite an unusual gate. His legs didn't seem to follow the usual up and down motion of a more normal runner. They would flail out on the upstroke and in on the down and his body always seemed to be trying to catch up with his outstretched legs.

The other kids were quick to associate his movements with that of a spider scurrying across hot blacktop. In reality, this peculiar motion didn't truly resemble a running spider, but that's the way the other kids saw it and they had no compunction about saying so. By the time Kevin reached high school the name Spider had become universally and indelibly associated with him.

High school in the late 1960's was no different than high school today and students then had no more compassion for the feelings of fellow students than they presently do. You could be merely a geek, a nerd, or a dip, or with the right deformity you could get your very own identity. Spider was just such a case.

Gym class was a particular Hell for Kevin, although the abuses he suffered there were by no means limited to that class.

Kevin could and did walk normally, but if he dared break into a run all hell would break loose—"S–P–I–D–E–R...SPIDER"! Spelling out the word in a rising crescendo and finishing off the chant at the top of their lungs with a final "SPIDER"! Then, of course, it needed to be repeated as many times as the closest teacher would allow. Verbal abuse *was* a major part of the daily life of Kevin "Spider" Reynolds, and summer and weekends were gifts from Heaven.

Even–keeled would pretty well describe Kevin. He got good grades, didn't drink or smoke, and never caused anyone any trouble, not even his parents. He was obedient and pleasant to be around, friendly and helpful around the house. In short, he was a good kid.

Apart from his peculiar gate he was a rather normal looking kid, standing an even six feet tall with straight blonde hair, worn in Beatle fashion, as was common around his school. He was a lean one hundred and seventy–five pounds of mostly muscle, and he could flash you a most ingratiating smile when amused.

Kevin did have two friends and they were pretty good friends, too, but both were also considered members of the general geek population of Carver High. Bryce and Wiley, each of which was an only child, had only each other and Kevin to serve as friends and companions. Kevin had an older sister, Carrie, up until the fall of last year when she had been killed in an automobile accident.

Carrie had been extremely popular at Carver High, but that had been before Kevin had moved up from middle school. He never had the opportunity to ride her coattails to popularity and she had long since graduated, so to the current kids at Carver, Carrie had never existed.

Carver High was a small school serving the community of ten thousand full time residents and everybody at school knew everybody else. It was not unusual to see seniors associating with sophomores or freshmen hanging out with juniors. But Kevin didn't associate with anyone he didn't have to, suffering all the abuse he could handle at the hands of his fellow seniors. Why go looking for more trouble, he reasoned. But Kevin was used to it. Years of the same experiences, being constantly messed with or messed up, had hardened him to it. But nevertheless, it never stopped hurting.

Carver High was the only high school in the alpine city of Carver. The building was modern and new, a replacement for the older, more charming building which was to become the middle school. The city leaders had decided to build the new school in Greenville, on the east side of the Saline River, where they had anticipated growth and development, which had not yet occurred.

The city of Carver was the very picture of alpine beauty, nestled into a high mountain valley, surrounded by three prominent peaks and subdivided by the Saline River flowing south through the heart of town.

Mount Crane stood to the east, rising to eleven thousand feet and towering four thousand feet above Carver. Jessup Mountain, which had replaced Crane as the resort area several years prior, rose forty–five hundred feet over the city and was responsible for the majority of Carver's revenue. The third peak, forming the trio, was Horse Tooth. This third peak had derived its name from the cubical appearance of its summit, which if one imagined hard enough, might resemble what the name implied. Horse Tooth was the short-est of the group stretching to reach its taller companions but falling short by several hundred feet.

The Saline River, a fast moving mountain stream, fed by perpetual snowfields and the spring melt, emanated above the resorts high up on Jessup Mountain. To the east of the Saline lay Greenville, so named for the rancher who first settled that side of the river, and to the west of the river was Carver proper.

Both sides of the Saline were actually Carver, but when Uriah Green's last living descendant passed on, Carver had annexed the area for itself. It had been know as Greenville ever since.

Two concrete rainbow bridges, the Upper and Lower Saline Bridges, connected Greenville to Carver, the Lower Bridge being the more heavily used, as it carried one directly into downtown Carver. The bridges were unique and an effort to have them listed in the state's historic register was underway. The two bridges were identical, with a concrete, rainbow shaped arch on either side of the bridges and pedestrian walkways outside each arch. Vehicular traffic passed between the arches in two lanes.

As you approached Carver from any of three routes in from the mountain passes you looked down on what appeared to be a pristine alpine village almost fairytale like in appearance. Coming down into town, and upon closer inspection, there were evident signs of the town's depressed state.

There were city streets in need of repair, buildings needing paint, and other telltale signs that the town was in need of a more substantial treasury. But the Jessup Mountain resorts had done a lot to improve things over the past three years and revenue was slowly starting to find it's way into Carver.

So Carver, situated comfortably in this cradle of alpine beauty, with its hiking, skiing, and hunting opportunities, should have been a wonderful place for a boy to grow up. And it was so for Kevin, as long as school wasn't in session.

Bryce Spencer was one of Kevin's two friends and lived just two blocks from Kevin, on Cutter's Lane. They were closer friends to each other than they were to anybody else. They were best friends.

Bryce never achieved the status of Kevin at school. He had no fancy nickname and no distinguishing characteristics other than fiery red hair. He was just a geek who went by the most common and mundane of names, such as Dipstick and Pinhead. "Carrot Top" or "Fire Head" were not names used in the Carver area to describe someone with hair like Bryce's. It was far too common a trait in Carver, having come from the original Coates family stock. In Carver you were more likely to be teased over black hair, than you were red.

So Bryce had gone through his life so far, as a *typical* geek, neither special nor distinguished. What got him in trouble with the other kids at school was his straight–laced, almost Puritanical attitude.

Bryce lived by one set of rules, imparted to him by his father. *"This is how life is lived–"* according to Dirk Spencer. There was no circumventing the rules, no bending the rules, and certainly, no breaking these rules!

Bryce was fine with it all, neither questioning nor defying his father's wisdom. You did not cheat, steal, lie, or in any other way go against the word of God. It was a simple plan for happiness and tranquility within their home and as a guideline for their daily lives.

Another important lesson that had come to Bryce, by way of his father, was that you *never looked the other way*, when others transgressed. There was no room in this world for apathy toward, or tolerance for the willful breech of God's Word.

So Bryce adhered to these rules, to a fault, and was therefore neither liked nor trusted by his fellow students. Their dislike and mistrust of him was something he simply could not fathom because life was supposed to be simple and well defined, with *everyone* doing, as they should and following the rules.

Bryce was the kid the teacher would ask to watch the class if she had to leave the room. Bryce was one of the hall monitors. He was honest and beyond reproach. Put simply, the other kids didn't trust him. They knew if he overheard their plans to do something irresponsible or wrong, he would squeal. If he saw someone cheating, he would tell. That was Bryce and it helped earn him his rep as a Carver nerd. Did he care? Not at all. His allegiance was to his two best friends, Kevin and Wiley. They accepted him just as he was.

Then there was Wiley Coates, Kevin's other best friend. If Bryce was heads on a coin, Wiley was tails. He was not as close to Kevin as was Bryce, but they were good friends and buddies. Wiley *had* achieved a status of his own. He was "Taxi"—"Hey Taxi! Better shut your doors!" or "Dumbo" to others—"Hey Dumbo! Have a smooth landing!" Yes, Wiley's ears stuck straight out from his head, a feature not overlooked or ignored by his classmates.

Wiley was different though, and didn't take the abuse as calmly as did Kevin and Bryce. Wiley had a short fuse and could be a smart ass at times. He never started trouble or instigated pranks, but when teased in public, he would turn as red as his own hair, and spit out some pretty harsh rebuttals. This earned him more than his share of razzing because his reaction would be, predictably, what the other kids wanted.

Take the Tuesday Wiley had returned to school, after missing Monday with a bad cold. He had arrived ten minutes before homeroom was to begin, going directly to his locker as usual. He had dialed the combination on his padlock, 27 Right, 47 Left, 16 Right, and had jerked the lock open.

He suddenly got a funny feeling, like he was being watched, and looked over his shoulder. There were several kids gathering at the other side of the hall, watching him as he removed the lock from its hasp.

They were standing there, trying to look inconspicuous, but it didn't look to Wiley like they were simply having a conversation. The kids were whispering among themselves and their eyes kept darting to him and glancing quickly away.

Wiley looked back at his locker and lifted the latch, which should have allowed the door to swing open freely. Usually the door would pop out toward him, as if on springs. It did not. He gave it a tug. Nothing happened and the door remained closed, fixed in place. He gave it a second tug; this time harder, and again it failed to budge.

By now Wiley was hearing the familiar sounds of snickering behind him. Determined to ignore them and not be duped again, he gave the door one last pull. It did not yield, and he had pulled with such force that his fingers lost their grip on the handle. He reeled backward, dropping his books, stumbled, and gained his balance just in time to avoid falling on his butt. The laughter started, outright and full.

Wiley spun on the small crowd and began screaming, his face red and twisted.

"Get the crap away from me you stupid jerks!" he yelled. "Who the hell do you think you are?"

The onlookers scattered in five different directions, running and looking back at Wiley, laughing and jeering. Wiley stood there, in the middle of the hallway, alone and angry.

Bastards, he thought, and then stooped to pick up his books.

Later, the resolution to his dilemma came in the form of a janitor who replaced his locker. Even the janitor couldn't pry open the locker door and Wiley's belongings had to be removed from the back of the locker, after the locker was removed from the wall.

Needless to say, the janitor was no more pleased than was Wiley.

"Who'd have done a thing like this?" the janitor asked. "Gluing your locker with epoxy glue. Damn those kids, anyway. Just makes a lot more work for me!"

Wiley *was* quick tempered and lashed out frequently, but he had always been 'all mouth'. The other kids simply saw him as humorous and harmless. But he also had a dark side, which neither Kevin, nor Bryce quite understood and the other kids never saw.

He would sulk for hours, wandering off alone, after one of his verbal retaliations to a prank or joke at his expense. His face would change, distorting into something Kevin considered strange and scary. He would turn within himself, withdrawn for hours, then shake it off and return to the Wiley that Kevin considered his friend.

After Wiley would return from wherever he had been and whatever thoughts he had been thinking, it was as if nothing had happened at all. This behavior of his was of concern to Kevin, but he knew how it felt to be ridiculed daily and he figured that this was Wiley's way of dealing with it.

The relationship between Bryce and Wiley was much the same as that between Kevin and Bryce. They too, were best friends. So it was Bryce who was loved by both Kevin and Wiley. He was the boy in the middle of the triad of friends. Bryce was the friend that cemented the three friends together, and it was also Bryce who would become the catalyst for life changing events to come.

Kevin may have grown up to lead a relatively normal life had it not been for Bryce, for it was Bryce, or rather what happened to Bryce, which was to change the course of Kevin "Spider" Reynolds' life. It would change his life and it would change Wiley's as well.

From that day on, Wiley and Kevin would become inseparable. Best friends. From that day on they would have a common goal. Beginning on that cold and miserable, second day of November, their lives would become as one, intertwined and with common purpose. But it would be Wiley, who would fan the flames of hatred, and keep the goal alive and in focus.

CHAPTER 2

Kevin, Wiley and Bryce, the "Three Mountaineers", as they had referred to themselves in their younger years, were inseparable. They had formed a coalition, which helped insulate them from the abuse they suffered at the hands of their fellow classmates. They resided in a world of their own creation, where they were safe and comfortable, apart from, yet parallel to, Carver. It was an after school and weekend world, where they could retreat from the cruelty and injustice of Carver High and its student population.

Their parallel world had geographical boundaries, like any other world might have. Some of these boundaries were physical and rigid, one other, flexible and ever expanding. The three main physical areas of their world were their bedrooms, where they would retreat for hours, talking, playing games, and making big plans for the future. One day it might be Kevin's bedroom, on another, Bryce's or Wiley's. It really didn't matter, as long as they were together.

The fourth fixed geographical location in their world was their shack, which was located in the forest behind Kevin's house. It was constructed of scrap lumber provided by Cutter's Mill and obtained by Kevin's father, at the boys' request. The "shack", as the boys referred to it, was neatly constructed about two hundred yards behind the Reynolds home. It was not visible from the neighborhood and the homes on Birch were not visible from it. It was their place totally away from every place else, where they could wile away the hours after school or on Saturdays and Sundays, undisturbed and sheltered.

The shack itself was square in shape, measuring ten feet on each side, and seven feet high at the top of the single pitched roof. The roof was constructed of the same rough sawn planks as were the sidewalls, and a duck canvas tarp had been affixed over it to keep the rain and snow at bay. The floor, made of the same wooden planks, had been laid first and the windowless shack had been built around it.

The truly unique feature was the shack's entrance with its three–foot tall door, which made entry possible on one's hands and knees only, and was neatly tucked between two large rhyolite outcrops. A ten to twelve foot approach down a two–foot wide corridor between the rock monoliths was necessary to reach the door. Then one was required to drop to their knees, unlock the padlock, and push the door open to gain entry.

The boys had built their shack up against these two twelve foot high stones, positioning the entrance, squarely behind and between them. To approach the shack from the neighborhood side was to likely overlook it. Approach to it from the forest side was nearly impossible, as the mountain swept up sharply behind it.

Inside the retreat there was a table and chairs, hand–me–downs from each of the boy's families, a throw rug beneath it all, and a lantern, suspended from the ceiling on a brass chain. It was cozy and secure, although there was no heat source for the colder days of winter. They had nailed tarpaper on the interior walls to keep out the bitter winter winds and the wind blown rains, but the cold during the winter months was a problem that limited their time there.

The fifth geographical location in their private world was the forests themselves. This was the flexible portion of their world, the portion they were constantly expanding. Every hunting or camping trip to a new location increased the territory they had laid claim to. As they had grown older and obtained "wheels", this boundary had expanded rapidly, providing even more insulating distance between them and their antagonists at Carver High.

As this new territory had become accessible to them, they had spent far less time at the shack, and it had begun to fall into disrepair. This bothered Wiley more than Kevin or Bryce, because for Wiley, the shack had always been more vital to his happiness and well being. The shack had always provided a haven from his father's drinking and his mother's crying. Home, for Wiley, was a lonely place and not always a very pleasant place to be. The shack, to him, was not about play, but survival.

The last week of October had ushered in some unseasonably mild weather, which had come as a relief to the previous five weeks of snow and cold. The base snow was in place for the start of the skiing season on Jessup Mountain, and that was all that mattered to the community. But the warm up had started Wiley thinking about the shack again.

As he, Kevin and Bryce, walked home from school, Thursday afternoon on the thirty–first, Wiley brought up the subject of the shack and its need for repairs.

"You know what I've been thinking about?" he began.

"What's that," Kevin asked, as Bryce also directed his attention to Wiley.

"I've been thinking about the shack. We haven't been back there in months and the last time we were, it needed some help. We should head back there today and do a little fixing up. Hell, what better way to spend Halloween than doing that!"

"Yea," said Kevin. "Can't let it get too run down, I guess. That's a good idea Wiley! What do you say, Bryce? Want to go back there today?"

"Sure, that's fine with me. We'll need to stop by your house, Kev, and get a hammer and some nails. The tarpaper was coming loose in several places the last time we were back there," he pointed out.

"And a candle, too," Wiley said.

"What do we need that for?" asked Bryce.

"There are a few small holes in the roof tarp that were leaking last spring. We can drip candle wax over them and seal them up," Wiley explained to him.

"Anybody have their key with them?" Kevin asked.

"I do," Wiley and Bryce answered, simultaneously.

"Good, because mine is back in my locker at school. I didn't think I'd be needing it until spring," he explained to the others.

"So it's settled then?" asked Wiley.

"Yep," Kevin replied.

"Sure, sounds like fun," answered Bryce.

The boys continued toward Kevin's house, their plans set for the restoration and improvement of the shack. It was understood by the boys' parents that they would be together, someplace, until suppertime, so there was no need to check in or get permission as long as they were on foot and home in time for their evening meal. If they were driving somewhere, there was a different set of rules that applied.

Of the three boys, Kevin was the only one who owned his own car, a black, 1960 Chevrolet Biscayne. It was a six cylinder with a "three–on–the–tree" shifter. He had earned the money for its purchase over the past summer by working at the mill with his father. The purchase had been made from old "Chief" Hailstones at Sleet's Fleet Auto Sales on the outskirts of Greenville.

"Chief" Hailstones was a native Blackfoot Indian, who had made a good living for himself selling used vehicles on the "Payday Plan", years ahead of its time. He generally had about a dozen good used vehicles on his lot at any given time, and Kevin had been watching the lot weekly, looking for just the right car.

Then one day, while riding with his dad on a lumber delivery, *there it was!* He had decided, right then and there, that he had to have it. There was just something about those big, horizontal fins that had intrigued him. He had talked his dad into stopping and loaning him a down payment on the Biscayne, and had driven it away, a happy camper. Every payday, for the following eight weeks, he had stopped by Sleet's and made a fifty–dollar payment. The car was now his.

He had so much looked forward to driving to school, but he rarely did so now. There were two reasons for this, each of which out-weighed the luxury of driving, forcing the boys to trudge through the winter snow.

First, and foremost, leaving the car at home deprived his adversar-ies at school of the opportunity to trash it for him. He had learned this lesson the first week back to school.

He had come out to the parking lot on the third day back, to find his "new" Chevy, "keyed" from stem to stern. The scratch was deep and straight, as if someone had walked past the car while holding a key waist high and had dragged it along the finish. Needless to say, he had been livid and had wanted to strangle the bastard that had done it.

On the fourth day back, he left the building to find his Biscayne covered in dried egg. He had found it necessary to use his ice scraper to remove the dried goop from his windshield, in order to drive home. *That* had been the last day Kevin had allowed himself the lux-ury of driving to school. From that point on, he had chosen to walk the mile to school rather than subject his beautiful Biscayne to the abuse of his "loving" classmates.

The second reason for not driving to school was simply a matter of economics. He was no longer working at the mill, as they had lain off all part–time workers. When school began Kevin was forced out of a job, so his gas money being in short supply, he preferred to save it for hunting and camping trips to the wilderness.

Arriving at Kevin's house the boys entered the side door to the kitchen, and procured a snack from Mrs. Reynolds. Finishing that, they gathered the tools and nails they would need for the repairs, and a candle and matches for Wiley. With all necessary supplies collected, they headed out the back patio door.

Kevin's back yard was about seventy–five feet deep from the patio to the forest, and beyond that was the densely forested foot of Mount Crane. Kevin's back yard lay right up against the unused west slope of the mountain. For a seventeen–year–old boy, who loved the forests and mountains, it was truly a picture perfect place to live. He had virtually grown up in the woods behind his house, learning to hunt with his pellet rifle, trap small game, and navigate the deer trails to wherever he wanted to go.

And so, the triad of friends began yet another trek into the familiar trees that concealed the fourth dimension of their world. They would refurbish the work of their youth, recounting old stories and revisiting old memories laid dormant until now.

They crossed Kevin's back yard and disappeared into the world of the ancient Indians, mountain men, and explorers. It was a world they rarely ever wanted to leave, once they had settled in, and Kevin's dinner bell was the only signal they ever acknowledged as reason to depart.

"How long has it been since we've been back here?" Bryce asked, stepping around the base of a giant balsam.

"Too long," replied Wiley.

"Think anybody has messed with it since then?" Bryce asked, always the talkative one in the group.

"I doubt it," Kevin answered. "Nobody knows it's here but us and the critters."

"I hope not," Bryce said. "I still want it to be just our place."

Upon arriving at the entrance between the outcrops, Wiley went in first.

"Seems narrower than it used to," he commented.

"Bryce, who had grown substantially over the summer, replied, "You're not kidding! This seems a lot tighter than it did before!"

Wiley knelt down before the door to their private domain and inserted the key in the lock. He gave it a quick turn and the lock popped open. Removing the lock from its hasp, he pushed the door inward and crawled into the darkness of his liberation. Kevin and Bryce followed in silence, speaking not a single word, as that was the way Wiley had always liked it to be. It was a ritual he had created years ago to initiate their transformation from schoolboys, to mountain men, for *that* is what they became when they entered this place.

Once inside, they lit the lantern and a soft yellow glow filled the tarpapered room. Wiley said the magic words, which always began their stay in "the shack":

"Oh great ghost of Jim Bridger and friends. We have arrived at rendezvous. We ask only for the warmth of your fire and the pleasure of your company. If you've a mind to share, your coffee smells inviting and your stew, delicious. Are we welcome at your fire?"

With the welcoming message spoken, Kevin and Bryce replied in unison.

"Welcome, mountain men. Join us at our fire and share in our bounty. Have you traveled far? What sights have you seen? Come, sit and tell us of your journeys."

With that, they all broke into laughter. It had been so long since they had done this and it felt so good to be back. Why, they wondered, had they let their maturation into young men get in the way of visiting this most wonderful of places.

They made a pact, then and there, not to let it happen again. This *world* of theirs was too special and unique to ever let it slip away. They put to work immediately, nailing up the fallen tarpaper, sealing the leaky roof, and dusting from the table and chairs, the accumulation of lost time.

It had been a glorious and joyful afternoon, filled with wonderful memories of the past and plans for the future. They had talked of future hikes in the Los Lobos, past trips to Robinson Ridge, and they had talked about their futures after Carver High. It had been an afternoon, which had sealed their commitment to one another and had belonged to them alone.

Kevin's dinner bell had rung—much too soon.

CHAPTER 3

❁

*T*he three boys did not share all the same classes, so it was impossible to stick together throughout the whole school day, although they certainly wished they could. The lunch periods at Carver High were staggered, so except for Kevin and Bryce, the three boys were split up even then. Kevin and Bryce did have each other's companionship at lunch, Wiley being the unfortunate one who had to eat alone.

Today, as Bryce and Kevin selected their seats at the back of the cafeteria, Kevin noticed Mary and Alicia sitting not ten feet away at an adjacent table. They were laughing and talking with each other about *who knew what* and justifiably, Kevin's paranoia kicked in and he was sure they were discussing Bryce and him.

"Damn," he said to Bryce, nodding toward the girls. "Look who's here…"

Bryce looked in the direction Kevin had indicated and shot a scowl back at Kevin.

"Can't even eat lunch in peace," he commented.

It was a scene that played out several times each month, on the days when they arrived late in the lunchroom and had little choice where they would sit. Today was just one of those unfortunate days.

Mary *had* noticed the boys sit down and Kevin had been right on the money in his paranoia; the girls had begun talking about them.

"Don't look now but dumb and dumber just sat down over there," Mary pointed out to Alicia.

"Yea, I saw them," Alicia answered.

"They really should have a separate room for those creeps to eat in," Mary spat. "It grosses me out to have to look at them while I eat. Especially that little drip, Bryce, the suck up snitch."

Alicia nodded in agreement with Mary's snide comments.

Mary made no attempt to keep her voice low; hoping Bryce would hear her, which he did.

"Did you hear that?" Bryce asked Kevin.

"Yep. Just ignore her Bryce, you did right. She's just pissed she got caught. Don't pay any attention to her," Kevin advised, through bites of his meal.

"Yea, I guess," Bryce said, shaking his head.

Strange as it may seem, of all the kids who gave the boys trouble, their chief antagonists were these two girls. Mary Clemmons and Alicia Koppe, who were as different as night and day, but seemed to share a common purpose in life; making the boys as miserable as could be humanly possible.

Mary was the debutante, born of wealthy parents. She and her family resided on the *right* side of the river, in the area of Carver referred to as "Pill Hill", the name derived from the fact that most of the local doctors lived there.

Mary could be aptly described as spoiled and took her position as a resident of Pill Hill far too seriously. Call it a superiority complex; if you will, but Mary believed, no she *knew* she was better than all of the other kids. Considering that she was a beautiful girl, with strong features, natural blonde hair, pristine blue eyes, as well as being tall and lean, and you had the makings of one conceited little girl.

Alicia, on the other hand, was from the Greenville side of the river, the daughter of a local shopkeeper. She was pretty, but petite. Her olive skin and dark brown hair went in perfect harmony with her cordovan brown eyes. Alicia was quiet, unassuming and shy.

Whatever social strength she possessed, she drew from her friend-ship with Mary. If Mary wasn't around, neither was Alicia, even when she was there in the room. But as different as their back-grounds and personalities were, they were united in cause. They were the self–appointed demons of Spider, Taxi, and the dipstick.

But for right now, Bryce was Mary's principal target. She had always given him a hard way to go, but ever since *the incident*, she had really grown to despise and torment him.

Bryce had always taken the other kid's criticisms the hardest of the three boys, and lately he seemed to be singled out by Mary for her most vehement wrath. He knew why, but he truly couldn't under-stand it. In his world of truths and principles, near the top of the list was *"You do not cheat!"* Mary had, and he had caught her.

Kevin noticed that Bryce had fallen silent and had withdrawn into private thoughts, probably about the rough time Mary had been giv-ing him since he turned her in for cheating. He decided to try to take his mind off the problem.

"Hey! Are you ready to go skiing tomorrow? It's supposed to turn cold again, so the shack is out for Saturday. Let's go skiing instead," Kevin suggested.

"Sure! Which slope do you want to go to? The lifts won't be run-ning on Crane, you know. Cougar is probably the easiest to climb up to the top of."

The thought of going skiing was working. Bryce perked right up at the chance to get away to the slopes.

"Okay then. You picked it, so that's the one we'll go to. Cougar, here we come!" Kevin confirmed. "I'll pick you up so be on your curb at six so we can get up there before anyone else," Kevin instructed. "We can ask Wiley about going after school."

Kevin and Bryce finished their lunches, chatting about this and that, and left the cafeteria as quickly as they could. They were glad to escape the cold, hateful stares Mary was shooting their way from the next table over.

Mary had been silently eavesdropping on the boys' conversation throughout their meal, something she was not above doing upon occasion; any occasion.

"Did you hear what Kevin said Alicia?" Mary asked.

"About going skiing?" Alicia asked.

"Yes. About going skiing tomorrow morning. I think I've got a way to get back at that little Spencer punk, if you're game?"

"Depends. What do you have in mind?" asked Alicia, wanting to know what was up Mary's sleeve before committing.

"Tomorrow morning, we get up early and get up to the Cougar slope before they do. We lay a trap for Spencer, one that will mess him up good," Mary plotted.

"You're crazy! We'd have to leave at five a.m., which means I'd have to get up at four on a *Saturday morning*! That's nuts!"

"Damn it, Alicia! When will we ever get a better chance to get even with him? He's right in the palm of my hand now! I know where he'll be and when, and I'm going to be there to screw him over, somehow! Now are you in or not?" Mary asked, forcefully.

"Okay. I'll do it, but four o'clock is awfully damn early to be getting up on a Saturday morning. What exactly do you have in mind for him? It had better be good with all the sleep I'll be losing!"

"Oh–it will be good, you can bank on that," Mary assured her.

Friday afternoon, the weather *had* changed, once again, to the winter cold everyone in Carver expected for early November. Yesterday's relative warmth of the shack would be gone today, and probably for weeks to come. As the boys made their way home from school, crossing the Upper Saline Bridge, Kevin mentioned the skiing trip to Wiley.

"We can go to Cougar, bright and early, and have it all to ourselves," he urged Wiley. "I'll drive, and we can leave at six. We'll be there by six forty five and get started."

"The lifts won't be running," Wiley reminded him.

"So we'll hike it to the top. We've done it before, besides, were doing Cougar, which isn't that hard a hike. Bryce is all for it, aren't you Bryce?"

Bryce nodded his affirmation.

"Cougar was his idea. Come on, Wiley," Kevin pleaded.

"I don't know," Wiley said. "It's getting pretty cold and a storm is due in tomorrow. That's what I saw on the weather last night. Maybe we should wait until next Saturday and see what the weather does."

"Come on, Wiley! What's the matter with you? Since when does a little cold and snow stop a mountain man from going where he pleases?" Kevin encouraged him, calling upon Wiley's sense of manhood to sway his decision.

"Okay, I'm game," Wiley relented. "What time will you pick me up?"

"Six o'clock, sharp. Be waiting at the curb," Kevin instructed. "I'll pick you up first Wiley, and then I'll swing by your place, Bryce, and get you."

They continued their walk home, deciding to go to Kevin's house and play Pong on Kevin's Atari. It was getting too cold to venture back to the shack and hang out there for any length of time.

On Saturday morning Kevin showed up at each of the other boy's homes, right on schedule. They liked to hit the ski slope early on Saturday mornings before any other kids showed up, not that many, if any, would. They had decided on the Cougar Run on Mount Crane because it *was* little used, and easily accessible when the lifts weren't running. They knew the lifts wouldn't be running Saturday morning because ever since the new slopes were constructed on Jessup Mountain, the Mount Crane slopes were all but abandoned. They were primarily just overflow slopes now, used by the locals when the holiday skiers would come to town on Thanksgiving and Christmas, swarming Jessup Mountain.

The boys had learned a lot about self-preservation throughout the course of their high school careers. Now that they were seniors, they pretty much had it all figured out. What it all boiled down to was *avoidance*. Avoiding the other kids allowed life for the three of them to proceed rather normally. So Mount Crane was the perfect place for them, close to home and little used, they usually had it pretty much to themselves. There was no reason to suspect, as they left home before daylight, that this day would be any different.

Mary had been looking for a way to get even with Bryce, the teacher's pet, ever since he had turned her in to Mrs. Collins for cheating on a history exam.

Her parents had grounded her for a month, and not only had her scholarship to Evans been revoked, but now they were saying her acceptance to the college was under *further review*. Bryce had screwed up everything for her and now it was going to be his turn to hurt.

"I hope Bryce comes down first," whispered Mary, her breath, hanging in the bitterly cold air.

"What if he doesn't," Alicia asked.

"Then we wait for Bryce," Mary instructed. "He's why we're here. I want to screw him up bad! Give him something to think about the next time he considers screwing with me!"

"That's fine with me, but maybe we'll get lucky and they will all come down together," replied Alicia.

"I hope not," snickered Mary. "They'll drag us halfway down the mountain!"

"Well whoever comes first better hurry before my ass freezes off!" Alicia complained, shifting her weight from her left cheek to her right.

Mary's plan had been a last minute affair, devised only shortly after she had overheard Kevin and Bryce discussing their ski outing in the school cafeteria.

At first, all she knew was where and when she would get her opportunity to get even with Bryce. She hadn't figured out right away how she was going to do it. Mary had considered rolling a log onto the slope in the hope that Bryce would hit it and go flying. But, upon further consideration, she had decided he might simply jump it, and besides that, she wasn't sure she could manage to roll a heavy log any distance or whether or not one would even be available.

She had thought of stretching a rope out across the slope, tied to trees at either side of the run, but again, he might see it ahead of time and either slide under it or jump over it. He was a good skier after all, one of the best in the area.

The rope idea was better than the log and she even knew where she could get the rope, but the element of surprise was still missing.

The idea to do—what she was about to do—had come from an old war movie she had seen on TV. The movie had been about World War Two Nazi mountain troops fighting the Americans somewhere in the Alps.

The movie had come to mind as she had been going to sleep last night, thinking about the rope in the shed, and while in that twilight zone of thoughts that randomly pop into one's head before falling into sleep. One particular scene from the movie, which she had thought was really cool, came swimming forward—*That was what she would do to Bryce!* It was perfect. A broken arm would be great; a leg would be even better!

She had rolled over and grabbed the phone to call Alicia right away.

"*I'll pick you up at four.*" She had told her. "*I'll explain later. Just be ready!*"

So—on this cold, November morning–the rope was carefully hidden just below the surface of the snow, tied to a tree on one side of the slope, firmly gripped by Alicia and Mary on the other. The trap was set.

Only moments passed before a shape appeared above them on the slope; one lone figure racing down the hill toward them.

"Who is it?" Mary asked, excitedly.

Alicia stared into the frozen mist and falling snow and replied, "It's Bryce!"

"Okay! Wait until I say, and then pull with all you've got," instructed Mary. "We'll send him flying! As soon as he flips, run like hell! We have to get out of here before the others come down."

Mary was responsible for the timing and she timed it just right. She gave the signal to Alicia and they jerked on the rope with all their strength. A plume of snow arose in front of Bryce, totally confusing him.

What the hell! Then out of instinct, or perhaps fear, he sat down on his skis. Then…he saw the rope…just before it caught him under the chin! He didn't have time to think about that. His legs shot out in front of him, his neck made a terrible snapping sound, and he slid lifelessly down the hill and into the forest.

Alicia had let go just in time and had fallen back down a small ravine, but the force of the collision had yanked Mary out of hiding and onto the slope. Alicia was just standing up and brushing herself off as Wiley went by. She saw him, but it did not appear as though he had seen her. She hunkered down a little as Kevin flew by. He hadn't seen her either, of that she was sure.

But…what about Mary? She thought.

She scrambled up the side of the ravine and ran to Mary, who was lying in the snow staring down the slope.

"Mary! Did they see you?" she asked.

"He's not moving," was her only reply.

"Did they *see* you?" she repeated, with more urgency.

"He's still not moving," repeated Mary.

"For God's sake, Mary! Did they see you? Did they get a look at you? Answer me!" screamed Alicia.

Mary finally turned to face Alicia and said, "Yes, they saw me. But he's still not moving, Alicia."

They could see Bryce clearly, up against a fir tree some ten to fifteen feet into the woods. He was motionless and twisted against the trunk of the tree, and it did not look good. They watched for movement from Bryce, but there was none. Not a foot, not a hand, not a finger. Wiley and Kevin had gone right by him without stopping or even trying to stop. It was obvious they had not seen him fall, nor did they see him lying there in the woods. Finally, Mary got to her feet, all the while remaining transfixed on the crumpled body below.

"Did he move yet, Alicia?"

Mary was trembling with fear. It was not fear for Bryce's well being that she displayed, but the fear that she had finally done something that was going to get her into some very serious trouble.

"God, Alicia, tell me he moved!"

Alicia put her hand on Mary's shoulder.

"Mary, listen. We have to get out of here. We have to get out of here *now*. The other two are at the bottom by now and will be wondering where Bryce is. They'll come back up here looking for him and we have to be gone by then. Bryce will be fine. He's probably knocked out, that's all. We *have* to get moving before they return."

Alicia was trying to be calm but forceful.

"Let's get going," she finally commanded.

Mary finally responded to her coaxing, and the two girls disappeared into the forest from which they had come. Mary stopped one last time to look back, then moved along again, into the forest and the uncertainty of her future.

CHAPTER 4

Wiley was waiting at the bottom of the slope when Kevin finally arrived, looking extremely excited about something.

"Wiley!" he yelled. "Did you see the wolf up there? That was cool!"

"That was no wolf," Wiley answered, bluntly.

"You don't think so? It looked bigger than a fox," Kevin stated.

"It wasn't a fox either, Kevin. Wolves and foxes don't have human faces."

Wiley was standing fixed, like a statue, staring up the slope. It was clear to Kevin that he was distressed over something. Kevin could see it in his furrowed brow and narrowed eyes.

"I didn't see any human face," Kevin replied, a little confused at Wiley's last comment.

"She put her face down to the snow as I went by," Wiley replied, still staring up the slope.

"She?" questioned Kevin, now even more confused than before.

"Mary. *Bitch* Mary."

Wiley had closed his eyes to mere slits now, as he continued to stare up the slope.

"Mary? What would Mary be doing up there?" Kevin asked, now more confused than ever. "That's crazy."

It was then that Kevin realized something was missing. He looked around in all directions and asked, "Hey! Where's Bryce?"

"I don't know," answered Wiley. "He never made it down. We better get back up the slope and find out. Something's not right. Something is *very* not right. Come on, Kevin, let's go."

It took the boys over half an hour to make their way back up to where they finally spotted Bryce, lying still in the snow. He was wrapped around a small fir tree and nearly covered in snow. They had almost missed him again, as they had on the way down.

As Wiley had predicted, a front had moved in as they had first arrived, and snow had been falling for over an hour, but now large flakes were falling heavily all around them.

They made their way over to Bryce, who still lay motionless.

"Bryce. Bryce! Can you hear me?" asked Kevin.

There was no reply. There was no movement.

"Bryce!" shouted Wiley. "Bryce!"

The silence was sickening.

"My God, Wiley. I think Bryce is, is dead," stammered Kevin.

"No way man. Damn! He can't be dead!" Wiley cried.

Wiley bent down and shook Bryce's lifeless body, but there was no response. Wiley shook Bryce again and his head flopped on his limp neck to a sickening, unnatural position.

"Damn, Kev! We've got to get him down to the hospital!" cried Wiley.

Kevin, always the calmer and more collected of the two, replied, "You stay here with Bryce while I go get the ski patrol. They will be able to get him out a lot more quickly than we can, and I can travel down to them more quickly alone."

With that, Kevin shoved off down the slope to get help for Bryce, knowing full well that there was no help for Bryce, other than perhaps, a prayer.

Wiley sensed this, too. He knew there was no help to be had for Bryce. But he was glad to stay behind, because he wanted to head up the hill to where he had seen Mary. He noticed a very strange mark on Bryce's neck, and it didn't look right to him.

What the hell is Mary doing up there, and what the hell did she do to Bryce, he wondered?

He made his way up to where he had seen Mary, but there was no sign of her now. The snowfall was beginning to obliterate everything on the slope and he almost overlooked the rope. He would have missed it entirely had he not spotted the knotted end around the tree trunk. He made his way over to the tree, worked the knot loose, and coiled the rope up around his lower arm.

Now, how can I get rid of this?

Wiley had now figured out what had happened to Bryce and a plan, was developing in his mind already. He wasn't sure how it would unfold just yet, but he knew this was the last straw. He, and he alone would resolve this issue. He was sure Kevin would feel the same. He knew Bryce was dead, he didn't need a doctor to tell him that, and he knew who was responsible.

I've got to dispose of this rope, he thought to himself. *Permanently, where it will never be found. The sheriff will notice Bryce's neck, too, and come looking for explanations.*

It took over two hours for Kevin to return with the ski patrol. The drive to and from Jessup Mountain, in the new fallen snow, had taken most of the time. Kevin found Wiley sitting alongside Bryce and holding his frigid hand.

"He's so cold," said Wiley.

"I know," replied Kevin, in a comforting voice. "He'll be okay now. The patrol will take him to the hospital."

Wiley looked up at Kevin with his eyes welling over and replied, "Right, the *hospital.*"

Both boys knew there would be no hospital involved. Bryce was gone and Wiley knew that Mary was to blame. He wondered if Kevin had come to that conclusion yet. He doubted it, because Kevin didn't know about the rope and he didn't know if Kevin had noticed Bryce's neck. These were things they would have to discuss. They would have to discuss these things *before* the sheriff started asking questions.

The patrol carefully loaded Bryce's broken body onto their sled and started down the slope. Kevin started to follow, but Wiley grabbed onto his arm and made a gesture indicating to Kevin to wait up.

"We need to talk," he said. "Let them get ahead a little before we start down."

Wiley's voice was firm and commanding.

Kevin said, "Okay," and thought, *What's up with this?*

CHAPTER 5

*W*iley knew that with the snow coming down as it was, all tracks and evidence of Mary's being on the slope would be eradicated in short time. He had made short work of the rope by dropping it down one of the many deep rock cuts that could be found along the east precipice of Mount Crane. Now, the only other evidence of Mary's presence up here was Kevin.

The ski patrol was moving quickly down the slope and had put a lot of distance between themselves and the boys. Wiley had suggested they walk down, rather than ski, as he wanted, no *needed*, the chance to talk with Kevin.

"Did you notice anything peculiar about Bryce?" Wiley began.

"Like what?" Kevin asked.

Wiley hesitated a moment.

Would Kevin go along with his plan, he wondered? *I'll need a partner in this. It's not something I want to try alone. Kevin loved Bryce, there's no doubt about that, but will he have the stomach for this?*

"Did you notice the strange mark across Bryce's throat?" Wiley asked.

"No, I don't think so. What mark?" Kevin asked.

"There was a mark across Bryce's throat, a rope burn," Wiley informed him.

Kevin stopped in his tracks and stared at Wiley.

"A rope burn? How the hell would he get a rope burn?" Kevin asked, incredulously.

Wiley began recounting what he had discovered while Kevin had been going for help. Kevin just stared, dumbfounded, in disbelief, saying nothing.

When Wiley had finished, Kevin spoke.

"She killed Bryce? That little bitch!" he yelled.

As if he were made of straw, Kevin collapsed to his butt in the snow. He sat there trying to make sense of what Wiley was saying. To lose Bryce like they had was terrible enough, but to try to comprehend that Mary had killed him was too much to assimilate all at once.

Wiley knelt down beside him and offered a comforting hand on Kevin's shoulder.

"Look, Kevin," Wiley began. "I got rid of the rope. With the snow falling like it is there will be no sign of Mary up here. No tracks, no nothing. The sheriff will notice the rope burn on Bryce's throat and we will be suspect. As far as they will know, we were the only ones up here this morning."

Kevin shot Wiley a worried and confused look. His mouth dropped open, but no words were uttered. Wiley waited for Kevin's thoughts to emerge.

"But we saw Mary! We can tell them we saw her," Kevin blurted out.

"No, we can't tell them that," replied Wiley, in a soft and reassuring voice.

"Why not? If we don't, they'll think we did something to Bryce. They'll blame us!"

"And we'll deny it," interrupted Wiley. "We'll play dumb and say that we came down the hill after Bryce and when we got to the bottom he wasn't there. *That's all we know.* We went back up the hill looking for him and found him dead. Period."

Again, Kevin was silent as he stared at Wiley in disbelief. After he had thought for a moment he asked, "Why would we do that, Wiley? Why wouldn't we tell them about Mary being up here? Why should she get away with this? Why in the hell would we want to help her and take the heat ourselves?"

"Come on," Wiley said. "Let's get moving before we're buried in snow. I'll explain it to you on the way down."

Wiley stood and helped Kevin to his feet. He wasn't sure what his plan would be yet. He hadn't had time to take it very far in his mind, but he was sure of one thing. Mary was *not* going to get away with anything. He also knew that Mary had not come up here alone. Mary never did anything alone. He knew that she would have had someone with which to *enjoy* her treacherous trick. There would have been no point in doing it alone.

He also had a pretty good idea of who it might be. He would share all this with Kevin, but he also knew something else that he would not share with him. He would not share this one piece of information with Kevin, because he needed Kevin to believe that Mary had *murdered* Bryce. He needed Kevin to develop the resolve to see this thing through. If he knew it was just a terrible accident, a prank gone badly, he may not have the balls to follow it through to the end.

After they had traveled a few hundred feet down the slope, Wiley began to unfold his thoughts to Kevin.

"Those bitches have been making our lives miserable for years. Now, they have finally *murdered* our best friend. I don't want the sheriff to arrest them and have them get off with a slap on the wrist. We are going to handle it ourselves. Not today, or even tomorrow, but we are going to make them wish they had never been born. We are also going to make their parents wish they had never been born."

Kevin stopped, grabbing on to Wiley's arm, and asked, "Who is *they*? I didn't see anybody but Mary—or, who you say was Mary."

"Oh, it was Mary all right, and who is Mary *always* with?" asked Wiley. "Do you think Mary came up here by herself?"

"No, I guess she wouldn't," Kevin responded.

"No, she wouldn't, and you know as well as I do that Alicia was probably with her. We didn't see her, but you can bet your ass she was there—somewhere."

Kevin thought for a moment about Wiley's conclusions and nodded in agreement. Wiley was right about that. If that had been Mary, and he had no reason to doubt what Wiley saw, then Alicia most definitely had to have been nearby.

They continued a little further down the slope. Again, Kevin stopped and turned to Wiley.

"Why do you think she meant to *murder* Bryce? Maybe it was just an accident. Maybe she just wanted to play another one of her dirty tricks on him. Just trip him up or flip him, just for *fun*. Maybe she didn't mean for him to get killed."

Wiley had his answer ready, for he knew this was coming. Kevin was a trusting person, and always tried to see the bright side of every situation. He was quick to give anyone the benefit of the doubt, and therefore, this was the one bit of information that Wiley would change. He needed Kevin's complete conviction to the plan.

"Look, Kevin. That's what I thought at first. But when I found the rope tied to that tree, *neck high*, I knew she did just exactly what she intended to do. Break Bryce's neck. Kill him. I don't know what she had against him that would make her want to kill him, but she did. You don't tie the rope, *neck high*, if you just want to trip him up."

Wiley was right, of course, but the truth be known the rope was actually tied knee high. Wiley knew it, *but Kevin never would*, not if he could help it.

CHAPTER 6

❀

By the time Mary and Alicia had made their way back to the service road where Mary's Gremlin was parked, the new snow had accumulated almost four inches. After the initial shock of what they may have done to Bryce had worn off, they had tried to run the majority of the way. They had found it necessary to stop frequently, to catch their breath, but they had not spoken another a word between them.

When they arrived at the car it was covered in new snow. They frantically cleared the windshield with their gloved hands, flung open the doors and drove away, as fast as one could go in the deepening snow. Mary prayed that they wouldn't get stuck, for that would surely spell the end for them. If they were going to get stuck, they had to at least make it back to a public highway where they could invent some story for being there.

"God! Do you think he's dead?" asked Mary, in a terrified voice. "Do you think we killed him? Why the hell did he sit down? Damn!"

The actual shock of the event had worn off and Mary was now simply frightened for her own well–being. She had been able to wriggle out of everything she had ever done in the past, but could she wriggle out of killing someone? Of *that*, she wasn't so sure. She seemed about to lose it when Alicia broke in.

"I don't know. Maybe he was just knocked out. He could have been unconscious. Right?"

Silence fell between the two girls, but only briefly. Alicia was worried about her culpability, too, but she had been listening to the voice of reason coming from within her upbringing, which she had chosen to put aside since losing Karl and becoming devoted to Mary.

"We have to go explain what happened," Alicia suggested. "We'll tell them it was an accident. We only meant to trip him up. We didn't mean for him to get hurt."

"It wouldn't matter Alicia. They wouldn't care whatever we said we meant to do. We would still be in a deep bucket of crap and I'm not going to jail over that twit!"

They drove on in silence for a while, both girls trying to sort things out in their own minds. Shortly, Mary calmed down a bit and pulled the car to the side of the road. She turned to face Alicia and began telling her what she had been thinking.

"Look, Alicia. For one, we don't know if he's dead. For two, we don't know for sure if they recognized me. I'm sure they saw me, but they were going by fast. Maybe they didn't get a good enough look at me to know who I was. For all they might know I could have been just another skier who had fallen on the slope. Someone who had gotten an even earlier start than they did."

"But what about the rope? We left it there," countered Alicia.

"What about it? There's nothing that ties that rope to us."

"But it's there, and that will tell the police that it wasn't an accident. They'll start an investigation, and we'll be screwed!"

Mary thought about that for a moment, and then replied, "Well—the snow will cover it up. Nobody will be up on the slope in this weather for a while. We'll go back and get it before anybody finds it."

"Now?" asked Alicia.

"No, not now. We'll go tomorrow morning, early, before daylight. There won't be anybody up there on Sunday morning that early. We'll go back up then and get the damned rope before it's discovered. In the mean time, we keep our mouths shut. We go home and we keep our mouths shut."

Alicia wasn't sure about all this, but Mary always called the shots, so why should it be any different this time. It made sense. And besides, what else *was* there to do? Maybe Kevin and Wiley hadn't recognized Mary. Maybe they hadn't thought anything of it at all. Maybe they hadn't seen the rope. They were going by very fast. They hadn't stopped at Bryce's body laying motionless in the snow as they went down the slope. It seemed they hadn't seen him on their way past where he lay. She remembered wondering why they hadn't stopped as she and Mary had begun running for the car. Maybe, just maybe, Mary was right. Maybe the police would just chalk it up to a terrible skiing accident. She did know one thing for sure. They had to get that rope before anybody found it. *That* was the key. *That* was a must.

She went through it all again, trying to dissuade reason's grip on her current thinking. Wiley had come down the hill *after* Bryce had come to rest against the tree. Wiley could not possibly have seen the fall or its cause. Wiley had probably seen Mary, but could he tell who she was? She had no answer for that at present. Had he seen the rope? That, she felt was doubtful, because it had been dragged out of the way by Bryce's momentum down the slope. Wiley had not actually skied over it. Snowing as hard as it was, he likely missed seeing it altogether.

She was still leaning toward the voice of reason, but perhaps there was enough doubt that she could afford to wait a while and see what developed. Perhaps Bryce was merely unconscious and would be fine. Why go asking to be punished when there may be no real reason to fear after all? If Bryce were alive, and not permanently disabled, Mary would find a way to get them out of it somehow. She always had.

Mary pulled up in front of Alicia's house. The drive from the mountain had taken three quarters of an hour, but it had seemed like much longer to her. There had been so many questions to ponder, and so many fears to allay. The drive had seemed to take forever.

There seemed to be an urgency to get safely back to her home, as if she had not been out at all that day. If no one knew she had been out, then suspicion would not fall on her. She knew the same was true for Alicia.

Mary's parents were out of town for the weekend, and she had no siblings, so there was nobody at her house to say any different. She thought about that for a moment then turned to Alicia, as she was opening the door to get out of the car.

"Does anybody at your house know you went out this morning?" she asked.

"No, not unless a neighbor saw me leave or something. Dad and Bill went out early to the shop," she answered. "Mom is at Grams."

Alicia lived with her mom and dad, but her mother was helping care for her grandmother in Liddelman, and had been gone since early Friday evening. Her father and brother had left for the shop before she had left the house that morning. Something about getting an early start on inventory. There was no one else at her house to say she had not been there all morning.

"Good," replied Mary. "Let's hope no one did see you, or me for that matter. My folks are out of town visiting friends. Unless some-one should say different, we've been home all day. Okay?"

"Okay," answered Alicia. "But what if someone does say different? What if someone says they saw us out early this morning? What then?"

"I don't know. We'll see. For now, go in the house and I'll call you later on."

Alicia agreed and went inside. She didn't like doing it as she felt she should be going straight to the sheriff's office and telling him what had happened, but beneath the voice of reason was the hope that Mary would figure out a way to slither them out of this mess, too.

She decided she would wait for Mary to call before making any final decisions.

CHAPTER 7

Kevin and Wiley made their way down the mountain to the bottom of the slope, where Deputy Phillips was waiting to talk with them. There was no sign of Bryce or the ski patrol, so they supposed that Bryce had already been taken to the hospital, or–to Keller's Funeral Home, by now. There was no morgue in Carver, so old Doc Abrams would look Bryce over at the funeral home and the mark on Bryce's throat would probably get the sheriff involved regardless of what they told Deputy Phillips. Still, he would have to be handled carefully.

"Hey boys!" the deputy greeted.

Deputy Phillips had a look of compassion in his eyes.

"Sorry about Bryce. I know he was a good buddy of yours."

"Is he–is he–you know, dead, Deputy Phillips?" Wiley asked, hoping for the answer he knew he wouldn't receive.

"Yes, I'm afraid so, Wiley."

"Where did they take him Mr. Phillips?" he asked, forlornly.

"Down to Keller's. There was nothing the paramedics could do for him. They told me he didn't suffer though. They figure he died instantly when his neck was broken. It was pretty severe, the said."

"That's good–I guess," Wiley lamented.

"Did either of you boys see what happened up there? I mean, how Bryce took that fall? I remember seeing him win the Founder's Day competition over on Jessup last year. He was a pretty darn good skier. So how did he come to take that fall boys?"

"It was a fox," Wiley answered.

"Well can you tell me about it for my records? His family will also want to know how it happened."

"Sure–Bryce started down first–then I followed. We were down the slope about a quarter mile. I was about twenty–five yards behind Bryce. A fox came busting out of the woods, probably chasing a rabbit, but I didn't see a rabbit. Anyway, the fox ran right into Bryce's path. He tried to turn sharp to miss it, and he did, but he lost his balance and fell. Then he started sliding down the slope and into a tree. That's where he stopped, all crunched up on that tree."

"I see. Anything else you can add, Kevin?" Deputy Phillips asked.

"No, sir. I was a ways back of Wiley. I hadn't come over the rise yet. When I got down to where Bryce hit the tree, Wiley was already there, trying to get Bryce to wake up. But he couldn't wake him up."

"Then what happened," asked the deputy?

"Well–I told Wiley to stay with Bryce while I went for help. I figured I could travel faster alone and the patrol could get him out faster than we could. So I went for help and Wiley waited with Bryce."

"And, Wiley, what did you do or see while Kevin was away getting help?"

"Nothing, sir. I just sat down and held Bryce's hand and tried to keep him warm, but his hand was so cold. I tried to keep the snow out of his face the best I could. I just held his hand and tried to keep the snow off his face."

"Okay, boys. I think you should head on home and get warmed up. If there is anything else I need to know, I'll get in touch with you at home. I'm sorry about Bryce. I know you boys were close."

"Thank you, Deputy Phillips," Wiley said.

"Yea, thanks," responded Kevin.

"Are you okay to drive, Kevin? If not, I can run you boys home and you can came back and pick up your car later."

"No thanks," replied Kevin. "We'll be okay."

They made their way back to Kevin's car in silence.

"Want me to drive, Kev?"

"No, I can drive," Kevin, answered.

"Sure?"

"Yes."

"Deputy Phillips didn't mention Bryce's neck," Wiley commented. "I mean the rope burn on his throat."

"Yea, I know."

"That doesn't mean that Doc won't bring it to their attention," cautioned Wiley.

"Doc's old. Maybe he won't mention it. Maybe he won't think it's anything other than where a branch hit him," suggested Kevin.

"Maybe, Kev, but we can't count on that. We have to come up with some sort of explanation for it, just in case Doc does recognize it for what it is."

"How are we going to explain a rope burn happening in the middle of the ski slope?" Kevin asked.

"Maybe it happened before that," Wiley suggested.

"That won't do. They can tell things like that," Kevin cautioned.

"Not if it happened *right before* he went down the slope. Like, just minutes before. Hell, we don't have a crime lab or coroner in this town, or even in this county. They won't send Bryce to a real pathologist unless they are real suspicious. We just need a logical explanation that the sheriff will swallow," Wiley said.

"And what would that be, Wiley?" Kevin asked.

"I'm not sure yet. Let me think about it for a while."

As they drove off, Wiley tried to visualize the morning leading up to the death of Bryce. He tried to picture every step they took and every move they made. Somehow, he had to find a logical, believable explanation for Bryce's neck.

He started with when Bryce first got in Kevin's car, early this morning. Was there a rope in the car? No, there was nothing there that would work. Then he pictured them arriving at the parking area at the bottom of the slopes. Again, looking through his mind's eye he saw nothing of use there either.

Damn! There has to be something, somewhere that will work!

He continued, picturing the ski lifts. They hadn't used them, because they weren't running. They had hiked to the top as they often did. He continued his journey in his mind watching every inch of the trail. Still, there was nothing. He finally reached the summit, almost out of breath from the mental journey. He stood at the trailhead and gazed around the top of the ski run. Wiley's "eye" fell on something, and as Kevin watched his expression change, he could almost see the gears of Wiley's mind, gnashing together.

"That's it!" he yelled. "That's it! Bryce had to take a pee!"

Kevin stared at Wiley in amazement.

"What?" he questioned. "He had to do what?"

"Bryce had to take a pee and he didn't want to do it out in the open. Even though nobody else was there, he didn't want to do it out in the open. You know how Bryce was about things like that. He would never take a pee in the open, and everybody that knows him, knows that."

"But, Wiley, how does that explain anything?" questioned Kevin.

"Okay–look! We are up there at the head of the slope. Bryce needs to take a leak, so he heads for the closest woods. What's in his way, Kev? What's between him and the woods? Think about it. Picture it. What's in his way?"

Kevin started trying to picture the top of the slope, the shed, and the woods beyond. Then it hit him, too.

"The rope barrier!"

"Right!"

"But how does he hurt himself on that?" asked Kevin.

"All right. He heads for the woods. It's slippery and he needs to step up over that rope to do so. He decides to use one of the poles for support, to rest his hand on for support. Just as he nears the barrier and reaches out for the pole, he stumbles forward. He grabs for the rope or the pole, but misses. His neck comes down square on the rope and he slides down it a foot or so! Viola! A rope burn!"

"Damn, Wiley! That might work!" Kevin exclaimed.

"You're damn right it will work! We can even tell the sheriff how we jibed him about it after that. '*Couldn't take a piss like everybody else. You had to go and stick your neck out!*' Yea, it should work just fine."

"Maybe we should tone it down a little. It's too perfect. He just fell forward on the rope. Period. We don't say that he hit his throat on it; we let them draw that conclusion. He just fell forward on the rope. Period. Forget the 'sticking his neck out' part."

Wiley thought about that.

"Yea, maybe you're right. We can't make it too convenient. It just needs to be a possible explanation that they can satisfy their doubt with. Okay. That's it, good thinking, Kev."

CHAPTER 8

❀

The sheriff's office in Carver was an anomaly, being the only building in Carver built in the Spanish architectural style. It reminded the sheriff of an old gas station from the 1930's which might have been converted to the sheriff's office at some time in the past history of Carver. Perhaps it had, but Al couldn't remember it being anything other than what it was now.

It was a freestanding building, the color of dry earth, with a portico in front large enough to shelter two cars. Inside were three rooms, one of which was a jail cell, the other two, Al's office and the reception area where Becky, their "Girl Friday" and dispatcher, monitored the phone and police radio. Having no office of his own, Stan shared this reception area with Becky at a desk set up in one of the far corners of the room. There was no second floor, and the basement, which was one large room beneath the entire structure, was used for the storage of files and supplies.

The building, located on Center Street, was completely surrounded by a macadamized parking lot and was accessible also from Carver Boulevard, which ran behind it. Its nearest neighbors were Olson's Oldsmobile one block to the south, and equidistant to the north, the Carver Laund–Ro–Matic, referred to by the locals as the LRM.

Sheriff Al Dramico had received word of Bryce Spencer's demise and sat quietly, looking out his office window at Mount Crane. What a tragedy for the Spencer family. What a sad thing that the Spencer boy had been killed in a skiing accident before he even turned eighteen.

Skiing accidents were nothing new to Sheriff Dramico, or Carver. There were always broken arms and legs every winter, but fatalities were rare, and usually befell the weekenders or the holiday skiers. The locals knew the slopes well, every turn, bump and dip. They usually held their own up there, with a few exceptions. He tried to think back to the last time a local had died on the slopes, but he couldn't think of a single time. If it had happened before, it was before his time.

"Afternoon, Sheriff." Stan Phillips had entered Al's office, unannounced as always, but Al's open door policy permitted that. Even if he had more formalities in the rules, his deputy was not one to stand on formality. But it didn't really matter, for there were few formalities associated with his office, and Al liked it that way. *"Small rules for a small town."* It worked okay.

Al Dramico was a big man, standing nearly seven feet tall and weighing every bit of three hundred pounds. It was a well–proportioned three hundred pounds, the focal points of which were his massive shoulders and chest.

To stand and talk with Al was to get a good impression of his size, but watching him walk through a doorway, filling the width of it completely and stooping to fit his Stetson beneath it, confirmed his bulk to anyone watching. His round face was cheerful and friendly and his personality was as cheerful as his face. Despite his intimidating size, Al's demeanor was unassuming and relaxed, never using his size as leverage with law–abiding citizens or tourists.

Al had been the sheriff in Carver since most of the younger people could remember. He wore a uniform, at the insistence of city council, but it was never adjusted quite correctly and rarely pressed. He preferred a Stetson cowboy hat to the city issue police cover he had been provided, and *despite* the council's opposition, he wore his Stetson proudly. On that point and on the choice of his vehicle, he would not relent.

Stan was a small man, or at least when he stood by Al that was the impression one got. He was actually an average five foot ten, slender though, probably in the neighborhood of around one hundred fifty pounds. He too, was congenial and friendly, both in appearance and personality. Stan was always sharply dressed, in pressed uniform and official cover. He liked driving his patrol car, unlike Al, who preferred his International Harvester Scout. Stan worked hard at his job, and liked working hard at his job. He was proud to be a Carver City Deputy, and it showed in his deportment and enthusiasm for the job.

Al swiveled his desk chair around to face Stan. "*Squeeeek.*" He hated that chair. He had always hated that chair. Three requisitions to council had still brought him no satisfaction. After the third request he had received a note back inferring that if he lost the Stetson and began driving his patrol car it would be considered. He had given it some thought, but the patrol car was out of the question. There was no way he was going to try to stuff his frame into one of those little cars.

I'll be stuck with this darn chair 'til the day I die, he thought.

"What is it, Stan?"

"Doc says the Spencer boy died of a broken neck. Pretty typical of the type of fall he must have taken. Probably happened when he hit that fir tree."

Al let out an audible sigh and said, "Well, that's what I expected. Darn shame. How are the other boys taking it?"

"Oh, they're doing okay. They're pretty upset and all, but doing okay."

"They say how he fell?" Al asked.

"Yes, sir. They said a fox ran out from the woods right in front of him. Made him swerve and he lost his balance and went down hard. Said he flip–flopped down the hill a ways and hit dead on into a fir tree."

"That's a darn shame Stan. Thanks for the report. Just type it all up and I'll go see the family."

"Okay, but Sheriff–There's one more thing."

"What's that, Stan?"

"Doc says the Spencer boy had what looks like a rope burn on his throat. Couldn't figure it. Doc says it isn't like a hanging burn. It's just across his throat, in the front."

"Fresh?" asked Al.

"Yep, Doc says it was real fresh."

"Now how the heck would he get a rope burn up there on Cougar Run? Maybe I better put off seeing the family until I check this out and know all the facts. Where are the boys now?"

"Probably home. I talked with them at the foot of the slope. Didn't seem any need to drag them down here."

"Thanks Stan. I'll take it from here."

As Stan left the room, Al swiveled back to his view of Mount Crane. It was bathed in a new blanket of snow and it was still falling.

Won't find anything up there, he thought to himself. *Fresh rope burn? Where the heck did that come from?*

Al was fast coming to the conclusion that this might not be exactly as he had pictured.

Maybe the boys can shed some light on this rope burn, he thought.

Al knew the boys pretty well. It was a small town and he knew almost everybody, although as he had grown older, he had been less able to keep up with all the new young faces and which families they all belonged to. He knew Kevin Reynolds and Bryce Spencer though, through complaints of harassment their parents had made on other kids in the community. He knew who Wiley Coates was, too; although he wasn't sure which Coates family he belonged to. Wiley had come along to give his side of the story on some of the complaints the Reynolds or Spencers had filed.

He knew the three boys were inseparable, and he knew their friendship was much like an island in a stormy sea, or an oasis in an arid desert. They stood together, alone in this town. He also knew they were good boys and good students. Not one of them had ever been in his station house due to a complaint on them or for anything he or Stan had caught them doing wrong.

They'll probably have a good explanation for that burn, he thought. *There's no way either of the two would hurt the Spencer boy. It's just not in them. There has to be a good explanation for it.*

By the time Al had reached his Scout he had managed to pretty much convince himself of the boys innocence in the matter. It was just a tragic accident, like he originally believed. Rope burn or no rope burn, it was just an accident.

"But where the heck did that rope burn come from? Maybe Doc was wrong about it being a rope burn. Maybe a tree branch had made the mark."

Al figured he'd drive over to the Reynolds' place and see if Kevin could explain the mark on the Spencer boy's neck. One way or the other, the weather forecast called for overnight clearing, so first thing Sunday morning, he'd have a look around up on the slope. After all, he *was* the sheriff, and he had to look at it from all sides, even if he felt there was no foul play.

I guess I can't put this to bed until I know about that mark on the boy's neck...

CHAPTER 9

*A*l pulled into the Reynolds' drive. Buck Reynolds' house was rather woodsy in appearance, located on the northwest edge of Greenville, just north of the confluence of Mount Crane and Jessup Mountain. The garage door was open and he saw Buck in the garage pulling the starting cord on his snow blower.

"Hey, Buck. How's it going?" Al hailed.

Buck worked at Cutter's Lumber Mill, a foreman of sorts, as Al remembered. He was a large man, nearly equal to Al in stature, but on the leaner side. The coarse muscles of his arm bulged beneath his skin as he pulled the starter cord, with such ease that it appeared it was attached to nothing at all.

"Hi, Sheriff," Buck greeted, looking up from his work.

"How's Nancy these days?" asked Al.

"She's doing pretty well, thanks. She's come a long way since Carrie's accident," Buck said. "What brings you out this way?"

"Looking for Kevin, Buck. Is he around?"

"Saturday morning–No, he'd be up on the slopes by now, Sheriff. Anything wrong?" Buck asked.

"Yea, Buck, I'm sorry to say there is. I know Kevin has been up to Mount Crane this morning; Stan already talked with him up there. Now he's all right, so don't worry, but there's been an accident. The Spencer boy, Bryce, had an accident up there this morning."

"Hurt bad?" asked Buck.

"He died, Buck. I'm sorry to say, he died," Al answered, lowering his eyes momentarily.

"Kevin?" Buck questioned immediately, letting go of the cord.

"No, Kevin is fine, and so is the Coates boy. Seems Bryce took a fall on account of a fox crossing his path and his neck was broken. Died instantly according to Doc. I just need to talk with Kevin a minute. Stan got his statement at the mountain, but there are a few things I need to clear up."

"What kind of things?" asked Buck, with concern.

"Oh–Nothing much. Just some loose ends Stan didn't cover up there. Do you know where the Coates boy lives, Buck? Maybe Kevin is over there. If I can catch them together I can make short work of this, I'm sure."

Buck looked at the ground for a moment and then raised his eyes to the sheriff. He had a disturbed look about him, an almost frightened look.

"Those boys would never hurt Bryce, Sheriff."

"I know that, Buck. I just need to get some details straight, for the record. You know how that is. Its just details."

"Okay. Just so you know they wouldn't hurt him," Buck replied.

"I know that, Buck. Truly, I do. It was just an awful accident. Now where can I find Wiley?"

"He lives a couple blocks over, on Mill. I don't know the number, but it's the only green house on the east side of the street."

Al thought for a minute, a furrow forming in his brow.

"Is Wiley, Calvin Coates' boy?" he asked.

"Sure is, Sheriff. It's hard to keep all those Coates families straight around here, but yes, Wiley *does* belong to Calvin, I can tell you that much for sure. He and Kevin have been friends for years."

"Thanks, Buck. Now don't you worry about anything. Its just details."

"Sheriff–After you talk to Kev, send him on home."

"I'll do better than that, Buck, I'll bring him home myself," Al offered, with a smile.

"Thanks, Sheriff."

"No problem, Buck."

Al backed out of the drive and headed down Birch. In just a few minutes he was on Mill.

Only green house on the east, he thought to himself. *I've been here often enough.*

Buck had been right about the Coates families in Carver. There were Coates families scattered throughout the valley. Coates was one of the original names in Carver Valley. Coates, Green, Carver and Dramico. Al's family was one of the original families also, and the only one of Italian descent.

It was Wiley's ancestors who had brought the proliferation of red hair to this area, and they had also done a good job of proliferating themselves! It was, by far, the most common name in Carver. There was the Coates Dry Goods Store, on Center Street, the Coates Theater, on Main, and the Franklin Coates Salvage Yard, out near the dump. This was to name just a few of the local businesses, which the Coates family members were into. Anyone coming into town for the first time might get the impression that the town was named Coates, if they had missed the Carver sign, at the edge of town.

When Al pulled up to Wiley's place, Kevin's car was parked at the curb in front of the house. He pulled into the drive just as Kevin was coming out the front door. Kevin saw Al at about the same time as Al had spotted him.

"Damn! What's he doing here?" went through Kevin's mind, like a shot. *"Doc must have said something about that burn. Damn!"*

"Hey, Sheriff," greeted Kevin, trying to be as cool as he could. He wasn't convinced that Wiley's idea was such a great one, right now.

"What's up?" he asked.

Al climbed out of his Scout and faced Kevin.

Damn, he's big, thought Kevin. The sheer size of the sheriff was already intimidating him. He wasn't sure at all if he could go through with this.

"Kevin, how are you holding up, son?" Al asked, with genuine concern.

"Pretty good, Sheriff."

"Wonder if we could go back inside and talk a little about all this? Is Wiley inside?"

"Yes, sir. Wiley's home, but I better be getting home myself, before my folks get worried," Kevin answered, trying for an out.

"I just talked with your dad and he knows I was coming over here to talk with you, so they won't be worrying. I told him all about Bryce and that you were fine. So let's just go inside and get a few things cleared up, son," Al insisted.

"Okay–Sheriff."

Kevin turned and they walked back to the house together, Kevin leading the way. Wiley had been watching from the window and opened the door just as they reached the top of the stoop.

"I saw you guys talking out there. What's up?" asked Wiley.

"Well, son. I need to talk to the both of you about Bryce's accident," Al answered.

"What about it, Sheriff?" asked Wiley.

"Can we go inside, Wiley? It's a bit cold out here," Al suggested.

"Sure. Sorry, Sheriff. Come on in."

Wiley proceeded to lead them into the living room where the boys sat down, Wiley in his dad's easy chair and Kevin on the sofa. Al remained standing, in the center of the room.

"Doc tells me that Bryce broke his neck in the fall. That's what killed him."

He stopped and looked at the boys, first Wiley, then Kevin.

"He said it looked pretty much like an accident to him, but for one thing."

Al paused again, and looked at each boy, in turn.

"What one thing, Sheriff?" Kevin asked, complacently.

"Well…"

The sheriff paused again and studied the boys' expressions.

"It seems that Bryce has a strange mark on his throat. Doc says that it appears to be a rope burn."

Again, Al paused to study the boys. They didn't appear to be overly concerned about what he was saying.

"Now, what I can't figure out is how he could get a fresh rope burn up on that slope?"

Al paused again, this time he would wait for some reply before continuing.

"Rope burn?" asked Wiley, in a dry, almost puzzled tone.

"That's what Doc says it looks like," Al replied.

The boys had been preparing for this ever since returning from the slope. They had decided not to know how it could have happened, at first. They would feign puzzlement, and then slowly, the light would come on. They decided they couldn't just blurt it out. They had watched enough TV to know that pat answers arose suspicions in the minds of law enforcement people.

The shock of Bryce's death should cause the previously humorous pissing event to drift to the backs of their minds. Forgotten, for the moment, until something would jog it out.

This is it, thought Kevin. *This is where we sink or swim. I hope Wiley knows what he's doing.*

"Sheriff–Maybe a tree branch or something caught Bryce in the throat," suggested Kevin, as if searching for an answer.

"That's what I was thinking, Kevin, but Doc says he thinks it's a rope burn. Now I know Doc is old and he is no fancy coroner or anything, but he's been around a long time. I've got to go with his beliefs until something proves him wrong. I can't put this behind us until I know what that mark is."

It was Wiley's *turn* to speak.

"He couldn't take a piss." Wiley swallowed hard. "Like anybody else."

A tear ran down Wiley's face.

Kevin was amazed.

He's actually crying, he thought.

"What was that, Wiley?" asked Al.

"He couldn't take a piss like everybody else," repeated Wiley. "We were kidding him about it at the top of the slope."

Al looked puzzled.

"Back up a bit, Wiley. I'm not following you," he said.

"You remember, Kevin," glancing briefly Kevin's way. "When we first made it to the top of the hill, Bryce had to take a leak."

Another tear ran down Wiley's cheek.

"He couldn't just do it. He had to go somewhere private. I mean there was nobody else there but Kevin and me. Anyway, he headed for the woods behind the shed, but when he got to the rope barrier fence he stumbled and fell forward. He landed right on the rope and he slid down it a foot or so. We laughed our butts off."

Another tear and a hard swallow followed. Kevin was even becoming convinced this had happened.

Damn he's good!

Wiley had stopped talking for the moment, as if he was lost in a deep thought.

"That's why he went down the slope ahead of us. He was pissed off at us for making fun of him. We kidded him about it all the way to the head of the run."

Another tear ran down Wiley's cheek.

"I guess he could have burned himself on *that* rope when he fell. I don't know. I didn't notice."

"That pretty much how you remember it, Kevin?" asked the sheriff.

Kevin couldn't muster a tear, but he swallowed hard and replied in his best, broken voice, "Yes, that's pretty much how it was, Sheriff."

"Okay, boys. Thanks for the chat. That clears up a lot for me. I better be getting along."

"Okay, Sheriff," replied Kevin.

Wiley just nodded, and wiped the last tear from his cheek.

"Kevin, I promised your dad I'd bring you home. I forgot that you would have your car over here, so I'll just follow you home, if that's okay with you?" Al asked.

"Sure, Sheriff. Whenever you're ready."

Al followed Kevin to his drive and tooted his horn as he went on his way. He was glad the boys were able to clear this up for him. It explained a lot. Still, he knew he would have to go up and see what they were talking about for himself. He didn't relish that, but he figured it was his duty.

He had never been up to the top of that slope before and he couldn't put something in his report that he didn't know for a fact existed.

Oh well, I'll just hike up there and back again, he thought.

He was not a skier. In fact, he didn't like heights at all, and the ski lift was out of the question, even though it really didn't get that high off the ground.

"Maybe I could send Stan up there to check it out," he murmured. He selected a Skeeter Davis tape and plugged it into his eight-track player. He sat back, relaxed and began singing along as *Set Him Free* came softly to his ears.

Damn she's good, he thought, and picked up the chorus again.

When he returned to the station, Everett Carson was waiting for him in the parking lot. He popped Skeeter out of the player and prepared himself for the inevitable questions.

"Hey, Al. What can you tell me about what happened on Crane this morning?"

"Not a thing, Everett. I'll give you a statement when it's official."

"When what's official? I need some details to print, Al. What can you tell me?"

Everett was the editor of the local Carver Journal, *and* it's only reporter. He was a mousy little man, with a pushy nature, all part of his job, Al had reasoned.

"You've got to give me something, Al. I've got a duty to the community."

"So do I, Everett. So do I. I'll give you a call when I can release the details."

Everett frowned at Al and walked back to his car. When he had reached it, he turned and yelled, "Okay, Al. I'll be back. You can't sit on this forever."

Having finished with Everett, for the moment anyway, Al went into the office, flashing Becky a smile as he passed by. He walked around his desk to his chair and sat down, putting his elbows on the desktop and resting his forehead in his hands.

How the heck did Everett get wind of this so quickly, he wondered?

He went back to thinking about the morning's events.

He believed the boys. He had no reason not to, but he hadn't actually seen this rope barrier Wiley had described. Something about that bothered him. There was something else he should be doing to make it really official. He knew he couldn't simply let this rest the way it was. He would talk to Stan when he returned and get this finished right. In the mean time, he would try to figure out what Stan should be looking for up there.

Al was a good sheriff, and he always tried hard to do things right, but he had never had any formal training. He had been appointed deputy to the previous sheriff and was elected sheriff himself when Sheriff Phelps had retired.

Stan returned after about fifteen minutes, which didn't give Al a lot of time for thinking about what he would say to Stan.

"Stan, there's something I need you to do for me," he began. "I need you to go up to the top of that slope and check on something for me."

"Okay, Sheriff. What's that?" Stan asked.

"I talked to the boys a little while ago and they described a rope barrier around the top of the slope up there. They say that the Spencer boy may have hurt his throat on that rope barrier just before they came down the hill."

"Do you believe them, Sheriff?" Stan asked, raising the bill on his cover.

"Yes. I believe I do Stan, but I can't just take their word for it without looking into it a bit. I need you to go up there and check this barrier out and see what you think."

"Sure, Sheriff. You want me to bring back a section of it for comparison to Bryce's injury? You know, to see if the rope and the burn match up?" Stan said.

"Yes–Stan. That's exactly what I want you to do," answered Al.

"You probably want me to make sure that it is all in tact up there, too. I mean, check that none of the barrier is missing, like it was used for something else, somewhere. Right?"

"That's exactly what I was thinking. You're getting good at this, son!"

Stan smiled broadly, and then said, "I'll be back shortly, Sheriff. I'll get it all checked out for you."

Stan lowered his cover and hurried out of Al's office.

He'll make a good sheriff one day, Al thought. *I'm sure glad he's been taking those academy classes in Bennett. He's turning into a real good lawman.*

With that thought, Al swung his chair around to look out at the mountain. *Squeeek*—Al grimaced.

CHAPTER 10

*I*t was mid afternoon and Alicia was getting nervous. Mary hadn't called yet and she was beginning to have second thoughts about trying to hide their tragic prank from the authorities. When she had been unable to wait any longer, she had tried to call Mary, but there had been no answer. That had her worried, too!

Maybe the sheriff had shown up at Mary's house and had taken her in for questioning, she had thought.

It was like being in a vacuum. She wanted desperately to know how Bryce was.

"Is he dead or alive? Is he paralyzed for life? God! What's going on?"

Her thoughts were racing around in circles, like a dog chasing its tail.

I know—I'll call the hospital—No—I'll call—I'll call—Who? Let me think!—Her mind screamed.

Alicia realized that she didn't really care how Bryce was, as long as he wasn't dead. She was terrified that she and Mary would be blamed for whatever had happened to him, more so, than she was worried over his physical condition. As far as she was concerned, Bryce deserved whatever had happened to him, as long as he wasn't dead. She could not live with *that. That* was not in the plan.

He was a jerk and a squealer, and he was responsible for the "F" Mary had received on her last history exam. He had *actually* told the teacher about her crib sheet!

What a faggot, she thought!

Although the idea, had been, to flip Bryce down the mountainside, she had secretly hoped he *would* break a leg or something like that. They weren't supposed to be seen though. That was the problem, that, and the fact that Bryce hadn't been moving after his fall.

She decided to give Mary a little while longer to call, while she made herself a sandwich. As she ate, she let her mind drift away from the problems at hand. Her mind needed to escape this pressure, and drift back to happier times, and safe harbors.

She found herself thinking about Karl, during the months before he had graduated from Carver. Those had been good times. Karl had been an upperclassman, and her friend. He had been more than just a friend; really, as she had felt a fondness for him since they had first met when she was just thirteen.

She remembered their first meeting, Karl riding up on his new motorcycle, and she wanting so badly to take her turn riding behind him as her friends had done. He had even asked if she was ready for her turn, but she had turned him down, knowing her mother wouldn't have approved of that at all.

They had never dated, the four–year difference in their ages, being more than her mother would tolerate. Her mom had allowed them to be friends, seeing each other during the daytime, but no *dates* at night had ever been permitted.

Time spent with Karl, had also been a juggling act with Mary. Mary had known that Karl and Kevin were friends, and Alicia's friendship with Karl, in Mary's eyes, had been intolerable. Alicia had made it quite clear to Mary that her feelings for Karl had nothing whatsoever to do with Kevin. Mary had eventually learned to tolerate it, but never came to like, or accept it.

Alicia had always envied Mary everything; her beautiful home on Pill Hill, her expensive clothes, her beautiful blonde hair, her lithesome body, and her own personal car. Ever since she had first met Mary, she had wanted to be just like her, in every respect but one. Her relationship with Karl was the one thing she had accomplished, that Mary had not. Mary had not acquired the ability to care for someone deeply. Mary had always, and still did, consider herself *above* any boy at Carver High, and Alicia did not envy Mary this.

Alicia thought back to the occasions when she and Karl had been together, cruising in his old Jeep, and once, actually going horseback riding, the closest thing to a date she had experienced with him. Karl had given her a kiss late one evening, and she remembered now, wondering at the time why he had done that. It had just snuck up on them in the blink of an eye. The kiss had been nice, just a brief and gentle meeting of the lips, the first and only between them and the first of her young life. But as warm a feeling as it had created, it had also created confusion in her. They had been, after all, just friends, or so she had thought. Now–however, looking back, she *did* understand.

Then, before a second kiss could be enjoyed, before anything had ever been decided between them, Karl had graduated and had gone away to college.

There had been letters from him, the last of them coming from somewhere in Arizona, which she had happily replied to, as she had the ones before it. But, then the letters stopped coming. They just stopped coming, without explanation.

She had tried to rationalize the loss away, by convincing herself that he was simply too busy to write. Whether she had believed it or not, it had helped, a little. It was at this time, that she had thrown her full devotion, toward Mary. It was at this time, she felt; she had begun to grow bitter. This had been the point in her life, at which she had allowed Mary to begin doing all of her thinking for her.

Her reverie was broken, by the sound of the phone.

"Hello," she answered, hoping it would be Mary.

"Alicia. Sorry it took me so long to call. I've been trying to find out more about how Bryce is," Mary apologized.

"How? We can't call anybody! We are supposed to have been in the house all morning. Remember?"

"Settle down, girl. I know that. I went for a walk with my dog. I went all around the neighborhood, stopping to talk to anybody who was out shoveling snow, or whatever. I figured that if they had heard anything, they would bring it up. Besides, I figured that if I am seen around the neighborhood, well, you know how bad people are about recalling time. It's not a perfect alibi, but it sheds some doubt on what time I was out in the neighborhood. I thought that if I stayed inside, nobody would see me at all, and with no one home to verify I was there, I'd have no alibi at all," Mary explained.

"Did anybody say anything? Did you find out anything?" Alicia asked, anxiously.

"No, not yet. I guess it's too soon for it to have gotten around yet."

"Well, at least the sheriff hasn't shown up at your house. That's a good sign. If Kevin or Wiley had recognized you the sheriff would have been around by now," stated Alicia.

"Yea, you're right. Maybe they didn't get a good look at me after all. We still have to get up that slope early tomorrow morning and get the rope. That's the one thing that could *hang* us, if it's found. I know they can't tie it to us, but, like we agreed before, it will start an investigation and we don't want that," Mary emphasized.

"No. That's the last thing we want," agreed Alicia.

"My parents will still be gone, so I don't have a problem slipping out. What about you?" Mary asked.

"Inventory usually takes two mornings. They stop counting when they open for the day, so Dad and Billy usually go in early both Saturday and Sunday mornings. Mom isn't due back from Liddelman until tomorrow night, so I shouldn't have a problem either," Alicia explained.

"What time do your dad and brother leave in the morning?" Mary asked.

"Usually about four. I'll call you as soon as they leave."

"Sounds good. I'll wait for your call and then I'll come pick you up. Once we get that rope I think we will be in the clear. See you in the morning, and remember to bring your snowshoes, and dress warmly," Mary reminded her.

As Mary put the phone back on the hook, she thought about the rope. It wasn't that the rope could be traced to her. It couldn't be. It wasn't hers, or even her father's. It had come from the storage shed on top of the ski slope. She had cut it from the large coil stored in the shed. That had been part of her plan.

She knew it was there from when she used to ski on that slope, before switching to Jessup Mountain's new slopes. She had snooped, as she was prone to doing, into the shed one day and had seen the large spool of rope sitting in the corner. She remembered it because it looked so out of place there among the snow shovels, tools, and spare lift seats. She remembered wondering at the time what the heck they needed all that rope for.

It seemed a whole lot safer to get the rope there, rather than to be seen carrying a rope up there, by some unseen person. She had worried that the spare rope might not still be there, but what was she going to do, go buy a new rope at the hardware?

The fact that the rope would be found, stretched out across the slope, was the bad thing. If the boys hadn't noticed it, then Bryce's fall would appear accidental. If the rope was found tied to a tree and stretched out across the run, right where Bryce went down, then foul play *would* be suspected. It would not only be suspected, it would be the sheriff's official determination. Even if neither of the boys recognized her, it would be only a matter of time before she and Alicia would be questioned. Everybody in town knew how they felt about those nerds.

They would be the logical suspects. They had played other tricks on Bryce in the past, some almost as dangerous. Like the time she and Alicia had put a bike chain through the spokes of his back bicycle wheel. He hadn't noticed it, as they had hoped, and when he took off the bike had stopped, almost immediately, and quite suddenly. Bryce had been pitched from his bike and lay sprawled on the ground. At least a dozen other kids had witnessed the prank, and others they had masterminded. So it would be only a matter of time before the sheriff got around to questioning them.

If, on the other hand, the rope were never found, that would change things entirely. There would be no evidence at all. The boys' word, that they had seen someone up there, would be all the evidence there was. It could have been anyone, a bird watcher, a hunter, or a hiker. It would have been better not to be seen at all, but what's done is done.

But, the rope problem could be remedied, and that was exactly what they were going to do.

CHAPTER 11

❀

*I*t was getting late in the day now, and the snow was still falling. Stan knew he had only a few hours of daylight left and there wasn't enough time to hike up to the head of Cougar Run. He was going to have to get Larry to fire up the old lift

It took only a few minutes to drive to Larry's Conoco on Highway 20. As he pulled in he saw Larry under the hood of a customer's car. Stan pulled his cruiser along side and gave the siren a short blast. Larry reared up and conked his head on the hood of the car.

"Damn! What the hell you doing, Stanley? You about scared the bejebus out of me!"

"Sorry, Larry," remarked Stan, trying to keep from laughing. "I've got some official police business I need your help with. Have you got anyone here to watch the station? " He asked.

"Yep, Lou's in the back, turning a rotor. He can watch her for me. What's up?" Larry asked.

Larry was a "good ol' boy", with a big heart, and an even larger curiosity. Anytime "police business" was mentioned, he would be the first person in line to help out. It wasn't civic pride or duty that formed his attitude, he just considered it cool to be involved.

"I need you to fire up the lift on the east slope so I can get to the top before dark."

"What do you need to do up there, Stanley?" Larry probed, looking for a clue as to what this "police business" was all about.

"I have to check something out for Al," Stan answered. "No big deal, but he wants it done today. We haven't much daylight left, so could you please go tell Lou and we'll get moving?"

"Sure, Stanley. I'll be just a minute."

Larry went inside and returned promptly. He jumped in the passenger side of the patrol car and they headed for Mount Crane. There was no doubt in Stan's mind that Larry would come along, even if it meant closing the station. There was just about nothing Larry liked better than getting a ride in the patrol car.

He was normally a rather somber man, but whenever he got a chance to ride in that cruiser, he was one big smile, from ear to ear. Stan could relate to that feeling. He remembered feeling exactly the same way as a kid, when Sheriff Phelps would let him ride, from time to time. It was a good feeling.

"How's business, Larry?" Stan asked, trying to make conversation.

"Pretty good, Stanley. It'll get better when the greenhorns get up here for the holidays, though. If the crowds get big enough to run the lifts at Crane, I'll be earning some good money."

"I don't ever remember a season where you didn't need to run them," Stan commented, encouraging Larry.

"Not since I've been doing it. I've run them every year since I took over for Cobb. Jessup keeps getting more popular every year. Maybe in another few years, I'll be running them full–time, you never know."

"No, you don't, Larry. Maybe you will."

By the time they arrived at the lift house Stan figured he had about an hour of daylight left, maybe a little more. The trip up the slope would take only ten minutes, once Larry got the lift running, so he should actually be headed back down before dark. That was good, because his plan was to ski back down and have a look along the slope.

That could be a little tricky, after dark, he thought.

Stan didn't know what he would be able to see or find along the way down, especially with the way the snow had been coming down all day. As he completed that thought, the lift sprang to life. It didn't sound a whole lot like it wanted to, but after a few grinding and whirring sounds, it did.

"See you in about an hour, Larry!" Stan yelled.

Larry waved to him and Stan took his position to board the lift. On the way up he kept a keen eye on the ground below, looking for anything out of place or that didn't look just right. He didn't see a thing other than a lot of deep snow.

The lift reached the top in about ten minutes, as he had expected. He jumped off and stood, studying the area. Stan had never been up here before, and he found the view breathtakingly beautiful. The next thing he noted was the shed, just a simple wooden structure, used for storage.

Stan had taken up skiing after Jessup had opened, so this was all new territory to him. He stared hard into the falling snow beyond the shed, but he didn't see any rope barrier, anywhere. He began trudging toward the shed, keeping his eyes peeled for the barrier that was supposed to be somewhere up ahead. He finally reached the shed and thought he'd better have a look in there, just to be thorough. He reached for the handle on the door, and realized it was only knee high. The snow had drifted hard against the door, and try as he might, he could not pull it open.

Just as well, he thought. *I'm supposed to be looking for that rope barrier anyway, and I don't have a lot of time to waste.*

He worked his way around the corner of the shed and headed towards the woods beyond.

Why didn't that boy just piss behind the shed? It would have been a lot closer than the woods. Go figure.

He was just about to give up, and head back, when–"Damn! What the hell!" He yelled. He had bashed his shin on something hard, hidden beneath the snow, but whatever it was, he couldn't see it. He knelt down on one knee and rubbed his shin. "Damn that hurt," he uttered audibly, and began digging in the snow for whatever he had run into. His gloved hand came in contact with something hard and round. He kept digging and brushing away the snow to discover what appeared to be a wooden post. Brushing away more snow, he discovered that the post had a rope attached to it, or rather running through a large metal screw eye, inserted in the top of the post.

Well, I'll be damned, he thought. *It is here.*

Stan had put up with about all of this mountaintop that he wanted. He wasted no time in pulling his knife and cutting a two foot section of rope from the barrier, and then folding it in two, he stuffed it into his back pants pocket.

"They can fix this next spring," he said, into the silence.

I don't think anyone will be up here before then, anyway, he thought.

He knew that wasn't true, but he didn't really give a damn. He was getting cold and wet, and wanted nothing more than to get the hell off this mountain.

Standing, he turned and headed for the slope. Half way there he stopped and took his skis and poles off his back and fixed the skis in place.

Should've done this when I first got up here, he thought to himself. *Stupid, I guess.*

Stan reached the head of the run and shoved off. He maneuvered down the hill, keeping his speed down to a bare minimum. He watched the sides of the run intently, but didn't see a thing out of the ordinary, or out of place. When he reached the bottom of the run, Larry was waiting in his patrol car.

He had shut down the lift when he was sure that Stan had reached the top. Now, he was just trying to keep warm.

"Hey, Larry, thanks for warming up the car for me. I'm freezing my tail off," Stan kidded.

"You?" replied Larry, with a smirk. "I warmed it up for *me*!"

"Well, thanks just the same," countered Stan.

"Did you find what you were looking for up there?" Larry couldn't wait to ask.

"Yep, sure did," Stan, said, cutting it off there, intentionally.

"Well?"

"Well what?" Stan teased.

"What did you find?"

"Larry, you know I can't discuss police business with you," Stan answered, sternly, but smiling all the while. "It's against the rules, and you know it."

"Seems to me—when you bring someone out on police business—and near freeze them to death—you could bend those rules of yours a bit," Larry said, between blows on his fingers, his feathers obviously ruffed.

"Sorry, Larry. Can't do. Say, by the way, do you know what's in that shed up top?" Stan inquired.

"Just tools and such, like shovels and plows and all," Larry answered.

"Okay. That's what I figured. I couldn't get the door open for all the snow drifted against it. Let's get the hell out of here. I'm hungry, tired and half frozen."

Stan dropped Larry off at his service station and paid him the standard twenty–dollar fee for the police business he had performed. That was something Sheriff Phelps had started years ago, to encourage citizens to get involved.

As he pulled out onto the highway, he began thinking about getting some supper. He was thinking through the list of possible restaurants he could stop by, when he realized that he didn't have time to eat right now. He wanted to get the piece of rope over to Keller's before Doc went *home* for the day.

Doc didn't live on Pill Hill with the rest of the town's five doctors. He wanted to be close to his work as Carver's only mortician, so he lived behind the funeral parlor in a small, but nice apartment. Despite the fact that going home meant walking through a door from the mortuary to his apartment, when Doc was off duty, Doc was *off duty*!

He enjoyed his personal time listening to concertos and reading, much too much to be disturbed by normal business. If you had an emergency though, that was an altogether different story.

Stan's piece of rope did not constitute an emergency, so he would not bother Doc with it until morning, if he had already retreated to his apartment. The only way to get Doc to come to the door, late at night, was to press the doorbell button marked, "For Emergencies Only". Stan would never do that, unless it *was* a matter of life and death. Doc was old, and needed his quiet time and rest. Besides, he had earned this level of respect, through years of loyal service to the community.

As Stan passed the last restaurant between Larry's and Doc's, he sighed.

Sure would be nice to have time to eat around here, he thought.

Stan was a bachelor, so there would be no supper waiting for him at home. There would also be nothing in the pantry or the fridge to fix.

I'll just swing by Mickey D's after I finish up with Doc, he thought. *It shouldn't take very long to get his opinion on the rope.*

He shifted his weight, settling into the seat a little further, turned on the radio, and smiled.

This really is the best job in the world, despite late suppers and cold mountaintops.

Doc's drive came up quickly, and he almost missed it, just as he always did. He would have missed it, if he hadn't been here so many times before.

"Doc really needs to put some lights out here," he muttered–*Or, at least light up the sign,* he finished silently.

Turning into the drive he noticed that the parlor's porch light was on. That was good, because that was the last thing Doc turned off, before retiring for the night. It was his signal to the world that he was now lost in the melodies of Mozart or wrapped up in the words of Shakespeare. Stan pulled the cruiser up to the porch, and parked.

Doc answered the door on the third ring of the doorbell.

"Hi, Doc. What took you so long?" Stan kidded. "You're getting slow in your old age," he poked.

"Wine is aged slow, too, Stan. What brings you out here after dark?" Doc asked.

"The sheriff wants me to show you something and get your medical opinion on it."

"Okay, son. Come on in," Doc said, smiling, as was his usual practice.

"Thanks, Doc. I didn't want to disturb you with this so late, but the sheriff needs an answer," Stan continued, apologizing for the disturbance.

"Sure–What's it all about, Stan?"

Doc was the classic country doctor and mortician, both in appearance and manner. His neatly pressed black suit and bow tie were something out of a storybook, and turn of the century. His white hair and mustache were classic, as were his wire rim glasses. His gold watch chain, looped gracefully into his vest pocket, completed the image. Stan had no idea how old he really was, but to guess, he would put Doc in his late eighties.

Stan reached around his back and pulled from his back pocket, the section of rope he had cut, then handed it to Doc.

"You said the Spencer boy had what appeared to be a rope burn on his throat. Al wants to know if that burn could have been made by this rope, or one just like it?" Stan explained.

"Well, let's have a look. Follow me back to the prep room and we'll compare a few things," he said, examining the rope in his hands. He pulled a small ruler from his vest pocket, and held it to the rope.

"Hmmm?" was all he said.

Still studying the piece of rope, he turned, and started walking toward the prep room. Stan followed, though reluctantly. He wasn't sure he wanted to go into the prep room. All he wanted was an answer, not a tour. The idea of visiting the prep room unsettled him, causing his empty stomach to churn.

Doc walked over to where Bryce Spencer lay, face up on a stainless steel table. Stan moved along side Doc and stared at the lifeless boy.

"What a damn shame," Stan whispered.

"You don't have to whisper, Stan. You aren't going to wake him up," Doc said.

"That's a bigger damn shame," replied Stan.

"Yes. Yes it is," whispered Doc.

They stood there is silence for a moment, and then Doc moved closer to the boy. "Let's see, Stan. We know this is the right kind of rope, because the burn was made by a rough rope, like hemp or sisal, not something smooth like nylon or poly. This piece of rope is sisal. The burn is also accompanied by bruising," Doc stated, assessing the damage to Bryce's throat.

"What's that mean, Doc?" asked Stan.

"It means that there was impact associated with the injury. The rope wasn't just raked *across* his throat. It hit his throat hard or his throat hit the rope hard," Doc explained.

"Like maybe he *fell* on the outstretched rope?" Stan suggested, leading Doc and hoping for that conclusion.

"Yes, maybe so. That could be one explanation for it," Doc stated. "Or,—"

"What other explanations could there be? And, is this the right rope?" Stan interrupted.

"It's the right type of rope and it is the right size. Could even be *the* rope involved. Though I can't be sure of that. As to other explanations, there aren't any. He either hit the rope or the rope hit him, hard." Doc paused a moment. "It was not just a glancing blow, but a direct blow to his throat," Doc finished.

"So, what you are saying is that he either fell on the rope or ran into the rope. It wasn't high enough for him to have run into it and he was probably not moving fast enough for it to do any real damage, anyway. He must have fallen on it then," Stan said, summing it all up.

"If he was skiing down that hill and ran into this rope, he was certainly going fast enough to do the damage, Stan," Doc suggested.

"Well, sure Doc, but the rope came from a barrier fence at the top of the ski run. The other boys say he stumbled and fell on the rope while he was going to take a piss in the woods. Sorry I didn't mention that before, but I wanted your opinion before telling you the details," Stan explained.

"I see. Is there anything else you neglected to tell me?" Doc asked, lowering his head and peering over the top of his glasses.

"No, Doc. That's it. Sorry, but I needed an unbiased opinion," Stan explained.

"My opinions are always unbiased, young man, but that aside, I can tell you that their story is plausible. This could definitely be the rope and the injury on this boy's throat could have happened just as they describe," he concluded.

"That's good to hear, Doc. That's what I was hoping I'd hear, and that's what I expected to hear," Stan said, with relief.

"I'm glad it appears to have turned out the way you wanted, Stan, but remember, I said it was a plausible explanation for what happened, not the *only* explanation. It's true the injury was incurred at approximately the time of death. If he fell on that rope up top, then started down the slope right away, then fell and broke his neck, it all fits. But my other explanation also fits. He could have run into that rope coming down the slope," Doc cautioned.

"But that's not where the rope was, Doc. That's what blows that theory," Stan countered.

"Not *this* piece of rope. Are you sure there is no other rope like this up there?" Doc asked.

"I skied down the slope, slowly, and looked carefully for any sign of anything out of place. I didn't see a thing," Stan informed him.

"Lot of snow fell up there today," Doc cautioned, again. "Might not be easy to find by now."

"Yea, I know. Maybe I better take another look tomorrow. Just to be sure," Stan said, thinking aloud.

"Maybe you had better," Doc advised. "Just to be sure."

"Thanks, Doc. Sorry I had to bother you so late," Stan apologized again.

"That's not a problem, Stan. I'm sorry I can't go along whole–heartedly with the boys' explanation of what happened. It's just that the bruise is barely a half–centimeter wider than this rope. Stan, you know I'm not a pathologist, but I don't think that would be possible if this injury happened even two minutes before his death. By my judgment, it should have expanded through the capillaries to at least four centimeters beyond the width of the rope. It didn't, indicating to me that the rope injury happened at or within seconds of the time of death. I don't know that the cold might have slowed the spread, perhaps it could. I'm not a pathologist."

Doc showed Stan out and he drove away feeling somewhat better, but not totally satisfied with it all.

Plausible, he thought. *Doc said, plausible.*

He didn't relish the idea of going back up that mountain in the morning, but he'd let Al make that call. If Al were satisfied with Doc's "plausible", then it would be good enough for him. He spotted the Mickey D sign, just ahead.

CHAPTER 12

*I*t was late Saturday evening before the snow finally abated. In all, a total of thirty–seven inches fell over most of Carver, Montana. Perhaps a little more had fallen on the slopes of Mount Crane, on top of the seventy–five inch base already present. By three o'clock Sunday morning the skies were clear, with a million stars ablaze, against the black velvet ceiling of the early morning sky.

Wiping the sleep from her eyes, Mary went to her bedroom window and peered outside into the darkness. She was not pleased that the snow had stopped falling. Falling snow covers up tracks, both human and automobile. Ideally, the snow would have continued for their journey up Mount Crane, but snowing or not, the rope was something that couldn't be overlooked or ignored.

The good thing about the weather clearing was the gibbous moon, shedding ample light on the snow, for their mission. It would reflect off the snow and make their trip through the woods much easier than if it had remained overcast. Finding the rope would be no problem.

She moved across the room to her closet and picked out some warm clothes to wear. It was going to be very cold up there before sunrise. She was just tying her bootlaces when the phone rang.

"Hello, Alicia?" she answered the phone.

"Hi, Mary. The coast is clear. You can come get me now," came the reply.

"Okay, I was just finishing dressing. Look, Alicia. You leave the house now, like you are going for a walk. I'll pick you up at the corner, by the park. That way if anybody happens to be watching, they won't see me pick you up," Mary instructed.

"Why would I be going for a walk at three fifteen in the morning? That's dumb. Just pick me up and let's get going! I want to get this over with. We don't even know if Bryce is hurt badly or not. There's been nothing on the radio or TV about..."

"There wouldn't be," Mary interrupted. "You know how Sheriff Dramico is. He thinks he has to protect this town from everything, and that includes losing the tourist bucks. He isn't going to say that *'there was an apparent accident today, that took the life of a local teenager'*, or, *'seriously injured a local teenager'*, now is he? He won't release a statement until he has to. Until he notifies the radio and TV stations in Bennett, there won't be any mention of the accident, other than in the local newspaper. Mr. Carson will snoop out the story, but the sheriff won't give it up to the outside until he's done thinking it over. *You* know that. We've seen it before. We won't know how Bryce is until the Journal comes out later this morning. We can't wait that long. We *have* to get up there and back down with that rope before anyone else has the chance to find it. Got it?" Mary asked, sternly.

"Yes. I've got it. So get over here and let's get this done."

I sure as hell hope Bryce isn't seriously hurt, because if he is, that girl is going to get us busted, was Mary's first thought after hanging up the phone.

The only reason she put up with Alicia was the simple fact that Alicia was the only friend she had that shared her interests in tormenting those nerds. Her other friends all had a little too much compassion for their feelings. Not much more, but enough to prevent them from going along with the really *good* jokes.

Alicia, on the other hand, although never the instigator, was always quick to follow her lead. A smile came to Mary's face as she thought back to how many times she had talked Alicia into one prank or another. Her smile quickly faded though, as her mind came back to the task at hand.

She ran down the stairs, snatched her coat off the hook and went swiftly out to the garage. She took her snowshoes down from the wall and placed them in the back of her mother's Wagoneer.

Won't get anywhere without these, she thought. *I hope Alicia remembers hers.*

Then, pausing for a moment's reflection upon what had just gone through her mind, she took her mother's snowshoes as well.

She pulled up to Alicia's house about twenty minutes later. Pill Hill was across the river from Greenville, and despite the Wagoneer's four wheel drive, the roads had been treacherous, and the driving, slow.

Alicia was waiting at the curb but started to back away as Mary pulled up. Mary lowered the passenger window and called to her in a low voice.

"Alicia. What wrong? Get in."

Alicia stared momentarily, then advanced.

"Mary?"

"Yes, get in!" she said, trying to keep her voice low.

"I didn't know it was you. You scared me," Alicia explained.

"I thought I'd better borrow Mom's Wagoneer, what with all this snow. We can't afford to get stuck up at the slope. You ready?" she asked.

"I guess," grumbled Alicia. "Let's just get moving."

The girls drove on in silence. In the forty–five minutes it took to get to the slope, not one word was uttered between them. The reality of the trouble they could be in had settled over them like a wet blanket. It was heavy and it was uncomfortable. The frustration of not knowing if they were in serious trouble was disconcerting.

If Bryce was seriously hurt or dead, they were in deep crap, if found out. If not, it still behooved them to get the rope and avoid the slap on the wrist, but the not knowing was gnawing at them incessantly. Whatever the outcome of Bryce's fall, the priority was getting the rope off that slope. Remove the evidence and avoid the suspicion–the prosecution.

"We're almost there," Mary said. "I'll park in the lower lot so we can't be seen from the road."

She turned into the upper lot and turned out her headlights. With the moon and the bright snow she could see just fine without them. She drove across the upper lot and shifted back into four–wheel drive before going down the ramp to the lower lot.

The county still plowed the Crane lots, probably because they always had, or maybe in hope of a big weekend and Jessup overflow. The lot was still snow covered, but it was nothing the Jeep couldn't handle.

Mary pulled into the deepest corner of the lot and parked the Jeep. She was careful not to leave her foot on the brake any longer than was necessary.

As necessary as this trip was in their minds, their bodies weren't sure if they were quite ready for this. Hiking half way up this ski slope in three feet of newly fallen snow was not going to be easy. They couldn't even afford to take the path of least resistance. They were going to be forced to take the path of maximum concealment. There was little doubt that they would be the only fools up here this morning, but this was not the time to gamble. They needed to get up there quickly, but *unseen* by anything other than indigenous wildlife. Yesterday it had taken them an hour to reach the shed and half an hour to get back to where they would set up their prank. Mary figured that with the new snowfall it would take the better part of an hour, or slightly longer, to reach the rope.

It was now almost four and sunrise would come in about three hours. She found herself wishing she had thought this out better, and had planned to leave a little earlier than they had. Still, if all went well they could get back to the Jeep before sunup and be out of there. Once they left the parking lot, they would be home free.

Mary was glad she had thought to bring her mother's snowshoes, because, just as she had feared, Alicia didn't remember to bring hers. They donned this most essential gear and headed up into the woods. They kept to the fringe, just off the ski slope, but where they could see the run and keep their bearings. It was hard going; really hard, but they were driven by purpose, or perhaps it was fear, which kept them going.

"There's the tree that Bryce hit," Mary pointed out to Alicia. "Not much further now."

Alicia was too out of breath to respond with anything other that a nod.

"We'll have to cross the run to get over to where we can untie the rope," Mary said.

Again, just a nod of recognition from Alicia.

"There's the tree!" Mary exclaimed, pointing it out to Alicia.

Mary picked up her pace as best she could, which wasn't very much, and cut a straight line for the tree. Upon reaching it, she fell to her knees and let out a cry, that Alicia was sure would be heard all the way back to town.

"What's wrong?" asked Alicia, in a tone that was unmistakably one of apprehension.

"It's not here!" cried Mary, falling backwards onto her back. "The damn rope's not here! God, Alicia! What the hell happened to the rope?"

Alicia was momentarily without thought. Her mind was blank. She tried to collect a thought, and blurted out, "Maybe it's just buried!"

In one flash of a moment Mary was on her knees again, digging feverishly into the new snow, which surrounded the tree's trunk.

"Dig!" Alicia shouted. "Dig!"

Then she too, fell to her knees and scooped the snow as fast as she could, until she finally hit the hard packed base snow. She stared at the base of the tree and began to cry. Mary was now digging up the frozen, crystalline, base snow with all the fervor of a badger gone mad.

"Mary–It's not here–The rope is not here. Stop digging, Mary. It's not here!"

She reached over and placed her hand on Mary's arm.

"Mary–Stop." Her voice had grown strangely calm. "It doesn't mean anything, Mary. Maybe we have the wrong tree. Maybe another skier found it later on, and took it. Maybe a hiker."

Mary finally stopped her digging and looked at Alicia. Her face was twisted in a fashion Alicia had never seen before. It was the countenance of fear, mixed with hate and confusion.

"Come on, Mary, let's go home. We can't dig up every tree on this damn mountain looking for that rope. If we can't find it, then no one else will either."

Mary's face relaxed, but ever so slightly. She looked straight into Alicia's eyes and her lips trembled.

"What if we can't find it because it isn't here, *anywhere*, Alicia? What about that?"

"I don't know," Alicia answered. "Like I said, maybe a hiker or skier found it. Maybe we do have the wrong tree. I don't know."

"What if the sheriff does have it, Alicia?"

Mary seemed to be coming apart. There was a look in her eyes that made Alicia *very* uneasy. If Mary fell apart, and wasn't able to think ahead of this anymore, then she would be lost for what to do next. She could always "fess up" to the fact that they had done what they did, and take her medicine for it. But, if Bryce were dead, that would be a bitter pill to swallow.

"Mary, listen. If the sheriff has the rope there is nothing we can do about that. But, if it is still up here and we spend any more time looking for it, we won't get back to the car before daylight. If we are seen up here, then there will be questions to be answered, questions we don't want to be asked. Now come on. Let's head back to your mom's car."

Mary seemed to see the reason in what Alicia was saying, and slowly rose to her feet. She brushed away the snow from her clothing, threw her shoulders back, and looked straight at Alicia.

"Alicia, I don't want to go to jail. I can't go to jail, Alicia."

She was barely hanging on to reality now, or maybe she was now seeing the reality of the situation, very clearly.

"We're not going to go to jail, Mary. Let's just get back to the car and go home."

The sun was just cresting Mount Crane as they arrived at the Wagoneer. They were exhausted. It was an effort just to remove their snowshoes and place them in the back of the vehicle.

Mary had gathered her wits on the hike back and was once again in control of herself. Alicia couldn't have been happier about that, because this plan to out–fox the sheriff had been Mary's idea, and without Mary, like she had thought before, she was lost.

Sitting behind the wheel of the Wagoneer, Mary started the engine and pulled out of the lower lot and into the upper. She stopped and looked around, then proceeded toward the highway.

"Just a few more yards and we're clear," she uttered, more to herself than to Alicia. "Just a few more yards."

She reached the highway and turned out. There were no other vehicles in sight and Mary sighed a loud sigh of relief. Now that they were back on the highway, the Wagoneer was just another car, going to somewhere, and coming from someplace.

They had traveled no more than a mile before Mary started laying out their next moves. Simply put, there would be only one.

"What we need to do now, is drive over to the mall in Bennett. Climb back in the back Alicia and cover those snowshoes with the blanket back there. Make it look neat and tidy."

Alicia did as she was instructed. It felt good, somewhat, to have Mary calling the shots again.

"What we will do is drive to Bennett, go to the mall there, and buy a few things. That will give us a reason for being out this morning. We need a reason for being out this morning. I don't think we have been seen by anybody yet, but going back home, now that it is daylight, will be another story. We have to assume that we will be seen, so we need a reason for being out.

By the time we reach Bennett, the mall will be opening. We wanted to get there early so we left at seven. Got that, Alicia? Seven. We left at seven to drive to Bennett to go to the mall. We've done that before. It's believable. There's no reason to account for the time before that because I'm sure we weren't seen. Don't you agree?" Mary asked, seeking confirmation.

"Yes, I agree. I don't think we were seen earlier," Alicia agreed.

"Then it's settled. That's what we did this morning. We went shopping, in Bennett, at the mall. We left at seven."

Her voice was stilted, her expression, blank.

Alicia stared at Mary.

She seems so, so mechanical…

Perhaps Mary wasn't as much in control as she had previously thought. Alicia found herself praying under her breath.

Please God…let Bryce be all right!

CHAPTER 13

Stan left the house early, Sunday morning. It was a beautiful, clear day, the landscape covered with a think blanket of fresh snow. He marveled at how beautiful it actually was, once it had fallen, and the county had it under control. These snowstorms were both a blessing and a curse. Without them there would be no Jessup slopes and no tourists or skiers. It was the "Winter Wonderland" aspect of Carver that brought anyone here at all.

On the other hand, while the snow was falling, like it had yesterday, emergencies could arise. Traffic accidents, stranded skiers, and lost hikers went hand in hand with these storms. Stan was glad this storm had hit *before* the actual opening of the winter season in Carver. Oh, it was winter all right, but nothing really got going up here until the Thanksgiving weekend, and that was over three weeks away.

He dressed hurriedly, strapping on his service belt, hurrying out the door, throwing his jacket and cover on, as he went. Stan was in a hurry to get to the office early to report to Al what Doc had told him last night. This was normally Stan's day off, but if Al were to decide to send him back up the mountain, he wanted to get an early start. Perhaps he would be able to salvage some of the day for himself.

The drive to the station was pleasant and relaxing. The pristine beauty of the mountains, in their new cloak of white, was breathtaking. The Carver area was definitely "God's Country" and, he was sure, as beautiful as any in the world. Having grown up in Carver, Stan knew no other home. Sure, he'd been away before and had seen some of the world beyond this valley, but this was home.

As far as opportunities were concerned, all he *ever* wanted was to one day be sheriff. He'd get his chance. Al had always done a good job and was doing so still. He was popular and would be hard to beat in an election, and that, Stan knew for sure. Others had tried over the years, but none succeeded in displacing Al from the job he loved. Stan had no plans along *those* lines, anyway. He was content for now to be the deputy. He liked Al, and Al *had* appointed him, after all. No, Stan would wait for Al to retire. He was fifteen years Al's junior, and that would give him plenty of time to enjoy later, as the man in charge.

He had arrived at the station before he even realized it, having been so absorbed in the beauty of the valley that he didn't even remember much of the drive there. Al's Scout was in its parking place under the portico by the front door, as he had expected. He pulled his cruiser alongside and went inside, stopping briefly to chat with Becky before entering Al's office.

"Morning, Sheriff," he said, addressing Al, cheerfully.

Al looked up from his paper and gave Stan a momentary, blank stare.

"You see the morning paper, Stan?" Al asked, quite sternly.

"No, sir. Why?" he asked.

"There's an article here, on the front page, about the Spencer boy," Al informed him, poking the paper with his finger.

"Yes, sir."

"It says here he died in a terrible skiing accident on Mount Crane."

Al's voice was becoming even more agitated with every word he spoke.

"I wasn't aware that we were finished with our investigation. You wouldn't know anything about how Everett picked up on this story would you? Please tell me he got it from the ski patrol, and not from you," Al said, seeking an answer.

"No, sir, not the patrol. He got it from me, sir. Everett caught me in the lot yesterday and wanted to know what had happened to the Spencer boy. Now how he found out anything had happened at all, I don't know. He may have heard that from one of the ski boys. He didn't say. I told him that, at this time, there wasn't any reason to call it anything other than a tragic accident. That's all I said, sir. I told him what the boys told me about how it happened, that it was just a terrible accident. I'm sorry if I spoke out of turn," he apologized.

"Stan–" Al paused, glancing back at the paper. "You know we have to be very careful what information we release before we have all the details. In this case there's probably no damage done, but in the future, I don't want *anything* said until I approve it. Are we clear on that?"

"Yes, sir. Very clear on that, and I'm sorry I said what I did."

Al settled back into his chair and swung around to look out the window. "*Squeeek!*" "Darn, I hate this chair," he grumbled. "Did you get a chance to get up on that mountain and take a look around?"

"Yes, sir. I fetched Larry and he ran the lift for me, then I skied back down checking along the way for anything that might be helpful to us," Stan said, filling Al in.

"See anything?" Al asked.

"No, sir. There was nothing unusual at all. Up top, I did find that rope barrier like the boys said. I cut a section from it and brought it back down with me for Doc to have a look at."

"Did Doc see it yet?" Al inquired.

"Yes, sir."

"What's he think?" Al swiveled back to face Stan.

"He says the rope I brought to him was exactly the right type and size to have caused that burn. Said he can't be certain that it was *the rope*, but it was the right texture and size. That barrier rope is made of sisal, and Doc says the burn was made by sisal or hemp, nothing smooth like nylon, or something called poly."

"Did you tell him what the boys say about how it happened?" Al asked.

"Yes, sir. After I got his first impressions. He says the boys' explanation is 'plausible'. That was his exact word. He said it may not be the only plausible explanation, but it is one that fits the injury. He said the Spencer boy either fell hard on that rope, or ran into it, going pretty fast. He said it was an impact injury, not just a glancing sort of thing," Stan explained.

Al thought for a moment, and then asked, "Did he offer up any other theory of his own?"

"He asked if the boy could have skied into the rope. I told him I didn't see how because the rope was at the top of the run, not on the slope."

"Was any of the rope missing from the barrier?" Al said, pressing further.

"Now *that*, I couldn't determine, Sheriff. I damn near broke my leg running into it when I first got up there. I smacked my shin dead into one of the poles. It was completely buried in snow. I couldn't even find the barrier at first. There was no way for me to check out whether it was *all* there or not, and still have time to come back down before dark. I wanted to check the slope while I could still see well enough to do so."

Al reflected on what Stan had said.

"Do you want me to go back up there today and have another try at it?" Stan asked, hoping for a "don't bother", or similar answer.

"Al looked up at Stan and gave a little smile, and said, "No. I really don't think it's necessary. I think it's just as the boys said it was. Bryce Spencer took a bad fall and died. It's a shame it happened, but there's nobody to blame but bad luck. No need to mention to anybody that we ever thought it could be any different. Case closed."

Those last two words were the best words Al could have said. Stan never believed that the boys could have done anything to hurt their friend. If it had not been for the rope burn, they'd have been taken at their word, instantly. Combine what the Doc said with the boys' story and it fit easily together, like a well used jigsaw puzzle. No reason to doubt it any longer. Still, Stan was not comfortable with not being able to complete his investigation in the manner he had wanted to. He wanted to *know* that the whole barrier was still there, and he had wanted to have a better, more thorough look at the slope, *but not now*. Not in all this snow. All in all, he was comfortable enough with the facts to sit easy with Al's decision to close the case.

CHAPTER 14

*A*licia felt that Mary was much more herself on the return trip from Bennett. They had spent most of the day there, shopping for little nick–knacks, blouses and shoes. Mary had her own Visa Card, complements of her father, so money had not been an issue. Mary had done all of the buying, as was usually the case, Alicia being, habitually, a contented window shopper.

Returning late in the afternoon there would be no problem with *anyone* seeing them arriving at their homes. Mary had relaxed considerably and Alicia was almost dozing in the passenger seat, listening to a Hank Williams song on the car radio. She was drifting in and out of thoughts of the events of yesterday and thoughts of how Bryce might be. Hank's song ended and a commercial for John Deere came on the radio. She was just about to ask Mary what the name of the Hank Williams song was when the news came on.

"Our top story of the afternoon: Yesterday–in Carver, Montana–seventeen–year–old Bryce Spencer was killed in a tragic skiing accident. A witness to the accident, seventeen–year–old Wiley Coates, a good friend of Bryce's, said a fox darted across Bryce's path as he was skiing down the Cougar Run on Mount Crane. Bryce, trying to avoid a collision, lost his balance and fell. A local doctor reported that the cause of death was a fracture of his neck, sustained when the boy hit a tree. Mount Crane's

slopes are little used overflow slopes for the popular Jessup Mountain
runs. In other news, a two car accident..."

"God!" cried Alicia, "He *is* dead! Oh my God. We killed him!"

Mary turned her head to face Alicia and said, with the slyest of
grins on her face, "One down. Two to go." With that, she broke out
into a cackle of a laugh and said, "Just kidding. Just kidding, Alicia."

The clear statement from the radio that it was a "tragic accident"
had not escaped her.

"There's no way the radio station would have that story if the
sheriff hadn't come to that conclusion and released it to them! We're
home free girl!" Mary exclaimed.

"All...Right!" chanted Alicia, her voice as loud as she could muster.

They stared at each other. Silence filled the Wagoneer. Each girl
was lost in thought. Then, Alicia said with a barely audible whisper,
"I *am* sorry he's dead though. I didn't think I would be, but I really
am sorry he's dead."

A tear ran down her cheek and dripped onto her blouse. She was
quiet for a moment, as if formulating another thought.

"I'm not sure if it's because he is dead or because I killed him. I
don't know," she confessed.

"We killed him, Alicia," interjected Mary, in a stern voice. "We
killed him. It's just as much on me as it is you. We planned it and we
did it. It got screwed up, but we did it just the same. So don't be too
hard on yourself."

Alicia forced a small smile.

"Okay," she replied.

"The important thing right now is that there will be no investigation. It's an accident as far as the sheriff is concerned and we are in
the clear."

They continued for home, feeling much relieved over the news
they had just heard. Each would have to deal with their own guilt in

their own way, but their common goal of eluding detection seemed to have been accomplished.

Willie Nelson was singing from the radio and the girls were just beginning to settle in for a peaceful, relaxed journey home. The tires seemed to hum in rhythm with Willie and the motor was purring the background.

"Hey! I like that song!" barked Mary.

Alicia had just reached over and turned the radio off.

"What did you do that for?" she asked.

"Why would Wiley tell the sheriff that a fox ran in front of Bryce? There was no fox," Alicia pointed out.

Mary looked at her in amazement.

"They did say that, didn't they?"

"That's the way I heard it. He fell because a fox ran in front of him. What fox?" Alicia questioned.

"Good question. I don't know what fox," Mary replied.

The girls fell silent once again, each trying to make sense of what the radio had said.

Why would Wiley say he saw a fox cause the fall, Mary wondered? *It doesn't make sense at all. If he had seen the rope he could never have mistaken that for a fox. Maybe there was a fox we didn't see. Maybe when Alicia fell down the ravine and I was sprawled in the snow, a fox did run across the slope. Maybe Wiley assumed that was what caused Bryce to fall.*

"Mary." Alicia spoke, interrupting her train of thought.

"What?" Mary snapped.

Alicia was staring at Mary with a huge grin on her face.

"What's so funny?"

"Look at you," ordered Alicia.

"What? Damn it, Alicia, spit it out!" Mary commanded.

"Look at your hat. Look at your coat and collar," Alicia told her, smiling broadly.

"So. I'm looking. What is it?"

Mary was becoming frustrated at the game Alicia was playing with her.

"You're the fox, Mary!" Alicia stated. "Your hat *is* fox fur. Your coat is some kind of fur and your collar is wolverine. *You* look like a fox. What I mean is, that lying there in the snow and Wiley flying by at close to fifty miles per hour, he might have thought you were a fox that had just crossed the run. Maybe that's why he never told the sheriff you were up there. Not just because he didn't recognize you, but because he thought you were just a fox. It wasn't full light yet, you were half buried in snow, you put your face down as he went by, and maybe all he saw was fur," Alicia explained.

Mary thought about that for a minute.

"You may be right," she acknowledged.

"Of course I'm right!" Alicia stated. "That's the only thing that makes sense. If Wiley had recognized you we would be in jail already. If he told the sheriff he saw someone lying in the snow where Bryce had fallen, he would not have released the story to the radio yet. He would spend some serious time trying to find out who was *also* up there before telling the news it was an accident. The report would have said something like:

"Authorities are seeking an unidentified person in connection with this incident. An as yet unidentified person was seen at the site of the death and Sheriff Al Dramico is seeking this person as a potential witness to the occurrence. If you have any information as to the identity of this potential witness, please call…"

"Oh, that was *good*," Mary, said mockingly. "But, it makes a lot of sense."

"Sure it does. It's the only explanation for the sheriff wrapping this up so quickly."

Alicia was quite pleased with herself. She had figured it out. It *was* the only explanation that fit the circumstances as they were.

No mention of a fourth party on that slope meant that no one ever realized they were there at all, thought Alicia. *The rope, wherever it was buried would not be found 'til spring, if at all. No one would be going up there then. The holidays would be over and the last skiers of the season would be at Jessup.*

She shared this thought with Mary, then added, "When the weather gets nice, we can hike in from the other side of the mountain, retrieve the rope and that will make it final."

Mary smiled and nodded in agreement. Alicia was very pleased with herself.

CHAPTER 15

Sunday morning found Kevin sleeping in. It was nearly ten o'clock before he opened his eyes to the clear blue sky out his window. He had been exhausted from both the physical and mental stress of the previous day, and had retired early. Awaking, he was surprised at how well he had slept. He remembered he had been worrying about their attempt to deceive the sheriff as he was getting into bed. Now, as he thought back to Wiley's performance yesterday, he chuckled—*He should get an Oscar for that job*—He looked out the window again and thought, *Looks like a pretty good day.*

His enthusiasm for the day waned as the realization swept over him that his good friend Bryce was gone. He couldn't help but see him lying there in the snow, crumpled up against the tree. Then his mind's eye wandered to happier times of great hunting trips, and fishing trips they had taken together. Then, unfortunately, back again. Kevin made an effort to force out the sadder thoughts and tried to focus on the happier ones. Next to skiing, deer hunting was his favorite pastime, and oh, he, Bryce and Wiley had surely had some great times on their hunting trips! Now it would be only Wiley and him, and this saddened Kevin, once again.

Kevin dressed and left the house without even thinking of breakfast. He wanted to get over to Wiley's house and discuss their next move. He also wanted to get Wiley's angle on what he thought the sheriff might be thinking. He didn't know what the punishment was for what they were doing, or even what the *crime* would be called. They weren't covering up evidence to protect themselves; they were doing it to take the law into their own hands. That, too, was something he needed to find out from Wiley.

What the hell has he got planned, he wondered?

It took him barely ten minutes to travel the two blocks to Wiley's and upon his arrival; Wiley was just putting the snow blower away.

"Hey, Wiley!" he called.

"Hey, Kev! What's up?"

"I thought maybe we should talk about all this," replied Kevin.

"Yea, good idea, let's go up to my room."

Wiley led the way inside. He seemed relaxed to Kevin and in control of the situation. Outwardly, Wiley didn't seem to be worried about anything at all. That, in itself, made Kevin feel more comfortable.

Wiley's room was rustic. Aside from being an excellent skier, Wiley was an exceptional woodsman. His room was a testament to that. There were rabbit skins, fox skins, and even a bear skin adorning the walls. In the space between his two windows was his prize trophy, a ten–point buck, mounted on a walnut base. It was a beauty! All four walls were wallpapered with a rough wood plank design and the woodwork had been grained to look similar. It was a *great* room, which Kevin envied greatly.

Wiley, like Kevin, was an avid hunter skilled in the ways of the forest. Both boys had benefit of fathers who hunted, like their fathers before them. The boys had spent days on end in the woods during the various hunting seasons each year. Both had been at it ever since they were old enough to tag along with their dads.

Kevin sat on the end of Wiley's bed facing Wiley, who had seated himself in his desk chair.

"Wiley, what do you think the sheriff is thinking about Bryce's accident by now?"

"I'd say he is thinking that it was just that; an accident." Wiley professed.

"Your story yesterday, about how it all happened, sure had me convinced," Kevin said, as he broke a big smile. "That was just awesome what with the tears and all!"

"Thanks–The tears were real though. I loved Bryce–That's why I am going to get those bitches and put them in their place, once and for all."

Wiley's face twisted with this last statement.

"I loved him, too. He was a cool guy," Kevin agreed.

Kevin paused a moment, then began again.

"How can we be sure we have fooled the sheriff? I mean, how will we know we are in the clear?" Kevin asked.

Wiley tossed Kevin the newspaper, which he had picked up from the hall table on their way upstairs.

"Look at the front page," he said.

Kevin opened the folded paper and began scanning the page.

"See it?" Wiley asked.

"Yea–I see it!"

Kevin's face had lighted up like a flare.

"Damn! It says 'tragic accident'! The sheriff bought our story!"

Kevin was beside himself with glee.

"Yep, looks like he did. Now, there's nothing in our way. We get the pleasure of doling out the medicine to those bitches. We get the pleasure of watching them squirm."

Kevin looked at Wiley in disbelief. He had never seen him this way. He had never heard him talk this way either. Wiley's face was all red and twisted, with deep furrows in his brow, his eyes mere slits, and his mouth was drawn tightly closed. It was kind of scary, but he couldn't say that he didn't agree one hundred percent.

"What are we going to do to them? I mean do you have a plan? How are we going to make them pay?"

Kevin realized that he was really getting into this. He, like Wiley and Bryce, had suffered the jokes, tricks, laughter and humiliations those bitches had been handing out to them for as long as he could remember.

"How are we going to make them pay, Wiley?"

"Don't know yet," was his reply.

"I thought you had a plan," Kevin said, a bit confused by Wiley's answer.

"I will come up with one, soon enough. For right now, we do nothing. That's the first step. Doing nothing."

Kevin listened intently as Wiley continued.

"Those bitches are probably scared to death by now. They planned to kill one of us. I've been thinking about it and they probably decided to kill whoever came down the hill first. Fortunately for you and I, that was Bryce. I don't know for sure. Maybe they *were* targeting Bryce. It's no secret that Alicia hates his guts and I'd bet my life that she was there with Mary. I figure when the rope went taught; Mary got jerked out in plain view. She hadn't counted on that and I saw her. I think she realizes I saw her. I half expected her to go to the sheriff and try to explain that it was just a prank and they didn't mean to hurt Bryce, but with the rope tied to the tree neck high, that would never have washed. Maybe she realized that. Anyway, she is running scared right about now and so is Alicia."

Kevin cleared his throat and interrupted.

"So—we do nothing and let them stew a while?" he asked. "Is that right?"

"Right. They never went to the authorities or we would have been called out by now on our story about the fox. If they had admitted what they did, our story becomes an outright lie. The sheriff would have been here by now, wanting an explanation."

"So we let them stew. Cool. How long?" asked Kevin.

"I don't know yet. There's no hurry. Pretty soon, they will relax and think they have gotten away with murder. They will see the news on TV, or read about it, and realize just like we did that the sheriff is satisfied with it being an accident. They will think they are in the clear and we are not going to do *anything* to make them think otherwise. Then, when the time is right, we will put the rest of our plan into action. We'll get our revenge."

"I like that!" bubbled Kevin. "I like that! We let them get comfortable with what they did and then we strike! Cool!"

Kevin was really getting into it now. Suddenly, the idea of being at the other end of the carrot, holding the stick, appealed to him greatly. He flopped back on the bed and laughed.

This is perfect, he thought!

He sat up again and looked straight at Wiley.

"So—what is 'phase two'? Do you have any idea yet, Wiley?"

Kevin really wanted to know how this was all going to unfold. He wanted to avenge Bryce, but he was also gaining enthusiasm for his new role as persecutor, a role he only knew from the other side, as the persecuted.

"Nope, none. I do know that I want it to make them suffer and I also want it to make their families suffer for raising those two bitches like they did. Don't worry, Kevin; I'll come up with something. In the mean time we just let them think they're sailing smooth waters. Then, when they least expect it we'll strike, and then we'll get our revenge. We'll make it hurt!"

Wiley's face had grown tense and contorted again, almost inhuman.

CHAPTER 16

Kevin and Wiley spent the rest of Sunday afternoon hanging out in Wiley's room. They played some Atari games and talked about some of the good times they had each had with Bryce.

There had been the occasional hunting and camping trips, which had been great, but it was the daily stuff that seemed to come to mind now. Visits to the shack, topped the list of course, but there was also the "snow tracking" and "sock dragging", which had been favorite pastimes for them all.

Of the two, the "snow tracking" had probably been the most fun. It was a game they played, right up until Bryce's death, whenever there was snow on the ground. Each boy, in turn, would be given a fifteen minute head start, into the forest, before the others would come looking for him. It was his "job" to use any trick at his disposal, to elude capture by the other two. He had thirty minutes to mislead the others, confusing his trail and finding a suitable hiding place. If, after one hour he was still undiscovered, he would head back to the starting point, as would the others, and the next boy would take his turn.

They spent hours at this game on Saturdays and Sundays, and occasionally, during the week after school. Wiley had always said that it would hone their tracking skills to a fine edge, but it was really just the fun of it that had kept them at it for so many years.

Although this game was sometimes played after school, the later months of winter, didn't allow enough daylight for each boy to have his turn. It was during those months that the after school game became "sock dragging". This was the game of choice also, when there was no snow available for the other.

They had been sock dragging for years also, but had not been able to play this game in over a year. The sock dragging game required the participation of a fourth, and key player. Boots, Kevin's white legged Sheltie, had been that participant. The game consisted of stuffing an old white tube sock, with rags or other old socks, tying the end in a knot and knotting it to the end of a short rope. The sock was supposed to represent a rabbit, or squirrel, or some other little creature of the forest. They would toss it to Boots, and let her play with it a while, tugging on the rope and generating her interest in it. Then, when her interest was peaked, Wiley or Bryce would hold Boots back, while Kevin would run into the forest, dragging the sock behind him. After fifteen minutes, or so, they would turn Boots loose and try to keep up with her as she bolted into the woods. By this time, Kevin had tucked the sock under some log, or bush, and had moved a short distance away to await the arrival of Boots.

The big question was supposed to be whether or not she would find the sock, but she had never let them down, not ever. Upon the successful completion of her mission, they would all gather together, praising Boots for her efforts, and Kevin would reach into his pocket and offer her a treat.

Wiley and Bryce swore that she was the best tracking dog in the county, but secretly, Kevin suspected it was the anticipated treat that actually led to Boots' success.

Whatever the reason for her unfaltering participation, it had all ended when a car, in front of Kevin's house, struck her and she had passed away. The boys had prepared a nice casket for her, lining an orange crate with old towels. They had held a small funeral service, just the three of them in attendance, and laid her to rest, alongside the shack.

These were the times they talked about today in Wiley's room. The good times they remembered sharing with Bryce. It was a good afternoon and it was made better by the passing of time.

Each hour that passed made them more comfortable with themselves and what they had chosen to do about the girls. There were still some lingering doubts in each boys mind as to whether they were really in the clear or not. The Journal made it pretty clear that the official status surrounding the circumstances of Bryce's death was *"tragic accident"*. Still, it was just a day later and the girls might take part of Sunday to decide to come forward. They may be discussing it and coming to the decision to tell what they had done without realizing that the case had already been classified an accident. So there was still some doubt, but with each passing hour the doubts diminished significantly.

Monday brought their return to school. They knew ahead of time that this would be hard, because they would see Mary and Alicia there. As expected, Bryce's death was the main topic of conversation in the hallways, the cafeteria and even in the classrooms. Attention was focused on Kevin and Wiley because everybody knew they were Bryce's best friends.

Mary and Alicia had never been friendly with or kind to either of them before, but today proved to be different. This particular Monday was the first time the girls showed any compassion toward them. But, they were not sincere feelings, but kind sympathies directed toward them out of nothing less than sheer contempt. What better way to revel in what they had done than to come face to face, in pseudo sympathy, with those whom it most affected.

Yes, Monday was interesting. It also brought the temptation to lash out at those bitches, but Kevin and Wiley were fixed in their determination to play out their hand in their own time. It was Tuesday that turned into the worst school day of the week for Kevin. It started normally enough, with the usual rebuffs to his greetings and the typical stares and whispers. The morning progressed pretty much as he had expected, until after lunch.

Lunch in the cafeteria was the usual ordeal, with the occasional piece of food hitting him in the back of the head, or one of the guys walking by and trying to snitch something off his tray. It was just another typical lunch period, the worst of which being that he and Wiley were on staggered lunch schedules, Wiley's lunch period beginning as Kevin's was ending. With Bryce gone Kevin was totally alone and on his own at lunchtime.

What really made the day turn sour was what Kevin found taped to his locker after lunch. He saw it as he approached, but couldn't make out what it was until he came nearer. What he discovered was a photo of Bryce, torn off at the neck, and taped to a crude drawing of a person crunched up against a tree. The caption, scrawled at the bottom of the page read:

"Bryce Spencer's first kiss, the kiss of death!"

Kevin was livid! *"How could she?"* he exclaimed, under his breath. He knew full well who had put this atrocity there for him to find. He looked at Bryce's face on the photo. It was a school photo, but an old one, probably eight or ninth grade. The round holes punched through it, slightly larger than pinholes, explained the longevity of the photo in Mary's possession. It appeared to him that it must have been used as a target on a dartboard, for quite some time.

Kevin yanked the vulgar display from his locker door, and carefully removed the photo of Bryce. Taking a piece of notebook paper from his binder, he wrote his own note:

Dear Mary,
I'm returning your target.
I have you in my sights!
Truthfully,
Kevin

He didn't know if she would interpret the note correctly, or not. Right now, he really didn't care. He folded the photo of Bryce in the note he had written, and walked to her locker, which he knew was number 27, as it was just two lockers away from Wiley's. He creased the folds sharply, and inserted the folded note through the vent slots in the locker door.

His retribution, so very uncommon of him, made him feel better, but he realized that he had probably just violated his pact with Wiley. He decided he would keep quiet about the whole incident. What Wiley didn't know, wouldn't upset him. Besides, Mary probably wouldn't understand what he was talking about anyway.

The week continued to pass slowly, with Wednesday bringing less attention to the boys. Kevin received no more *messages* from Mary, nor did she mention his message to her. He didn't really expect to hear back from her about it, as he knew she would not give him the satisfaction of acknowledging his rare burst of bravado.

Bryce's funeral service was Thursday morning, and Wiley and Kevin were excused from school to attend. No other students had made the request, and none were in attendance at Keller's.

The service was nice, an open casket visitation, and Doc had done a wonderful job of capturing the vitality that was once Bryce Spencer. So much so that Kevin had almost spoken to him, as if to awaken him from a nap. Bryce was dressed in his best Sunday attire, his hair neatly combed, which was the one mistake Doc had made in his living appearance. Bryce wore a smile on his face; just enough to appropriately capture his once friendly and loving personality.

The attendance was small, with only twelve concerned friends and family members present. Kevin and Wiley were there of course, as well as Kevin's parents and Bryce's parents. Millie Coates, Wiley's mom, made the effort, although Calvin did not. Two of Bryce's aunts from Liddelman and one uncle from Casper, Wyoming, came also. Those in attendance were completed by the appearance of Al and

Stan, who would lead the funeral procession to the Glen Laurel Cemetery, as well as pay their respects.

Following the thirty–minute service, Stan and Al led the five–car funeral procession through Carver, across the Lower Saline Bridge, and through Greenville to the Glen Laurel Cemetery. The Spencers had owned a plot in the older Oak Meadows Cemetery on the Carver side of the river, but had decided that they would buy a new one for themselves and Bryce near Mount Crane. Glen Laurel was located at the foot of Mount Crane, and it had seemed appropriate that their son rest near the mountain he had loved so much. Bryce was laid to rest at two in the afternoon, Thursday November 7, 1968, five days after his final run down Mount Crane's Cougar Run. After the funeral, each boy had each gone home to his own room to think privately about Bryce and all that he had meant to them, collectively and individually.

By Friday afternoon, it was like any other Friday afternoon at school. The only thing on any of the student's minds was the weekend. Mary and Alicia had gone back to their usual ways, that of ignoring all but their small, select circle of friends. There were no more sympathetic words, phony or otherwise, for the boys. It was business as usual at Carver High.

When the final bell rang on Friday afternoon, signaling the beginning of the weekend, Kevin and Wiley walked home together, as they had three of the previous four school days since the *accident*. On Monday and Tuesday they had gone to Kevin's house, and to Wiley's on Wednesday. Kevin liked going to Wiley's because he loved Wiley's room. It was just what he wanted his room to be like, but his mother would not allow animal skins in *her* house. The one exception was the bearskin his father was allowed to keep on the wall of the garage, not technically *in* the house.

"Hey, Wiley, let's go to you place today," Kevin suggested, as they walked down the school's front walk, toward the street.

"Sure."

"Deer season starts next weekend and we should start making some plans," Kevin suggested. "Have you thought about where you want to go yet?"

"No, not really. Have you?"

"No. All I've thought about lately is Bryce, but I'll start giving it some thought. Did you get your license yet?" Kevin asked.

"Yea, I got my license last week, but I didn't get a doe permit this year. Waited too long," Wiley commented, forlornly.

"That will make two of us hunting a buck then. I haven't even been to get my license yet, but I'll go down to Schooley's Hardware tomorrow, and take care of it."

"Good. I checked the moon phases for this season and we will have a sliver past a new moon the first weekend. Should be good hunting," Wiley told Kevin.

Kevin knew that was good, and Wiley's comment needed no further explanation. With a new moon, or nearly so, the deer would bed down all night, rather than browse, as they would with light from a full or gibbous moon. Kevin knew the deer would start moving at first light, after he and Wiley were in their stands, waiting for a big one to come along.

Kevin replied knowingly, "Great! That's cool!"

During the past week Kevin *had* been doing some thinking about making this hunting trip special, something different, but he hadn't been ready to discuss it with Wiley yet. It should be something of a memorial to their lost friend who would not be accompanying them this year, or ever again. This would be the first time in six years the three would not be together, on some mountain, for the first morning of deer season. The past two years they had gone alone, just the three of them. Prior to that their father's had led the expeditions into deer country letting the boys tag along to learn the ropes and gain experience. Now it would be just the two of them and that meant that this hunting trip had to be something special and different. To go to where they had always gone and do what they had always done would be hard to handle. No, this trip had to be unique. This hunting trip had to be special, a tribute to Bryce and his memory.

Kevin lay on Wiley's bed looking at the ten–pointer between the windows. Wiley had taken that buck on the first trip they had made alone to Robinson Ridge. It was a beauty, but he remembered all too well the difficulty they had packing it out.

That was one heavy buck!

He rolled onto his stomach and looked at Wiley, who was deep into a game of Pong. Kevin decided that now was as good a time as any to bring up his idea for this year's hunting trip.

"Wiley, I've been thinking," Kevin started.

"Now we're in trouble," chuckled Wiley.

Kevin smiled.

"I've been thinking that we should make this trip a tribute to Bryce. We should go somewhere different, somewhere Bryce would have really liked. It should be someplace none of us have ever been to before, or ever dreamed of going to."

Wiley turned from his game and faced Kevin.

"Like where?" he asked.

"I don't know–Bryce was always talking about going up to Blind Valley…"

"Blind Valley!" Wiley interrupted. "That's crazy! He wanted to go up there to explore, *not to hunt!* There's no way you can pack a buck out of there. Hell, it's damn near impossible to climb up into there on your own, let alone pack a deer out."

"I know, but it's where he always wanted to go," Kevin insisted.

Wiley shook his head, then lowered it, looking at the floor.

"Kevin, that is about the most ridiculous idea you've ever had. My dad went up there once. He told me that it's a five hundred foot climb up into that box canyon. You don't need climbing gear or anything, but he said it's a damn hard climb. There's no other way in. Nobody hunts up there because they *know* they can't pack their kill back out. In fact, nobody goes up there at all. It's too damn hard to get in there." He thought for a second, then added, "Or out!"

Kevin stared hard at Wiley. It was obvious he was upset.

"Well–*That* is where I want to go…for Bryce. Maybe we won't hunt this trip. I think we should go up there just for Bryce, because he always wanted to and never got the chance. We could just camp out and maybe hunt small game. Then we wouldn't have to worry about packing out a deer."

Wiley was still staring at Kevin with that look of incredulity he had often displayed when Kevin had previously shared some of his own ideas.

Not hunt? But, he could see the resolve in Kevin's face. This seemed to be pretty important to him.

"Tell you what, Kevin. I'll think about it, okay?" Wiley conceded.

"Okay, but while you're thinking, think about this. Maybe we'll get a glimpse of the Blind Valley Hermit!"

"Right, like he exists. That's just a legend bonehead," Wiley jibed.

"Legends are grounded in fact, Wiley. They get embellished, but they are grounded in fact. My grandpa says he exists. He told me *he* got a glimpse of him when he was a teenager."

"Right," Wiley said, mockingly. "What was your grandpa doing up there?"

"He went up with his dad to hunt deer. It was in the winter of 1907 and it was a bad one. All the deer had disappeared from the usual places, he said, and his dad had the idea that they may have retreated to Blind Valley and other places similar to it. He said that Blind Valley is a sheltered valley and the deer may have gone there when the food supply dwindled around here. They were dependent on the deer for their own food supply, so they went looking in Blind Valley out of desperation. Their plan was to butcher the deer up there and pack the meat out on their backs. Anyway, Gramps said they were up there hunting their stand when he caught a glimpse, out of the corner of his eye, of a man watching them through the forest. He turned to see an old man, all dressed in fur with a long beard, moving silently and ever so slowly through the trees. He walked all hunched over like he was very old, but managed to move without a sound as he watched them from behind one tree, then another. Gramps tapped his dad on the shoulder and motioned for him to look, but his dad was too late. Gramps said the old man disappeared as quickly as he had appeared. He was gone, vanished like smoke," Kevin finished.

"And you believed it? You would you cluck. It's just a legend I'm telling you. Did you know the Montana State Police went up there looking for him? I think it was during World War II. It might have been Korea, I'm not sure."

"No, I didn't," Kevin answered, a bit surprised.

"My dad told me about it. He said they wanted to fingerprint him just to be certain he wasn't hiding out from the law up there. They planned to use the war as their excuse for probable cause to print him. Something about making sure he was registered for the draft and hadn't already been called to duty."

"Hoaky," Kevin interjected. They didn't find him, did they?"

"No they didn't, and why? Because he didn't exist. He didn't then and he doesn't now. They never found a trace him and they never found where he lived. A man experienced in the woods might be able to stay out of sight when he knows folks are up there looking for him, but he can't hide his cabin. They would at least have found his home, and they never did. Why? Because *it* didn't exist either!"

"Gramps wouldn't lie to me Wiley. He exists," Kevin insisted.

"Okay, let's say he *did*. I say did because even if he had existed, he'd be long dead by now. The legend has been around forever. Your grandpa said he saw an *old* man in 1907. This is 1968. That was sixty–one years ago. If he ever existed he would have to be at least a hundred and twenty years old by now. Think about it."

Kevin was silent. He flopped back down on the bed and then bounced right back up again.

"Damn, I guess you're right, but he *did* exist. I'm telling you he did."

"I'll tell you what, Kev. We *will* go up there next weekend, if for no other reason than to prove you wrong. We'll search every inch of that valley for his cabin, or the remains of it. That will make it an adventure and I like adventures, almost as much as hunting."

Kevin beamed with joy.

"Then it's settled?" he asked.

"Yes, it's settled. We'll leave early Saturday morning."

"One more thing, Wiley. We can't let my folks know where we are going. Every time my Gramps told that story and I showed an interest in going there myself, my dad would warn me that I was not to go up there. He says it's a dangerous place to get in and out of. *"Too dangerous for a boy to try."* So we can't say we are going there, okay?"

"Sure. Ditto for my folks, too. They would probably say no also," agreed Wiley.

With that settled, Wiley started to stand, and then sat back down hard.

"Damn," he said in disgust.

"What?" Kevin asked.

"That trip is going to take us more than just two days, counting having the time to search and all. We can't possibly be back in time for school Monday."

"So—we skip school Monday, and Tuesday, too, if necessary. Hell, it's deer season. We won't be the only ones out of school those days," Kevin reminded him.

Wiley was deep in thought again, gazing at the floor and rubbing his brow.

"That's true enough, but it's our folks I'm worried about. What are we going to tell them? We can't just disappear for two extra days. We have to have an explanation for where we are going and how long we'll be gone," Wiley said, searching for an idea.

"Upper Los Lobos," Kevin stated, flatly.

"What about it? Why there?" he asked Kevin.

"This is the first year they are opening it to doe permits. It's over-populated this year. I saw it in the Journal," Kevin informed him.

"That's two hundred miles from here!" Wiley exclaimed.

"So—we're not really going there. That's just what we tell our folks, to account for the extra time we'll need. If they give us a hard time about it, we'll tell them it's our *senior trip*," Kevin suggested.

Wiley thought about it.

"But we don't *have* doe permits," he reminded Kevin.

"Does you dad know that yet?" Kevin asked.

"No, come to think of it, I haven't mentioned it yet," Wiley, replied.

"Then what's the problem?" Kevin asked, smiling broadly.

"None, I guess."

"Then it's settled?" asked Kevin.

"Settled."

Kevin was elated. He had dreamed of going up there ever since his grandpa had told him about spotting the Blind Valley Hermit. That was one of the reasons why Bryce had wanted so badly to go. Kevin's grandpa had shared his story with Bryce one evening at Kevin's request. It had intrigued Bryce as much as it had Kevin. Going some-place new was one thing, but how often did you get to go on an adventure like this would be? Searching for a legend would be the ultimate adventure!

They spent the rest of the afternoon planning their adventure and debating the existence of the Blind Valley hermit.

CHAPTER 17

The weekend passed into Monday morning and the return, once again, to school. Kevin and Wiley found things at school had gone back to complete normalcy. With the exception of themselves it seemed as though Bryce had been totally forgotten, a faint and fleeting memory of someone who once occupied a front row seat in every class he attended.

The taunts and teases had resumed with fervor, Kevin and Wiley being the most popular targets. It didn't matter that they had just lost their best friend to a tragic accident. It made as little difference to the other students as does rain to a fish. As the week passed along, each day brought its usual torment, but each ensuing day also brought something new and cruel. With each passing day a new "Bryce joke" was being added to the ever–growing magazine of ammunition the *in crowd* had been building over the years.

The majority of the students were mute, neither offering condolences nor taunting the boys. It was as if they didn't know what to say, so they tried to steer clear of Kevin and Wiley all together. A casual nod as they would pass in the halls was about all the recognition they were prepared to offer. As far as the boys were concerned, that was fine with them. It was a whole lot better than being harassed, and besides, they didn't know how to talk to these people anyway.

They were the fringe element, the casual tormenters who never started anything with them, but were always quick to support the efforts of those who did, the *other* group, which had Mary and Alicia at the top of its organizational structure.

This *other* group was comprised of the kids who could put their pants on, "both legs at a time". The self–appointed panel who determined which kids were cool and which were geeks. Bryce's death had not changed any of this, not in the least.

With each passing day it was as if Mary and Alicia were gaining confidence that they had not been found out. With each passing day they became more emboldened. They, of all people, were making up Bryce jokes, and this enraged the boys and hardened their resolve to "make them pay".

"How did Bryce manage to hit that tree…? He was 'rubbernecking'!" they would say, or *"How fast was Bryce going…? At 'break neck' speed!"*

They had heard the comments around every corner. Most of the kids would only say these things when they thought neither boy was present, but Mary would tell these jokes to her friends knowing full well that one or the other, or both were present, then turn her head in their direction, smiling her coy little smile.

God I hate her, they would think! *You'll get yours.*

What made this second week of school even close to bearable was the anticipation of the upcoming adventure to Blind Valley. The more they thought about it the better it was beginning to sound. They wanted, no, needed to get away, into the forest where they were free from their tormenters. They needed to be free from the constant taunts and reminders of Bryce's *accident*. Most of all, they felt that they must put some space between themselves and those bitches. *That* was imperative. It took all their resolve to keep from lashing out at Mary, or for that matter, at Alicia.

Mary was by far the worse of the two, but Alicia was getting her barbs in, too, whenever the two of them were together. They had killed Bryce and believed they were free and clear of all responsibility. They felt they had put one over on the boys, and were it not for their desire to remain free, would have flaunted it in their faces. The girls were pushing their *knowledge* of their involvement to the edge, just shy of *taking credit* for Bryce's demise.

Wiley felt that he had to get away from them before he broke his own pact with Kevin and blurted out something that would give away *his own* knowledge of what happened to Bryce. He was not so worried about Kevin losing control as he was for himself. He knew the taunting and joking was adversely affecting Kevin, but he believed, mistakenly so, that Kevin's fuse was long, unlike his own. Kevin would keep it together okay, but could *he*? Saturday was just around the corner. He would brace himself for one more day of this Hell and then he'd be in the mountains, free of this place and the people it contained.

Kevin was not feeling as confident about avoiding a confrontation as Wiley believed him to be. He was finding it harder, with each passing day, to keep his cool and not lash back at them. He had already broken the pact once, and was trying desperately, not to do it again. But those bitches were so unbearably cruel.

If only we had a plan, he thought. *Maybe I could look past all this, to the day we'll get even with them.* But, with no plan for their retaliation in place, it was just one day at a time, with no satisfaction in sight.

The late afternoons and evenings had been a blessing, providing release from the bonds of the classrooms and corridors of Carver High. They would spend them in one boy's room or the other, planning their excursion to Blind Valley. They made lists of the provisions they would need, of the equipment they would take, and of things they needed to accomplish before leaving.

At the top of the list of things to obtain was a map of the region. Not a street map or county map, like you could get at the gas station, but a *real* map, showing topography and water sources, peaks and valleys, and of course, names of known features on the landscape. There might be information to be derived, from what those who had gone before them had chosen to name things. One never knew.

The map was Kevin's idea. He had looked at the maps they had which included the Blind Valley area, and had concluded that none of them were detailed enough. None of them showed topography.

"How steep is this hill, or how deep is this valley?" he had pointed out on their maps.

None of them showed small features, or names of features in the area. He had explained to Wiley that a survey done in June might yield a name on a good map, like "Dry Spring". *"But we're going up there in November, and in November the spring might not be dry,"* he had explained. This was *"important information"* they might need, Kevin had said. Wiley had agreed with Kevin's reasoning, and the map became priority number one, followed by number two, candy bars, *"for quick energy"*, Wiley had argued.

Each boy had presented his case to his parents for the need of a *senior trip* to Los Lobos for the new doe season. Wiley's father was cool with it all, encouraging him to bring back some good venison for their locker. Kevin's father, on the other hand, was not so sure it was a good idea. He had argued that it was a long trip, into country they weren't familiar with, but Kevin had eventually won out, using the age old argument that he'd be eighteen years old next month.

"I'm not a little kid anymore, Dad!" He had pleaded. *"We're even going to Bennett, after school Friday, to get a topo map of Los Lobos,"* he had explained, his fingers crossed behind his back.

So the late afternoons and evenings helped derail the building frustrations of each day completed in the confines of Carver High. The late afternoons and evenings helped bond them in their resolve to remain "cool" at school. These late afternoons and evenings, left alone to their own devices, became the crucible in which their futures were being formed.

CHAPTER 18

✿

"Got everything?" Wiley asked. The car was packed and ready to go. It was five o'clock Saturday morning and it could not have come too soon. Wiley had just finished double–checking his equipment and supplies. Once they climbed up into Blind Valley, there would be no coming back down for matches, rope, food, or anything else they might need.

"Yep," replied Kevin. "I think so."

After school Friday afternoon, they had driven to Bennett. In Bennett, they had visited the U.S. Geological Survey office and obtained a topographical map of the Blind Valley area. They would scour the valley, grid by grid, either proving or disproving the hermit's existence. They were now approaching this trip with all the meticulous preparation of archeologists leaving on a quest for a lost civilization. *Their* lost civilization consisted of a one–man colony, the cabin of the Blind Valley Hermit. This was *truly* shaping up to be a glorious adventure!

"Map, compass, binoculars, flashlight. I think I've got everything," Kevin declared.

"Good, let's shove off. We should be there by daybreak," replied Wiley, with great anticipation in his voice. "This is gonna be great!"

Wiley's prediction was right on the money. Daybreak found them pulling off Highway 77 and onto a dirt access road used by the forestry service, which would lead them up to the embarkation point. They had studied their map Friday night to find the best place to head up into the Blind Valley area. This little access road was it.

The terminus of the road would leave them with a steady uphill hike of some three miles to the base of Oriel Peak. Then there would be an even steeper assent of another five miles to the foot of the escarpment, which climbs into Blind Valley. This was where the going would get extremely hard. Access to Blind valley sat five hundred feet up the escarpment.

They arrived at the end of the forest access road at sunup and pulled Kevin's Chevy into the forest, as far as they could go. Kevin felt his car would be safer back in the woods, out of sight of the road, just in case anyone else should happen to find their way back there. It wasn't likely that anybody would, as there was absolutely no sign that anybody ever came back this way, at all. There were no littered beer cans, no trash piles, or discarded appliances and furniture, the likes of which you were certain to see at the end of many, more frequented roads. It appeared to them that nobody ventured back here, ever.

The car safely hidden, the boys threw on their backpacks, consulted their map and started the long hike to the base of Oriel Peak. According to their map, Blind Valley was like a giant sugar bowl, nestled into the side of the mountain. Oriel Peak rose above this point to 13,950 feet, starting its rise on either side of where the boys would enter the valley. There was no other way in.

The really intriguing fact they learned from their map was that the floor of the valley would be below them by the time they had climbed to the base of the escarpment. They would have to go up, to go down. In climbing the five hundred foot escarpment the boys would be climbing fifteen hundred feet above the floor of Blind Valley, before descending down into it from the lip. Down into the bowl. Fortunately, the map indicated a much more gradual descent, after reaching the crest.

The boys knew this would be the hardest climb they had ever undertaken. The elevation lines on their map all converged at the escarpment, forming what appeared to be, one thick line and that meant *steep*! The escarpment stood five hundred feet tall and nearly all five hundred feet was at an angle of fifty–five degrees from horizontal. There were also short climbs along the route that were as steep as sixty degrees. They didn't know these details at the time, but they would soon find them out. As hard as they studied the map, there was no other way around it, through it, or over it. This was not only the most practical route in; it was the *only* route that would not require climbing equipment and a lot of rock climbing experience. It was easy to see why a hermit would pick Blind Valley, and why it was so rarely visited.

If climbing the escarpment wasn't enough to discourage one from trying, there was no trail to follow up to that point either. Anyone wanting to go there, including the boys would have to rely on a compass, map, and skill, to navigate the eight miles of forest that lay between civilization and Blind Valley.

Fortunately, Oriel Peak was on the leeward side of the Hatcher Range and the snow was only a few inches deep. They had brought their snowshoes thinking they would need them, but had found them unnecessary upon their arrival.

They plodded up the steep grade and through the thick forest without speaking, for almost four miles. In part they were simply enjoying the sights and smells of the forest, taking it all in, in reverent silence. They saw mountain jays, nutcrackers, and tuft–eared squirrels in the trees. They spotted ground squirrels and marmots, darting in and out of the rocks, in the talus slopes they passed. Where the snow had been blown from the ground, their boots crunched softly on the weathered alabaster and conifer needles, which formed the floor of this alpine area. It was a glorious day, and they were completely lost in its beauty and wonder.

As they broke the tree line, they found the need to become acclimated to the "thinner" air they were encountering. They weren't flatlanders, so they were used to the rare air at 7,000 feet, where they had started hiking, but they had now ascended to nearly 11,000 feet, under heavy exertion. They were becoming breathless and light–headed and decided to stop for a moment's rest.

Kevin bent over to study an Indian Paint Brush flower he had spotted, and upon standing, a minute later, fainted and fell on his backsides before regaining consciousness. Wiley enjoyed a good laugh over that!

"Hey *mountain man*. How high are we?" Wiley asked, still laughing.

Still sitting on his rump, Kevin pulled the map from his coat.

"According to the map, we are at about 11,000 feet," he replied, speaking between gasps for air and efforts to clear his head.

"How high will be going?"

"The base of the escarpment is at 12,300 feet," he answered, still breathing hard.

"So we are going to climb over a mile by the time we reach the lip of the valley!" Wiley exclaimed, in awe of the heights they would be reaching.

"Looks like it," Kevin said.

"Wow! This is awesome! We'll be on top of the world!"

"Pretty close to it, at least for around these parts," Kevin acknowledged.

Kevin folded the map and placed it back in his coat pocket. Shaking his head and taking a deep breath, he attempted to stand. His second attempt found him back on his feet, but wobbly and slightly disoriented.

"Wow! That was wild!" he exclaimed. "We better keep moving. We don't know how hard this is going to get or how much time it is going to take to get up the escarpment. I want to get into the valley and get our camp set up before dark," Kevin advised.

"That's for sure," Wiley agreed. "You can't pick out a campsite in the dark, in country you don't know," he added.

They pushed on, as the terrain changed from forest to scattered scrub pine and low ground foliage. It was windy up here, and the little snow that had fallen was mostly blown away. The crunch of the alabaster and the soft whisper of the wind, were the only sounds that met their ears.

An occasional scrub jay would swoop silently before them, darting randomly from bush to bush. Bright patches of orange and green lichen could be seen blanketing much of the rocky terrain. Breathing was becoming more difficult than ever, and the escarpment loomed just ahead, rising into view as they moved onward and upward. A half an hour later, Kevin and Wiley stood shoulder to shoulder, staring up at the escarpment. It was a forbidding sight to behold.

"Wow!" gasped Kevin in awe of the sight before him.

"You got that right," Wiley confirmed.

"Think we can make it?" Kevin asked, his trepidation apparent.

"We have to," replied Wiley, wiping his brow. "You're not getting cold feet are you?"

Kevin smiled at Wiley, slapped him on the shoulder and replied, "They've been cold all day. Let's rest a spell, *and then* hit it. We've made pretty good time so far."

Wiley looked up at the sun and commented, "Looks like about one o'clock. What do you say?" he asked Kevin.

Kevin looked at his Timex and replied, "12:50. Pretty good, Wiley! That's pretty good."

Each of them picked what looked like a comfortable rock and sat down to rest. Wiley rummaged through his pack and came up with a Hershey Bar, with almonds, and Kevin pulled his favorite, a Chunky, from a coat pocket.

He thought to himself as he chewed, *Chunky. What a chunk o' chocolate!*

Kevin had always loved that commercial. He couldn't remember the actor's name that spoke those famous words, but he never failed to crack Kevin up, every time he saw it.

Wiley, finishing his Hershey Bar came to his feet.

"Ready to go, Kev?" he asked, suggesting it was time to start.

"Ready," Kevin stated. "Let's do it!"

They each stuffed their candy wrapper into a pocket, put their packs back on, adjusting them securely, and approached the daunting task before them. Wiley laid out a visual route, then started up, while Kevin said a little prayer, and followed in his footsteps.

CHAPTER 19

*T*f God had created a more beautiful place, Wiley couldn't imagine where. He was standing at the portal to Heaven, he was sure. He had reached the top of the escarpment, just ahead of Kevin, and was looking down on the most awesome sight he had ever seen.

He turned and yelled back to Kevin, "Hurry up, Kev! You are not going to believe this!" He turned again in the direction of the valley. There before him was a vast depression with sheer black cliffs rising above all of its other walls, rising on either side of him to the summit of Oriel Peak. In front of him though, lay a sloping downgrade, into the fifteen hundred foot deep bowl that was Blind Valley. Most amazing of all was the descent into the bowl dropped back below the tree line and the floor of the valley was a vast forest.

"*God, this is cool,*" he murmured under his breath.

"Kevin! Hurry up!"

His words echoed throughout the valley before him.

Kevin reached the top moments later. He stood next to Wiley in total silence, his mouth hanging open, and his eyes as wide and round as silver dollars.

"Damn," was the only word he could muster. Then again, "Damn!"

Wiley threw his arm around Kevin's shoulders and tugged him against his side.

"Kevin, we made it! Damned if we didn't do it. Have you ever seen anything so damn awesome in you life?"

It was a rhetorical question of course. Wiley knew neither of them had ever seen anything like this before, nor had most other people, even those who traveled the world and sought out the most beautiful places to visit had probably never seen anything that could top this.

"No, Wiley. I have never seen anything so awesome before. But it's a whole lot more than just awesome. It's unbeatable! It's magnificent! It's, it's–" Kevin had run out of descriptions for what lay before his eyes. He wasn't even sure if he had come close to describing it yet.

"Look, Wiley!" he said as he pointed into the distance, down into the bowl. "There's even *clouds down there!*"

The two friends turned to look at one another, simultaneously, with the look of children coming down the stairs on Christmas morning. Together they began down the slope into Blind Valley, first at a measured walk, then breaking into a run with arms uplifted to the sky, whooping and hollering as they went. Their exuberance lasted for about fifty yards before they became totally winded. They slowed their descent to a stop and panting and smiling, they hunched over, resting their hands on their knees. They were facing each other, breathing very hard and laughing so hard that tears ran down their cheeks. It was truly their time, shared by no one else but these *two* close friends. They seemed to realize this and a somber look came over Kevin's face.

"God, Wiley–Bryce would have loved this place," Kevin lamented.

Wiley's smile faded to an empty expression. His eyes looked haunted by some inward vision or ghost, and he said nothing, as his face became contorted. It was clear to Kevin that Wiley had drifted into some place other than Blind Valley. Some dark place where his thoughts had turned to something that Kevin wasn't sure he wanted to know right now. He sat down on the slope and looked caringly at Wiley.

"You okay, Wiley?" he asked with concern.

"Sure, I'm okay, Kev," Wiley spoke softly. "I was just thinking."

Wiley paused for a moment, wiping the tears from his cheeks and chin.

"Get that map out and let's see what looks like a good place for a camp," he suggested.

Kevin smiled and pulled out the map.

"Sure, let's find a place to set up," he agreed.

They spent the next ten minutes looking over the map. They noticed an area along the west wall where the elevation lines on the map seemed to cross over others of the lines.

"What's this?" asked Wiley, pointing to the spot on the map. "Is that an overhang?"

"I'm not sure, but it appears to be. I haven't seen anything like that before on any other maps," Kevin confessed.

"Well, if it is an overhang, it would be a great place to pitch camp," Wiley suggested. "It'll be sheltered from above. If we get rain or snow we'll stay high and dry. Come on, let's check it out!"

Kevin took a reading with the compass, plotted their course, and they headed out in the direction of the strange markings on the map. As they descended to the tree line, within the bowl, Kevin noticed something quite strange. Although the trees seemed to be the same species of fir, balsam, and pine as they had encountered on their way up to Blind Valley, they were much shorter and less densely needled, as if they were stunted in some way.

"Do you notice the trees, Wiley?" he asked.

"They're puny," Wiley replied, looking around at them.

"What's with that?" Kevin asked.

"I'd say their growth is stunted."

Wiley looked up and around in all directions.

"They probably don't get enough sunlight down in this hole. That's what I'd say," Wiley theorized. "That's just a guess, mind you, but I can't think of any other reason for it."

Kevin thought about that for a second or two, studying the trees and the surrounding area.

"Yep, you're probably right. Not enough sunlight, that's interesting."

They took another look at the map and another compass reading and then ventured into the forest of stunted trees. They walked on, Kevin studying the map and checking his compass, Wiley taking it all in. There was no snow in the bowl and their feet fell quietly on the bed of needles that was the floor of Blind Valley.

"Hey, Kevin."

Wiley was the first to break the silence.

"When we get back home and discuss this place, where we might be overheard, we are going to refer to it as 'Short Pines'. This is going to be *our* place, our *secret* place. Okay?"

"Sure, Wiley, that's a cool name for this place," Kevin replied.

He liked the idea. It was their own secret place, where nobody would be able to find them or bother them. A place they could come to and explore. A place away from the rest of the world, and just their own. He liked the idea a lot.

They continued on their plotted path until they finally broke the forest. There before them rose a massive cliff of dark gray granite. It was fully shadowed, the sun having already withdrawn its light from its face by late afternoon. It appeared nearly black before them and rose a thousand feet up into the deep blue sky. The map had been right. This monolithic mass of granite leaned toward them, perhaps as much as five degrees from the base to the midpoint, and then angled even further forward from that point on to the top. It appeared firm and solid, with practically no talus beneath the overhung structure. In fact the floor beneath it was virtually free of fallen rock. It looked safe and would provide several hundred feet of sheltered ground on which to pitch their camp.

"This is awesome!" Wiley yelled in total exuberance.

"Yoooooooooo!" he sounded, as loud and long as he could hold it. His 'Yo' echoed throughout the valley, coming back to them at least a half dozen times, before fading back into silence.

"Let's move to the base and pitch our tent. We can gather some firewood and build us a big campfire, heat up some food and plan our search for tomorrow. How's that sound, Kev?"

"Sounds like a plan to me," he replied smiling and swelling with enthusiasm.

"This is gonna be just awesome!" Kevin exclaimed.

They picked up their packs, which they had dropped to the ground as they first stood in awe of the massive cliff wall. Hiking them into position they moved forward, looking up at the solid rock ceiling forming above them as they proceeded ever closer to the base.

It was a good two hundred feet to the foot of the wall; all under the granite ceiling that would shelter them. Wiley selected what appeared to him to be the perfect spot for their camp. Kevin agreed that it looked good, and they broke out their gear and pitched their pup tent, with the opening toward the wall. Wiley reasoned that this would afford them maximum protection from the elements. Kevin didn't think that was necessary and complained that the view would be *better* if it faced the other way.

"What the hell do you think you are going to see after dark?" Wiley argued.

They flipped a coin. Wiley won.

This minor disagreement put aside, they began their gathering of firewood. It was plentiful, and they had a roaring fire going in minutes. The boys sat by the fire and sorted through their provisions, each selecting what he would heat up for his first supper in 'Short Pines'. Kevin chose beans and franks, and Wiley went with beef ravioli. Although these had always been among their favorite foods, they had never tasted better than they did right now. Steak and potatoes could not have been more rewarding. They savored their first meal in Short Pines, eating slowly and talking about all that they had experienced during this most wonderful of days. As they finished their last bites, Kevin suggested they start planning out their search for the hermit's cabin.

"I've been reconsidering that idea, Kev," Wiley said.

"Reconsidering what, Wiley?" Kevin asked.

"I think he built a home pit, like the Aleuts did in Alaska," Wiley postulated.

He had done some reading about the natives of the Aleutian Islands and how they had dug circular pits in the ground, over which they had constructed sod domes, for protection from the prevailing high winds.

"In all these years that he has been talked about and even searched for, no one has ever found where he lived. *If* he existed, I can understand why *he* was never found, because he was probably good at staying hidden and he knew this place like the back of his hand. But, he couldn't just move his home around to avoid folks looking, so it must have been very well hidden and totally inconspicuous. That's what I think," Wiley suggested.

"Sounds logical," Kevin agreed. "But where? Where do we start looking? This *is* a big place!" Kevin reminded him.

"If I were him I'd want to be located where I had the most protection from the elements. I'd take advantage of this overhang for one thing. It's also the west wall of this valley, which provides the most protection from the prevailing westerly winds. I think we start our search along this side of the valley, close to the wall first, then expand it outward."

Kevin thought about it for a moment.

"That sounds good."

Pointing to a spot on the map, he continued.

"We'll start in this quadrant here, where the slope we entered on gives way to the cliff."

"No," interrupted Wiley. "That's a waste of time. I don't think the hermit ever planned to leave this place once he found it. The only reason for locating up there would be for easier access in and out of the valley, a shorter distance to travel coming and going. No–I think he would have buried himself deep into the valley."

Wiley pointed to another location on the map.

"Here–close to this corner, where the west wall turns east. *That* is where I would build my home. Maximum protection and maximum distance from the intruding world."

Kevin was amazed at Wiley's apparent understanding of how the hermit would have thought. It all made sense to him, but neither of them knew if Wiley would be right. They had to start somewhere and only Wiley had come up with a logical reason for where they should begin, so he agreed.

"That's good thinking, Wiley," he commented with an air of awe in his voice. "You've given this a lot of thought."

"Not really," he replied. "That's just what *I* would do if I chose to live up here and not be bothered. Come on; let's hit the hay. I want to get started at daybreak. We've got a lot of ground to cover tomorrow."

Night had fallen as they had talked by the fire, and they were exhausted from their climb into this place and the excitement of their adventure. Kevin threw a few more logs on the fire and they curled up in their sleeping bags, where, in a matter of hours, they would greet their first morning in Short Pines.

CHAPTER 20

Kevin slept well, very well. He awoke to the sound of his wristwatch alarm, set for six o'clock. Wiley was still sound asleep, snoring softly, completely hidden within his mummy bag. Kevin yawned and reached for the tent flap, pushing it outward. It was still quite dark and the fire had died to embers. He crawled from his bag, slipped on his boots and went out into the darkness. He selected a few logs from their pile and laid them carefully on the glowing embers. The wood, seasoned and dry, immediately burst into flame. The added warmth from the growing flame was a welcome visitor.

He turned his eyes to the sky above and saw only blackness. Puzzled, he gazed to the eastern sky and was relieved to see the familiar Milky Way, the wide white ribbon that wrapped the velvet black ceiling of night. He realized he had totally forgotten about being beneath the overhang.

"*That explains it,*" he though.

Still, from his vantage point it was a very interesting perspective with half the sky devoid of Heavenly lights and the other brightly shimmering, like a billion little candles in the distance.

Kevin lowered himself to the ground, sitting cross–legged, and poked at the fire with a stick. He'd give Wiley a few more minutes of sleep before waking him from his slumber. After all, there was plenty of time before daybreak, and he was enjoying the solitude of the morning, the warmth of the fire, and the spectacular stellar display to the east.

He took a little skillet from his mess kit, placed three strips of bacon in it, and placed it on the fire. The smell of bacon cooking began to permeate the cold air, and Kevin inhaled deeply, through his nose. He knew right then that this was a very special place and he would be back many more times to come. He was just finishing his first strip of bacon when the tent flap popped open. A sleepy face appeared in the firelight.

"Morning, Kev. How long have you been up?" Wiley asked, hazily.

"About thirty minutes. Come on out and I'll throw a few more strips of bacon on for you," he offered.

Wiley crawled slowly from the tent.

"Damn, it's cold out here," he complained.

"Its fine over here by the fire. Come on over and warm up," Kevin suggested, motioning for Wiley to come join him.

Kevin placed three more strips of bacon in the little skillet and put it back in the fire.

"It'll be daybreak in about thirty minutes," Kevin stated. "Better eat up as soon as it's ready. We've got some exploring to do."

"Right, will do," Wiley, said, through a yawn.

Wiley looked up toward the sky and with a double take, asked, "Where's all the stars?"

"Kevin laughed and said, "Look east, young man."

Wiley turned his head as instructed and smiled.

"Pretty cool," he said, as he discovered what Kevin had figured out only moments before. That's pretty damn cool."

Kevin began wiping the skillet clean and looking up from his chore, addressed Wiley, in a somber, low voice.

"I wish Bryce could be here."

He waited for a response.

Wiley nodded and completed Kevin's though for him.

"He would have loved this, I know. And…" Wiley stopped, then continuing in the same breath. "He would be if it weren't for Bitch Mary and her little bitch puppet."

Kevin nodded in agreement. He never thought those girls would ever go so far as to murder one of them. They were mean and nasty to them, always. They were cruel and took great pleasure in humiliating them at every opportunity, but he never realized that their hatred for them ran *that* deep.

"I still find it hard to believe, Wiley. I mean, that they would murder Bryce like that," he stated.

"You better believe it. I saw the rope. I saw how they tied it. Neck high. If it had been a wire it would have taken Bryce's head clean off."

Wiley's face had drawn tense and perverse, as it did every time the subject of Bryce's murder came up. Kevin was totally in favor of *getting even* with those bitches, but he still had no idea of what Wiley had in mind or how far he would take his revenge. He could cloak his plan, whatever it would be, in the guise of justice, but it was really revenge he was seeking. Kevin knew this, and he was okay with it. What they had done to his best friend justified revenge. Revenge in this case *was* justice. What he had no idea of, yet, was just how far Wiley intended to take his revenge, or in what form it would come. Every time he would ask, Wiley's response was the same. *"I don't know yet."* He suspected that Wiley had some rough ideas that were juggling around in his head, but he hadn't come to a final decision as yet. Wiley had responded once, to his curiosity with, *"It has to be perfect. It has to punish both them and their parents. They raised the bitches!"* Kevin figured Wiley was still trying to think up the *perfect* punishment. That was okay though. The first step of the plan, which *had* been decided, was to let them get comfortable with what they had done. Let them think they were *home free* for a while.

Kevin set the skillet aside and looked across the fire. Wiley was licking his fingers clean of the bacon grease and staring into the fire.

"It's daybreak, Wiley. Are you ready to get going?" he asked.

"Yep, ready. Let's shove off."

Wiley extinguished the fire while Kevin made one last check of the map. They would head straight along the west wall to where it would begin turning east. That would be where their search would begin in earnest.

As they hiked along the face of the cliff, Kevin kept an eye peeled for scats and tracks. If the hermit had existed, he would have to eat. So far, the boys had spotted no game in the bowl. They had seen an occasional ground squirrel and a tuft–eared squirrel, but nothing you could exist on for a lifetime.

They hadn't traveled very far when he spotted his first encouraging sign.

Deer droppings, he thought to himself. *Good.*

A little further along he saw the unmistakable tracks of a hare, being followed, or tracked, by a fox. There seemed to be game up here, the question was whether or not it was plentiful enough to sustain the hermit all the years he must have been here, if he had been here. Then, like music to his ears, he heard it. The shrill whistle of an elk, then another in answer to the first. Perhaps the game *was* abundant enough after all.

Kevin had also been concerned about the availability of water in the valley. They had not run across a brook or spring since arriving. There were none marked on the map, nor was there any indication of a lake or pond in the bowl. Surely the cartographer would have indicated a lake if there were one. But now, it didn't really matter. If deer, fox and elk were thriving up here, they were getting water from somewhere. He was sure they would come across the source, given enough time to search for it. They would eventually come across a deer or elk trail and follow it to their *watering hole.*

"We almost there, Kev? What's your map say?" Wiley asked.

"Look up ahead, Wiley," Kevin hinted. "You don't need a map to see that cliff turn."

In the shadowy light of the overhang they could see clearly where the massive structure made a sharp curving turn to the east. This was their destination for this morning. It loomed just ahead.

As they had hiked, Kevin had been trying to get the hang of thinking like the hermit might have.

"Well, if the hermit did make his home in this section of the bowl, you can bet the water supply is elsewhere."

He reasoned that anyone looking for him or coming up here for an extended stay would first try to locate a water source. They would probably do it by following game tracks. Then they would make camp and center their activity on that camp. The hermit would not want to *live* anywhere near that water for fear of being discovered. It would stand to reason that the more activity and moving about in an area, the more likely they would be to come across his home.

Although finding a water source was not their mission on this trip to the valley, if they planned to return in the summer for a longer visit, they would need to find it first. There was no way a person could pack in enough water for more than a few days duration. So it was an important detail for future adventures to Short Pines.

Arriving at what appeared to be the mid–point of the bend to the east, the boys stopped for a short rest. Wiley pointed out to Kevin that they were to look for anything out of the ordinary, no matter how insignificant it may seem. He was going on his theory of the Aleut's homes as he spoke.

"Look for low rises in the ground. If he built something like the Aleuts did, it will blend right into its surroundings. The only indication that it is there will be the domed shape."

"Okay, where do we start?" Kevin inquired.

"Right here, Kev. What we will do is walk a crisscross pattern so we can stay within earshot of each other. You walk out fifty yards in that direction, keeping your eyes peeled. I'll walk out in that direction at a ninety–degree angle, the same distance. Then we will each turn a ninety–degree turn, me to the right and you to the left. We'll cross paths and continue in that fashion until we have each made four turns. Then we head in a straight line back to here. Understand?"

"Yep," Kevin acknowledged.

"Good. Now, if you see anything, yell. Let's go."

They began their crisscross search pattern with enthusiasm, catching sight of one another twice along the way. Kevin was the first to return to the starting point, so he sat down on a boulder and awaited Wiley's return. In less than five minutes they were reunited. Wiley took a seat on another rock facing Kevin.

"See anything," he asked.

"Nope, nothing," was Kevin's response. "What do we do now?"

Pointing in an easterly direction, Wiley stated, "We move over there, fifty yards, and we do it again."

Kevin looked around in all directions. He was beginning to realize that at this rate it would take *weeks*, not days, to search this whole valley. He told Wiley as much.

"Don't get discouraged so soon. I'm sure he would have set up in this area. It's the only logical place. We won't have to search the whole valley. We'll find his place here in this area," Wiley assured him.

"Okay," answered Kevin, but if we find water in this area, we move to the other side of the valley and search there."

Wiley looked puzzled.

"Why would we do that?" he asked.

"Because, I have been trying to think like the hermit, too, and I have a theory of my own," Kevin informed him.

He explained his theory to Wiley, about the hermit not wanting to reside near a water source. He had been doing some more thinking on the matter, too, so he explained to Wiley that since the map showed *no* water sources, anywhere, there was likely to be only one. He reaffirmed that there had to be at least one to support the lives of the game he had seen and heard sign of. A little to his surprise, Wiley agreed whole–heartedly with him.

"Good thinking, *Mr. Holmes*," he said, when Kevin had finished. "We'll search this area until we have exhausted it or until we find water, whichever come first."

"Or," added Kevin. "Until we find his damn house."

They moved to the east and began their second search pattern, once again seeing each other twice along their respective routes. Again, Kevin returned first and found a place to sit and wait for Wiley.

He hadn't sat for very long when he heard Wiley yelling for him. Kevin jumped up, excitedly, and ran in the direction of Wiley's voice. He yelled for Wiley to get his bearings, and heard Wiley respond not far off to his left. He went in that direction and spotted Wiley intently studying something on the ground.

"What is it, Wiley?" Kevin asked, breathlessly.

"Looks like a campsite," he responded. "There's a fire pit and rock ring and all."

"Whose is it, I wonder?" Kevin asked.

"I don't know, but it's not old," Wiley commented. "From the looks of the ground around here it has been used frequently and fairly recently."

"Maybe hunters?" Kevin guessed.

"Maybe, I'm not sure. They clean up well after themselves, who-ever they are. There's no litter or anything else left behind. Maybe they're just hikers, but if so, they've been here more than once. Look around, they've made a clearing, and there's hardly any available loose wood lying about for fire building. They've picked the immedi-ate area clean."

"I thought nobody ever came up here, Wiley. Who could they be and I wonder how often they come up here?" Kevin asked.

Wiley gave Kevin a sly smile and said, "Maybe they're *hermit hunters*, too!"

Kevin laughed and replied, "Well whoever they are, they're not here now, so let's go find *our* hermit!"

They went back to the starting point of this, their second search pattern, and moved another fifty yards east to begin a third pattern.

Kevin suggested that before they start their next search, they sit down and enjoy a candy bar. It was now getting to be lunchtime and those three strips of bacon had long ago worn off. This time, Wiley pulled a Baby Ruth from his pocket, while Kevin chose to stick with his favorite, a Chunky. Neither boy could remember a time when candy had tasted so good or was so satisfying. They chewed in silence, except for the occasional "Ummmmm" or "Ahhhhhhh" and the smack of their lips. When they had both finished, each took off for a separate tree, behind which, to take a dump.

"You got the toilet paper, Wiley?" Kevin yelled from behind his tree.

"No! Don't you?" Wiley yelled back.

"Crap!"

"Exactly!"

Neither Wiley nor Kevin explained to the other how they had handled the situation and neither asked. They started their third search pattern, each a little more embarrassed than the other. They passed within sight of one another once and continued their individual patterns. They expected to see each other again, as had happened in the previous searches, but before that ever occurred, Kevin let out a yell, which echoed thunderously throughout the canyon.

Wiley began running in the direction of Kevin's call. Kevin yelled again, louder this time, or maybe he was just closer now, he wasn't sure, but Kevin sounded awfully excited about something. Wiley grew more excited with anticipation with every running step. He broke into the clearing that existed between the forest's edge and the cliff, to see Kevin jumping up and down and waving his hands high above his head.

When Kevin saw Wiley break out of the woods he yelled at the very top of his lungs, "I found a cave! I found a frickin' cave, Wiley!"

Wiley crossed the remaining thirty yards between he and Kevin in Olympic class time. By the time he reached his friend he was breathless, but managed to utter, gasping, "Where? Where is it?" He leaned forward resting his hand on Kevin's shoulder.

"Wait a minute–Let me catch my breath." He took several deep breaths, still using Kevin for support. "Okay, now, where is this cave? Show me."

He stood erect once again and Kevin turned to lead the way.

"Come on, follow me," he said, with total excitement pouring forth. Kevin led him to a small rise at the valley's edge.

"There! There it is!" he said, pointing toward the granite wall.

Kevin's search pattern had brought him to this exact spot. It was a good thing it had, because to move five or six feet in any direction, other than toward it, caused the illusion to disappear completely. The opening, if it was that, seemed to be recessed deep in the granite wall, perhaps six feet or so. If you moved back down the small rise, it vanished behind the rise. If you moved laterally, in either direction, the granite wall, jutting out around it, obscured it completely.

Wiley squinted and looked into the shadows, which lived on the walls throughout most of the day. He saw what looked like a near vertical slit in the wall, which, without going closer, appeared to be no more than a darker shadow resting on the cliff.

"What makes you think that's a cave, Kev?" Wiley asked with skepticism.

"I went over there, that's what," he replied, smiling his slightly crooked smile.

"You did! What's in there?" Wiley asked, with anticipation.

"I didn't go in, it's pitch black. I could see only a foot or so in," Kevin explained.

"So you don't know for sure if it's a cave or not. For all you know it might be nothing more than a three foot deep crack in the wall– right?"

Wiley's skepticism had returned.

"Well, it's worth a look. You said to yell if I saw *anything* out of the ordinary. So–I did."

"I know–you did right. We can't afford to overlook any possibility. Let's check it out," Wiley said, hoping for the best.

When the boys reached the slit, Wiley studied it intently. It was an opening in the wall, barely two feet wide and rose from the base to a height of about seven feet, before tapering quickly down to nothing. It *was black* in there, Kevin was right about that, and try as he did Wiley could see absolutely nothing. He turned quickly and ran back to the edge of the forest where he retrieved a fallen sapling trunk, about eight feet long. Breaking off some of the dead branches as he ran, he returned to the slit.

"Now we'll see if this thing goes anywhere," he informed Kevin.

He reached into the slit with the pole. It ran into nothing. He looked at Kevin, smiling.

"Well, we know it's at least *that* deep," he stated.

"Yep," replied Kevin.

With that, standing sideways to the entrance, Wiley swung the pole back with both arms and heaved it in. He smiled a wide grin. It had hit nothing that they could hear.

"I figure that went in about fifteen or twenty feet!" he said with glee. "That's well worth exploring!"

"But the flashlights are back at camp," Kevin interjected. "It will be dark before we can get back here, even if we leave right now."

"So–? It will be dark in the cave no matter what time we go in. So what's the difference? We'll go back to camp, get some provisions and the lights, and check it out tonight," Wiley suggested.

"And sleep in the cave?" Kevin questioned, with total apprehension.

"Yes, we can sleep in the cave. That'll be cool!"

"What if something is already *sleeping* in there?" Kevin asked. "Like a bear," he added. He was thinking *black bear*, even though since arriving, he had seen no bear sign. He was remembering having had a similar experience before, with Karl, an older boy who lived three doors down from him. They had been good friends, not through school, but by virtue of having grown up together, on Birch. Karl had graduated from Carver High three years ago and now Kevin would see him only occasionally when he came home to visit his parents. Karl had initially attended Bennett Community College after leaving Carver, but had since transferred to a college somewhere in Arizona, so he didn't come to visit very often.

Their similar experience to what Kevin was feeling now had taken place in November also, when Kevin was twelve years old. They had found an old mine shaft cut horizontally into a solid rock wall, not far from their homes. He and Karl had been exploring the woods behind Kevin's house when they came upon it. Kevin had run home for a flashlight, following his tracks home and back again so as not to get lost. Upon his return they had entered the shaft and had walked about a hundred feet in on hard ground. At that point, the ground had turned muddy under their feet.

"I shined my flashlight down to the ground to see just how muddy it was and that's when I saw them; *bear tracks*, lots of bear tracks, and all the clawed toes were pointing *into the shaft!*" Kevin said, recounting the experience to Wiley. "Karl saw the tracks, too, at just about the same time as I did. Without a word or signal between us we started backing out of that mine! Wiley, I'm telling you, you have never seen two kids put it in reverse so fast! We were scared out of our britches! There was no room for a bear to get around us so if we had disturbed him he'd have had to go *over* us to get out! At least we hoped he'd go over us, and not stop to eat us! I'm telling you, Wiley, I have never walked backwards so far or so fast as I did on *that* day! Not ever! It was something; really something!"

Having finished revisiting his adventure with Wiley, Kevin waited for Wiley's response.

"That's nuts, Kev. There's no bear in there. That slit's two narrow for a bear to get through. Come on, it'll be cool," Wiley encouraged.

Kevin was not so sure about the "*cool*" part of this whole idea, but he knew Wiley; so he also knew there would be no changing Wiley's mind about this. He agreed, reluctantly, but added one condition.

"When we go in there, Wiley, you go first–and if the ground turns muddy–*look down!*"

*B*ack at camp by dusk, the boys sorted through their gear, selecting what each thought he would need for their stay in the cave. The trip back to camp had given Kevin time to think of other reasons why this did not seem like the best of ideas. He had still seen no sign of bear and that worry was becoming less intense as he thought about it. He knew that it wasn't likely a bear would find that narrow slit inviting, but still, it was hard to shake the feeling he had experienced as a kid in that mineshaft.

What was really starting to bother Kevin was the idea that the slit may not open up into a cave at all. It may just remain a slit, barely wide enough to lie down in. The thought of sleeping in a narrow slit, pitch black and cold, would be like sleeping in a coffin. Kevin wasn't claustrophobic, but this was pushing his limits *to* the limit. He shuddered.

"Let's get moving," Wiley said, interrupting Kevin's last thoughts at just the right time. The less he thought about the possibilities, the better.

"The more ground we can cover before dark, the more battery life we'll have for the cave," Wiley advised.

Kevin was amazed at Wiley's thought processes.

So damn practical, he thought to himself. *He thinks of everything,* he thought sarcastically. Kevin was *not* into this yet.

"All right, I'm ready," he lied.

"We can make it most of the way back to the cave before we'll need the lights. Don't turn it on until you absolutely have to," Wiley ordered.

"Right," Kevin replied, dryly.

Neither boy had imagined spelunking as a part of this trip, so neither had thought to bring extra batteries. Kevin's batteries were relatively new, and he hoped Wiley's were also.

They had plotted out a course that would be a straight line back, cutting off the curve of the valley wall. If they stayed on course, they would make it back to the cave with minimal battery use. At least that is the way Wiley had it figured. As it actually turned out, Wiley was wrong. Total darkness found them nowhere near the imposing cliff upon whose wall the cave was located. They could see it looming before them in the distance. The absence of stars in the space it occupied should have been the only indication that it was there at all, but Wiley noticed something else. There was a faint halo of light outlining it against the blackness of the sky.

What do we do now, Wiley?" Kevin asked. "If we start using our lights now, they'll be dead before we get to the cliff."

"We wait," replied Wiley.

"For what? Morning?"

It was clear Kevin was extremely agitated. His apprehension was evident in his voice. The one thing perhaps worse than sleeping in a slit in a rock wall, was the thought of sleeping in the cold, black forest, with no sleeping bag or tent.

"No, not morning–the moon," Wiley informed him.

Almost as if on queue, the moon appeared over the southeast rim of Short Pines. As it slowly rose over the rim, it revealed itself as merely a small crescent, no more than a sliver, but there it was, cresting the peak and shedding the faintest of light down into Short Pines. There wasn't much light, but it was enough to avoid walking into the trees. The forest that had melted into darkness just moments ago, slowly materialized before them. The light was so dim that it was not even perceived as such.

It reminded Kevin of the moments just after turning off his bedroom light, when he would lay in what appeared to be total darkness, and then his furniture would slowly appear, followed by the walls, and eventually, the whole room would become visible. It was that kind of light, just enough to allay total darkness.

Kevin thought to himself.

Even when he's wrong, he's right, thinking of how Wiley *almost* got them stranded in the blackness of night.

"Damn, Wiley, you're the luckiest SOB in the world! I can actually see again!" Kevin remarked, smiling broadly.

Wiley looked at Kevin with an expression that said, *"Of course— What did you expect?"* Then he smiled at Kevin, one of his Wiley smiles, patted him on the shoulder and said, "Come on brother, let's get crackin'."

They moved on through the trees, toward the cliff, skirting the dimly lit trees and rocks before them. Kevin glanced up at one point, noticing that Saturn had followed the moon into the velvety black sky, and had come to rest on Orion's shoulder.

It was slow going, but they eventually reached the wall without serious incident. There had been a few stumbles, scrapes and bruises along the way, but no serious injuries. They discovered quickly that traveling by the light of a sliver moon was no easy feat.

They were more than thankful when they finally reached the cliff, thankful *and* surprised. The course they had plotted had brought them to the cliff only thirty or so yards off their mark. Entering the darker shadow of the cliff they had been forced to begin using their limited electric resource. They moved carefully along the wall, trying to hurry as much as safety would allow, until they reached the slit.

"Come on, Kev! Let's go caving!" Wiley said, cheerfully coaxing Kevin on.

Kevin stepped back and replied, "You first, remember? And, keep one eye on the ground," he reminded.

"Okay, but the last one in's the one the *arriving* bear will eat first," Wiley kidded.

"And the *first* one in is the sleeping bear's appetizer," countered Kevin.

They laughed, and Wiley disappeared into the dark slit that was hopefully, *the cave.*

It was a tight fit, but navigable. They proceeded, single file by necessity, for the slit had not yet widened any over the first thirty feet or so. Kevin was cautiously following Wiley, checking every foot of ground he covered, when suddenly; he crashed into Wiley's backsides.

"What's wrong?" he questioned Wiley. "Why'd you stop?"

"Shhhhhhh," he hushed. "Bear tracks." His voice was *barely* a whisper.

"Back up, quick, back up, Wiley!"

Kevin was using his softest whispering voice and had already put it in reverse, covering half the distance back to the opening before Wiley let out a roaring laugh!

"Just kidding, Kev. Gottcha!" he laughed.

Kevin wanted to throw his flashlight straight at Wiley's head, but thought better of it. He settled for, "You dumb cluck! That's not funny! Someone ought to kick your ass!"

The thought having arisen, Kevin made an attempt in the close quarters to do just that. He advanced, swung his foot, missed, and fell on his back in the powdery dirt.

"Damn!" he complained as he lay there in the settling dust.

"Get up numb nuts. Geez, you're such a dork!"

Wiley could hardly get the words out through his laughter.

"I'm sorry, I just couldn't resist," Wiley said, still laughing softly.

Kevin started to push himself off the floor when he felt something unusual under his fingertips, something cold and smooth. He manipulated it into his hand and shined the light on it.

"Damn," he said as he stared at it curiously.

"What is it, Kev?" Wiley asked, as he noticed Kevin staring at something in his hand.

Wiley stooped down for a closer look at whatever Kevin was studying.

"What'd you find?" he asked.

"A half dollar, I think. It's got a lady on it."

Wiley looked closer and shined his light on it, too.

"That's a *Seated Liberty* half dollar, Kev! Can you make out a date?"

Kevin wiped away more of the crusted dirt from the coin and said, "1876! It says 1876! Wow–awesome!" Kevin exclaimed.

"Let me see that, Kev," Wiley asked.

Kevin handed the coin to Wiley, who studied it further.

"It's hardly worn at all. It's probably been lying back here since close to 1876!"

Wiley was excited. Kevin could almost see the wheels turning in his head.

"I wonder who dropped it here?"

"The hermit," Kevin postulated.

"Maybe, but this is not proof of his existence, Kev. For all we know your grandpa dropped it here," Wiley cautioned, not willing to concede the hermit's existence just yet.

"In 1907? You said it was almost like new. If Gramps had dropped it in 1907 it would have thirty years wear on it. If Gramps had found this cave, he'd have mentioned it to me in his story. Nope, it's the hermit's," Kevin insisted.

"It's definitely cool, Kevin, but it's not proof."

Wiley handed the coin back to Kevin and continued, "Come on, we've got to finish checking out this passage before we lose our lights."

Wiley turned back, facing into the unexplored passage before them, and walked into the darkness again. Kevin followed closely behind, scanning the ground before him. The tunnel made a very gradual turn to the left as they proceeded. They couldn't really see it, but sensed the gradual change in direction. They had now traversed about two hundred feet of passage when Wiley stopped once again.

"What's wrong," Kevin asked. "Why'd you stop?"

Wiley was silent.

"Wiley, why are we stopping?" he repeated.

"Because it's a damn dead end, that's why!" Wiley spit.

Wiley was pissed. His tone was unmistakably a mixture of anger and disappointment.

"It just stops dead, Kev. There's nothing but solid rock on all sides. The passage is a lot wider up here, but solid rock on all sides just the same! It goes nowhere!" he informed Kevin, unmistakably disappointed.

"Damn!" Kevin hissed. "Now what?"

Kevin's neck and back were stiff. He had been walking in a hunched position the whole way. When he noticed the stiffness he thought about why it felt that way. He noticed he was bent over in a very uncomfortable position, a posture he hadn't been aware he had assumed until now. It wasn't necessary. They had noted at the outset that the ceiling of the slit was seven feet tall. He stood erect.

Plenty of room, he thought.

Then he gave it some more thought.

I guess when you can't see what's above your head; you tend to protect yourself from hitting your head on any unseen objects by walking all hunkered over.

He shined his light upward and noticed that the ceiling had risen much higher than seven feet. It looked closer to twenty feet high back here at this end of the slit.

He had been fully aware of the other two dimensions of the slit, width and length, but height had gone unnoticed. It hadn't mattered. Maybe to a bat, coming and going, it would matter, but not to Wiley or him.

"Hey, Wiley, look up," he instructed. "The ceiling is twenty feet high here."

Wiley shined his light straight up at the ceiling above.

"You're right–When did that happen?" he questioned.

"I don't know. I just now noticed it," came Kevin's reply.

Wiley studied the ceiling above, shining his light all around the roof above and then slowly down the wall in front of him, then back up the wall to his left. As the beam moved slowly up the dark granite it disappeared, absorbed into a dark hole about nine feet above the floor.

Look, Kev! A hole!" he yelled, excitedly.

The hole appeared to be nearly as wide as the passage they were standing in, but no more than three feet high, a crawlspace actually, *if* it went anywhere.

"Kevin, give me a leg up!" Wiley's voice was filled with excitement. "Hurry!"

Kevin cupped his hands together and Wiley placed his foot into the saddle they formed.

"When I say three, lift, with all you've got. One—Two—Three—"

Kevin thrust Wiley upward as Wiley pushed off the floor with his other foot. As his arm cleared the lower edge of the hole he reached quickly into the dark of the hole hoping to find a handhold. His hand came to rest on something hard and cylindrical. He grasped onto it and tried to pull himself up, but the object began moving in his direction with the pressure he was exerting on it. It kept coming his direction as he fell backwards against the wall behind him, and then down to the floor of the slit.

Kevin was barely able to get out of the way, having tried to break Wiley's fall, but failing to do so. The boys lay there in the fine dirt and dust, taking inventory of their injuries. There were none serious.

"What the hell happened, Wiley?" Kevin asked.

"I'm not sure. I grabbed on to *something* and when I tried to pull myself up, it moved and I fell," he explained, as he dusted himself off.

"Moved? Like it was *alive*?" asked Kevin, preparing to exit quickly, if necessary.

"No, not like that. It slid toward me. It didn't hold me. Moved. Like that," Wiley tried to explain.

Wiley felt around for his flashlight, which had apparently gone out in the fall. He located it by his side and tried to turn it on. He shook it a couple of times before it lit. He pointed it upward and through the settling dust he saw it.

"Look, Kev! A frickin' ladder!"

They lay there with the dust settling upon them, staring up at a solidly built ladder, protruding horizontally from the hole. It was hand made, nothing you could have purchased at a store. It wasn't what one would likely picture when thinking of a hand made ladder, crudely lashed together with leather lacing. This was a fine ladder, made of round and solid wood. The rails and rungs were devoid of bark and smoothed finely, almost as if sanded. The two rails were bored through every foot and the rungs fitted into the boreholes snugly.

"Damn, look at *that*!"

"Cool!" Kevin affirmed, equally spell bound. "Wonder where that came from?"

"I don't know," Wiley answered. "Let's find out!"

CHAPTER 22

It was an extremely tight fit, even with the widening of the passage, but Wiley managed to work the ladder down into place across the slit. It was just tall enough to reach safely to the hole above them on the left wall, as if it had been made for exactly that purpose, as Wiley was sure it had been. The ladder stretched across the tunnel, its base against the bottom of the right wall and its top just high enough to reach into the hole above, on the left. They would have to mount the ladder from the side, but that was no big deal.

"You still want me to go first, Kev?" Wiley asked. "It's your honors. I never would have thought to look *up*, so it's your find."

Kevin smiled at Wiley and said, "Sure, you go first, Wiley, let's not change anything at this point. We wouldn't want to change our luck or jinx ourselves."

"Okay then, here goes."

Wiley side stepped onto the second rung of the ladder, positioning himself squarely on the ladder, and started up. He stopped after a couple of steps and looked back down at Kevin.

"We better go up one at a time. Let me take a look up there first and if it looks safe, then you can follow. Okay?"

"Sure, sounds good," Kevin, replied, in full agreement.

Wiley proceeded up the ladder and over the top, disappearing into the hole on his hands and knees. Kevin kept his light shining up into the hole to give Wiley as much light as possible. He was a little nervous for Wiley up there alone in that hole. He didn't know why. Bears certainly don't use ladders, so he had discarded that fear when they had come to this juncture.

No, it wasn't bears he was afraid of now, it was probably the fear of seeing his best buddy go off into the unknown. It was nothing rational at all. Just the same feeling you sometimes get when a loved one goes off on a long trip. You expect them to return, but sometimes, well sometimes they just don't. Like when his older sister went off to college and was killed by *that* drunk before she ever arrived on campus. It was that sort of feeling he was struggling with now.

Wiley was gone for only a few minutes maybe ten minutes, at the most, before he popped his head out of the hole. Kevin directed his light straight into Wiley's face to discover a wide grin staring back at him.

"What is it?" He asked with overwhelming anticipation. "Where's it go?"

"It goes up slightly and back about ten feet. It never gets any bigger, so you have to crawl the whole way," Wiley explained.

"The whole way to *what*?" Kevin asked anxiously.

"A huge room!" Wiley blurted out, almost bubbling over with excitement.

"What's in it?" Kevin urged.

"I don't know. It's so big my light beam just disappears into the darkness without hitting anything. It's huge! I could see the floor though. I shined my light down after I almost fell and I could see a few feet of the floor, but that's all," Wiley continued.

"Fell? What do you mean you almost fell?" Kevin asked.

"I was crawling up the hole and all of a sudden when I put my hand down there was nothing there. I rocked forward, but caught myself and backed off a bit. Then I edged closer and shined my light down and saw the bottom, about nine feet down on that side, too. I shined my light in front of me, and all around, and saw my light beam disappear into nothing in every other direction. It's huge!" he exclaimed.

"Wow! That's neat!"

"Come on up!" Wiley invited. "We've got to check this out!"

Kevin stepped across the ladder, straddling it, and stepped onto the first rung. He began climbing into the unknown, one rung at a time.

"Make room for me up there, Wiley!" he yelled up into the hole.

Wiley backed up in the hole to give Kevin the room he would need to exit the ladder and enter.

"Made it," Kevin said, as he climbed over the top of the ladder and into the small passage.

"What's next?" he asked.

"Okay, Kev, pull the ladder up and feed it back over your head as you do. It may help to lie on your back and pull it up that way, passing it along this way to me. I'll pass it over me and lower it down on the other side, into the room. Then I'll climb down into the room and you'll follow. Simple. I have the feeling someone did it like that hundreds of times before us, but probably alone," Wiley explained.

"Unless it was Indians," Kevin suggested.

"Yea, that's a possibility, I guess, but I don't think this is an Indian made ladder. I don't know why, it just seems like something a white man would have made."

Kevin did as Wiley had instructed and it worked as smoothly as a puck skims the ice. It was just a matter of a couple of minutes before Wiley was descending the ladder into their newly discovered world, and Kevin was following him down. The boys stood at the foot of the ladder, shining their dim beams into the absolute blackness of the room.

"You were right, Wiley. The beams just seem to dissolve into nothing. I can't see a thing," Kevin said, confirming Wiley's previous statement.

"Let's move forward, *slowly*. Keep your beam on the floor in front of you," Wiley cautioned, "and watch for drop–offs. There could be more tunnels like the one we came through, but they may *go down!* *Straight down!*"

Kevin didn't like the sound of that very much, but began edging slowly forward, keeping a sharp eye on the floor ahead, his light beam sweeping left and right before him. Wiley was by his side moving just as cautiously, the arc of his beam crossing into the path of Kevin's and out again.

At first, they saw nothing but the powdery floor of the cave, its light gray dust puffing up from beneath their feet with each small step forward. About thirty feet in Wiley's beam fell upon what he thought was a large boulder. He moved closer to examine it and discovered that it was not a boulder at all, but part of the floor, which rose up like a smooth gray dome. He began moving the light up the side of the dome, and when the light reached its curved crest, it fell upon the third man–made object they had encountered since leaving the outside world. This was perhaps, the best find yet, for this meant someone had spent some time here in the past.

The lantern was very old, the hurricane type, fueled by oil or kerosene. Kevin saw it in Wiley's beam and brought his to rest upon it, too.

"Wow," he said, in awe of the find.

Wiley confirmed the feeling.

"Yea, wow!"

Kevin stepped forward and reached up to the top of the four–foot high dome. He reverently took hold of the lantern and gave it a little jiggle.

"Sounds empty, Wiley," he remarked, flatly.

"Now that's a damn shame. How are we going to explore this place with the little battery power we have left? We'll need most of what's left just to find our way back out to the valley," Wiley grumbled.

"I guess we'll have to come back another time, with our Coleman lanterns. That's all I can think to do," Kevin suggested.

"But we're here, *now*," Wiley argued, showing his frustration.

Kevin thought for a minute. He really wanted to come up with a solution. It would be terrible to be forced to leave now, not having had the opportunity to explore this wondrous place. He didn't want to have to wait another week to come back, and he knew Wiley was having the same thoughts. Without speaking he moved to his right, carefully circumnavigating the dome, shining his light all around its base.

"Yes!" he exclaimed.

He knelt down and picked up a large metal can. He had not seen one like it before and it looked at least as old as the lantern. He shook it.

"Yes!" he repeated.

He hurriedly unscrewed the cap and took a whiff of the can's liquid contents.

"Coal oil, I think. Anyway, it smells like *some* kind of oil! Let's try it in the lamp!" he suggested.

Wiley reached up and took the lamp from its resting place and placed it on the ground. He unscrewed the small cap from the fuel reservoir and placed it on his knee. Kevin tilted the can, ever so gently until the oil trickled slowly out and into the lamp. Wiley noticed that the oil didn't smell like kerosene at all. The odor wafting from the can put him in mind of skinning a marmot. It had a gamy odor and he wondered if it had somehow been rendered from animal fat.

Kevin tilted the can back and replaced its cap while Wiley screwed the cap back on the lamp. He lifted the lamp back to its proper resting place and turned to Kevin.

"Give me the matches. Let's see if this dog will hunt," Wiley said.

Kevin reached into his pocket and began rummaging around, then tried another pocket. He reached behind his butt and patted each back pocket, then tried his coat.

"Damn!" he cried. "They're not here!"

"What?" Wiley bellowed, his eyes wide and his mouth agape. "What do you mean, 'they're not here'? Where the hell are they?" he asked, complaining profusely.

Kevin buckled over in laughter, handing the tin match holder to Wiley.

"Got *you* this time!" he exclaimed, trying to bring himself under control. "You should've seen your face!"

"Funny, very funny, dork."

Then, Wiley chuckled, too.

"Let's try this antique out."

Wiley removed a waterproof match from the cylinder and replaced the cap. He turned it upside down revealing the striking pad on the bottom.

"This is nice, Kev. I'm gonna get one of these when we get home," Wiley said, complementing Kevin's match case.

"Scraaaatch…" The match burst into flame with a familiar hissing sound.

"Lift the glass, Kev."

Kevin pulled down on the lever that would lift the glass and Wiley put the flame to the wick. It flickered and sputtered at first, than gradually the flame spread over the top of the wick. Wiley twisted the little knob that lowered the wick and Kevin slowly released the lever, allowing the glass globe to settle into place.

The room slowly came to life as the little flame brightened. A warm glow filled the dank air and the walls and ceiling came into view. The boys looked up and were transfixed. They had noticed as they walked in that the floor sloped downward as they moved ahead, but the ceiling was a perfect sphere. It was like standing in the rotunda of a great domed building and looking up at the ceiling from within.

"How the heck did this get here?" Kevin asked, as he stood in awe of the sight.

"Magma chamber," Wiley stated, with authority.

"Magma chamber?"

"Yea. I think Blind Valley is an ancient caldera. It was probably formed when the main magma chamber blew. The top of the chamber collapsed, forming the bowl," Wiley explained.

"Think so?" asked Kevin.

"Maybe. That's what I think happened, anyway. I think I remember something like that from earth science class. I also think this smaller magma chamber vented at that time, through the passages we entered, but this chamber never collapsed. There are probably more beneath us," Wiley said.

"How do you figure that?" Kevin was fascinated by it all.

"This dome on the floor is probably hollow. It's probably where some volcanic gas pushed up from below and formed a bubble," Wiley explained, stating his theory.

"Cool!" exclaimed Kevin.

They began surveying the room and noticed that there were other domes on the floor of varying sizes, the largest of which, within their limited view, was nearly twelve feet high.

"This place is awesome!" Kevin yelled, hoping to hear an echo.

"This place is awsommmmmmmmm..." echoed back to him. He chuckled.

"Hey hermit!"—*"Hey hermitttttt–"* "Where are you?"—*"Where are youuuuuu–?"* Wiley hollered, breaking into a roaring laugh.

"Come on, Kevin, let's do some speeeelunkin'!"

They moved further into the chamber, working their way slowly through the maze of domes on the floor. Some they could see over, some they could not. It was one of the neatest places they had ever seen. It was absolutely cool, to say the very least.

So far, the only signs of prior human presence they had seen were the half dollar, the ladder, the lantern and the oilcan. It was as if they were in the foyer of a great building and the lantern was the welcoming light.

Kevin began thinking about the possibilities.

"So why was the lantern here? Are there other rooms, possibly, the lantern placed here to light the way? Just what was this place, anyway?"

They rounded another rather tall dome and spotted atop a lower dome, another lantern. It had also run dry, so Kevin ran back to get the oilcan. The boys knew the routine now, and had the second lantern lit in a matter of minutes.

Kevin was beginning to get warm and removed his coat. It was designed for cold weather and the temperature in this chamber was much higher than it had been outside. Outside, the temperature was hovering around twenty–five degrees, but in here it felt fifty, or maybe a little warmer. Wiley had begun to notice it, too, and followed Kevin's lead, removing his coat and placing it atop Kevin's on one of the lower domes.

"What do you say we bed down here for the night? I'm bushed. There's no telling how much more of this place there is to explore. We can get up early and check it all out in the morning," Wiley suggested.

"That's fine by me," Kevin replied. "I'm getting tired too."

As if on queue, he yawned and rubbed his eyes.

"We'll explore the rest of this place in the morning then."

They dropped their packs from their backs and spread their bags out on the soft gray powder that seemed to cover the entire floor area of this domed room.

"Let's leave the lantern lit, Wiley. Okay?" asked Kevin.

"Sure, Kev. We'll leave it lit," Wiley said, comfortingly, as if he were making a kind gesture or a friendly concession. In truth, Wiley had never considered blowing out the lantern, either of them.

Wiley drifted off to sleep trying to solve a dilemma. Ever since finding this place he had been bothered by a question rattling around in the back of his mind.

"If you had to climb into this place using a ladder, and leave by the same method, why was the ladder up in the passage?" It didn't make

sense to him. If this were your home, it would make a lot of sense to pull the ladder up behind you upon entering the second passage. That would provide security and concealment. But, you would put it down on the other side, as Kevin and he had done to enter the domed chamber, leaving it in place there until you left again. You wouldn't; no *couldn't,* shove it back up there into the passage, unless you were eight feet tall, or close to it. You wouldn't do it anyway, even if you could. It wouldn't make sense. Wiley soon drifted off to sleep, his question still unanswered.

Kevin drifted off to sleep, thinking about the events of this amazing day, of who had left these lanterns and who had dropped the coin. He thought about this cave they were about to sleep in, and how Wiley had guessed it had formed. The last thoughts he remembered, upon waking in the morning, were, *In here, how would he know when morning actually came? Or whether it was day or night?*

CHAPTER 23

*K*evin opened his eyes to the soft glow of lantern light.

Is it morning already, he wondered?

He turned his wrist to take a peek at his watch. It was an inexpensive, analog alarm watch, which gave no indication of day or night.

Eight thirty–seven.

Kevin assumed it was morning, although he could not be sure. He had come to realize that he had absolutely no concept of time here in this chamber. Day and night were defined only by whether the lanterns were lit or not. It was like at home, when you would lie down in the afternoon for a nap, and awaken after dark not knowing if you were late for school or not. Then, you slowly remembered lying down for the nap and your heart would start beating again.

He was relieved that the lantern oil had lasted throughout the night, and that he had awakened to lantern light, and not darkness.

He rolled over in his bag to face Wiley, who was still fast asleep.

"Wiley," he summoned in a low voice. "I think it's morning."

Wiley opened his eyes.

"Think?" he questioned.

"Well, it's eight forty. We've either been sleeping thirteen hours or one hour. Take your pick, but it feels more like thirteen to me."

"Okay," Wiley said, yawning and stretching his arms to his sides.

"Let's get up and see what we have here."

Wiley crawled out of his sack, stretched again and said, "First things first. We check the lanterns, then we eat."

Kevin understood what he meant. He slipped out of his sleeping bag, moved to the lantern and, holding the base, carefully unscrewed the filler cap. He looked in the hole, but could see nothing. After a moments thought, he stuck his pinkie into the hole and removed it.

"Looks like about half," he reported.

"Good," Wiley replied. "Then they are good for about twenty–four hours, on a full tank."

There was nothing in the immediate vicinity with which to build a fire, so there would be no cooking breakfast. The boys settled for chocolate bars again, and although good, Kevin found himself long-ing for Canadian bacon and eggs, rather than another Chunky. Wiley, on the other hand, was completely content with his Clark Bar. They washed their *breakfast* down with swigs of water from their canteens and prepared to explore this wonderland further.

"Let's just leave our gear here for now. No sense in toting it with us all day," Wiley suggested.

"Makes sense to me," Kevin agreed, and they moved further into the unexplored chamber.

Wiley estimated from what he could see in the lantern light and from the curve of the dome above, that they were about two–thirds of the way across the room. He began explaining the ladder dilemma he had been thinking about to Kevin.

He explained how it didn't make sense to him and that the ladder should never have been where they found it. Kevin began putting his mind to work on the problem. He gave it some serious thought and tried to imagine he lived here and how he would deal with coming and going. Finally, Kevin stopped walking and said, "Maybe he only used that ladder on the outside. Just to come and go from the second passage. Lowering it to leave and then pulling it up behind him as he returned."

They began walking again as they talked.

"Yea, that *makes* sense," Wiley responded. "But then, how did he get up and down from the passage into and out of this chamber?"

"A second ladder?" Kevin guessed, shrugging his shoulders.

"Okay–So where is it? If whoever came and went from here left, and never returned, it would still be there in place. For that matter, the ladder we found would not have been up in the second passage. If whoever used this place came in one last time and never left again, the ladder *would* be where we found it, but still, where's the second ladder? It should still be standing there on the inside of this room. He wouldn't *jump* down and risk breaking an ankle or something, and how would he get back up there the next time he needed to leave?" Wiley was stumped.

The light from the second lantern had grown very dim as they continued walking. It was getting very difficult to see very far ahead as the darkness of the cave was creeping back in at this point.

"Maybe I better go back and get the lantern," Kevin suggested, looking back over his shoulder. As he finished that thought, the boys rounded one last dome and spotted a third lantern.

"Nope, just the can of oil, Kev."

Kevin returned shortly, toting the oilcan, and they filled and lit the third lamp. The darkness faded away, revealing the end of the chamber. Twenty feet or so beyond where they stood was the back wall, curved like the others and rising seamlessly into the domed ceiling. They had come to the end of this new subterranean world and the only vestiges of the former inhabitant they had found, were behind them now.

They stood, frozen in their tracks, staring at the remaining expanse of the chamber. They had crossed the entire diameter of this hemispherical world, nearly seventy yards, and had found nothing more than a ladder, a coin and a few lamps. Disappointment settled over them like an overcast day, dampening their spirits and dashing their hopes of proving the existence of the Blind Valley Hermit.

Someone had been here before. *Someone* had used this chamber for something, but it had revealed no clues as to what that might be. They leaned back and rested their butts on the small dome behind them, staring up at the downward sloping roof that was the end of the room. The two boys sat there, slowly gazing around in a circular, sweeping motion. With the third lantern now lighted, the chamber was a well–defined hemisphere, like the top of a giant bubble, roughly two hundred feet in diameter and rising to a height of approximately one hundred feet at the center. It was a magnificent sight to behold, and although they were elated by its discovery, it had revealed nothing of the hermit to them, and that was a let down.

A one–time visitor, a prospector perhaps, could have left the coin, ladder, and the lanterns here. There was no evidence that this was a *home* to anyone at any time.

"Well, Wiley–Now what?" Kevin asked, with disgust in the tone of his voice.

"I guess we go back. We'll take a different route."

Wiley pointed to the right.

"We'll go around that side on the way back and see if there is anything over that way. Who knows, maybe we'll stumble across *something* that will tell us about this place."

"All right," Kevin replied. "Should we blow out this lantern before we go?"

"No, not yet. If we don't find anything on that side, we'll circle around the other side and come back to here, so we'll leave it burning for now," Wiley instructed.

"Okay, let's shove off. Time's a wastin'!" Kevin said, with a little more enthusiasm now.

They headed off on a curving route toward the far side of the dome. As they embarked, Wiley returned to the topic of the ladder mystery.

"So–he comes in from a day of hunting, climbs his ladder and pulls it up behind him. Then he lowers it over the other side and climbs down into the chamber. Maybe he *is* really tall and shoves it back up in the passage where it won't be in the way."

"In the way of *what*, Wiley?" Kevin asked, poking a little fun at his friend.

"Yea, you're right, in the way of *what*?"

Wiley was a little embarrassed by thinking of that theory.

They had now made their way around to the outer perimeter of the room. The light had grown dimmer here, as they had traveled away from the lanterns in the center area of the room. Wiley was looking upward, studying the walls and ceiling above, when Kevin spoke.

"You know that ladder thing you have been worrying about?" he asked.

"What about it?" Wiley answered, without looking down.

"I *think* we just found the answer," Kevin said.

"What? What answer?"

Kevin pointed ahead and Wiley's head slowly turned.

"YES!"

What lay before them was another floor dome, but this one was different than the rest they had seen so far. This one had one side "blown" out of it, as if the pressure from below, when it was formed, had become too much to withstand. It had a gaping hole in it and one quarter of the side they were viewing was missing. Protruding from the hole at a fairly steep pitch was a three–foot section of ladder, which disappeared down into darkness. The ladder was of the same material and construction as the first and probably built by the same hands.

"Answers that question," Wiley stated. "There *is* a second ladder! Whoever lived here moved it around as he needed. He would come down into this chamber from the second passage, and take the ladder with him to here. That explains why there was no way down from up there without using the *outside* ladder. Why build three ladders when you can move the second one around in here, as need be? Right, Kev?"

"It sounds like you have it figured out there, Wiley, but–where does this ladder lead?" asked Kevin.

"Hell if I know," Wiley answered. "Let's find out!"

They approached the hole slowly; their eyes locked onto it, as if to look away would be to lose it forever. Their disappointment, only minutes before, had turned to great expectation. Upon reaching the dome they peered down into its depths, eyes wide in anticipation of what they might see. As it turned out, they could see very little.

"I wonder how deep it goes?" Kevin asked, in a low whisper.

"I don't know–it's too dark to tell. Give me your flashlight."

Kevin handed his light to Wiley. They stared into each other's faces for a moment, and then Wiley switched the light on. He turned, leaned into the hole, and trained the beam down the rungs of the ladder. The beam found the ground below and the base of the ladder.

"Looks like about ten feet," he stated.

"Do you see anything else?" Kevin asked.

Wiley moved the light as much as the angle would allow.

"I can't see very far from the base of the ladder, but there is something there."

He tried to lean a little further in and moved the light again.

"Yes! There's another lantern down there, sitting on a box!" Wiley exclaimed.

He pulled back out of the opening and looked at Kevin.

"Go get that oilcan, Kev. We're going down!"

CHAPTER 24

Wiley was the first one down the hole, stopping half way to receive the oilcan from Kevin, who handed it down to him from above. Kevin followed, and soon both boys were standing in the dark. Wiley flicked on the flashlight and located the lantern sitting on an old wooden crate. The flashlight was nearly exhausted and shed barely enough light to search out the lamp.

"Hurry, Kev. The lights going fast."

He spoke as he twisted off the filler cap on the lantern. Kevin knelt down and carefully filled the lamp. Wiley was striking the match as Kevin was lifting the globe. The wick danced to life, sputtering at first, and then growing brighter. They boys sat down on the ground awaiting the room to fill with light.

This lantern played tricks with them though. It was as if it was fighting to keep its secrets hidden from their anxious eyes. The wick sputtered and almost died, then flared up brightly, but with such short duration they were not afforded time for a good look around. It died down again sputtering and flickering dimly. Eventually, the wick's antics gave way to a steady flame. The room below the dome slowly brightened and revealed itself to the intruding young men within it.

It seemed only natural to look up as the light spread. They noticed first the ceiling, domed sharply and blackened with what appeared to be soot from the lantern. It occurred to Wiley that it must have taken years for that much soot to accumulate.

Kevin was noticing the smaller hole, opposite the ladder hole they had entered through. He hadn't seen it from above, having not ventured around the dome to that side. It put him in mind of a window. He could see the light from the other lanterns through it, which made this chamber more like a real room than the chamber above. What they could see of this chamber was very much smaller than the main cave, measuring perhaps, only thirty feet across. The highest point of the ceiling was a mere fifteen feet overhead.

Kevin and Wiley stood at precisely the same moment, as if something had signaled them it was time. As they rose, their eyes were drawn to the same spot in the room, just beyond the lantern, perhaps ten feet away. It was as if something had told them, *"Look over here. Over here."* And, they did.

Kevin was the first to react, retreating to the furthest wall in one mighty leap, breathless and unable to even muster a scream. Wiley ducked to the floor lying as flat in the dust as he could manage. He clawed at the dirt as if he was digging an escape tunnel, but in reality he was merely trying to find the coordination to crawl out of this place. Then, they froze. Like two statues, one erect and one having fallen over with time.

Kevin was pressed against the rear wall, hands over his face, peering through his parted fingers. Wiley had become as still as a frozen lake, lying on his side and rolled into a ball against an adjacent wall. He too, was peering through parted fingers, as if somehow his hands could hide him from doom. They remained in their respective positions for several minutes, trying to make out the intentions of the specter before them.

As they peeked through their fingers they confirmed what each had thought they had seen. There was a crude bed, fashioned in much the same way the ladders had been made. Sitting on the bed, with his back resting against the headboard, was a man, dressed in skins and fur from head to foot. His cap appeared to be made of rabbit fur, his shirt of buckskin, laced at the neck. He wore buckskin pants as well, but his moccasins were of a lighter colored material, probably the more durable hide of an elk. His chin was lowered to his chest; the black holes that were his eyes were watching them intently. Lying across his chest, in his folded arms, was a rifle. His fingers were slender, appearing to no more than bone, for that is exactly what they were. As the boys' eyes became accustomed to the low light, they realized that they had found the skeletal remains of the Blind Valley Hermit.

"Wiley–Wiley–Do you see him?" asked Kevin, in a voice barely audible.

"Yes," came the reply from across the room. "I see him."

"He's dead, right?" Kevin asked, with only slightly more volume.

"I sure as hell hope so!" replied Wiley.

"Good. I mean, not good, but good," Kevin stammered.

"I *know* what you mean," Wiley affirmed.

"What should we do now, Wiley?" Kevin asked, still not sure if he should raise his voice and risk waking the *sleeping* hermit.

"We take a closer look, that's what," Wiley stated.

There was a momentary silence between the boys, as if they were waiting for the hermit to object. He did not, but the lantern flared at that moment, nearly causing Kevin to have an *accident*.

"You first?" asked Kevin.

"Okay, me first," Wiley answered.

Wiley gained his feet, noticing that his legs were still wobbly beneath him. He moved cautiously, reverently, across the room. Kevin began to follow behind him, but only after he was sure the hermit would not respond to Wiley's advance. They came side by side at the foot of the bed, studying the old man carefully.

"He knew he was going to die," Wiley stated, bluntly. "He just sat here with his rifle and waited."

"I wonder how he knew?" Kevin responded, accepting Wiley's premise without question.

"I don't know, but he knew." Wiley stated, with authority.

They looked about the room to see what else it might reveal, but it was hard to keep their eyes from gravitating back to the hermit, peacefully sitting in his bed.

They noticed he had fashioned a crude night table out of another wooden crate and had placed it along side his bed. Upon the table lay a Bible and an old pair of reading glasses. Kevin wondered why he had chosen to hold his rifle, rather than his Bible, as he drifted off that final time. It puzzled him, but he knew he would not find an answer to that question. He could only guess, that although apparently a religious man, it was his rifle that had brought him through many hard times. His faith had surely helped, but, *The Lord helps those who help themselves,* he thought, and up in this wilderness that was probably more true than elsewhere.

Wiley had wandered over to the far side of the room. Here, the floor fell away into a lower room under an adjoining roof, like a double bubble. It had its own dome, but it connected to the first. There was a gradual slope down a few feet to this lower level, which was no more than three feet below the main floor.

"Hey, Kevin," Wiley summoned. "Here's his living quarters and stash."

Kevin joined Wiley at the top of the slope. They surveyed it from above, noting a hand made table and chair in the center of the area. Along one side were stored dried or smoked meats, cut into strips and hung on a wooden rack. On the other side of the space there was a rock fire pit. Sitting on the remains of the last fire it had seen, was a cast iron kettle. Above the kettle was fashioned a wood rack, probably used for smoking meats. To one side of the hearth was a good supply of firewood, perhaps enough for a week of daily use. Directly above the fireplace, in the ceiling, was the hole Kevin had thought looked like a window. He now saw the functionality of it and wondered if the old man had knocked it out himself, as a smoke hole.

They walked down the short slope for a closer look at the provisions wall. There were ammunition boxes, perhaps two–dozen, some still containing rifle shells, and others, dried berries. There were no canned goods, which Wiley attributed to their weight. He would have had difficulty bringing in any supply of canned goods when he first came here. Wiley also surmised that he had probably had a pack mule when he first made the trip up. The kettle and lanterns, the oil-can and his initial supplies to live on, indicated to Wiley the necessity of a mule.

He explained all this, his theory, to Kevin, and added, "The mule had died years before the hermit had, and was probably buried outside the cave, somewhere in the valley." Kevin questioned why the hermit would go to the trouble of burying it, and Wiley explained, "Because, it was his friend, his only friend. And, besides that, he couldn't leave it lying in the open to rot. Eventually, someone might come along and find its skeleton. That would give them good reason to look in this area for him."

"If, anybody *was* looking for him," Kevin interjected, on a rather sad note.

With that, the boys went back up the slope to the main room. They stood in awe of the hermit, once again.

"Look at him, Wiley. That's a mountain man from the 1800's. We're looking at history!"

Kevin was fascinated with the old man.

"Mountain man?" Wiley scoffed. "He's a hermit!"

"Not *just* a hermit, Wiley. He *was* a mountain man. He might have even known Jim Bridger, ever think of that?" Kevin asked. "Look– Look at his rifle, Wiley. Do you know what that is?" Kevin asked.

"Old?" Wiley snapped. "It's just an old damn rifle!"

Kevin was stunned. Wiley was getting that all too familiar look on his face. His complexion was turning red again, and his facial muscles were growing tense.

"Seriously, Wiley. That's an 1874 Sharps .45–70! That's a buffalo gun, Wiley, a buffalo gun! He was probably a buffalo hunter at one time too! What do you say to that, Wiley?"

"Yea, yea," sarcastically responding to Kevin's fervor. "A buffalo hunter, right."

Kevin heard the sarcasm in Wiley's voice.

"What's wrong with you, Wiley? Don't you think this is awesome, looking into the face of history and all? Coming face to face with a mountain man and buffalo hunter from another time in history? What's wrong with you?"

Wiley was silent. He was thinking again, but not about the *mountain man* or his history. Wiley saw that Kevin was really intrigued by the old man and the history he might represent. He didn't want to step on his enthusiasm, but he didn't want him to become too attached to the old geezer either. He didn't want Kevin to start thinking of this place as sacred or a shrine or anything.

He finally responded, "Look, Kev. Yes, I think he's cool. Yes, he was probably a buffalo hunter. So what? He's dead now."

Kevin was shocked. He *knew* Wiley thought this was awesome. He *knew* Wiley thought the mountain men were the greatest Americans in our history. He had heard him say on more than one occasion that it was the mountain man who was responsible for opening up the west for settlement. He'd heard Wiley say that they'd braved the elements, the Indians, and the grizzly bears, all for the chance to live free and unencumbered by the rules and regulations of the civilized world. He *knew* that Wiley thought this was cool!

"Why are you acting like this, Wiley?" Kevin asked again. "I don't understand."

"Look, Kev. I've got plans for this place. Big plans. I don't want you thinking that this place is hallowed ground, or something like that," Wiley stated, angrily.

"What plans?" Kevin interrupted.

"I haven't worked it all out yet, but this place will be part of it and I can't have you balking on me," Wiley stated, firmly.

"What plans, Wiley? What the hell are you talking about?"

"I'm talking about those bitches, Mary and Alicia. That's what I am talking about!" he shouted.

Kevin was silent. He wished Wiley had not brought that up. Not here. Not *now*. Finding this place and the hermit was about the greatest thing in his life. He didn't want to think about those girls now. He didn't want to think about what they had done to Bryce. *Not now*, and certainly, *not here!*

He looked Wiley straight in the face and with the sternest voice he could find, he said, "Wiley–I don't want to talk about that now and I don't want to talk about that here! Got it? Not now, not here!"

Wiley backed up a step. He had not seen Kevin take a stand like this, *ever*. He put his hand up, palm forward, and motioned for Kevin to stop.

"Okay, I won't say another word about it, *now*. But, we are going to discuss it later, and you are going to go along with it. We're in this together and there won't be any backing out. *You got it?*"

Wiley turned abruptly and began climbing the ladder.

"I'll wait for you up here while you say your good byes!" he yelled back over his shoulder.

Kevin stood at the foot of the bed, looking at the mountain man sitting there peacefully, just as he had years before when he was full of life. Just as he had as he let go of life. Kevin tried to imagine all that this old man had seen in his lifetime. Herds of buffalo, Jim Bridger, maybe even Sitting Bull. Kevin wanted to say good–bye to the old man and wish him to rest in peace, but he realized he didn't even know his name.

His eyes fell upon the old man's Bible. He didn't think the mountain man would mind him looking in the Bible. "Sir," Kevin said respectfully, addressing the old mountain man. "Would you mind if I took a look at your Bible?" There was no objection, so Kevin took it in his hands and opened the cover. He stared at it briefly, then closed it gently and placed it back on the table, beside his glasses. He took one last look at the old gentleman, turned and began climbing the ladder. On the third rung, he stopped and turned his head back to the room.

"Good bye, Sam Elliott," Kevin whispered. "Rest in Peace."

CHAPTER 25

When Kevin reached the top of the ladder, Wiley was sitting on the ground facing him. Kevin stepped off the ladder and sat down to face Wiley.

"Hey," Wiley said.

"Hey, yourself," replied Kevin.

"Look, Kev. I'm sorry about down there. Really. I just got to thinking about Bryce when I saw that rifle the old man was holding. I lost it, that's all."

"Why?" Kevin asked. "What about the rifle?"

"You've forgotten already? I know Bryce had to tell you about that rifle? He was constantly bending my ear about it! He always said you weren't a real deer hunter until you took a deer with a Sharps. I don't know why, he just loved those rifles. He wanted to buy one, you know, a real one, but figured he'd have to settle for a reproduction. He was always showing me pictures of the one he wanted, with a thirty–two inch octagonal barrel and tang sight. He said you could drop a deer at five hundred yards on a windy day with that rifle, and even a thousand yards on a calm day. He never discussed it with you?"

Wiley was almost in tears, talking about it.

"No, Wiley, he didn't. He never mentioned it to me. I do remember seeing a magazine picture of a Sharps on his bedroom wall, but I never asked about it," Kevin replied. But, then again, we never really talked about guns. When we were hanging out we talked about hunting and hiking, but he never mentioned having a favorite rifle he wanted.

Kevin was a little confused. How could he have not known about something that important to his friend?

"*That* was the catalogue photo. *That* was the very one he wanted!"

"I didn't know, Wiley. I guess you were his gun buddy, or maybe I never gave him a chance, talking all the time about the Ruger I want. Maybe he was so sick of hearing about my Ruger he didn't even want to mention his Sharps to me. I don't know."

"Maybe? Kevin, you do run that Ruger into the ground sometimes. Anyway–when we came back up to that upper room and I looked at the old man again, I realized *that* was Bryce's rifle in his arms. It hadn't hit me before that. I lost it. I started thinking about Bryce and how he would have loved to see that Sharps in the hands of a real mountain man. Then I started thinking about why he isn't here today and what those bitches did to him. *That's* when my plan came together. *That's* when I knew what I wanted to do to them!"

Kevin was a little afraid to ask, but he did.

"What's that, Wiley? What *do* you want to do to them?"

"No–I told you I wouldn't talk it about it here, and I won't. We'll discuss it later, outside," Wiley told him.

"Okay, thanks, Wiley."

"No problem, buddy. Let's head back to our gear and pack up. What time is it anyway?"

Kevin looked at his Timex and replied, "Noon."

"Okay, plenty of time."

They started for their gear and Wiley began thinking about whether or not Kevin had bought his story about the Sharps. He hadn't had much time to think it up and he wasn't so sure it was convincing. But, Kevin was easy, not at all hard to manipulate. He *had* lost it down there, but it wasn't for the reasons he had told Kevin. He needed Kevin for his plan to work and that meant keeping him on the edge. He had already convinced him that the girls had *murdered* his best friend. *That* didn't matter to him, but it would matter to Kevin. As far as he was concerned those bitches had it coming, *whatever* happened to them.

If Kevin knew that Bryce's death had simply been an accident, a prank gone terribly wrong, he would actually come to forgive them in time. That couldn't happen. He had to keep Kevin believing they were murderers. He would also have to fuel the hate, because Kevin wouldn't maintain it on his own. He was too forgiving and understanding. It wasn't that he didn't love Bryce enough; it was simply that he didn't have the capacity for hate if left to his own devices. He *would* find a way to be okay with it all.

"Hey, Wiley." Kevin said, breaking Wiley's chain of thought.

"Yea, Kev, what?"

"There's still something I haven't figured out."

Wiley wasn't prepared for this. It sounded to him as though Kevin had found a hole in his story. He'd have to do some fast thinking if Kevin found something wrong with what he had told him.

"What haven't you figured out?" Wiley asked, cautiously.

"Where the heck did Sam get his water? He had to have water."

"Sam?" Wiley asked, surprised and a bit confused.

"Oh–I didn't tell you, did I? After you went up the ladder, I looked in his Bible and his name was there. It was Sam Elliott. Do you ever remember reading about a mountain man or buffalo hunter named Sam Elliott?" Kevin asked, hoping Wiley had.

"No, I can't say that I have," he answered.

"Me neither. I guess he wasn't one of the famous ones. But, that doesn't mean he didn't *know* Bridger, or at least cross paths with him sometime," Kevin said, optimistically.

"No, it doesn't, Kev. Maybe he did."

"Anyway," continued Kevin. "I was wondering where he got his water. At first I thought he wouldn't live anywhere near its source, but now, I'm not so sure."

"Why's that?" Wiley asked, becoming interested in this puzzle. After all, Kevin *was* right, Sam would have needed water, at least a couple of gallons a day, and it wouldn't be easy hauling it into here from outside somewhere.

"Well, it's pretty darn hard to get in and out of here. Water is pretty heavy and bulky when you are talking about how much he would have needed daily."

"That's *exactly* what I was thinking just now, Kev," Wiley interrupted.

"Really? Well, I can't see him coming and going every day, fetching water from some stream or spring out in the valley. It wouldn't be practical. In fact, it would be damn hard to do," Kevin speculated.

"He was a tough man. He'd do what he had to do to survive up here," Wiley suggested.

"Yes, he would, but still, I don't see him leaving here every day bringing back the water he would need for the day, and that is about all he would be able to drag in here on one trip."

Wiley thought about that for a second, than asked, "So what are you suggesting? That he was getting his water in here somewhere?"

"It's the only thing that makes any sense," Kevin said, with finality.

"Okay, where?" asked Wiley.

"I don't know, but we should look for it. If I'm right, and we find it, we could come up here next summer and stay in here as long as we wanted. We could do more exploring and all, and visit Sam again," Kevin said, his voice rising.

"Okay, Kev. So we'll look for it, but we can't waste a lot of time on it. We have to get back to our original camp before dark so we can get an early start for home tomorrow. Our parents are expecting us back sometime Tuesday and I don't want them getting suspicious about what we've been up to if we're late," Wiley warned.

They stopped heading in the direction of their gear and went back to Sam's 'home'. They would start there, where they left off, and continue down that side of the chamber, looking for a water source. Then, if they found nothing they would complete the circuit, back to the third lantern. They had just begun their new search when Kevin brought up another thing he had been thinking about.

"How do you suppose Sam knew about this place?" he asked.

"I don't know, maybe he didn't. Maybe he just found it, like we did, while looking for shelter or just exploring the valley," Wiley suggested.

"Maybe, but not likely. We were searching, looking specifically for anyplace he might have lived. If I hadn't happened to end up at that exact spot, I'd have never found it," Kevin explained.

"Maybe he was searching, too. For a home, a place to live out the rest of his life," Wiley countered.

"I guess, but I don't think so. He was a mountain man. Maybe an Indian told him about this place. Told him where it was and how to get in, even where to find water."

"Hey, anything's possible," Wiley agreed.

"Well, that's what I think," Kevin said. "I think an old Indian told him about the place and he came here to live, knowing it was here just waiting for him."

"Think what you want, buddy," Wiley said, kindly. "But I haven't seen anything that would suggest Indians have ever been here, just your mountain man—Uh..."

"Sam, Sam Elliott," Kevin reminded him. "And I didn't say the Indians *lived* here, just that they knew about it. Maybe it was a sacred place or something," Kevin suggested.

"Maybe, Kev, just maybe," Wiley said, flatly.

Wiley wasn't very comfortable with the way Kevin was thinking. *Sacred place!* he thought, uncomfortably. He was beginning to think that this place was getting too important to Kevin, perhaps to 'sacred' to bring those bitches to. He would have to work on that, and soon.

CHAPTER 26

Continuing their circuit of the domed chamber, now in search of water, they neared the first lantern and Kevin came to an abrupt halt. He hadn't noticed it in the dimmer light over by Sam's house, but as the light grew stronger, he saw it now. Here, as they approached the first lantern they had encountered yesterday, it was evident. The fine gray dust, that everywhere else covered the floor of the chamber, was not present at his feet now. He was walking on hard solid rock. Kevin looked to his left and the dust reappeared, and looking to his right, he found it present also. It had not been obvious as the rock and the dust were the same color, making it difficult to detect by lantern light. He looked ahead and noticed the narrow ribbon of rock floor running off into the distance across the chamber, perhaps fifty feet, before vanishing. It appeared to Kevin as though the floor dropped off at that point.

"Wiley, look! We're on a trail!"

"Trail?" Wiley questioned, not having noticed what Kevin had.

Kevin pointed to the ground before them, raising and lowering his outstretched arm to indicate its path.

"Yes, look. The dust is missing along here. We're walking on rock. It's a trail. Sam must have made it coming and going frequently along here."

Wiley's face lit up.

"Going for water maybe!" He exclaimed, his voice rising to an excited pitch.

"Sure," responded Kevin, adding, "Once the dust was displaced from his frequent movement through here, there would be nothing to disturb it. No wind or rain, or anything."

"Not very careful of him, being a mountain man and all," Wiley suggested.

"Outside, yes, but in here, what did it matter? He was the only one who came in here," Kevin reminded him.

"Yea, right," Wiley said, sorry that he had made that remark.

"Come on, let's follow it!" Kevin exploded. "Let's see where it goes!"

Kevin ran ahead and grabbed the lantern, leading the way, with Wiley following close behind.

"The path appears to head straight for that wall over there." He pointed down the path. "There may be another room over there."

They ventured further down the path. The floor beneath them dropped off suddenly, going down at a relatively steep decline.

"Look, Wiley," Kevin pointed out. "It goes down under a ledge."

They continued following the trail by the light of the lantern Kevin carried. The ceiling in here was low, just inches above their heads, and the floor continued to drop away. They had left the main chamber behind and were now in a new passage, as wide as ten feet in places, as narrow as six in others. The ceiling remained at a constant six inches overhead, following the floor ever downward, with no sign of leveling off. The boys began to wonder how deep it would go and where it would lead them. They had traveled about twenty yards down, into this newest of discoveries, when Kevin stopped in his tracks.

"Look, Wiley," pointing to a large rock. "Carvings!" he exclaimed, excitedly.

Wiley leaned forward to get a closer look at what Kevin had found.

"I'll be damned," he commented. "You may have been right. Maybe Sam *did* find out about this place from the Indians."

The boys were staring in awe at "pictures" carved into the rock, like hieroglyphics from Egypt, only different. They had no way of determining what the pictures meant, but Kevin speculated that the three wavy lines etched into the granite on the top of the rock, had *something* to do with water.

"Looks like *flowing* water to me, Wiley," he stated.

Wiley agreed, by way of an affirmative nod of his head.

They followed along the path, now some forty yards in, but not knowing how deep they may have gone. The passage began to open up gradually, first ten feet, then twenty, and finally, some sixty yards into this new passage, they found themselves in a room. In the dim light of their lantern they could see that it was not a big room and not particularly tall. The floor before them was littered with pottery pots and vessels. Some were broken, some remained in tact. Kevin held the lamp at arms length before him; head high, in an attempt to shed more light into the room.

The far side of the room was only dimly lit, but it was sufficient light to see that the floor was not gray over there, but black. From left to right, the width of the small chamber and perhaps six feet out in their direction, it was *black*!

"Do you see that, Wiley?" Kevin asked, not looking away from the sight.

"You mean the black floor?" Wiley questioned, already knowing the answer.

"Yes, the black floor."

"I see it, Wiley answered. "What do you make of that?"

"I don't know... Let's go see."

As they approached the black band on the floor, Wiley reached out and took Kevin's arm, holding him back.

"Be careful, Kev, it may be a drop off," he warned.

They approached with caution, inching toward it, so as not to slip on the sloped floor and slide into the blackness. When they reached the brink, Wiley stooped down and put is hand warily into the void.

"Water!" he exclaimed. "*Cold* water!"

Kevin stooped along side Wiley and stared at the water, putting his hand in to test it, and withdrawing it quickly.

"That is cold!" he confirmed.

He thought for a moment and continued.

"I wonder how a pond got way down here? Where's the water come from?" Kevin questioned.

"I don't think it is a pond. I think it's a stream, Kev," Wiley suggested.

"But it's just sitting there. It's *not* moving," Kevin countered.

"Give me a match, Kevin."

Kevin took a match from his case and handed it to Wiley.

"What's that for?" Kevin asked.

Without answering, Wiley dropped the matchstick into the blackness. It sat motionless for a moment, and then began drifting ever so slowly to the right. They watched the little ship cruise a course toward the right wall of the room and then disappear, apparently beneath it.

"It *is* a stream!" Kevin exclaimed. "I wonder where it comes from?"

"It's probably snowmelt from the snowfields on top of Oriel Peak," Wiley suggested, with an air of certainty in his voice.

"Think so?" Kevin asked.

"Yep, I do. I can't think of any place else it could come from, can you?"

"No, I guess not, but does that mean it will dry up in the summer?" Kevin asked, thinking that perhaps it would be dried up when they returned next summer.

"Not necessarily. Some of those snowfields may be perpetual, lasting throughout the summer. They'd be marked on the map if they were. Let me see your map," Wiley said.

"It's in my coat, back with our gear," Kevin replied, upset that he had not brought it with him. "Damn!"

"Okay, so we'll check it when we go back," Wiley assured him.

For the next ten minutes the boys checked out the ancient pottery and further studied the room. At one side there was an old fire pit, the ceiling above, blackened by smoke from many fires. By the fire pit was a stone, suitable for sitting on, and around it thousands of small shards of chipped flint and obsidian. There was also, on one side of the stone, a small pile of obsidian, which appeared not to have been worked yet. On the other side of the seat were three finished bird points and a knifepoint, laid neatly side–by–side. Beyond the sitting stone there was a sleeping mat of woven fibers.

"Something happened to him, Kevin," Wiley said, breaking the prevailing silence. "He never made it back here the last time he left. He intended to return, but he didn't."

Kevin turned and looked at Wiley.

"What makes you say that?" he asked, genuinely wanting to know the answer.

"He planned to come back," Wiley said. "But, something happened to stop him from returning. I think he used this place like a camp when traveling from place to place. Others probably did also. It was probably a place to stop off on a journey and have shelter and water. He would stay here for a while and make arrowheads and other tools he would need in the future. Then, he left one day, planning to return, or else he never would have left behind those finished points and blade. He just wouldn't have done that," Wiley explained, as if he had it all figured out.

"I wonder who he was?" Kevin pondered.

"Just some Indian," Wiley answered.

"Wiley, I'll bet there's a whole lot more to this place than we know. When we come back in the summer, to stay awhile, I wonder what else we'll find?"

"Who knows?" Wiley answered, shrugging his shoulders. "Who knows?"

Before leaving, the boys filled their canteens with cold, *black* water. As they ascended the sloping passage to the main chamber, Wiley suggested they head back to their gear, eat a little something and start back to their original camp. Kevin agreed. As they passed the dome from which they had taken the lantern, they put it back in its proper place, then turned and headed for their stuff.

Wiley sat munching, this time, on an Almond Joy while Kevin snacked on another Chunky. They sat and talked about how good it was going to be to get back to their camp and have a real meal for a change. They had been sustaining themselves on candy bars for far *too long!* They rolled up their sleeping bags and tied them to their packs.

"Ready to head home?" Wiley asked.

"Yep, ready to go," Kevin answered.

"Okay then, blow out that lantern and we'll be off."

Kevin leaned over and gave a short puff into the top of the globe. There was still plenty of light to navigate by coming from the other two lanterns, and Wiley headed off first, in the direction of Sam's house.

"Hey, Wiley, it's shorter this way," Kevin called to him, pointing out their original route in.

"I know, but we have to do like Sam did when he would leave. It'll be a lot easier. Come on," Wiley called back to him.

Kevin followed Wiley around the circuitous path that would lead to Sam's house. When they arrived, Wiley climbed down the ladder and emerged shortly thereafter with the oilcan. He sat it on the ground and pulled the ladder up from Sam's quarters.

"Kev, grab the can," he instructed. "I'll take the ladder."

They cut across the chamber to the center lantern, Kevin carrying the can and Wiley dragging the ladder. Wiley puffed this one out and they proceeded to the first lantern.

"We leave this one burning so we can see to get out of here. Put the can down here," Wiley instructed, pointing to the base of the lantern dome.

"I think this is how Sam did it when he would leave. That's why the can was by the first lantern. It would always burn out while he was away hunting or whatever," Wiley theorized.

"Then how did he see to get *this* far when he returned? He didn't have a flashlight like we did," Kevin asked, and again, he really *wanted* to know the answer.

"He probably had it all paced out. You know, like blind people do, to get around their houses," Wiley answered.

That made sense to Kevin and he told Wiley so. Wiley smiled and dragged the ladder to the exit passage.

"Kev, you climb up first and pull that ladder up behind you. Put it down the other side. I'll put this ladder up and follow you," Wiley instructed.

Kevin did as Wiley instructed and soon they were in the original passage, the slit.

"Now what?" Kevin asked. "How do we get the ladder back up in the hole so nobody finds it?"

"We don't, and Sam didn't either. It's too high up and would be nearly impossible to do," Wiley stated.

"I can see *that*," Kevin said, sarcastically.

"When Sam would leave, he would take it with him and hide it somewhere outside, somewhere nearby, but well hidden. He probably had a trench dug to lay it in and then he would cover it with limbs and stuff until his return," Wiley replied, again, seeming to have it all figured out.

"How do you think of all this stuff, Wiley?" Kevin asked, genuinely impressed.

"I don't know. I just try to put myself in his place, I guess. Anyway, that's what we are going to do. Come on, let's get moving."

Kevin led the way with Wiley following after him, dragging the ladder behind. Finally, they saw daylight, for the first time in nearly twenty–four hours.

CHAPTER 27

When Wiley and Kevin reached the end of the slit they discovered that they had plenty of daylight left by which to hide the ladder and make it back to their camp. Having not brought shovels along, Kevin wondered how Wiley planned to dig a ditch for the ladder. Digging a ditch in this rocky soil would not be easy, so he watched with interest as Wiley looked about and apparently came up with an idea.

Wiley laid the ladder flat, alongside an old fallen tree trunk. It was just the trunk; the top portion of the tree had broken off about twelve feet up from the base. Kevin moved around to see what Wiley was up to, and noticed the trunk was hollow.

"Come on, Kev, give me a hand. Help me roll this baby up on top of the ladder," Wiley said, soliciting Kevin's help.

They slowly rolled the log over, until it rested on top of the ladder, the trunk concealing all but the rails, over which Wiley brushed dirt and rock, until the ladder had vanished from sight. The hollow tree trunk hadn't been nearly as heavy as it had appeared, and Wiley could likely have done the work all by himself. Kevin was once again impressed with Wiley's spontaneous thinking.

"If anybody comes up here, they sure won't see that ladder now," he insisted. "And, we will be able to locate it easily enough, when we return."

"Pretty sweet, Wiley," Kevin complemented. "I'm starving. Let's get back to camp and cook up some supper."

"Sure, but first, let's check your map for those snowfields, before we forget again." Wiley suggested.

"Oh, yea, we did forget, didn't we," Kevin replied. "Okay, here," Kevin said, as he handed the map to Wiley.

They sat down on the ladder log and looked at the map.

"Chances are we'll have water in that room all summer long," Wiley stated. "Look here," he said, pointing to the map. "Here's one cirque with a perpetual snowfield called Freemont Snowfield, and here's another named Blessing. Here's a third one called Liddle, but it's on the other side of the mountain. It probably doesn't feed our stream, but one of the other two on this side probably does. I'd say we are good to go as far as water is concerned."

"Awesome!" exclaimed Kevin. "That's just what I wanted to hear! Now we can make plans to come back next summer and stay a while!"

"Oh yes we will, Kevin. You can count on that," Wiley replied.

They got to their feet and headed back to camp. Wiley had suggested that they follow the cliff around, rather than cut through the forest.

"Don't want to get lost now," he said. "I don't want dark to catch us in those woods."

Wiley had noticed the sky was now overcast.

"There won't be any moon to help us out this time. Better to follow the cliff back to camp, so we're sure to get there. I'm too damn hungry to spend the night in the woods," he proclaimed.

As they walked on, Wiley was beginning to worry about the campsite they had found during their search of the valley. Now that he had plans for this place, the possibility of *visitors* was not a welcome thought, and he began going over the possibilities in his mind.

Who were these people who came up here regularly, and repeatedly, to this valley? It was clear that the site had shown a lot of wear, with multiple people on repeated trips to that spot. What did they do here when they came? Were they 'hermit hunters'? I doubt that. Not deer hunters for sure. Maybe they were simply campers from Bennett looking to get away from it all.

Wiley couldn't be sure of who they were, or why they came, but their possible presence during his planned activities here could become a problem for Kevin and him. There was nothing to be done about it now though, and besides, what was the possibility they would all show up here on the same weekend?

They continued their chosen path around the edge of the canyon, and when their camp came into view, the sight of it was a sheer delight. It meant that their aching stomachs would soon be filled. Kevin began preparing the fire immediately upon their arrival; while Wiley lowered their pouch of provisions from the tree limb they had secured it in, from the chance of a marauding bear. They hadn't seen any bear, nor bear sign, but you couldn't be too careful out here in the wilds.

By the time Wiley had the pouch down from the tree, Kevin had a roaring fire going and was greasing up the skillet. Wiley sliced the onions while Kevin sliced the potatoes, each throwing his contribution into the skillet. Kevin then sliced a pound of bacon into little squares and tossed the slices into the mix.

While that fried they ate two hard–boiled eggs each, prepared at home before leaving. When the main course was finished cooking, they scarfed it down like they hadn't eaten in days, which, except for a few candy bars, they hadn't.

By the time they finished their meal, referred to by Kevin as "Camp Hash", dark had fallen over the valley. Kevin wiped out the skillet and scraped the plates with the spatula, wiping them all clean with a cloth. It would have to do for now, as they hadn't enough water to be wasting it on cleanup. Kevin lay back on his back and looked up at the overhang, then eastward. He wished that it hadn't clouded up, because after sleeping in the cave, the Milky Way would have been a very comforting sight.

Wiley sat by the fire and whittled on a piece of wood. Kevin wondered what he was making, but didn't want to disturb him to ask, as he had that *Wiley look*, that only Wiley got when he was deep in thought about something. Kevin had learned that it was not a good time to disturb him when he wore that face.

He took one more look to the east, to see if the clouds had parted and he might be treated to another glimpse of the Milky Way, but they had not. He rolled over and crawled quietly to the tent, not disturbing Wiley, and slipped into his mummy bag.

He lay there a moment, wrapped in his bag, mulling over all that had transpired the past two days. It had been the experience of a lifetime. He couldn't help but think of Bryce and how much he would have loved this trip. Then he thought of Bryce lying in the snow, all broken and cold, and pictured Mary, making jokes about it. *"He was a neck breaking speed skier,"* he had heard her tell one girl, laughing her wicked laugh.

He thought about how Wiley had talked him into seeking their own brand of *justice*. Now, he wished he had been able to talk Wiley into telling the sheriff what they knew, but he hadn't even tried. He had let Wiley call the shots and now it seemed as though it was too late to change it. The die was cast. To tell the police now would be to invite prosecution for impeding justice...*"interfering with an official investigation"*. To do nothing would be to let the girls off scot–free. *Something* had to be done, that was absolute. Those 'bitches', as Wiley would put it, had to pay. Kevin was simply not sure he had the stomach for whatever Wiley had in mind. But, then, did he have a choice? He didn't think so. *One always has a choice,* he thought. He hoped so.

He drifted into slumber to the sound of the fire crackling softly and Wiley's whittling. Later, he awoke screaming!

"What's wrong?" asked Wiley, startled out of sleep. "Are you all right?"

Kevin was sweating and shaking. He sat upright, stiff with fear.

"Kevin?"

Wiley nudged his arm.

"Kevin, are you okay? What's wrong?" he asked.

"Dream, no, nightmare. Sorry, Wiley."

Kevin's speech was stifled and broken, as if trying to come back to reality, but finding the path a difficult one to travel.

"Nightmare? What about?" asked Wiley, with apparent concern.

"Bryce," Kevin stated, almost under his breath, and barely audible.

"Bryce? Damn, Kevin. We're going to take care of Bryce. You'll see," Wiley said, trying to comfort him.

"I know, you keep saying that, but this was different. It wasn't about the fall or him lying there against that tree."

Kevin was shaking visibly now.

"What was it then?" Wiley asked, again.

"I'm not sure. I mean I don't know what to make of it," Kevin confessed.

"Tell me about it, Kev. Maybe I can make sense of it. It'll help to talk about it. Really," Wiley coaxed, trying to determine what was upsetting Kevin so.

Kevin didn't respond right away, and then he looked at Wiley. His face was drawn in anguish. The light from the fire flickering over Kevin's countenance made it all the more ghastly.

"Okay…"

Kevin was collecting himself ever so slightly.

"I'll try to tell you about it."

"Good, just take your time and tell me what you saw."

"We were back at the chamber, the main chamber. We had decided to go back there to see if Sam had any water vessels we could use on our return trip. You know, or did we have to bring some of our own, like that. We put the ladder down the hole and climbed down to his home. Sam was there, just like we found him. Just sitting there with his Sharps folded in his arms. We continued past him and down to his kitchen, or whatever, where he did his cooking."

Kevin paused.

"Go on," Wiley urged. "Then what did we do?"

"We looked around for whatever he may have used to tote his water, and store it. We found what looked like a little reservoir he had built, like a well, to store water in. We looked on the wall and saw several skin vessels, with shoulder straps, hanging on a rack he had built to hold them. We took one down, deciding to take it with us. Fill it at the stream, and take it along for extra water on our way home."

Kevin stopped again. He began to shake more violently.

"Settle down, Kev. It was only a dream. Tell me what happened next," Wiley urged.

"I threw the pouch over my shoulder and we went back up to the main room, the bedroom, where Sam was. We were leaving, heading for the ladder."

Kevin shuddered hard.

"Go on, Kev. Take it slow. What happened then?"

"There was a voice! From behind us! He said, *"Where are you going with my water pouch boys? I need that."* We turned around and…"

Wiley rubbed Kevin's shoulder, comfortingly, and urged him to continue.

"And it wasn't Sam sitting there anymore! It was Bryce! I mean the clothes were all the same, the rabbit hat and all, but it was Bryce! And–The Sharps wasn't resting in his arms anymore! It was pointed right at us!"

Kevin began crying and shaking. He couldn't speak.

"Okay, Kev. Take your time. Take a deep breath and tell me what happened next. Hang in there, buddy and finish the story," Wiley said, still trying to comfort Kevin.

"I saw the blue smoke come exploding out of the barrel and heard the roar of the .45–70 as it went off!"

Kevin paused again, looking at Wiley, as if waiting for his response.

Wiley thought about it for a moment. Then in a comforting, soothing voice, he said, "Well, he didn't shoot you, Kev. They say you never hear the gun that kills you. You heard the gun," Wiley pointed out to him.

"I know, Wiley. He shot *you*. I saw your head explode all over the wall!"

Wiley stared at Kevin, shocked and in disbelief.

"It was *just* a dream," Wiley said, and rolled over, turning his back on Kevin.

Kevin sat there for a moment, looking out the tent flap to the dying fire.

It was just a dream, he thought, trying to convince himself. *It was just a dream.*

He lay back down and rolled over, his back to Wiley's.

"See you in the morning, Wiley," he said quietly.

There was no response.

CHAPTER 28

✿

$\mathcal{E}$xiting the tent, the first thing Kevin noticed was the brilliant blue sky. He had feared that it might snow during the night making their exit from the valley difficult, if not impossible, but it had not. His watch read nine o'clock and the fire had died. If he had remembered to set his alarm last night, he hadn't heard it go off. He looked at the sky, once again, and then went back into the tent, shaking Wiley's foot as he entered.

"Hey, Wiley, we overslept. It's nine o'clock."

Wiley rolled over to face him and smiled.

"You okay?" he asked, with sincere concern.

"Yes, I'm okay, thanks," Kevin, replied.

That was all that was said about the night before.

"Didn't you set your alarm?" Wiley asked.

"I don't remember, maybe not."

"That's okay. We still have plenty of time to get home by tonight, but we better get moving."

They gathered their gear and rolled up the tent, packing everything for transport home. Kevin spread the ashes from their fire to be sure it was out, and scattered them about. He then broke up the circle of rock he had built around it, pitching each in a different direction. The campsite looked almost as natural as it had when they first arrived.

Satisfied that they had not overlooked anything, the boys set a path for the saddle in the valley that would take them up to the escarpment. Once again, they hiked in silence, taking in the beauty of Short Pines and Oriel Peak, looming above.

As they began the long climb up to the escarpment, Kevin noticed something that made him break the silence.

"Hey, Wiley. Look!" He was pointing high up on Oriel Peak. "The snowfields!"

Wiley stopped and looked at the peak.

"Yep. There's your water supply, Kevin. Fall, winter, spring, *and summer,*" Wiley said, laughing a little as he said it.

"They'll shrink a lot once spring arrives, but they won't disappear."

Kevin smiled back at Wiley and resumed his climb up the saddle. The crest was just above, and the escarpment.

Kevin reached the top first and awaited Wiley, who had fallen behind. Kevin sat down on a boulder and watched Wiley as he made his way toward him. It appeared to Kevin that Wiley had fallen behind because he was daydreaming, or thinking, and not paying attention to the route. When he finally reached the top he plopped down next to Kevin and let out a long breath.

"Boy, that climb sure takes it out of you," he said, trying to catch his breath.

"Sure does," replied Kevin.

They sat there on the crest for quite a while, first looking at Oriel Peak, then in the direction of the escarpment, looking out over the vast Rocky Mountain Range. They could see for miles, and it was a beautiful sight.

Wiley dropped his pack and turning to it, reached in and pulled out his rope.

"How much rope did you bring?" he asked Kevin, studying his own rope.

"A hundred feet, like always," Kevin answered.

"I brought a hundred feet also," Wiley said. "It's not enough, but we can add to it later."

Wiley began uncoiling his rope from its neatly wound spiral. Kevin watched for a moment, curious, but silent. When Wiley had the rope unwound he began tying knots in it, one every foot or so. He looked at Kevin and stopped.

"Get started, Kev," he ordered. "Start knotting your rope."

"Why? What are we doing?" Kevin asked, unsure of what Wiley was up to.

"We are going to build a rope hold up the escarpment. We'll join our ropes together. That will give us about a hundred and seventy–five foot, more or less. The knots will take up some of our length. We can come back up in a little while and add more to it. By summer we will have a rope hold all the way up the escarpment. It'll be a hell of a lot easier to get up here with a rope to pull on," Wiley explained.

Kevin looked Wiley in the eye and said, "It wasn't all that bad, Wiley. We don't *need* a rope hold. Besides, that takes some of the adventure out of it."

"Yea, I know. Too bad for us, but the bitches *will* need a rope hold. I'm not going to carry them up here!"

"The bitches?" Kevin asked, alarmed and confused.

"Yes, the bitches. I told you I wouldn't talk about it back there in Sam's world, but now we're out. We're bringing the bitches up here, to the cave, and we are going to keep them there! Here–I made this for you last night."

Wiley tossed something toward Kevin, which he snatched from the air. He looked at the object in his hand. It was a crudely carved letter "B". A leather string was strung through the upper opening, fashioned into a loop, like a necklace. Kevin looked up from it into Wiley's eyes. They were narrow and fierce.

"*That's* to remember Bryce by, and what the bitches did to him!" Wiley screamed into Kevin's face. "Put it on! Wear it! *Don't* take it off!"

Wiley froze, staring into Kevin's face. His features were taught and drawn grotesquely. His face had grown red and fierce.

"We *will* do this Kevin! There will be *no* backing out! Those bitches *will* pay!"

Wiley stopped again, just staring. He was shaking with rage. Kevin had drawn back at the onslaught, frightened and confused. Was this his friend he had shared so many fun times with, or someone he scarcely knew?

"Wiley," Kevin said, hesitantly. "No one's backing out of anything. I *know* what they did to Bryce. I know they must pay, and I *want* them to pay. But what do you expect of me? *That*, I don't know."

Wiley's expression softened a bit and the redness in his face paled.

"I just want you to help. To go along with the plan, that's all," said Wiley.

"But I don't know what the plan is. You said we are going to bring them up here. *"Keep them up here,"* you said. For how long do we keep them, Wiley? How long do we keep them up here? What do we do with them up here? What do we do with them, after we are done keeping them up here? Tell me the plan, Wiley," Kevin pleaded, "So I'll at least know what to expect."

Wiley relaxed even more. He seemed to be coming back from someplace terrible, dark and horrible. But, he seemed to be coming back. He was beginning to look more like Wiley. Kevin could actually see the tension melting from his face and neck.

"I haven't got it all worked out yet," Wiley responded, in an almost normal tone. "It comes to me in pieces. For now, I know we will bring them up here and keep them in the chamber, with us. We'll make them fetch water for us and we'll leave them in there, in the dark, while we go hunting. They won't know when, or *if*, we are going to return. They won't know if we are going to hurt them or not. They won't know if we are going to rape them or not. The fear of the unknown, the uncertainty of their future, will drive them crazy."

Wiley paused, and smiled a sly little smile. He continued.

"Their parents will be terrified. They won't know what happened to their precious little bitches. They'll stand by the window from morning to night, watching for them to walk up the lane. Out of exhaustion and the fear, they'll drop into a chair and sleep, restlessly and briefly, before going back to the window to watch again. As time passes, they'll lose all hope of ever seeing their little bitches again."

Wiley stopped talking again, as if reflecting back on what he had just said, savoring it, living it.

Kevin had listened in disbelief. Where had this hatred come from? This was beyond justice, way beyond justice, or even simple revenge.

"How long, Wiley? How long does this continue?" Kevin wanted to know.

"I don't know. As long as it takes," Wiley replied.

"We can't stay up here forever, Wiley. No more than a week at the most, right?" Kevin questioned.

"I said, I don't know!" Wiley barked. "It will last as long as it takes!"

"Okay, so it takes as long as it takes. What then? What then, Wiley? Do we just let them go? Do we kill them? What then, Wiley?"

Kevin was going to get some answers, and he was going to have them right now.

Wiley looked directly into Kevin's eyes. He smiled, and for the first time since they had arrived on the crest, his eyes smiled, too. He answered Kevin in a calm and level voice.

"No–We don't kill them. We just go home. We blow out the lanterns for the last time–and we just go home. We never return, that's all," Wiley stated, simply and evenly.

"And what about the girls, Wiley? What do they do?" Kevin persisted.

Wiley smiled again, and looked directly into Kevin's anxious eyes. "They stay with Sam."

CHAPTER 29

❀

*K*evin sat on the crest, watching Wiley knot his rope. He wasn't sure if he could go through with this plan of Wiley's or not. He began knotting his own rope.

"Leave them in the cave, forever."

He stopped knotting and reached up to his chest, taking the carving in his hand. He looked down at it and thought, *They murdered Bryce, and Bryce is going to be dead forever. Maybe it is justice.* Kevin thought about that, several more times. He began knotting his rope again. Maybe he would go along with Wiley after all. He didn't like being on the fence about this, or anything else. He needed to be either in, or out. He decided he was in.

"Wiley, I'm in," he said, pointedly.

Wiley smiled the old familiar Wiley smile. He knew Kevin well enough to know what that meant. Wiley knew now that he had finally pushed all the right buttons to get Kevin out of the middle of the road, and over to his side.

"Okay, buddy, you're in," he said softly.

Wiley finished his rope first and looped one end over a large smooth boulder. He secured it with a handsome bowline and gave the rope a few tugs.

"Looks secure," he commented, speaking primarily to himself. "Let's see if it holds me."

He started backing down the escarpment, allowing the rope to support his weight. He went down about thirty feet, and then headed back up, pulling hard on the rope for assistance in the climb. The rope held and Wiley was back on top in no time at all.

"It may take some of the adventure out of it, but it's sure as hell a lot easier!" he exclaimed, smiling brightly at Kevin.

"Okay, smart ass, I get the message," Kevin chuckled, and went back to his knotting.

Wiley sat on a rock and watched as Kevin completed his task.

"Now that you're *in*, I'll tell you that I haven't worked out yet where or when we will snatch the bitches," Wiley said, honestly. "I do know that it won't be until late spring or early summer. We can't take the chance that we'll snatch them and then find that this place is snowed in."

"Right," Kevin replied.

"Besides, part of the plan is for them to become comfortable with what they did and the feeling that they got away with it, remember?"

"Yep. That's the first part of the plan." Kevin replied. We've already started that."

"*Yes we have*," smiled Wiley. "Yes we have," he said aloud.

Kevin finished his knots and coiled the rope over his shoulder.

"Ready to go, Wiley," he said.

"Okay. We'll climb down to the bottom of my rope and tie yours to it. We'll get some more rope this week, whatever we can afford, and come back up Saturday and add it on. We're going to need another four hundred feet of rope to make this work, so we'll have to come back up here and add on as we can afford to buy the rope," Wiley suggested.

"Sounds good," Kevin agreed.

At the end of his rope, Wiley attached Kevin's, using a square knot to make the connection. He gave it a few sharp tugs and leaned back, holding the rope tightly. Wiley shoved off the escarpment, as if to rappel, becoming suspended in air momentarily, and screaming, "Geronimo!" He settled back in place.

"Well, it held!" he laughed.

Kevin laughed and replied, "Lucky for you, fool."

They made their way down the escarpment, using the rope until they reached its end. Wiley started to turn to begin the rest of the descent when Kevin stopped him.

"What about the rope?" he asked.

"What about it?" asked Wiley?

"What if somebody finds it, that's what?" Kevin replied.

"Let 'em use it. It'll take all the *adventure* out of their climb," Wiley said, smiling his 'gotcha' smile.

Kevin shook his head and smiled back.

"Come on, let's get down from here and hit the road. I'd like to make it home for supper."

Wiley agreed, and they continued down the escarpment.

Adventure or no adventure, Kevin found that backing down, using the rope as a brake, was a lot easier than going down frontward or backward without it, trying to keep his feet from sliding out from under him. If they did, there was no telling where he would finally come to rest, or in what shape he'd be! Kevin began to concede that Wiley's idea was a *good* one after all. Not that he would ever admit it to his friend.

It wasn't long after they had departed the end of Kevin's rope, that Kevin had found something else to worry about. It was a valid concern though, and it began to trouble him. Going down the escarpment was extremely rough, and although he tried to focus on his new worry, he had little success.

This would not be a good time for a broken ankle, or worse!

Without the aid of the ropes, it was actually harder coming down than the ascent had been. So Kevin decided to wait until he reached the bottom, before discussing this new concern with Wiley. The escarpment required his full attention. As they had discovered on their way up, it was steep and the footing, crumbly. It was *not* a good place for a conversation.

They did make it down the escarpment without incident and took a breather, each sitting on his own rock. Being on solid ground again was a good feeling.

"The rope hold sure made coming down a lot easier," Wiley stated. "At least what there was of it."

"You think so, Wiley?" Kevin replied, as if not very interested. "I didn't notice much difference."

Wiley looked at Kevin, as if to say, *"Liar,"* but said nothing, smiling and winking at Kevin instead.

"But, like you said, the girls will need it to get up there," he finished, trying not to look Wiley in the eye.

Kevin reached back over his shoulder and retrieved his rifle. He began gently blowing the escarpment dust from it as he took a cleaning rag from his breast pocket and wiped the gun down. The Marlin was his favorite rifle, the one he preferred for deer hunting. It was a brush gun, a lever–action .30–30 he had received as a hand–me–down from his uncle.

"Better clean the grit off your rifle, Wiley," he suggested.

Wiley agreed and reached back for his Winchester. Wiley preferred his .243 for it's higher velocity and flat trajectory. It was a good canyon gun, one with which you could drop a buck across a valley. He never missed a chance to remind Kevin of this, but Kevin always countered with, *"Who wants to shoot a deer across a canyon. The idea is to 'hunt', not target shoot!"* On this point, Kevin was right. Most of the hunting they had done was in heavy brush, at close range. Wiley's lighter .243's were much more likely to be deflected from their target by branches, than were the heavier .30 caliber slugs Kevin's gun spit out. Of course, Bryce would have poohawed both guns in favor of the Sharps, or so Wiley had said. Now that gun would do *both* jobs, and then some.

There was no need to clean the barrels or chambers, as they had not had an opportunity to fire them on this trip to the mountains, and *That* was exactly what had been bothering Kevin as he had descended the escarpment.

"Wiley–I've been thinking about a little problem we may have," he started.

"What's that?" Wiley asked. "What problem?"

"We are experienced hunters, right?"

"Yes, I'd say we are experienced," Wiley answered, puzzled at where this was going.

"We told our dads that we were going up to Los Lobos to hunt doe. They know about Los Lobos being opened this year for doe because of the overpopulation of the herd," Kevin continued.

"So," Wiley responded. "So what?"

"Well how the hell are we going to explain coming home without a doe when the whole place is swarming with them? I mean, don't you think that will make them a little suspicious? How are we going to explain *that*?" Kevin wanted to know.

Wiley thought about it. It *was* a good question, and it *may well* lead to a problem. Kevin was right on the money with this. Given their experience and rifle skills, there is no way they would come home without a deer, each. That *was* going to get their dads asking questions.

"What do you mean you didn't see any?"–"How the heck could you miss?"–"You had two full days up there, and then some. What did you do with your time, piss it away drinking beer?"—"Where did you really go?"

That last question was the question that couldn't be asked. Once that was asked, the seed would be planted, that maybe they had lied about where they were going and what they had been doing. Wiley didn't want it to come to "*Where did you really go?*"

"You're right, Kev. That is a problem," Wiley replied, seriously. "Let me work on that a while."

They slung their rifles back over their shoulders, hitching them just right, and began the long hike back to the car. It was a magnificent day and they made a few stops along the way to watch the jays and ground squirrels going about their routines. At one point Kevin spotted an aspen glen and pointed it out to Wiley.

"Look, Wiley. Elk sign!"

The elk had come down from the higher elevations now and Kevin had spotted the tell tale sign on the aspen.

"Look where they chewed off the bark!"

It was a day fit for a king, or two seventeen–year–old boys, doing what they loved most.

The alabaster crushed softly under their feet, and for right now, there was no place they would rather be. They crested a small rise and spotted the car.

Kevin thought it similar to the feeling he had often felt when he had been enjoying that most perfect of breakfasts, bacon, fried eggs and blueberry waffles. That had been this weekend, enjoying and savoring every minute of it, every bite. It *had been* like eating the perfect breakfast, lost in the moment, thinking random thoughts and delighting in the wonderful tastes gracing your pallet. Then, you look down to your plate and notice that there is but one bite of bacon left, nothing else. *That* was the feeling seeing the car evoked in Kevin, that sense of disappointment as the weekend was ending, the last bite of bacon all that remained on his plate.

CHAPTER 30

It had been an interesting weekend. That could be said of it, without hesitation. That it had been a good weekend could also be said. The boys discovered new wonders they never imagined, nor ever expected to see. They had come face to face with a real mountain man, a buffalo hunter, no less. They had found the ancient workshop and shelter of a migrant Indian arrow maker. But perhaps the greatest find, was that which every young boy wishes for, a cave to explore! Yes, it had been a great weekend, but it was now time to leave for home and ultimately, back to school.

The boys loaded their gear into the trunk of Kevin's car, took one more longing look at Oriel Peak, and backed out of the woods onto the access road.

The issue of having no deer to take home had not been addressed, nor had it been mentioned again. Kevin was sure Wiley was thinking about it though. He had that look about him, the same look he had seen on the mountain, several times, and he hoped *that was* what Wiley was thinking about. It needed a resolution and they were running out of time.

The obvious solution, in Kevin's eyes, was to stop along the way home and poach a couple of doe. That would work out just fine, if– they got away with it. But if the game warden busted them, they would really be in a bind. The deer would be confiscated, their rifles forfeited, his car seized, their parents would be notified, and their dads would know they had lied about having doe permits. It was a solution that had major risks of its own. He searched for an alternative, another solution that would be risk free, or relatively so.

Try as he did, he kept coming back to the idea of poaching. Not that time had made the idea sound better, but because somewhere in that thought he felt that he had missed something. He went over it again in his mind, trying to come up with what it was that he was missing, or overlooking.

We could poach two doe.

Of *that* he was pretty certain.

We might get busted.

Of that, there was a good likelihood, during opening weekend.

*The deer would be confiscated and–That–*that part–that was it!

"Wiley! Try this on for size!" he exclaimed, bouncing slightly in his seat.

"We left for Los Lobos early Saturday morning. *That*, our parents know. We arrived there around noon. We hiked in deep and located a good campsite, pitched the tent, built a fire pit, gathered wood and started a fire. We took the provisions we would need for supper, and secured the remainder in a tree. Then, we settled in, cooked supper and ate. After cleaning up, we went to bed so we could get an early start in the morning. With me so far?" Kevin asked.

"So far. Where's this going?" Wiley asked, curiously.

"Hold on, I'm getting there. Sunday morning we awoke early and went scouting the area in search of good stands. Having never been up to Los Lobos, we traveled far into the area, taking in the sights and scouting for sign. Eventually, we came to a spot that was so cool that we decided to relocate our camp, so we spent the rest of Sunday breaking down camp and resetting it in our new location. By dusk, we were bushed."

"Kevin, get to the point," Wiley demanded.

"I'm getting there. I'm accounting for the time right now. I'll get to the deer in a minute. So–we were bushed. We ate and went to bed, deciding to scout our new area Monday, which we did. We found two great spots to build our stands along well–worn deer paths. Tuesday morning, today, we were up before dawn and in our stands, you up one tree, and me in another about a half mile away. You took your shot first. I heard it. It was a clean shot, and you had your doe. Moments later, I had my chance and we each had our doe. We joined back up and headed back for camp. Got it so far, Wiley?" Kevin asked.

"Yes, so far, but how does all this help?" he quizzed, getting a little impatient with Kevin's story.

"Okay, here it is. The problem was that someone else heard our shots–a game warden. He came to investigate. He had good reason, we found out later. He intercepted us in route to camp and wanted to know where we had shot the deer. We explained to him the best we could and he informed us that he would have to confiscate the deer and our doe permits."

"Why?" interrupted Wiley, confused. "Why would he do *that?*"

"Because, we had wandered outside the boundaries of our permits. We were no longer in the Upper Los Lobos permit area! The warden pointed out on our permit maps where we were and where we said we had taken the deer. We were now back in the official area, but we had been outside it when we killed the deer."

"Cool, Kev! You're brilliant!" Wiley praised.

"Thanks! There's a little more though. Then he said that because we were honest about where we had shot the deer, and because it was an honest mistake, he would not issue us a citation or confiscate our rifles. *'I'm just going to keep your permits boys. Your doe hunting is over for this year.'* That's what he told us, and we went back to camp, packed up and headed home, after thanking him, of course."

"I've got to hand it to you, Kev. You come through in a pinch. Good job, buddy!" Wiley praised him.

"Then you think it's a good story? We can use it?" Kevin asked.

"I think it's a damn good story, and yes, we'll use it. It's official!" Wiley declared.

Kevin was quite pleased with himself. It was a good story, a brilliant story, with no risks attached. It explained their not bringing deer home, it explained why, and it accounted for their time while they were away. He felt proud to have concocted it.

"Wiley, what do you suppose the wardens do with the deer they confiscate from poachers?" Kevin asked, again really wanting to know the answer.

"I read, or heard someplace, that they donate them to St. Gregory Orphanage. At least that's what I believe they do with them around these parts." Wiley said, partly speculating, but partly thinking he actually did remember that from someplace.

"That's a good thing," Kevin replied. "I'm glad they go to good use."

The boys drove on, moving ever closer to home, school, and a chance to try out Kevin's story. They knew they would both get the opportunity to *share* it with their fathers, like it or not.

CHAPTER 31

*K*evin pulled into Wiley's driveway and helped him get his gear out of the trunk. It had been a long day and they were both exhausted. Kevin wished Wiley good luck with the story, but warned him not to bring it up until questioned about not bagging a deer.

"We don't want to volunteer information without being asked," he said. "It may sound suspicious to your dad if you just blurt it out. Make him sort of pull it out of you, but be convincing," he urged.

"I know how to do it, Kev. Don't worry your buttons over it, but, you're wrong." was Wiley's reply. "The way to do it, as far as my dad is concerned, is for me to go in there and act pissed off as hell about losing my deer to the warden. You handle it your way, but I know my dad, and he will expect me to be pissed off over this and come in cussing!"

"Well, maybe so, for you, but my dad would expect me to be quiet about it until asked, like maybe I was reluctant to mention it to him out of embarrassment for having screwed up like that."

"Like I said, Kev, you handle it your way and I'll handle it mine. I'll talk to you later."

Kevin backed out of the drive and turned down Mill Street. It was only two blocks to his house, so he quickly went over his story one more time. As he finished his final review, he turned into his drive, parked and unloaded his gear.

Well, here goes, he thought to himself, as he opened the side door and went inside.

"Hi, Mom," he greeted, as he tried to slip past his mother who was standing at the kitchen sink.

"Hi, Kevin, welcome home," his mother greeted, preoccupied with what she was doing in the sink.

"Thanks, Mom."

He was almost through the kitchen and into the hallway.

"Where's that ten–pointer?" she asked.

Kevin could hear the jest in her voice.

"We went *doe* hunting, Mom. They're *no–pointers,* all of them," he said, with a laughing ring to his voice.

"Really? I do declare," she responded, laughing softly.

Kevin kept moving into the hallway toward the stairs. He didn't hear his mom speak again. He knew she wasn't really interested in the hunt; it was just her whimsical way of greeting him as he returned.

His dad though, was a horse of a different color. He *would* be interested in the hunt, and he would want to know all about it. If he could just get upstairs to his room, he might be able to put this off until tomorrow evening when his dad came home from the mill. That would give him a little more time to rehearse.

He crossed the hall and latched onto the newel post with his left hand, swinging around it like a tetherball on a rope. He was just stepping up the third riser when he heard his dad's voice coming from the den.

"Kevin, is that you, Son?"

Kevin froze, like a deer in the headlights of a Mack truck.

"Yea, Dad, it's me," he whimpered, trying to sound normal.

"Come in here, Son, and tell me about your trip," his dad requested.

"Sure, Dad, I didn't know you were in there," he replied, wondering if that sounded normal or contrived. He figured he would soon find out.

Kevin backed down the steps, and headed slowly for the den. *Oh hell,* he thought, as he entered the room.

His dad was sitting across the room in his Lazy Boy, going over some paperwork from the mill. He put the papers aside when Kevin entered the room.

"Hi, Son. How was the trip?" he asked, as he leaned forward, clasping his hands in front of him.

"Fine, Dad. It was a lot of fun," Kevin answered.

"So tell me, how was Upper Los Lobos? I've never been up that way myself."

"It was beautiful, Dad. You should have been there. We found the neatest campsite. It was too cool," Kevin said, enthusiastically.

"Did you drop your doe off at the lockers, or did you get lucky and get a buck?" his dad asked, smiling an inquisitive smile.

"No, no buck. We didn't even see a buck," Kevin replied.

"In all that time you were up there you didn't spot a buck? That's strange," his dad said, resting his chin in his hand.

"Not really, Dad. We spent a lot of time scouting for sign and searching for good stands. We also set up camp a second time when we found that really cool campsite. We moved everything from our original camp to the new spot. We did more scouting and exploring than hunting. We never took to the stands until this morning," Kevin explained.

"Well, that's what new places are for. It's sometimes more fun just to see where you are and get the lay of the land than it is to sit in a stand," he said, seeming to understand completely.

"Yea, right, Dad. That's the fun of a new place!" Kevin said, in complete agreement.

"So did you drop your doe off at the lockers then?" his dad asked, again.

"No, I didn't, Dad. The game warden confiscated my doe, and Wiley's, too," Kevin confessed.

"What the hell for? Your permits were in order weren't they?"

Kevin's dad was getting red in the face; distressed.

What kind of shenanigans was that warden up to, anyway? He probably took advantage of the boys, he thought.

"Yes, they were in order, but Wiley and I kind of got bewildered up there and we wandered out of the permit area before we shot our deer. The warden heard our shots and came to investigate whether it was buck or doe we had taken. He didn't catch up to us right away, not until we were back in the permit area, but we didn't know we had ever left it. When he asked where we had shot them, we told him," Kevin explained. "It turned out that we had been out of the permit area a good half–mile or more."

"So how much is that going to cost you?" his dad interrupted.

"Nothing, Dad. He was really nice. He said because we were honest about it and that it was an obvious mistake, he was just going to keep the deer and our permits. He let us keep our rifles and didn't give us a citation," Kevin bubbled out, acting relieved for that small kindness.

"That *was* nice of him. He could legally have kept you guns, I guess you know that," he informed Kevin.

"Yea, I knew that and I was worried about it, but he didn't take them," again, Kevin feigning relief.

Buck leaned back into his chair and laced his fingers behind his head. He smiled at Kevin and said, "Well, that's a good thing. If he had taken your uncle's .30–30, I'd probably have to hold your hand while you cried yourself to sleep tonight, and I have too much work to do for that."

He laughed and then continued in a serious tone.

"Let that be a lesson to you, Son. Keep your map handy and know where you are at all times. Sorry about your doe, but that's just part of the lesson," his dad said, wisely.

"Yes, sir, that's good advice. I *know* that now," answered Kevin, as if he had just learned his lesson well.

"Okay, Son. Run along now. I've got some paperwork to finish up. Did you say hello to your mother yet?" he finished.

"Saw her in the kitchen, Dad. See ya later."

Kevin left the den thinking to himself, *That went rather well.* He ran up the stairs to his room and shutting the door behind him, plopped down on his bed. He lay there, staring at the ceiling. He was hoping that Wiley had played it so cool. Knowing Wiley though, Kevin knew Wiley had plenty of experience with this sort of thing; he had not. This was really the first time he had ever outwardly deceived his father. Well, other than telling him he was going to Los Lobos in the first place, but that was one in the same.

Sure, there were the little *white lies* that every boy tells to avoid a spanking or being sent to his room without supper. But he had never actually *deceived* his father before. The feeling of achievement slipped into regret, mixed with a little bit of shame. He was finding that deceiving his father left a bad taste in his mouth. But it was necessary, wasn't it? They had done what they had done and they had enjoyed a great time. Why suffer through the long and miserable punishment that would result from telling the truth. It wasn't going to change anything. *Besides,* he thought, *this way dad still feels proud of me and he got a chance to impart some of his wisdom on me. It's a win–win situation.*

Kevin rolled over, onto his side, and looked out the window. He wished that it faced in the direction of Oriel Peak, but it did not. He knew he wouldn't be able to see it from here anyway, but it would be off in that direction, and that would be somewhat satisfying. It had been a wondrous place to visit. Finding Sam there, in the cave, made it almost a sacred place. He didn't think Wiley saw it that way though. Sure, Wiley thought it was a neat place, and finding Sam was cool, but Wiley didn't seem to hold it in the same reverence as he did.

Kevin felt that a decision needed to be made. He needed to stand up to Wiley on one thing, if nothing else. He needed to find the conviction not to be talked out of this, nor frightened out of it either. Kevin decided. He set his jaw and made a pact with himself that he would stand his ground on this one matter of importance. He would not let Wiley threaten him into submission. He would not let Wiley rationalize it into something unimportant and trivial.

Kevin had told Wiley that he was *in*, and he was, all the way, the entire plan. Bryce would have his justice and rest in peace, *but not at the expense of Sam.* Sam was one of only a few people who have willfully buried themselves at the end of their lives. He sat in his bed, beneath the earth, knowing it was the end. He sat there with his rifle in his folded arms, his Bible by his side, and waited for death to come and take him away.

It was a sacred place, Sam's final resting place, and he would not allow Wiley to let the girls get anywhere near it. Wiley could keep them in the main chamber, or down by the stream, but they were never to go down into Sam's home. *That* would be a condition for his *staying in* on the plan. Without that one concession, he was out, and Wiley could then go screw himself for all he cared.

Kevin rolled over again, away from the window, and closed his eyes. He could almost see Sam sitting on his bed. He tried to imagine his face, what he had looked like in life. He tried to imagine his voice and what he might have said had they found him before death.

How'd you boys get in here? You must be two of the wiliest mountain men in these here parts, to have found me in here like you did, Kevin imagined him saying, and then wondered, *Or—would he have just shot us with that Sharps?*

He curled up in a ball, fetal, and lay there. There was so much to think back on and so much ahead. Thinking back to all they had experienced in Short Pines and the cave was relaxing, but thinking ahead was frightening. There was so much uncertainty ahead and too many "what ifs".

The "what ifs" began with—*What if someone sees us abducting the girls?* And continued endlessly from there. Kevin felt that if he started a list he would be writing all night. He decided that he would begin by resolving the first "what if". This was Wiley's plan, but the rest of *his* life was at stake. Wiley may come up with something brilliant, his mind seemed to work that way, but Kevin wanted a plan of his own, just in case. He had let Wiley call all the shots so far, but now that he was *in*, he was going to have some control over the outcome.

He undressed and slipped under the covers. He'd think about it more tomorrow. There was plenty of time between now and spring, and he was too tired to think on it now. His thoughts returned to the present, and he remembered his mom in the kitchen as he had arrived home. He wondered what she had been making for supper. He was hungry, but so tired. Kevin rolled on his side, closed his eyes, and drifted off into sleep.

CHAPTER 32

$\mathcal{K}$evin hooked up with Wiley at the corner of Mill and Cutter's Lane. It was Wednesday morning and they were headed back to school. The only good thing about that was that this would be a short week. The trip had been a great retreat from the indignities and humiliations of Carver High, but for now, they would have to face the reality of their everyday lives.

Their first day back went pretty much as expected. There were the usual references to their supposed sexual orientation.

"Hey, queer bait. Where have you and Wiley been shackin' up? Been on your honeymoon?"

These sexual assaults, questioning their sexual orientation, were relatively new and were the worst affront to the boys. They were hunters, campers, and mountain men. How could their classmates say things like that to them? It infuriated them far more than the usual cuts about their appearance or physical attributes.

Still, the abuse continued, and the boys could see no end to it coming. Their lives were what they were in the here and now. Their lives had been what they were in the past. There had been no difference in the way they were treated, then or now. Only the nature of the abuse changed, evolving into more sophisticated persecutions as their tormentors grew in age.

How could they see that anything might be different if they went on to college? There had been no change between grade school and middle school and nothing had changed between middle school and high school. School for them, throughout their entire lives, had been one day of malevolence, followed by another.

Wiley and Kevin had made their own separate decision not to go on to college. Each had decided, that for the first time in their lives, they had a choice. College was just another school where they would be the brunt of the jokes and innuendos their new classmates would contrive. Why put yourself in such a position when there was a choice?

Kevin had chosen to follow in his father's footsteps and hire on at the mill. He had worked a few summers there and liked it pretty well. After graduation he would sign on full time, and maybe one day, work up to foreman, like his dad.

Wiley, on the other hand, had big dreams that a work–a–day place like the mill could not fulfill. He wanted to see the country. Not the cities or towns, but the mountains and deserts. His dream was to explore the Rockies, from the Canadian border, all the way to Mexico. He would finance the dream by becoming a government hunter, a hunter in the employ of the Department of the Interior, Forestry Service.

Wiley would become one of the hunters the government would send to hunt down a rogue grizzly bear in Wyoming, and relocate it to the wild. He would be sent to New Mexico to capture a puma that had been dining on sheep, and whisk it back into the hills, before the ranchers could trap and kill it. He had it all figured out. Realistic or not, he would try to see his dream through to fruition. College was simply not an option.

Bryce, on the other hand, had always said that college would be different. He had been looking forward to it. It had been his belief that the kids would be different, that they would be more mature.

The new kids they would meet at college would not be concerned with their appearance or bearing.

As nice as it had sounded, Wiley and Kevin had not bought into Bryce's vision of the future. They saw only that the abuse would grow more sophisticated, once again, and graduate to a new level of subtlety. Besides, what had Bryce known about it anyway? He had only been repeating what his parents had told him in encouraging him to continue his education. They had heard it at home themselves. But, despite the encouraging words from their parents, they could not see beyond the history they had experienced for so long.

So Wednesday passed as expected into Thursday and then Friday, each day just another song on the album of their lives, an album labeled *"School Sucks!"* But just as there is a Monday through Friday, there is also a weekend, and Saturday finally arrived.

Neither Kevin nor Wiley felt much like skiing lately, and the weather had turned too cold for hanging out at the shack. The heavy snows of late made a trip to the escarpment out of the question, and pointless as they had not yet been able to buy more rope. So Kevin and Wiley found themselves spending Saturday morning in Kevin's room, talking and playing video games.

Kevin was glad they weren't doing any thing specific today because this was a good opportunity to discuss with Wiley the *condition* he was going to impose on the plan. This was where he would take a stand and lay down the law about keeping the girls out of Sam's house. Wiley would either agree, or he would be *out!* Bryce deserved his justice but Sam deserved the privacy the grave should afford one.

"Wiley–I need to talk to you about something," Kevin started, breaking into Wiley's game of Break Out.

"Sure, hold on a minute–Damn! Lost that one!—Okay, Kev, what's up?" Wiley asked, turning from the game.

"It's about the plan to take the girls up to the cave. I want to tell you that..."

"Kevin! Kevin, are you up there?"

Nancy Reynolds' voice came up the stairs and into Kevin's room.

"Hold on, Wiley—Yea, Mom! What is it?" Kevin yelled back.

"You had better get down to Carl's! Next Thursday is Thanksgiving you know, and Gramps will be here! I don't want you looking like a ragamuffin! The money's on the table down here in the hall!"

"Okay, Mom! I'm going! Be right down!" he assured her.

"Looks like you'll have to tell me later," Wiley said, smiling at Kevin as if to finish the sentence with, "*Mama's boy*".

It was an inside joke between them and Kevin understood well what the smile had meant. He also knew that Wiley wished someone at home, anyone, cared enough to tell him what to do and when to do it.

"Yea, meathead, I'll tell you on the way to Carl's. Come on," Kevin said.

They went downstairs and collected the money from the table and headed out to Kevin's car. Carl's was across the Saline in Carver, so Kevin would have about fifteen minutes or so to discuss his ultimatum with Wiley on the way. But, Kevin's *best–laid* plans were simply not working out for him today. Either Wiley didn't want to hear what Kevin had to say, or he was genuinely interested in listening to Kevin's new eight–track tape featuring Merle Haggard and his latest hit, *Mama Tried*. As soon as Kevin had backed out of the drive, Wiley had popped it into the player and had begun singing away, *First thing I remember knowin'–was a lonesome whistle blowin'–*and he wouldn't stop, all the way to town.

"Hey, Wiley! Hey, Kevin!"

"Hi, Carl. How's it going?" Wiley asked, taking a seat next to Kevin.

"It's going okay, kinda busy all morning though. Is there something going on at the school that I don't know about, maybe a prom or something? It seems like every boy in town has been in here this morning." Carl remarked.

"No, not that I can think of," Wiley answered, "Kevin? Can you think of anything going on?" redirecting the question to his buddy.

"Nope. Nothing I'm aware of."

"Well it must be general sprucing up for the holidays then," Carl concluded.

"Must be," Wiley answered, picking up the latest issue of American Rifleman from the table by his chair. "That's why Kevin's here."

Wiley looked around the shop and began figuring out how many people were ahead of Kevin. He counted four, and with Bob not here to help Carl, he was in for a long wait.

The Carver Valley Barber Shop was a small business with three chairs and two barbers. Wiley never could figure out the logic in that. Maybe the third chair was for the *guest* barber. *"And today, our guest barber is, someone from Liddelman."* but guest or not, he was never there, whoever he was. And, whoever he was, he was sorely needed! Both Carl and Bob did almost as much talking as they did hair cutting, and with Bob absent, it was going to be forever.

"Hey, Carl, where's Bob today?" Kevin asked, as if he were reading Wiley's mind.

"He's over at the hospital with Clara, hopefully having that baby by now, if it's not another false alarm," Carl answered, shaking his head and frowning. "If it is, this will be the fourth time in the past two weeks he's left me high and dry with a shop full of customers!"

Wiley looked around the shop and noticed that under Carl's porcelain pedestal barber chair there was a mound of hair trimmings on the white tile floor. It completely surrounded the chair and was predominantly red in color. That never ceased to amaze him, knowing that the red hair came from his original family in Carver.

"Looks like you've had a bunch of my cousins in here today, Carl," Wiley stated.

Carl looked down around his feet and laughed.

"It's always that way, Wiley! You must be related to three–quarters of the kids in this town from the looks of my floor! If there were a market for red hair cuttings, I'd be a rich man by now!"

Wiley smiled. "Yes you would, Carl, but I get half, remember that!"

Carl's wasn't a bad place to hang out on a Saturday afternoon, if you had no other place to be, and right now, Wiley and Kevin didn't. They could talk here just as easily as anywhere else, as long as they spoke in terms of 'Short Pines' and 'Sam's Place', rather than Blind Valley and Oriel Peak.

"Wiley, you're going to listen to what I have to say now, or else," Kevin began again.

"Or else what?" Wiley kidded.

"Or else I'm gonna be pissed as hell, that's what!" Kevin replied.

"Okay, buddy, shoot."

"It's about 'Sam's place'. I don't think they should be allowed in 'there'."

"Do you mean the 'whole place', or just 'his house'?" Wiley asked, becoming a little concerned over the direction of this conversation.

"Just 'his house'. I'm okay with them going to the 'main place', Kevin answered.

Wiley's face was growing taught. He was thinking and Kevin could almost see the gears meshing. Then, as quickly as it had tensed up, his face relaxed.

"Okay, I can live with that," Wiley said, calmly.

"Sure?" Kevin asked.

"Sure," confirmed Wiley.

Kevin was taken by surprise by how easily Wiley had agreed. He thought at first, when he saw Wiley's face tense up that he was going to have a fight on his hands. He didn't know what went through Wiley's mind just then, but apparently Wiley had found a way to be all right with his ultimatum, although it had never gotten that far.

Good, Kevin thought. *This is very good!*

❧   ❧   ❧

Thanksgiving fell on the twenty–eighth of November, and November gave way to December. Both boys approached a milestone in their lives. The month of December would see them both become men, emblematically speaking, as each had their eighteenth birthday just around the corner. Turning eighteen had its benefits and its perils for Wiley. For Kevin, it was just benefits he was looking forward to, like maybe a new Ruger handgun.

Kevin was exempt from the draft, his bout with polio rendering him ineligible. Viet Nam was a large concern for boys their age, and it was so for Wiley. Turning eighteen meant registering for the draft, and the possibility of serving a tour in Southeast Asia, something that would totally mess up his plans of becoming a government hunter. He would be safe until he graduated from high school, but without plans for college, he would then become fair game for the Selective Service. So as their birthdays grew ever nearer, Kevin viewed his with great expectation, while Wiley approached his with a modicum of trepidation.

Wiley's was the first of the birthdays, reaching his manhood on the twelfth of the month. When asked, he told his parents he wanted money as a present. He had things he *"wanted to buy"*, but hadn't made up his mind which was more important than the others. What he had in mind, which he had not mentioned to them, was more rope. He wanted to buy enough rope to complete the rope hold up the escarpment.

Kevin and he had not ventured back up there since their initial trip. The weather had turned bad and there had been a lot of snow. One weekend was wasted on Thanksgiving and family stuff; the other two had just gone by the way as the snows fell. Wiley realized that the snowfall would be less severe on Oriel, but it might still be substantial. They had decided not to risk it until the weather had let up some and they could get enough rope to make the trip worthwhile.

His birthday turned out to be a bust. Not only could his parents not afford to give him enough birthday money for even one coil of rope, but he also spent that Thursday in Bennett at the Selective Service Office, getting his new draft card.

Kevin's birthday fell on the twenty–third of the month. It was always combined with Christmas and he would be receiving one present representing both occasions. Because it was always a two for one celebration, the present was generally substantial in nature and always presented to him on Christmas morning.

This year he had asked for a sidearm. He had done so in the past, but his father had always come back with the same answer…"Son. A rifle is one thing and a handgun is another. When you turn eighteen we'll talk about a handgun. Not before."

His father had said that they would *talk about* a handgun, but had never committed to the idea of actually buying one. Kevin knew exactly what he wanted and since this was to be his eighteenth birthday, he had brought the subject up again.

He had explained, leading into the discussion, that what he wanted was a pistol, powerful enough to be real protection in the forest. He wanted a weapon capable of discouraging a bear from coming any further toward him in a pinch, and it had to be powerful enough to take a deer if his rifle malfunctioned. He had explained that he liked the look and feel of the old western style single action six–shooters, and that Ruger had a new model out that was safer than the old type. It was called the *New Model Blackhawk* and was available in a .357 magnum caliber, which is what he was hoping for.

Kevin's father had listened intently, but had made no judgment that he was divulging at the time. Kevin had finished his pitch, saying that he hoped for the six–inch barrel, adding, "for accuracy and range."

His dad had nodded, in recognition of all that Kevin had described, but had made no commitment other than having promised to give it consideration. As Kevin had turned to leave the room, his dad had asked, almost as if in afterthought, "What about the holster?"

"A Hunter, Dad. Model 158, Large. What else?"

Kevin had gone upstairs to his room; feeling like his dad had finally taken seriously his desire for a handgun. Perhaps, just perhaps, this *would* be the year he would get one.

Christmas morning arrived two days on the heels of Kevin's eighteenth birthday and his hopes were high. Ever since his sister had been killed on her maiden journey to college, the family had dispensed with awakening early on Christmas morning and looking under the tree for gifts. Kevin's mom and dad would sleep in until they felt the need to arise. Christmas had been rough for them ever since Carrie's passing. Now, it was just the three of them, and none of the three approached Christmas with the same vigor as they had before the accident.

Kevin would always be up first, trying to pass the time as best he could, until his folks emerged and came downstairs. *Then it was time for presents!* It was no different this year, as he went downstairs to the living room to await them.

Kevin finally heard the sound of his parents coming down the stairs to join him. His long wait was about over. He grew excited about what he might find in the nicely wrapped package marked with his name. His folks entered the room together and took a seat, side by side on the sofa.

"Go ahead, Son. Open your present," his dad said, gesturing toward the box under the tree. "But, Son. Please don't be too disappointed with what's in the box."

"Okay," Kevin said, scooting across the floor and worrying about his father's last comment.

He carefully removed the wrapping paper, working methodically. He wanted to rush to get it off in anticipation of what he hoped to find within the box, but he was holding himself back in fear that it would be something mundane. Something like new hiking boots would be nice, but not the brass ring. He had not been able to tell earlier from the weight of the box, nor from shaking it gently, what treasure lay unseen within. Then, his dad had made that crushing comment, leaving him in total apprehension.

The first thing he noticed when he removed the lid, were the walnut grips, with the distinctive Ruger logo precisely fitted into the rich oiled wood. He folded away the tissue paper, which was hiding the remainder of the treasure and discovered a .357 magnum, New Model Blackhawk, with a six–inch barrel! It was comfortably nestled in a Hunter, Model 158 holster, with gun belt!

Kevin stared at the precision beauty of the weapon and the craftsmanship of the leather holster. He was mesmerized by its appearance, frozen in the moment, and then it hit him like a blast of hot air; *"This is mine! It's really, actually mine!"* He turned to his father with the look of a child who had received a new puppy, his grin stretching from one ear to the other, and rushed to throw his arms around him.

"Thanks, Dad! This is the greatest!" he said, with genuine sincerity.

"You're welcome, Son. You've come of age now. We'll talk *safety* after breakfast," his father said.

Kevin's mom prepared a nice Christmas breakfast of ham and eggs for her men, and they all sat down at the kitchen table to enjoy the meal, as well as each other's company. It was no more than two minutes into their meal when they heard the sound of their front doorbell.

"I'll get it," Kevin said, scooting back his chair.

Buck said, "I wonder who that could be, Nan?"

"Yes–I wonder–she said, but she already knew, or suspected. "I'll put another plate on for Wiley."

CHAPTER 33

*W*iley knew what to expect of Christmas morning also. It had been the same as long as he could remember. He would awake and go downstairs to find his father passed out on the living room couch. It was always that way, and not just on Christmas morning. Wiley's father, had for years, spent far too much time in the bottle, and far to little time with him and his mother. It was an illness, he was told. Wiley figured that illness was as good an explanation as any.

His father was not a mean man and he worked hard, supporting the family. The problem was simply that once the groceries were in the pantry his dad would find himself a way into the bottle. It happened all the time, nearly daily.

His dad worked at the rendering plant on the outskirts of town. It was a smelly job, one that Wiley insisted he would never do. His dad, despite his drinking, had never hit Wiley or his mother. He rarely lost his temper and when he did, it was as likely to be when he was sober as when he wasn't. He was a good man, but one who had somehow slipped into the habit of spending too much time with his Mescal.

So Wiley knew what to expect of Christmas morning and he found just what he expected. His dad was passed out on the couch and his mom was still asleep upstairs. Under the tree he saw an envelope with his name scribbled on it. It had obviously been written while his dad was near the bottom of the bottle.

Wiley opened the envelope to find a check, made out to him, for fifty dollars. The handwriting on the check was the same as on the envelope. It too, had been written as his dad had sucked on the worm. He turned and looked at his father's unshaven face, lying there in his work clothes, and said softly, "Thanks, Dad," and walked from the room.

He was glad to have the check, but embarrassed to cash it. He would though, even if it meant watching the teller look at the check with inquisitive eyes, trying to make out what was written there. It would be embarrassing, but he had done it before. This was rope money, needed to buy the rope that would make it possible to get the bitches up into Short Pines. But even Wiley didn't want to think about that on Christmas morning. He folded the check neatly and placed it in his shirt pocket.

"Merry Christmas, folks," he mumbled, as he went out the kitchen door and into the snow—*I wonder if Kev got that Ruger he wanted*, was his only other thought. He trudged down the drive and turned onto Mill.

Kevin answered the door.

"Hey, Wiley! Merry Christmas!" he greeted.

"Merry Christmas, Kev," Wiley said, returning the gesture.

"Come on in, we're just about to have breakfast; join us."

"Are you sure there's enough? I don't want to impose," Wiley said, with concern.

"Sure there's enough, come on." Kevin answered.

Kevin started for the kitchen, but Wiley grabbed his arm and asked excitedly, "Wait, did you get it? Did you get your Ruger?"

"Right on I did! I'll show you after we eat!" he said, excitedly.

They joined Kevin's parents at the kitchen table and ate a marvelous Christmas breakfast together. Mrs. Reynolds had prepared more than enough in anticipation of Wiley's arrival.

It was actually Bryce's year for Wiley's drop–in Christmas breakfast, but under the circumstances she had expected Wiley to show up at her house. She had noticed the pattern over the past six or seven years, and had subconsciously kept track. So she had prepared a breakfast for Wiley, too, *knowing* he would be around. She had shared her insight with Buck, so he was not surprised to have Wiley join them either.

With breakfast behind them, the boys went up to Kevin's room. Kevin was busting to show Wiley his new Ruger and Hunter holster. His father had withheld the ammunition until after they could "talk safety", which probably meant a few lessons out at the dump as well.

Wiley took the pistol in his cupped hands, feeling the heft of it. He turned it over and over, examining every detail of the craftsmanship, the fit and finish.

"This is sure one nice gun, Kev," he commented, on several occasions. "It must have cost your dad a bundle!"

"I guess, but it's a birthday *and* a Christmas present," Kevin answered.

"Still. That's a lot of bread he spent on you, and he got you just what you wanted," Wiley marveled.

"Yea, I know," Kevin said, thinking back to how he had deceived his dad, and swallowing a little lump.

"So, Wiley, what did you get for Christmas?" Kevin asked, trying to change the subject.

Wiley patted his shirt pocket and replied, "A check for fifty bucks. Rope money!" he explained, happily.

Kevin's face soured at the mention of the rope money.

"I really don't want to talk about that today, Wiley. Not today, okay?"

"Sure, Kev, me neither. There's plenty of time for that another day," Wiley agreed.

Wiley looked back at the pistol in his hand and then placed it in the holster.

"So when do you get to shoot this thing?" he asked.

"Probably later today, I hope. Dad wants to talk safety first, and then I hope he will take me out to the dump for some target practice. If he does, Wiley, do you want to come along?" Kevin asked.

"Naw," replied Wiley, "That's for you and your dad to do the *first* time. I'll go along another day."

The boys spent the next hour talking about Sam, the Indian arrow smith, and Short Pines. There was no mention of the girls, or the plan. That was for discussion on another day. Finally, around eleven, Buck yelled up the stairs to Kevin, "Hey, Kevin! Do you boys want to go shoot that pistol now?"

Kevin yelled back down the stairs, "Are you kidding? Does a bear shi...poop in the woods?" Kevin had put the brakes on that thought just in time! "We'll be right there!"

He threw the gun belt low around his waist, buckled it and tied it off on his thigh.

"Just like a gun slinger," he said to Wiley, cracking a big smile.

"Yup. Better git out thar and face the sheriff, pardner. It's high noon," Wiley offered, laughing.

They flew down the stairs, Kevin leading the way, to where Buck was waiting by the front door.

"You coming along, Wiley?" he asked. "You're more than welcome," he said, with a genuine smile.

"No thanks, Mr. Reynolds. My dad and I are going to scout out a new hunting spot today," he lied.

"Okay, son, you go have a good time with your pop. You can come along and shoot this *canon* some other time," Buck said, with kindness in his eyes.

Wiley smiled at Buck and said, "Thanks, Mr. Reynolds. I'll do that."

Wiley went out the door, back into the snow, and headed down the street. Buck watched him go and mumbled under his breath, "Shame, damn shame."

Then, after Wiley had disappeared around the corner, he turned to Kevin, who had also been watching Wiley go, and said, "Come on, Son. Let's go kill us some tin cans!"

Kevin felt that little lump in his throat again, swallowed, and said, "Right, Dad. Let's do just that!"

Kevin and his dad went down the hall and through the kitchen to get their coats and hats from the mudroom. Mrs. Reynolds was just finishing up the breakfast dishes and asked where her two men were going.

"I'm going to take Kevin out to the dump and let him shoot his new canon," Buck replied. "And I know–Be careful!"

"Exactly!" Nancy cautioned. "And don't forget that the Whitleys are coming over for Christmas supper tonight, so be home no later than four."

Carson Whitley worked with Buck at the mill and they had become fast friends over the years. Eventually, Buck had brought their friendship home and Carole Whitley, Carson's wife, and Nancy had also grown close. The Whitleys were an older couple than were Buck and Nan, with several children, the youngest of which, Jason, had graduated from Carver three years ago. He was now a junior at Reedmore College in Reedmore, Montana, about six hours away on the far eastern side of the state.

Kevin had met Jason on several occasions when he would come with his parents for supper at their house, but with Jason away to college it hadn't happened often. They had hit it off okay, spending time talking after supper or watching TV while their folks played gin.

One Saturday afternoon last summer, when Carson had come over to visit Buck, Kevin had taken Jason back into the woods behind his house to show him the shack. He knew that would piss Wiley off if he found out about it, but Jason was cool and Kevin wanted him to see it. Jason had thought the shack was pretty neat, but had seemed more interested in the outcroppings, which so neatly concealed it.

He had told Kevin that they were rhyolite, and that he might find garnets in it if he chipped away at it enough.

Jason was into rocks and rock hounding. It wasn't hunting, which would have been perfect, but rock hunting was cool in Kevin's book. He was pretty sure that mountain men had some interest in rocks, and if not, it still got you out into the wilderness and that was all that was important.

Jason was cool in another way too. He knew the names of every tree in the forest, and not just the conifer forests either. He knew hardwood forests just as well, and could tell a maple from a sycamore or a box elder from an ash. That wasn't real useful information around Carver, but it was cool.

So Kevin and Jason had hit it off pretty well, right from the start, and he always looked forward to his visits. Kevin could never quite figure out though why he and Jason, like he and Karl, got along so well. Neither of them made fun of him or thought he was nerdish, and they both seemed to like him for who he was, just Kevin. Perhaps it was because they had outgrown that sort of thing, if one prone to that behavior ever does, or maybe they simply weren't trying to impress other friends. Kevin wasn't sure and he didn't question it too far, because for him, friends were too hard to come by.

Kevin had also liked keeping these older two friends separate from his relationships with Wiley, and at one time, Bryce. On the relatively rare occasions that he would spend time with these other two boys, he felt something special. Like perhaps there were other people out in the world that would accept him for whom he was. Wiley and Bryce had always been around for as long as he could remember and those friendships had arisen out of the three of them being forced together as school nerds. What was the saying? *"Misery loves company."* That was how he and Bryce and Wiley had fallen together. But with Karl and Jason it was different. There was no basic underlying *need* for them to be friends. It had just happened and it felt good.

Kevin and his dad returned from the dump at four, just as they had been instructed by Nan. Buck had instructed Kevin on the proper safety measures to follow when handling a handgun and then they had "killed" a few dozen tin cans. Actually, they had had a contest with Kevin coming out on top, twenty–two cans to Buck's twenty. Only eight rounds from their box of fifty had gone astray.

Buck was impressed with Kevin's shooting and the fact that he had actually beat his old man. After all, Buck had at one time been camp champion on the handgun range at Fort Benning. He was, admittedly a little rusty, but Kevin had done him proud just the same.

Supper with the Whitleys was nice with Nan serving up a large Christmas ham and yams. Following supper the adults retired to the den for a few games of gin, while Kevin and Jason went up to Kevin's room and talked and played Atari games. It was a pleasant evening all around and Kevin felt that special feeling once again as he spent time with a friend who had materialized from common interests alone, and not merely the need satisfied by *safety in numbers.*

CHAPTER 34

Carver, and the surrounding area, stayed pretty well socked in through April. On May 4, Kevin heard on the TV that the jet stream had made a major shift and warmer air out of the Pacific was headed for Montana by way of Mexico. It appeared as though the temperature would be rising into the upper 50's for the next five to ten days.

Kevin figured that Wiley must have been watching too, because the phone rang immediately and he heard Wiley's voice on the other end of the line.

"Hey, Kev, it's going to warm up some," he said, excitedly.

"Yea, I just heard it on the news," Kevin replied.

"They said 50's for the next ten days," Wiley continued.

"They said five to ten days, Wiley. I heard it too," Kevin corrected.

"Well, five days is enough to melt off some of this snow. We can get back up to the escarpment and finish our rope hold."

"I guess we could," Kevin replied, but with little conviction.

"Sure we can. It's Sunday. Five days of near 60 degree weather will melt down a lot of the snow. Especially over on Oriel, where there won't be so much, anyway," Wiley pointed out. "By Saturday, we'll be able to get up there easily."

"Okay, Wiley. Do we have enough rope?" Kevin asked.

"I think we do. I have three hundred feet now, and you have two, right?"

"Yes," Kevin confirmed, with little enthusiasm.

"Well then, that should be plenty! We'll leave early Saturday and be back before anybody misses us," Wiley said, lightly. "You *in*?"

"Yea, I'm in, but you better be right about the snow. I'm not going to wade through eight miles of snow up that mountainside. Not for you–Not for nobody!" Kevin insisted.

"You getting soft on me, boy? I thought you were a mountain man?" Wiley laughed.

"I am, and mountain men are no fools!" Kevin retaliated, bursting into laughter. "We'll do it, but the snow better be gone, or damn shallow up there!"

"Or what?" Wiley questioned.

"Or you'll be making the hike by yourself, that's what!"

Daybreak Saturday morning found the boys at the terminus of the access road from Highway 77 into the Oriel Peak area. Wiley had been right again. There was scarcely two inches of snow here, by contrast to the deep base still on the mountains around Carver.

They had told their parents the night before that they were going on a day hike, and to expect them home by dark. If all went according to plan, that would not be a problem.

Kevin was afraid to pull into the woods this time for fear of getting stuck in the saturated ground, so they parked on the edge of the road, as out of the way as they could.

"You think the car will be all right here, Wiley?" Kevin asked.

"Sure why not? I don't see any No Parking signs anywhere," Wiley replied, poking some fun at Kevin.

"Seriously, what if someone sees it here, out in the open like this?" Kevin said, expressing concern.

"Kevin, we are not doing anything wrong. Don't be so paranoid about everything. If someone sees it, so what? We're hiking, or looking for elk sign, it's no big deal," Wiley assured him.

"I know that, Wiley. I was thinking that I don't want it stolen or trashed!" Kevin explained.

"Quit worrying," Wiley told him. "No one is going to come up here today."

Wiley looked back the road they had traveled and turned back to Kevin.

"Look. Ours are the only tracks on this road. No one has been up here in weeks and no one is going to come up here today. Now quit worrying and let's get a move on," Wiley insisted, ruffling Kevin's hair in a mischievous gesture of friendship.

"Okay, I guess you're right," Kevin finally conceded.

They retrieved their packs and rope from the trunk of Kevin's Biscayne, looked up at Oriel Peak, then lowered their gaze to the ground and began their eight–mile trek up the side of the mountain. The snow remained shallow and the going went smoothly. They found themselves looking up the escarpment before noon.

There was more snow on it than the last time they attempted to scale it, but they found it to be scaleable. It was slower going and the ropes were heavy, but they were making good headway despite the extra weight. They had compensated for the weight, somewhat, by leaving their tent behind. They didn't like going out into the wilderness without *all* their gear, but the weight of the rope was a concern they had not overlooked. This was not an overnight, so they elected to leave the tent in the car, even though an unforeseen emergency might prove that an error in judgment. What was done was done, and for now anyway, they were glad they left it behind.

By one o'clock they had reached the beginning of their partially constructed rope hold. Wiley took the rope in his gloved hands and gave it a stout tug. It held fast.

"Good!" exclaimed Wiley, smiling broadly. "It's still strong and secure."

During much of the previous week, in their spare time, they had been engaged in knotting the ropes they had purchased. They had reasoned that it would save a lot of time and be a lot easier to do, if they did it at home before leaving. It would make the rope a lot bulkier to carry, but that was the price they would pay for expediency.

Wiley tied off the first section, using another square knot. Kevin knew what was coming next. "Geronimo!" Wiley yelled, as he *tested* the link. He settled back to earth and said, "Looks good, buddy!" Wiley took the lead and they started backing down the escarpment, using the newly attached rope of their lengthening rope hold.

As they started back down, a funny feeling cut through Kevin, like a knife. He was awash with an overwhelming feeling of sadness. To come this far up Oriel Peak and then go back, without visiting Sam, was disheartening. He felt as though they should be going on, to pay their respects to their friend in the mountain. He knew they did not have the time for that on this trip, but still, the feeling was there.

"I'll stop by for a visit next trip, Sam," he told Sam, telepathically. *"Next trip up, I'll pay my respects,"* he said, apologetically.

They had now come to the end of the newest section of their rope hold. Kevin sat down on a small rock and unraveled another section of knotted rope, tossing one end down the grade. Again, Wiley tied it off with a square knot. He gave it a good tug, and then, "Geronimo!" and he lightly touched down. "That's two!" he exclaimed. He looked over his shoulder, down the escarpment, and said, "Looks like two more will do it, Kev." Then he began his descent on the newly set section. Kevin followed in his wake, down another eighty feet, to the end of the newest section.

Kevin unraveled another section of rope, again pitching one end down the face of the escarpment. Wiley started to tie it off, but Kevin reached over and stopped him.

"Let me do it this time?" he asked.

Wiley smiled at him and replied, "Sure, Kev. Have a blast!"

Kevin tied the new section onto the old with a square knot, just like he had watched Wiley do. He cinched it up tight, gave it a hard tug, and "GERONIMO!" he yelled, so loud that several crows took flight from a nearby boulder. He came to rest in his own footprints, from which he had launched.

"Pretty damn good there, Kevin!" Wiley praised, patting him on the back. "That was a perfect take off and landing. A '10', I'd judge."

Wiley sat down on the ground and laughed a hearty, sustained laugh. Kevin did likewise.

"*That* was a lot of fun!" Kevin exclaimed, after containing his laughter. "A *lot* of fun."

Wiley composed himself, too, and said, "Three down and one to go. That should do it. Let's get moving."

Kevin started down and Wiley took hold of the rope, turned his back down the cliff, and followed above him. They ascended to the end of this section, and they both took seats on rounded boulders, near the bottom of the escarpment.

Wiley looked down the remainder of the cliff below and said, "Yep, one more should do it."

Kevin began to unwind one more section of rope, feeding it down the slope as he did. He handed the upper end to Wiley, who began tying it off. He stopped with half the knot completed and looked at Kevin.

"Hey, Kev. It's still your turn, if you want," he offered.

"That's okay, Wiley, you go ahead. Have a blast! You thought it up in the first place."

Wiley finished tying the square knot. He looked at Kevin and gave the rope a solid pull. He launched, "GERONIMO!" and it was loud and long! Kevin had the feeling that this last "Geronimo" was designed to be the loudest and longest of the day. He also saw that it was by far the highest. Wiley had outdone himself this time, soaring a good three feet higher than on any previous jump. He came back down, but this time, his feet slid out from under him instantly. Wiley had no time at all to react. The rope jerked from his hands and he tumbled down the escarpment, careening off one rock and then another. He had no way to stop his downward momentum and tumbled to the bottom of the cliff, eighty feet below.

Wiley lay there screaming, thrashing in the snow and writhing in pain. Kevin was frozen in place. Wiley screamed in pain again and Kevin jumped to action, grasping the rope and backing down the grade as fast as was safely possible. He reached the bottom quickly and rushed to Wiley's side.

"God, Wiley! Where's it hurt?"

"Everywhere!" he screamed, "But mostly my leg!"

He was clutching at his thigh as he spoke, crying and moaning. Kevin looked at his thigh and saw nothing. He moved to the other side of Wiley and saw the glistening white bone protruding from his jeans. Kevin almost vomited, but gagged, and fought it back.

Wiley's femur was sticking through his faded jeans. There was blood, but it was not spurting or running profusely from the open wound. Kevin thanked God for that and tried to calm Wiley.

"Look, Wiley. Listen, please. Your leg is broken…"

"I know!" he screamed. "I felt the bone!"

"Let me finish, Wiley. It's broken, but no arteries are cut. There is very little bleeding. You are going to be fine," Kevin reassured him.

Kevin's voice was soft, but firm. Wiley began to listen through the pain and understood what Kevin was trying to tell him.

"Okay, I won't bleed to death, but how am I going to get down from here? It's getting colder…I can feel it. I'll freeze to death before you can get back with help!" Wiley cried, fearing the worst.

"Wiley, listen to me again. It is not getting colder. It's in the 50's. Remember the weather report, 50's for ten days, remember? We have plenty of time."

Wiley nodded as if he understood, then his eyes rolled and he fell unconscious.

Kevin was happy that he was temporarily out of pain, but very worried about Wiley slipping into shock. He had lied about the temperature. It *was* dropping, and quickly. The weatherman was right about the five days, but dead wrong about the ten. He came to the realization that going for help would do no good.

Kevin took off his coat and covered Wiley. *I have to keep him warm,* he thought. He raced to the edge of the forest below and came back with two stout, three–foot long sticks, and fashioned a split to Wiley's bent leg, securing it at the ankle with his belt. He carefully unbuckled Wiley's belt, gently slipping it off, and secured the top of the splint, high on his thigh. With that, Wiley came back to consciousness and began crying in pain.

"Wiley. Can you hear me? Listen closely. I've put a splint on your leg to try to immobilize it. Don't try to move your leg, okay?" Kevin cautioned.

Wiley looked up at him with terrified eyes. He nodded to Kevin.

"Okay. Now listen again. I am going to build a litter and pull you off this damn mountain. If you fall asleep again, and you wake up and I'm not here, it's because I have to go down to the trees and cut some wood for your litter. Okay? Do you understand?"

Wiley looked into his eyes and blinked, then gave a small nod.

"Okay then. I'm going now, but I'll be back very shortly," Kevin assured him.

Kevin dropped his pack from his back and removed his hatchet and several small rolls of leather lacing. He placed the pack beneath Wiley's head, adjusted his coat squarely over him again, and ran for the forest.

As he ran he was concerned over Wiley having stopped his screaming. The pain was subsiding, which was good, but he thought it might also be bad. He thought that it might mean that shock was setting in. That worried him a lot. He didn't understand what shock was, technically, but he knew it could kill you, somehow. He picked up his pace at that thought, arriving at the edge of the woods moments later.

He scouted the area quickly and selected two small trees, which looked as though they'd do nicely for the side rails of the litter. He selected two more to fashion into the slats, and began chopping. He cut two ten–foot long rails and eight slats, each progressively longer than the next, from two feet to four. He laid out the side rails and the four–foot slat on the ground, in the shape of a triangle, and lashed them all together. Next he took the two–foot slat and lashed it across the front end of the litter, in deep notches he had formed, so it would not slip. This would be his *handle*, to push on. He then laid the other seven slats in place, lashing each at both ends to the side rails.

It looked good, so he stepped into the front of the litter and raised it using the handle located in front of him, and pushed. *This will work fine,* he thought. He made his way back to Wiley as fast as he could manage up the steep grade.

Wiley lay motionless, still unconscious. His face was ashen and he trembled, ever so slightly. Kevin set the litter down next to Wiley and maneuvered him onto it, a little at a time, trying hard not to disturb his broken leg. He threw his pack onto the litter next to Wiley, and their rifles between the pack and Wiley's body. Kevin stepped into position and lifted.

"Damn!" He had not even considered Wiley's weight. It was too much to hold up while he pushed the litter. He figured he'd be lucky to get a hundred yards behind him, let alone *eight miles*. He lowered the litter and sat down to think.

It *was* getting colder. The temperature had dropped another several degrees as he had worked to build the litter. Sitting there, he was beginning to notice it now. It was getting cold enough for him to need his coat again, but he realized that Wiley needed it more. He would have to tough it out. He had no choice.

He had come to a standstill and Wiley was dieing because of it. He needed to come up with a solution. He looked about and took notice of everything, trying to jog his mind into coming up with an idea. Then it hit him as his eyes fell on his Marlin. *"My rifle sling!"* Kevin lunged to his feet and removed the leather sling from his rifle, extending it to its full length. He stepped into the litter and knelt down, lashing the fittings to the rails at each end of his handle. "Yes! This is going to do fine!" he cheered, to the empty mountain. "This will work fine!"

Kevin lifted the leather sling and stooped beneath it, letting it rest across his shoulders. He lifted with his legs and began pushing, the weight of Wiley's body resting comfortably across his shoulders. "YAHOOOO!" he bellowed at the top of his lungs. "Yahoooo," echoed back from the peak.

He began the long trip down the mountain, his friend in tow. He prayed he'd make it to Bennett in time.

CHAPTER 35

*K*evin awoke in a waiting room, alone and worried. It had taken him hours to get Wiley off that mountain. How many, he wasn't sure. He had completely lost track of the time up there in the freezing cold. There were times when he thought he would drop, and never wake up. But somehow he had made it to the car and managed to get Wiley laid out on the back seat.

Most of the drive to Bennett was a blur, a barely remembered dream. He did remember making the decision to come here to Bennett, rather than go home to Carver. He had almost started for home, but then he had remembered that Bennett would be slightly closer, and had a hospital equipped with a twenty–four hour emergency room. Other than that conscious decision, the only other thing he remembered was turning the heat up to high and the blower to full, and leaving them there the whole trip. How long he had been waiting here in the hospital he had no idea.

Upon Kevin's arrival at the emergency entrance the staff had spirited Wiley away, taking him down a short corridor and into surgery. The doctors had also examined Kevin and dressed his bleeding shoulders. There had been no necessity to admit him, so Kevin was escorted to a waiting room, to await word on his friend.

But, that was hours ago, he was sure. He wanted to get up and go check on Wiley, but he was too exhausted and sore to move. He was sure someone would come around and tell him how Wiley was doing as soon as there was something to tell. Kevin drifted off into sleep once again.

Someone shaking his shoulder gently, and speaking his name, awakened him.

"Dad?" He said, confused.

"Hi, Son. How are you doing?" his father said, softly.

"Fine–What are you doing here?" Kevin asked, still not quite awake.

"Ed called me," Buck said.

Kevin looked at his dad with a puzzled expression.

"Doctor Cranpool, one of the doctors attending Wiley. We went to high school together. We've been talking while you were sleeping and he tells me you saved Wiley's life."

"Is he okay, Dad?" Kevin asked, afraid of the answer he might hear.

"He will be, Son, in time."

His dad rubbed his arm gently.

"Ed told me he was suffering from a concussion, shock and hypothermia when you brought him here. The break to his thighbone was clean, no severed arteries or veins. He was lucky, damn lucky," Buck explained to his son.

"So he'll be okay then?" Kevin asked, again.

"Yes, he will. But it will take time. One of the other doctors told me that if another half hour had passed before getting him here, they might not have been able to save him. You did a fine job, Son," his father praised.

"Thanks, Dad. He'd have done the same for me."

Buck smiled at his son and gently rubbed his arm.

"Ed says your shoulders were rubbed raw and bleeding when you arrived. How'd that come to be?" his dad asked, after a moment.

"That's from the litter I built to pull Wiley out. I had to support his weight with my rifle strap slung over my shoulders," he explained to his dad.

"Litter?" Buck asked. "How far in were you?"

"About eight miles, more or less, but it was all downhill," Kevin stated, downplaying his achievement.

Buck smiled and let out a little chuckle.

"Downhill or not, that was some pretty good thinking and a long way to haul him. You did real good, Son, really good. Where'd all this happen, anyway?" Buck asked, curiously.

"Oriel Peak, just below the escarpment," Kevin let slip.

"Oriel Peak? What were you doing up there? You know you aren't supposed…

"I know, Dad," Kevin cut in. "We didn't go into Blind Valley. We didn't even try. We were just exploring the area, looking for elk sign and hoping to get lucky and spot a herd. That's all," Kevin explained, twisting the truth of the matter.

"Well?"

"Well–what, Dad?" Kevin asked.

"Did you get lucky and spot a herd?" his dad asked, showing interest in their explorations.

"No, just sign. We saw aspen that had been all chewed up by them," Kevin said, truthfully.

"Well, then it wasn't all for nothing. How did Wiley manage to break his leg like that? Ed said it was a pretty severe break."

"Yea, he fell pretty far. We were up at the tree line and he decided to climb a tree to scout out the area. He was reaching for a branch overhead when the one he was standing on broke away. He couldn't hold on with his one hand and he fell, landing sideways on a big rock. I heard his leg snap, Dad. It was terrible and I almost puked when I saw his leg bone."

Kevin had *twisted* the truth again, but the escarpment was *off limits*, so he had to get around that truth somehow.

"He was a lucky boy to have *you* up there with him, Son. You did a fine job of saving him. Come on, let's get home."

"But what about Wiley, Dad?" Kevin questioned.

"Ed told me that he was taken to intensive care after surgery. He won't be allowed any visitors, other than immediate family, for a few days. There's nothing for us to do here, Son. Let's head on home. Your mother's waiting, and she was pretty worried about you. She's fixing you a big supper by now, I'm sure, and it's three hours home. We better get moving or you'll be eating it cold," Buck stated, smiling and gently ruffling his hair.

"Did Wiley's folks come up here, too?" Kevin asked his dad.

"Not that I know of, Son. I called Calvin's house twice before I left to let him know what had happened and to offer him a ride up here, but no one answered the phone either time. They were either not home or not answering the phone."

Kevin knew what that meant without his dad having to come right out and say it. Mr. Coates was passed out on the couch again and Mrs. Coates was deep into her Quaalude–induced sleep.

"What time is it anyway, Dad?" Kevin asked.

"Four in the morning, Son…Why?"

"Maybe you'd better call Mom and tell her to make that breakfast, instead of supper," Kevin joked.

"Maybe I'd better. Come on, Kev; let's get home. You can come back up and see Wiley in a few days, when they move him to a regular room," Buck assured him.

On the drive home Kevin followed his father's Bronco and thought back over the events of the day. He had learned a stern lesson today, one he would not soon forget. He had discovered that the difference between a mountain man and a mountain *boy* was foresight. As much fun as the 'Geronimo' thing had been, a true mountain man would not have done it, because a mountain man would have foresight.

They lived dangerous lives, true, but they did not take *unnecessary* chances. They had foresight. They could foresee that a broken leg sustained hundreds of miles from help was not *simply* a broken leg. It could be a death sentence, and often was. It wasn't an issue of bravery. They were brave. It was simply prudence that would keep them from doing what Wiley and he had done, that, and foresight.

If Sam Elliott's ghost still roamed that valley and had seen what had happened to Wiley, Kevin was sure he knew what Sam was thinking now...

Stupid boys. Don't come back up here, to my valley, until you're ready to act like men.

It was good advice, an admonition he would not soon forget.

He drove on in the blackness; the only visible landmarks were his father's two taillights.

A strange thought came to mind, there in the blackness of pre-dawn. He began to wonder what Sam Elliott would think of their plan. Did mountain men believe in retribution? If someone had killed his best friend, how far would Sam go to seek revenge, or justice? Kevin thought about that for quite some time, and eventually, arrived at a conclusion.

He figured that Sam lived by a code of ethics and conduct, as every man does, to some extent. Sam's code would have been molded by hardships and the dangerous life he led. It would have been firm and unyielding, incapable of being bent to the slightest degree. Sam would have befriended those who respected his code and would have mistrusted those who did not. To break his code, in a manner that directly affected him, would subject the transgressor to swift retribution. Of this, Kevin was certain.

But how did this relate to the events Wiley and he were planning, he wondered?

If a good friend of Sam had been killed by an acquaintance of his, Sam's reaction would be based on the circumstances of the death. Kevin was sure that Sam was a reasonable man. If his friend's death was determined to be accidental, Sam more than likely would have the capacity to forgive, and would probably do so. If, on the other hand, the death were an intentional murder, he would certainly seek swift justice for his friend.

Kevin thought for a moment about how Bryce had been murdered. He tried to visualize Sam's reaction to such a crime. It became very clear to Kevin that if Sam's friend had been murdered in such a sneaky, spineless way, Sam would go to the ends of the Earth to seek out the cowardly murderer, and give no quarter!

Kevin's conviction to the plan was cemented. He too, would give no quarter. He looked ahead to his father's taillights. He felt the lump again, but it was smaller than before. How easily he had twisted the truth about their trip to Oriel Peak. It scared him to think how easily he had deceived his father this time. His father loved him, that was undeniable and unquestionable, and he was sorry that his dad had been forced to drive all the way to Bennett, in the dead of night. Kevin was sorry that his dad had to make the long trip, but he was happy that he did. It would have been a long, lonely drive home, without him. There was something comforting about seeing his father's taillights up ahead. He wasn't alone, out here in this all–enveloping darkness.

He drove on toward home, following the familiar taillights before him, and the sky began to change from black to dark blue.

Daybreak, he thought to himself. *A new day.*

And, it was a new day. He was eighteen now, a man. He had just been through his trial of manhood with Wiley, and had emerged complete. As much as he hated deceiving the man driving ahead of him, he had also loved Bryce, and Bryce deserved the justice Sam Elliott would have met out. It would now be up to Wiley and him to insure that this justice was served. The method and means were all that were in question.

If it took a few lies to achieve this end, then as much as deceiving his father bothered him, it had to be done. It was a necessary evil required to achieve a noble goal, justice for Bryce.

The sky lightened to a brighter blue and the blackness gave way to the surrounding landscape. Kevin crested a small rise in the road. As his father's Bronco dropped below him, Carver came into view, nestled snuggly in the valley below.

CHAPTER 36

Wiley and Kevin had not been the only people who had taken advantage of the early May warm up and melt down. Deputy Phillips had noticed it, too. Stan had been uneasy all winter about his inability to give Mount Crane the attention it needed. Sheriff Dramico had seen fit to close the case on the Spencer boy, and rightly so. There was no evidence indicating that the death of Bryce Spencer was anything more than an accident. Still, he had not done the investigation he would have done under better weather conditions, and this early May warm up would be his first opportunity to do so.

By Saturday morning, the snow had melted down significantly. There was still a good three feet up there on top of the icy base, he was sure, but that was about what had been present on the day of the accident, before the storm set in.

Stan swung by Larry's Conoco station around six o'clock. It was early, but he wanted to get an early start, ahead of any skiers, however unlikely, that might decide to use Mount Crane today. When he arrived at Larry's, Lou was pumping gas for a customer.

"Hey, Lou," Stan greeted, waving out the patrol car window.

"Hey, Stan!" came the reply.

"Is Larry around anywhere?" Stan asked.

"Nope. He went up to the slope to check out the equipment and all," Lou answered. "Memorial Day. It's coming up soon, you know."

"Sure is, Lou, it won't be long now," Stan, replied, waving good–bye as he drove out of the lot. "Thanks, Lou!" he yelled back to him.

Memorial Day was the last of the big skiing holidays for Carver. Jessup Mountain would be packed, and Crane would get the overflow, mostly locals not wanting to mingle with the weekenders. Larry, of course, was responsible for maintaining the slope and the lift. It all had to be ready to go when Memorial Day arrived.

Stan pulled into the lower lot at Mount Crane and parked next to Larry's truck. As he exited the car, he heard the distinctive sound of the lift motor, purring away. Stan took his skis and boots out of the trunk, put them on, and polled his way up to the lift. Larry was nowhere to be seen.

Must be up top, Stan thought, polling his way to the pick up. He positioned himself and the seat swept him away, up toward the top of Cougar Run.

As he hopped off the seat he could see clearly for the first time, the rope barrier, which had been buried in the snow last November. He also saw Larry, close by the barrier, and walking toward the shed.

"Hey, Larry!" Stan hailed, waving his arms above his head.

Larry stopped in his tracks, as if he thought he'd heard something, but wasn't sure what.

"Larry! Over here!" summoned Stan, still waving.

Larry looked in Stan's direction and began waving, then started toward him as Stan began polling himself toward Larry.

"Stanley! What in blazes are you doing up here?"

"I was hoping to find you and get a lift up the hill, but now, that's done," replied Stan, smiling.

"Well, good then, Stanley. Why'd you want to come up here?" Larry asked, curiously.

"Just doing a little unofficial investigation, Larry, into that Spencer boy's accident," Stan confided, although he had probably said too much already.

"I see. Anything I can do to help, Stanley?" Larry asked, wanting in on the action.

"I'll let you know if there's anything I think of. What are you working on up here?" Stan inquired.

"Ah, someone cut a hunk out of that rope fence over yonder, so I've got to put up some new," Larry griped.

"Sorry, Larry. I'm afraid that was me that cut your rope. I needed a piece of it for my investigation," Stan told him, apologetically.

"Well, shucks, Stanley. Why didn't you say so? I could have cut you a piece from the roll in the shed," he explained, giving Stan a slight lashing.

"You didn't mention any roll of rope in the shed before, Larry; when I asked you before what was in there," Stan said, surprised by Larry's comment.

"No? Well, I must have not thought about it then. That's all I can figure. Sorry, Stanley, was it important?"

"It may be. I'd like to take a look at that roll now though, if that's okay with you, Larry," Stan said, motioning to the shed.

"Sure. C'mon," Larry replied.

Entering the shed, Stan saw the large spool of rope stored in the far corner. It was a big spool of half–inch sisal.

"How much rope comes on a spool like that, Larry?" Stan asked.

"Five hundred feet," he answered.

"How much of it do you use for the rope fence, each time you string it?"

"Exactly one hundred and fifty feet."

"So you can replace it three times from one spool then, right?"

"Right. That I can, three times." Larry answered.

"So what do you do with the other fifty feet when you get a new roll?" asked Stan.

Larry hesitated. He looked at the floor, and then at Stan, dragging his foot across the floor from left to right.

"Well–Stanley–I take it home with me, but don't you tell no one, hear?" he confessed.

"That's none of my concern at the moment. Now, listen. How many times have you strung the fence off of this roll?" Stan wanted to know.

"Once is all, that's it out there now," Larry replied. "The one you cut."

"And you haven't taken any home from this roll, right?" Stan continued.

"No, sir. Not from this roll," Larry answered, holding up his hand as if taking an oath.

"So we should have three hundred and fifty feet left here. Let's roll it out and see if that checks out," Stan instructed.

Larry jumped to the task, and helped Stan roll the spool outside. They tied the exposed end to the shed's door handle and started rolling the spool across the snow until they had played out all the rope that was there.

"So how do you measure it out for the fence?" Stan asked.

"Just like we're doing now," Larry stated. "'Cept I don't roll it *all* out. Then I step it off."

"Go ahead, Larry, do it exactly like you always do," Stan instructed, motioning for Larry to begin.

Larry walked back to the door handle and started pacing off the rope walking toward Stan. He came to the end of his march and stopped.

"Is that it, Larry?" Stan yelled.

"Yep."

"Okay, cut her off and we'll string it." Stan said.

They took the measured rope over to the fence and pulled the old rope out. Larry tied a heavy knot at the end of the new section and started feeding it through the eyelets, one at a time. After stringing the rope through the last screw eye, he tied another large knot at the end of the rope. It fit perfectly.

"See, Stanley, just the right amount of sag between each post," Larry said, smiling with pride.

"Great job!" Stan praised him. "What else can I say, except, lets do it again, Larry."

They went back to the unused rope and began again. This time though, when Larry finished his measuring march, he was about twenty feet past the end of the rope. He had held up at the end of the rope, but Stan had instructed him to finish so they could see how short they were.

"Well–Larry. Counting the fifty feet that *should* be left over for your personal use, and the twenty feet we're shy of the third section, I'd say we're missing about seventy feet of rope, wouldn't you?" Stan asked.

"Looks like, Stanley," Larry confirmed.

"And you didn't take any at all from this roll?" Stan asked, again.

"No, sir. None at all."

"And you're sure about the roll being brand new before you strung that section that I cut up last November?" he double checked.

"Yes, sir. Sure as rain," Larry reaffirmed.

"Has this ever happened before Larry, coming up short like this, I mean?"

"Not in twenty some years of doing it, it hasn't," Larry answered, raising his head high.

Stan thought for a minute, rubbing his chin and surveying the area.

Seventy feet missing. Where would seventy feet of rope go way up here on this mountain?

He couldn't imagine anyone would come up here to steal rope unless they had a use for it *up here*. He turned back to face Larry.

"Tell me, how often do you change the rope on the fence?"

"Every other spring. A new roll lasts me six years," Larry stated, with certainty.

"And you take *your* fifty feet from the end of the roll, every time?" Stan asked.

"That's right, Stanley, the last fifty feet. There's nothing up here I have need of it for, so I take it on home with me and put it to good use. No sense in wasting it," he said, justifying his pilferage.

Stan felt like he had all the information he needed from Larry, but out of curiosity, he had to ask.

"What do you do with the fifty feet of new rope you get every six years? Just curious, mind you," he explained.

"Anchor rope for my fishing boat," Larry said, smiling and dragging his foot through the snow. "Got no use for it up here. Waste not want not, they say. You've heard that before, haven't you, Stanley?"

"Sure have, Larry. That's good advice," Stan assured him. "Thanks for your help. I'm going to ski down the slope and stop off at the site of the accident and have a look around. I'll see you later."

"Okay, Stanley, be careful. Snow's a little wet today," Larry warned him.

Stan skied down to where Bryce had come to rest against the fir tree. He looked the area over, then removed his skis and began hiking up the edge of the slope. He was thinking back to what Doc had said about the Spencer boy, possibly *"running into the rope"* rather than just falling on it. The injury could have happened either way. With seventy feet of rope missing from up top, he was beginning to wonder.

Stan had climbed about a hundred feet up the side of the run when he decided to stop and rest for a moment. He wasn't a teenager anymore, and this was a steep grade, on snow no less. As Stan stood there, catching his breath, he looked around for anything out of the ordinary. There was nothing.

He started to move up the slope, but as he stepped forward, he saw something out of the corner of his eye. He turned in that direction for a more direct look. It was faint, but he thought he could see a trail in the snow, running off into the woods, diagonally and away from him.

He moved in that direction and stared closer, discovering that it was *two* trails, running parallel to one another, and weaving through the trees into the distance. He went for an even closer look, intercepting the trail and kneeling down to examine the marks in the snow. They appeared to be depressions in the older, more crystalline snow, filled with newer, more powdery snow. He gently brushed the newer snow away, discovering boot prints in the crusted older snow. They weren't distinct enough for an impression of any kind. Time, evaporation, and freeze and thaw had played havoc with them, but he was certain that they were indeed boot prints. He turned to follow the tracks back toward the ski slope.

The tracks did indeed lead him back to Cougar Run. Then they seemed to disappear. He thought about that for a minute and walked onto the run, about ten feet, and knelt. He gently, ever so slowly and carefully brushed at the snow, removing the smallest layers he could with each stroke. There were tracks here too. Much less distinct, and apparently an attempt had been made to brush them out. He looked back to where he had come from and projected a mental path, following the same course, to the far side of the run. He went there and stood, looking around at everything.

The closest object to him was a small pine tree, several feet away. There were muted tracks all around it, ones that had not been brushed away. Stan knelt again and examined the tree's trunk. He spotted a small area where the delicate bark had been broken and scathed. He craned his neck to look around the side of the trunk and found another similar mark. He moved around and there was another, then another, forming a circle around the trunk. He stood, and stared at it. It was no more than twelve inches above the snow.

It didn't take Stan long to come to the conclusion that a rope had been tied around this tree. A rope upon which considerable force had been applied, twisting the rope on its anchor. He looked across the slope to the other side and thought, *About fifty feet to the other side, interesting.* He crossed the slope, going back to the other side, pacing it off as he went. He reached the edge of the run.

Fifty–five feet"

He continued into the forest.

Seventy feet.

He hunkered down. He was pretty well concealed at this point, but he could still see the ski run clearly through the trees.

Interesting, he thought to himself...*Very interesting.*

CHAPTER 37

Stan caught up with Al at Laura's Diner. Al was off duty and enjoying a late breakfast at the counter, as he usually did on Saturday mornings. Laura's was buzzing with activity, also usual for any given Saturday morning.

Laura's was a typical diner, with a Formica counter running the width of the restaurant, and eight booths along the front wall by the windows. The fifteen counter stools were the single post type, their round padded seats swiveling on top of fixed pedestals, and each pedestal, firmly bolted to the floor.

The floor itself was linoleum, and appeared to be one large sheet of black, and once upon a time, white squares. It had the appearance of a big chessboard whose white squares had dimmed to a ruddy tan with time.

The tabletops in the booths were constructed of the same Formica, as was the counter, with multi–colored "binkies", little boomerang shapes, adorning the white background. Each booth had its own chrome plated song selector, which played the favorite 45's of the day, through a colorfully lit Wurlitzer juke box located on one end wall.

Laura was a heavy set lady, somewhere in her fifties, with graying hair and 'cat eye' glasses, which were usually seen hanging around her neck on a gold chain. She had remodeled her diner in 1955, and it looked it, a throwback to that time. The fact that the building was much older was apparent by the painted tin ceiling tiles, nailed above the incandescent light fixtures and the ceiling fans. She had never bothered to replace the ceiling tiles, as she simply liked the look of them, and she preferred the incandescent light to the more modern fluorescent you saw in most businesses.

As Stan entered he took note of an empty booth in the corner, by the front window, and approached Al at the counter.

"Morning, Al," Stan said, tapping his boss on the shoulder.

"Morning, Stan. What's up?" Al asked.

"Can we go over to that booth and talk?" Stan requested, nodding in the direction of the empty table.

Al could see in Stan's face that something was troubling him.

"I suppose so, Stan, what's the problem?" Al asked, showing concern for his deputy.

"No problem. Let's go over there and talk though," Stan insisted.

Al picked up his plate and coffee cup and they moved to the vacant booth. Once they were seated Stan began.

"Sheriff. I did a little looking around up on Mount Crane this morning. I wanted to let you know what I found out."

"Okay, Stan, shoot," Al, replied. "This is about the Spencer boy...I presume."

"Yes, sir. It's been bothering me all winter, like a sore tooth," Stan replied, analogizing the situation. "I never got a chance to really scout it out before because of the bad weather. You remember that, right?"

"Yes, I do," Al, confirmed.

"Well, I kept on thinking about what Doc had said about how the Spencer boy's neck injury might have occurred. He could have fallen on that rope hard, *or* run into it hard. Remember that?" Stan asked.

"Yes, it's in the report, but we decided he *did* fall on it. There was no way he could have run into it—you said, if I remember correctly.

In your opinion, it wasn't high enough to run into with his neck," Al reminded him.

"It wasn't, but I got to talking to Larry up there and we discovered that he is missing seventy feet of replacement rope from the spool he keeps stored in the shed up on top."

"Did you locate it?" asked Al.

No, sir, but I did find something very interesting just above where the Spencer boy died," Stan informed him.

"Really? What was that, Stan?" Al replied, his curiosity peaked.

"Well, first of all I found tracks along the side of the run, in the older, more icy snow. The snow is now about as deep as it was that morning. Almost all the newer snow has melted. These tracks in the older snow were very deteriorated, but I could see them coming and going through the woods. Two sets. Sheriff, I don't think those boys were alone up there that morning," Stan suggested.

"They were with some other friends? Why wouldn't they tell us that? Maybe those tracks you found were just some hiker's tracks, Stan?" suggested Al.

"No, sir, I don't think so. I don't think the boys were with anybody else and I don't think they knew about whoever else was there. The tracks appeared to come through the woods and across the ski run, just above where the Spencer boy died. The tracks on the run appeared to have been brushed out some; concealed."

Stan paused, awaiting the sheriff's reaction.

"Go on, Stan. What else?" he asked.

"Well, I followed the tracks across the slope, best I could, to the other side. I found a pine tree with its bark all cracked and scarred, in a circle around the trunk, like a rope had been tied to it and then twisted hard around it."

"How far across the slope was this pine tree?" Al asked, very interested now.

"Fifty–five feet. Seventy feet put me in good hiding along the slope's edge, but I could still see the slope just fine," Stan told him.

Al was painting the picture in his mind as Stan talked.

"So you think somebody else went up there and took seventy feet of rope from Larry's shed, went back down the slope and tied it off on a tree. Then they hid in the woods and waited for the Spencer boy to come down, and when he did, jerked the rope up and broke his neck. Is that what you're thinking?" Al asked, having put all the pieces together.

"Yes, sir. That's what I think, but there's a problem with that, too," Stan suggested.

"What problem?" Al inquired.

"The rope was only a foot off the ground, maybe sixteen inches at most. I don't think it was intended to hit him in the throat. I think it was intended to trip him up, to give him a nasty fall, but not intentionally kill him, like it did."

"A prank then? Or, someone wanted to give him something to think about? Get even with him? There's a lot of possibilities there, Stan," Al told him. "Furthermore, if it was like you describe, how did the boy take the rope in the throat?"

"I don't know, sir, something went wrong, I guess. Maybe they pulled the rope too soon and he saw it coming. Maybe he tried to slide under it. It could have happened like that, I guess," Stan theorized.

"Okay, Stan. Bottom line. Did you find the rope? No, and you probably never will. Are the foot prints clear enough to cast or photograph?"

"No, sir. They're hardly footprints at all any more, just depressions in the snow," Stan said.

"Did you find any other physical evidence up there, like a dropped belonging, or anything?" Al asked.

"No, sir, there was nothing I could see. I followed the tracks back the way they came through the woods. They led to a little service road off the lower parking lot. But, I didn't find anything dropped along the way."

"So we have nothing concrete, just a lot of speculation and a little circumstantial evidence, at best. Is that right? Am I overlooking anything?" Al questioned, having already spelled it out for Stan.

"Yes, sir, I mean–no, sir, but it's enough to open the case again, isn't it?"

"Perhaps, Stan, but we have to think of the Spencers," Al cautioned. "Opening up this can of worms all over again will be hard on them, very hard. I don't want to do that unless we have something very concrete to go on. If we *officially* reopen this investigation and can't take it anywhere, it's just going to cause a lot of hurt."

"Yes, sir, I understand, but there's something in all this, I can feel it. It's not right. There's more to what happened up there that morning than we *officially* know about," Stan pleaded.

"I agree. Perhaps you should drop by the school Monday and *unofficially*, and *discretely*, find out who might have wanted to hurt the Spencer boy. Talk to a few of his other friends, not Reynolds or Coates mind you. I don't want to believe it, and I don't now, but they may have some involvement in this. We don't know that they were unaware of someone else being up there. If it was a prank, they may have been involved, too, or have knowledge of it, and could be covering for their friends. I doubt it though. That would be a pretty dangerous prank to pull on a friend. It doesn't really fit. But just the same, talk to a few of the Spencer boy's other friends. See what they have to say. See if you can find out if he had any enemies, but remember, keep it on the q.t.

Unless we come up with some concrete physical evidence, I'm afraid the only way we can *officially* open this back up is with an eyewitness, or a confession. That's not a whole lot likely to happen, I'm afraid to say."

"No, sir, that's not likely. I'll see what I can find out Monday, without raising too much dust," Stan promised.

They sat there a minute thinking about the new developments, and then Al asked, "Have breakfast yet, Stan?"

"No, sir, not yet," Stan answered.

"Well–the hash browns are really good this morning. Order up, son, it's on me!"

CHAPTER 38

$\mathcal{A}$t eight a.m. Monday morning, Stan was already sitting in the Carver High counselor's office, waiting for Miss Haley to arrive. He wanted to find out from her who Bryce's associates might be, beyond Kevin and Wiley. Stan knew he could get the information from almost any of the other kids, but Al had warned him to be discreet. In other words, start asking the kids and everyone would know he was asking questions, whereas he felt he could count on Miss Haley's confidentiality.

Stan explained the situation to her, providing only the information that was absolutely necessary, and obtained a list of four names. He was a little surprised that the list of names was so limited, but Miss Haley explained to him that Bryce was not the most popular of students. Before Stan left she assured him that she would speak of his or her meeting with no one.

Stan's plan was to wait until after school to talk with the boys, at their homes and in private. In the interest of discretion, he did not want to be observed interviewing the boys at school. *That* would start everyone speculating and devising all sorts of stories to explain his presence at Carver High.

Stan remembered how vivid the imaginations of teenagers could be. It had not been so very long ago that he had roamed the halls of Carver High, not in this new building, but the old building, which to him had always seemed more like a high school than this modern structure. He was a product of the old high school and he wasn't sure he would have liked it here, although his memories of the former building weren't all that wonderful either. He had suffered much the same abuse as had Wiley, Bryce and Kevin during his high school tenure. This trip into his past brought back some very bad memories. Memories he thought he had buried deeper than he apparently had.

Perhaps that was why he had become a lawman, to have some authority, and gain self–respect. He wasn't positive about that, but he was sure of one thing, what kids like Wiley and Kevin needed to realize, is that ten years down the road, none of these kids will even be a part of their lives. This high school is just a stopping off place, temporary, at most. Ten years from now they will be in an entirely different world, and this place will be just a collection of fading memories, some good and some bad.

Stan left Miss Haley's office and the building, while the first bell classes were still in session and the halls were empty. He drove by the elementary school he had attended as a child and parked by the playground. Soon, the children emerged from the building, screaming and shouting. Some of the kids headed straight for the play equipment, several swinging on the old tire. A chain of eight little girls formed, hand in hand, and swept across the play area, screaming and laughing, while other children kicked a ball about and still others ran aimlessly to and fro.

Closing his eyes, Stan listened. Was there a more wonderful sound in the entire world? The sound of children playing compared to no other sound on earth, a symphony within a cacophony of random noise, which played like a finely tuned violin.

Stan opened his eyes and began looking for the Kevins and Wileys on the lot. He knew they were here; they always were, just as he had been. Those two or three kids, sitting by themselves on a bench or on the ground and not participating in the fun of the others, not welcome in their glee. These were the Bryces of the future, the Kevins and the Wileys. Some would adjust as he had and others would not, remaining on the fringe of society throughout their entire lives. Some would grow up okay and others would find a lot of trouble for themselves. It was a sad thought and his heart went out to the three boys he spotted, sitting alone.

Stan had plans though, plans he had discussed with Al in the past. He wanted to start an after school program for kids, a program in which all who participated would have the opportunity to discover what they could do better than anyone else. He would build their self–esteem on that one thing they excelled in and instill pride in them for that which they accomplished.

Al had done that for him, after school at the station house, or riding in the cruiser. Al had unknowingly made him aware of the love he had for police work and had given him the encouragement to pursue it. Now, Stan wanted to return the favor to as many children as he could. As he thought about it, the feeling that perhaps Al had known what he was doing, swept over him like the shadow of a passing cloud.

Al had said that he would give his plan consideration, but nothing had come of it yet. Stan had waited patiently for Al's decision, but perhaps now, he would wait no longer. If nothing continued to be done, he *would be* the sheriff one day, and *that* would be as long as he would wait.

He pulled his cruiser back onto the street and drove in the direction of Greenville.

Later that afternoon, Stan made the rounds to the boys on Miss Haley's list, finding three of the four at home. He discussed with each the need for remaining silent about their conversation, and obtained feedback from each as to which kids they felt might have had it in for Bryce. After finishing with the final interview, there was one name at the top of the list of people who might have wanted to see Bryce get hurt. It had been unanimous, actually, with all three boys naming the same person. Stan felt as though he had more than enough justification to drop by and have a word with Mary Clemmons.

It was almost seven o'clock when he pulled into Mary's drive. The house itself was intimidating, largely so, and he felt quite out of place pulling into the circular drive. The entire neighborhood was upscale and luxurious, but the Clemmons home was the showpiece of Pill Hill. It was a massive white brick colonial with four boxed pillars reaching from the full–width front porch floor to the eaves of the roof. The house stood two and a half stories tall and sported, along the front, twelve double–hung sash windows with sash green shutters, alongside each.

In the driveway were parked a cream colored Mercedes Benz and a black Cadillac, both of which appeared brand new. In the separate garage, he could see through the open door, a green Gremlin and an old vintage automobile of some sort, red in color, perhaps an MG Roadster, although he wasn't sure about the make. The garage itself stood at a right angle to the house, facing it, from about eighty feet away. Behind the garage was a tennis court, which was adjacent to the swimming pool.

Stan got out of his cruiser and looked around. This place was unbelievable, and intimidating for someone like him. He was half–a–mind to turn around and leave, but how would he explain *that* to Al? He warily approached the huge double front doors and pulled the knob, which rang the doorbell. An elegantly dressed lady in her late thirties or early forties answered the door.

"Oh, hello, Sheriff. What can I do for you?" she asked, surprised at his presence on her stoop.

"Deputy, ma'am, Deputy Phillips. I need a word with your daughter, Mary, please," he said, respectfully.

Stan had actually expected a butler to answer the door, and was taken aback a bit when Mrs. Clemmons had appeared.

"You want to speak with Mary? Whatever for? Is there a problem–Deputy?" she questioned.

"No, ma'am, I just need to talk with her about a matter she may have information about," he replied, calmly and evenly. He didn't want to alarm her unnecessarily.

"It's not a big deal. Just a few questions for my report, is all."

Mrs. Clemmons looked at Stan, suspiciously, and then motioned for him to step inside.

"Mary is upstairs–in her room. I'll call her and you can talk in the parlor," she said flatly, and pointed to a room to Stan's right.

"Please, Deputy, go in and have a seat," she instructed with a pleasant, yet commanding demeanor.

Stan did as requested, passing through the French doors and into the parlor. It was an elegant room, well appointed with antiques and expensive looking paintings. Stan looked around the room and selected an antique rocking chair across from an antique settee. He looked down at the rug beneath his feet and thought; *I'll bet it's Persian. He looked up at the paintings on each wall and thought, Original oils, I'll bet. This is one fine room.*

He heard a rustle to his left and looked to see Mary entering the room, followed by another girl. They sat side by side on the settee, facing Stan.

"Hi, Deputy," Mary began. "What brings you here?" she continued, flashing a flirting little smile his way.

"Hi, Mary. Just a few questions I need to get some answers to. Who's your friend?" he asked.

"Oh, I'm sorry. Please forgive my manners. This is Alicia. Alicia Koppe. She's my best friend," Mary volunteered, flashing that same smile again. "What questions?"

Stan smiled and said hello to Alicia, then continued. "Alicia, are you Lucas Koppe's daughter?"

"Yes, sir, I am," she answered.

"Well, pleased to meet you. I know your dad from Milner's, nice guy, Lucas."

"Thank you, sir," Alicia responded.

"Okay–Mary, I'd like to start by asking if you have ever been up on Mount Crane, to Cougar Run, specifically.

"Well then, by all means, Deputy, go right ahead," Mary, quipped, still smiling her flirtatious smile. "Ask me."

"Okay–Well have you? Have you ever been up there?" Stan asked, getting a little flustered by her smile.

"Certainly, I used to ski up there," Mary replied.

"When was the last time you were up there, Mary?" he asked.

"Oh, years ago, before Jessup was developed," she replied, coolly.

Alicia's name had also come up, several times, while talking with Bryce's friends. Stan turned his attention to her.

"How about you, Alicia? How long has it been since you were last up there?" he asked.

"I don't ski, Deputy. I've never been up there," she replied, calmly; then added, "Except to watch, from the old lodge, when it was still open."

"Is that what this is about, Deputy?" Mary asked, taking charge of the conversation. "Have kids been partying up in that old lodge again? I'll bet they finally burned it down, didn't they? That's what this is all about, isn't it?" Mary blustered, trying to divert the conversation.

Stan was taken a bit by surprise. She was either the coolest cookie he had ever run across, or she had nothing to hide. That *had* been a problem over the years, since the lodge closed. Al and he had been out to the lodge on numerous occasions, running off the older kids who found it a convenient place to party. They *had* almost burned it down one winter; that was a true enough statement.

Not being thrown off by the diversion, if that is what it was intended to be, Stan continued with his line of questioning.

"Where were you, Mary, on the morning Bryce Spencer was killed?" he asked, immediately, not wanting her to think her previous comments were even considered.

Mary didn't even flinch, not a twitch or even a blink of an eye. Her smile did begin to fade though, into a slight frown. She looked directly into Stan's eyes and starred for a brief instance.

"I was right here, Deputy. All morning," she answered, without a hint of hesitation.

"Can anyone verify that? Your mom or dad, perhaps?" he questioned.

"No, sir. They were out of town," again, with no hesitation.

"Is there anyone else who might be able to corroborate your story?" Stan probed.

Now, Mary did flinch. But it was not what Stan had expected at all. Her face became filled with rage and she pointed her finger directly at him, shaking it in his face.

"Story?" she blurted out. "What *story*? I got up around nine and I called Alicia on the phone. We talked most of the morning about going shopping at Bennett Mall, on Sunday. We heard about Bryce on our way home Sunday, on the radio! I wish I *had* been up there to see him break his neck, the little prick!"

Mary paused her tirade, taking a deep breath.

"So, apparently, you didn't like Bryce?" Stan suggested.

"I hated the little bastard. He cost me my scholarship to Evans, maybe even my acceptance. He got me grounded for a month. He was a pain in my ass for as long as I can remember," she bellowed.

"So you're not sorry he's dead," Stan stated, bluntly.

"No, I'm not sorry for him. Maybe for his parents and family, a little, but not for him."

"So what you are saying is, that if you had the chance, you would have 'pulled the trigger', so to speak?" Stan said, trying to push the right buttons.

"No, I'm not—Deputy. I may have hated him enough, but I still have a future, Evans or no Evans. I wouldn't throw it away on the likes of him," Mary said, pointedly.

Stan was solidly on the fence. This young lady sure hated Bryce, but she sure wasn't afraid to reveal it. She didn't seem to be hiding anything.

"Alicia, what about you?" Stan asked, turning his attention again to her.

"Me? What about me?" Alicia asked, appearing rather surprised.

"How did you feel about Bryce, and can you verify Mary's being on the phone with you all that morning?" he clarified for her.

"Yes, we were. We talked about shopping in Bennett and other stuff, like she said, nearly all morning. About my feelings for Bryce—" Alicia thought for a moment. "I didn't like him much, but he never crossed me up like he did Mary. You couldn't trust him. That's what I didn't like. He was a snitch. I'm sorry he died, but I don't miss him."

Stan looked at her sincere expression and turned to Mary.

"So did you go shopping at the mall on Sunday? You say that's what you talked about, so did you go?" Stan asked, pushing her story forward.

"Yes, we did?" she answered.

"What did you buy?" Stan asked.

"Shoes and girl stuff. I don't know, just things. It was months ago, I don't remember exactly what I bought," she answered.

"Have you got receipts from the mall you could show me?" Stan asked, digging deeper still.

"That was six months ago, I doubt it!" Mary flared, appearing to be getting agitated with Stan's questions.

"It would help if you did. It would help verify all that you have told me," Stan pointed out, backing off just a little.

Mary thought for a moment. This was something that she had expected, but six months ago, not now. But, *when* didn't really matter at all. She knew the best way to verify their alibi would be with the receipts from the mall, but who saves those? That would be too convenient. But, most people *do* save their credit card bills. Why, she didn't know. No one ever looks at them again, but people do, so this was her ace.

"No, I'm sure they are gone. I wouldn't have saved them," she replied, with some certainty.

"Did you pay cash, or charge the items," Stan asked, playing right into her scheme.

"I used my Visa card. I always do," she replied, as if to say, *doesn't everybody?*"

"You have a Visa card–of your own?" Stan asked, a little surprised at that.

"Sure. Dad gave it to me for my sixteenth birthday," Mary answered, again, like it was no big deal.

"Who pays the bills?" Stan questioned.

"I do, out of my allowance, why?" Mary asked, perfectly concealing that this was exactly where she had hoped this conversation would go.

"Would you still have the invoice from last November?" Stan continued.

Mary's face lit up. It was perfectly timed and just right.

"Yea, I'll bet I do! Hold on a minute!" Mary exclaimed, as she jumped up and headed for the hallway. "I'll be right back!"

She went up to her room and took the invoice from where she had placed it for safekeeping. Then, she sat on the bed and waited for a few minutes.

I have to find it first, she thought to herself.

After what seemed about the right amount of time, she headed back downstairs.

"Here it is, Deputy."

She beamed with delight at having found it. Stan took it from her hand and looked it over.

"Mind if I hang onto this for a while?" he asked.

"No, sir–keep it," she answered.

"Thanks, Mary–Alicia. I'll be running along now. I'll drop by if I need anything else," Stan said, as he rose from his chair.

Mary showed him to the front door.

"Bye, Deputy," Mary said.

"Yea–bye," added Alicia.

Mary closed the door behind Stan and turned to Alicia, who looked terrible.

"Mary, I'm scared," she whimpered.

"What's to be scared about, Alicia? He bought the whole ball of wax! Trust me!"

Stan turned the corner and headed down from Pill Hill to the rest of the city below. He wasn't sure what he would do now. The one person who had the most against Bryce, and the only person with a real reason to harm him, seemed innocent enough to him. He felt he was barking up the wrong tree with the two girls. Maybe Bryce's death truly was an accident, or rather, a mistake. Maybe he was the victim of mistaken identity. Maybe Kevin, or perhaps Wiley, was the intended target.

He thought about that.

Now, I am grabbing at straws, he thought.

CHAPTER 39

*T*uesday morning was crisp and clear, the temperature had plum-
meted back into the twenties, but it was only May, and that was
to be expected, upon occasion. Stan pulled into the station lot and
went inside to report his findings to Al.

He found Al exactly where he expected to, sitting in his swivel
chair at his desk, looking out at the mountain.

"Morning, Sheriff," Stan said, cheerfully.

"Morning, Stan. You sound cheerful this morning," Al remarked,
swinging his chair around. *"Squeeek!"–"Damn!"*—I hate this damn
chair!" he said to Stan.

"Yea, I know," Stan said, with a slight laugh caught in his throat.

"How did your investigation go? Find out anything interesting?"
Al asked.

"Yes, sir. I talked with Bryce's best friends other than Kevin and
Wiley, and they were all unanimous in their opinions. They all
agreed that Mary Clemmons was probably the worst thing that had
ever happened to Bryce," Stan explained.

"Now—who's she?" Al asked, leaning on one elbow.

"She a doctor's daughter who lives up on Pill Hill," Stan answered.

"Did you talk with her?" Al asked.

"Yes, sir, I did. I talked to her and her best friend, Alicia Koppe.
She was visiting Mary when I arrived."

"Okay, now who is this Alicia Koppe?" Al asked, placing his other elbow on the desk.

"A shop keep's daughter from over in the Greenville area of town. You know her dad; he's the fellow that runs the dry goods store on Milner, for Old Man Swanson. You know–Lucas," Stan said, jogging Al's memory.

"Oh yes, Lucas. I don't believe I ever knew his last name. His daughter you say?"

"Yes, sir. It was her that I talked with at Mary's house, along with Mary herself," Stan continued.

"Did they give you anything to work with?" asked Al, resting his face in his hands.

"No, sir, not really. Their story of where they were that morning can't be verified, but it makes sense. They have each other for an alibi, but that's all. They said they were both home talking to each other on the telephone most of the morning when Bryce Spencer took his fall. I guess I *could* check the phone records, come to think of it. I didn't think of that until just now," Stan said, a little disappointed in himself.

"Nope, that won't do you any good. It's a local call from Pill Hill to Greenville. The phone company doesn't keep records of local calls, only long distance," Al informed him.

"Okay, scratch that idea. Anyway, they say they were talking about going shopping at Bennett Mall on Sunday, among other things."

"Can that be verified?" Al asked.

Stan handed Al the Visa invoice.

"Visa!" Al exclaimed, a little surprised. "How old is this Mary?"

"Just turned eighteen, sir. Her daddy gave her the card for her sixteenth birthday. She pays the bill each month from her allowance," Stan explained, as it had been told to him.

"Kids with credit cards. What's this world coming to, anyway?"

"It's not such a bad idea, actually, Al. I was thinking about that myself, and I suppose it can teach them some responsibility, some-how. You think?" Stan asked, trying to put reason to it.

"I suppose it could–somehow. So what was your impression of her and her story? Your gut feeling?"

"Well, I think she was being truthful enough. She didn't try to hide her dislike for the boy, that's for sure. She isn't even sorry he's gone, but for his folks' feelings. I think she was being straight with me," Stan summarized.

"Good–Any other ideas?" Al asked.

"Not that aren't pretty far fetched," Stan answered, thinking of his previous thoughts.

"We don't need that, but we do need something solid or we drop it altogether," Al declared.

"What about what we do know?" Stan asked, feeling like they had been left out to dry, once again.

"We save it in the back of our minds, we add it to the report, and we don't forget about it. That's what we do and that's all we can do–for now."

Al stopped and thought for a moment. He looked over his shoul-der at Mount Crane, standing tall and white outside his window, and spoke as if to the peak itself.

"And, to be thorough and to stay on the safe side, Stan, you go up there again with a camera. You shoot what you can of the tracks in the snow. Take some shots from where you think whoever held the rope was located, over to the tree, and then you take some close–ups of the tree trunk and some pictures of the tree itself. Take a chainsaw with you, too, and cut that tree down *above* the scars, and then cut it off below. Bring back that section of trunk and put it in storage in the basement, along with the photos."

Al looked back toward Stan.

"After you have done all that, Stan." Al paused. "After you have done all that, go have a talk with the Reynolds boy. He's not as callus as his buddy, Wiley. He's the weaker link if there is something they aren't telling us about that day. I want you to probe him a little, without Wiley present. I don't think he'll give anything up, and I'm not at all convinced that he knows any more than he has already told us, but do it just the same. Let me know what your gut tells you about him," Al directed.

"Okay, Sheriff. I'll get the camera and a chainsaw and head on up there now. I'll let you know what I find out after talking with Kevin."

"See you later, Stan. Be careful up there. Don't cut a leg off or anything," Al warned.

They both laughed, and Stan turned to leave.

"One more thing, Stan."

"Yes, sir. What's that?"

"Good work. I like the way you're sticking with this. Shows you care."

"Thanks, Sheriff!" Stan beamed. "Thanks a lot!"

Stan left the station feeling pretty good about himself. It wasn't often that Al noticed his efforts, or if he did, ever bothered to mention them. Stan was the kind of guy that liked a good pat on the back once in a while. Not because of ego or anything of that nature. He simply liked to please those who depended upon him. Praise was a measure therefore, of his success at doing that.

Al was a good sheriff and a good boss. Stan had the feeling, now looking back, that perhaps Al had *expected* him to follow up on this case all along. Al had closed it, officially, but Stan was now beginning to think that had been just a formality.

He knew I'd pick it up again come spring, Stan thought to himself. *He knew I would.*

Stan asked Becky to get him the Polaroid out of the cabinet behind her and went outside. He looked up at Mount Crane and said, "Here I come–again." He jumped in his squad car and drove in the direction of Larry's filling station. He didn't need Larry to run the lift, He'd hike up to the tree, but Larry owned several chain saws, and he was going to need to borrow one.

CHAPTER 40

Kevin returned home from school at around three–thirty. The hospital had promised to call as soon as Wiley was allowed to have visitors. The call had not come by the time he had left for school this morning, so he rushed in the house and called for his mom. He heard her respond from the basement, where she was doing the wash. He bounded down the basement steps, barely touching a third of them.

"Mom! Did the hospital call yet?" he asked her, anxiously.

"No, Kevin, I'm sorry they haven't called yet," she responded, sympathetically.

"Darn!" Kevin exasperated, clenching a fist and thrusting it downward.

"When are they ever going to call?" he asked, both angry and annoyed at their silence.

His mom gave him a sympathetic look and shrugged her shoulders, ever so slightly.

"Thanks, Mom," he said, as he turned to go back upstairs.

Kevin had called the hospital several times over the past two days, just to see how his buddy was doing. He had been informed on each occasion that Wiley was holding his own, but still in intensive care, and each time they promised to call him if there was any change.

Kevin was getting tired of waiting, impatient to see and talk to Wiley again.

He was just swinging around the newel post, heading for his room, when the doorbell rang. He pulled the front door open to find Deputy Phillips standing there.

"Hi, Deputy, how you doing? If your looking for Dad, he's still at the mill," Kevin offered, not showing any consideration to the possibility that Stan might be there to see him.

"Hi, Kevin. Actually, I wanted a word with you. Mind if I come in?" Stan asked, politely.

"No, sir, come on in. What do you want to see me about?"

Then it hit him.

Curve ball, he thought.

"Oh! You probably want to know about Wiley's fall! Is that it?" he asked.

"No, not actually, Kevin. I am here to talk about Bryce," Stan said, laying it out immediately, and watching for Kevin's reaction.

"Bryce? What about him?" Kevin asked, starting to become somewhat wary.

"Well, there have been a few new developments in the case that materialized after I was able to get back up on the mountain and have a look around Cougar Run. It seems to the sheriff and I that you boys might not have been alone up there that morning," Stan informed him.

"Who else was there?" Kevin asked, with apparently, genuine curiosity.

"We're not sure. We were hoping that you might be able to tell *us,* son. Did you see anybody else up there–at all?" Stan asked.

Kevin realized that this was his opportunity to come clean about seeing Mary up there. But, he was *in,* and was not about to give Mary up to the law. She was theirs to deal with now, and they would, in time.

"No, sir–nobody," Kevin answered coolly.

Stan looked into the den from where they were standing in the hallway and motioned toward the doorway.

"Can we go in there and sit for a minute?" he asked.

"Yea–sure," Kevin replied.

They moved the conversation to the den where they each took a seat facing each other.

"Kevin, I'll be honest with you. We don't think Bryce fell of his own accord, fox or no fox. We think he was tripped up with a rope as he came down the slope," Stan said, staring directly into Kevin's eyes. "We think someone intentionally tripped him up on that hill. We don't know why, but someone wanted to give him a nasty fall," Stan said, dropping his bomb.

Kevin was speechless.

Where did all this come from, he wondered? Then thinking, *Wiley said he hid the rope where it would never be found!*

"You found a rope up there?" Kevin asked, fishing for answers.

"No, but we know there was one and we know where it came from. What we don't know is where it went or who used it–or why," Stan told him.

"Any suspects?" Kevin went fishing again.

"Not at the moment, and that's why we were hoping that you might be of some help to us. We're stumped at the moment," Stan said, actually scratching his head like he was perplexed or something. "We haven't got a clue to go by, other than the tree."

"Tree? What tree?" Kevin asked.

"The one the rope was tied to. The rope left some scarring on the bark when it was jerked taught and dragged around it a bit. The scar was about twelve to sixteen inches off the snow pack," Stan revealed.

Kevin didn't say a word at first. There were too many thoughts bouncing around in his head, and he remained silent for several moments. He was beginning to realize that this conversation had to be turned around. If there was a rope, *down the hill,* then what of their story about the rope barrier up top? He *had* to turn this conversation around, and now!

"Kevin, did you hear what I said?" Stan asked, looking curiously at Kevin.

"Yes, sir, I heard, but I thought…"

"You thought what, son?" Stan asked, leaning a bit closer to Kevin.

"The sheriff told Wiley and me that Bryce had a rope burn on his throat," Kevin started.

"Yes, and you told him that Bryce fell on a rope fence up top, remember?"

"He did, just like we said he did, but we didn't see any burn on his throat. You had Doc check him out and the sheriff said Doc found a rope burn. We just accepted that as a fact, we never said *we* saw it. We didn't!" Kevin explained, hoping his instantaneous explanation would wash.

"But it was you boys that brought up the rope fence as the cause of the burn," Stan pressed.

"No, we took your word that there was a burn and then we tried to figure out how it could have happened. We remembered him falling on that barrier and figured that must have been it. We never actually saw the burn," Kevin stated, bluntly.

Stan thought about that for a minute.

"So you're saying that there might not have been a burn when he started down the slope. Is that right?" Stan asked.

"Maybe not, we never saw it," Kevin said, almost in tears. He was definitely getting better at deceiving people. It was coming so easy now.

"Then the burn could have come from the rope being stretched across the slope down below!" Stan said, triumphantly, as if he was actually patting *himself* on the back.

That's when it hit Kevin, like a rock smacking right into his forehead. He fumbled in his head for the right questions.

"Deputy—Did you say the rope was tied about a foot high on the trunk, a foot above the snow?" he asked, slowly, and with caution.

"Yes, that's right, Kevin."

"Is the snow maybe deeper up there now than when it happened?" Kevin was fishing again.

"No, actually it is just about down to the older snow pack that was there before the storm. The newer snow has all but melted completely," Stan explained.

"Then how did the rope hit Bryce in the throat?" Kevin asked. This time Kevin *really* wanted to know the answer to his question.

"That's what the sheriff and I were wondering, because the rope was obviously set just high enough to trip Bryce up and send him flying. It was a dangerous thing to do and we don't know why anyone would do that to him, but it looks like a bad mistake, like a bad prank gone deadly," Stan explained.

Kevin was in shock. *That* was *not* what Wiley had told him. Wiley had said the rope was tied *neck high*. He thought again for a moment, and then asked again, "So how did the rope hit his throat, Deputy?"

"We're not sure, Kevin, but it looks to us like Bryce saw it coming and started to fall down just before he went under it, or almost under it," he explained.

Kevin was now reeling with confusion. Had Wiley been mistaken or had he out and out lied to him? Or—was the deputy trying to coerce a confession out of him, by minimizing the severity of what they had found out to be true? He could always say later that he was wrong about the depth of the snow. Maybe he *is* wrong about the depth of the snow. There was no way for Kevin to know what was true and what was either fabricated, or simply inaccurate.

He decided to stick with the story, at least until he had a chance to confront Wiley with this new information.

"Yea, I suppose it could have happened that way. I hadn't come over the rise yet, so I didn't see Bryce fall. Wiley said he saw a fox though, what about that?" Kevin inquired.

"Maybe he did see a fox run across there. Maybe that's what he thought tripped Bryce up. Maybe the fox was the reason Bryce fell in the first place. Maybe he never did see the rope coming. There are a lot of maybes, but there was a rope, and there was *someone* on the other end of it, *that* I can tell you for sure," Stan stated, without hesitation.

"Yea, I guess so," Kevin responded.

"So you're sure you didn't see anyone else up there? Not even something that might have been a person in the woods maybe, a flash of color from their coat, or anything?" Stan asked, probing at Kevin's mind.

"No, sir, I didn't even see the rope and I must have skied right over it. It was snowing pretty hard as we were coming down Cougar," he reminded Stan.

Okay, son thanks for your help."

"Sure, no problem," Kevin said.

As Stan drove away he realized that his interrogation of Kevin had turned into no more than a conversation. It was more an exchange of information, a fact–finding mission, than an interrogation. Stan realized that he believed Kevin, completely. At some point between when he arrived and when he left, he had come to trust what Kevin was saying. It was just a gut feeling, but then that was what the sheriff had sent him to get.

He went back to the station and reported his gut feeling about Kevin to Al. They were right back where they had started. They had evidence that was now stored down in the basement, but no suspects. It was back to keeping things in the back of their minds and keeping their eyes and ears open. In other words, they were really not anywhere, but as Al reminded Stan, that was better than *nowhere*.

$\mathcal{A}$s Kevin came up his street Wednesday afternoon, he noticed his mother's car wasn't in the drive. He walked up his front walk and noticed a white piece of paper, taped to the door. It was folded and bore his name, written in his mother's handwriting. He snatched it and began unfolding it in anticipation of what it might say. He fumbled with the note and finally got it unfolded. It was short and to the point:

> *Wiley is out of intensive care.*
> *Being moved to Carver Mercy.*
> *Please be home by 11. Love you. Mom.*

Kevin's face lit up. "Yes!" he exclaimed, in a low hissing tone as he threw open the door and ran inside. He went straight to the kitchen, pulled open a drawer and removed the phone book. As he fumbled for the number, he wondered why Wiley wasn't being sent home, but driving to Mercy would be far better than driving to Bennett.

Carver Mercy was a relatively new hospital, built on the outskirts of Carver. It wasn't a full service hospital as yet, although there were plans for future growth and additional services. It had an emergency room, but it was only staffed during the hours that the Jessup Mountain slopes were in operation. It was The Jessup Group, a collection of outside investors that had pushed for a new hospital and had partially funded it for the benefit of their growth. It was an integral part of the group's plan for the growth of the Jessup Mountain Resort.

Kevin realized that if Wiley were still in serious danger, they would not move him to Mercy. So why not just send him home? Kevin fumbled through the phone book and came up with the number.

"Carver Mercy," a lady with a pleasant voice answered.

"Yes, hi. Has Wiley Coates been admitted yet?" Kevin inquired, impatiently awaiting her answer.

"One moment please, I'll check," she offered.

Kevin waited, drumming his fingernails on the kitchen counter.

"Sir?"

"Yes."

"Mr. Coates was admitted this afternoon and is in room 127," she informed Kevin.

"Thank you—no wait, does he have a phone number yet?" Kevin asked.

"No, sir. There are no phones in the ward rooms," she answered.

"What about visitors? Can he have visitors yet?" Kevin said, nearly begging for a positive answer.

"Yes, sir, he is allowed visitors from eight a.m. to eleven p.m.," she informed him.

"Thanks!" Kevin exclaimed, as if the operator was responsible for the decision herself.

Kevin slid the book back into the drawer, grabbed a handful of chocolate chips from the cookie jar on the counter and headed for the front door.

"Damn!" he said, as he got halfway down the hall, and turned back for the kitchen. Grabbing a piece of chalk he scribbled a note on the small chalkboard beneath the wall phone:

Borrowed 5 bucks for gas.
I'm at Mercy. Be home by 11. Kevin.

He opened a cabinet and removed a large crockery jar, grabbed a five–dollar bill, replaced the jar and bolted for the door. Carver Mercy, although located on the far side of town, would take Kevin only fifteen minutes to reach, but even that seemed too long.

As he waited while Lou pumped five bucks worth of gas into his car, he thought of all Wiley and he had to talk about. There were so many questions to ask, and one in particular, for which he needed an answer, now.

Lou finished pumping his gas and moved toward the hood of his car. Kevin leaned out the window and said, "Oil's fine, Lou." Lou nodded and came over to his window.

"How's your friend, Wiley, doin'?" Lou inquired. "Heard he took a nasty fall."

Kevin had worked at Larry's one summer, pumping gas and doing minor repairs when Lou had been hobbled with a broken knee.

"I'm on my way to visit him now, Lou. They just moved him from Bennett to Mercy today," Kevin answered, wanting to get on his way.

"Well, you tell him Lou says howdy–hear?"

"Will do," Kevin said, handing Lou the five–dollar bill. "I've gotta run. Talk to you later, Okay?"

"Okay, Kevin. Take care," Lou said, as Kevin was already pulling away.

Kevin entered Room 127 and saw immediately why Wiley hadn't been sent home. Or, at least what he saw was probably the reason. There was Wiley, flat on his back, with his leg suspended in the air by some contraption he had never seen the likes of before. His eyes surveyed the rest of Room 127, which was a four–bed ward with the other three beds vacant.

"Hey, Wiley," Kevin greeted him, cheerfully.

"Kev! Good to see you, buddy!" Wiley returned, equally as cheerful in his response.

"So how are you doing?" Kevin asked, studying the stainless steel frame that Wiley's leg was suspended from.

"I'm good, thanks to you."

His tone was sincere and his face, serious.

"I've had some time to think about what you did for me up there...

Kevin cut him off in the middle of his thought. It was simply no more than something that had to be done. You couldn't leave your best friend to die on a mountaintop.

"Wiley–it was nothing," Kevin said. "So what's this contraption they've got you in?" Kevin asked, changing the subject. He had motioned toward the framework holding Wiley's leg in the air.

"They call it traction. I've got a stainless steel pin in my leg. Now *that's* cool! A stainless steel pin! This gizmo is supposed to hold it all in place while it heals, or something like that. This whole room is rigged with them. It's the *skier's ward*."

"How long do you have to be hooked up to it?" Kevin asked, intently studying the apparatus.

"Six weeks," Wiley scowled.

"Six weeks!" Kevin exclaimed, his mouth gaping wide.

"Yea, and then I'll be another six weeks in something called a body cast. At least that's what they think will be necessary," Wiley commented, and frowning as his voice dropped off to a mere whisper.

"Then what?" Kevin asked, a little shocked at the time it was going to take to get Wiley back on his feet.

"Therapy–maybe–they say. I'll be on crutches though for sure, after I get out of the cast. It'll take at least a month of exercise to get back to normal strength they're saying. Damn, Kevin! There goes my whole summer!" Wiley protested.

"Damn. That's a bitch," Kevin agreed.

Kevin pulled up a chair and they visited with each other for a while, talking about things in general, and nothing much about anything important. It was just good to be back together again, talking with one another. But, there were also important matters to be discussed.

"Wiley–Deputy Phillips dropped by to see me yesterday," Kevin said, ending the previous amenities.

"Yea? What did he want?" Wiley asked, his countenance changing from carefree, to one of concern.

"He's been back up on Mount Crane, looking around Cougar Run," Kevin answered.

"And?" Wiley asked, urging Kevin to continue.

"And–he has it all pretty much figured out, Wiley. He knows there was someone else up there and he *knows* about the rope and all," Kevin informed him.

"Does he know that *we know*?" Wiley demanded.

"No, I don't think he suspects we do. He found footprints up there and a rope scar on a tree, he said, but he doesn't know the who, or the why of it yet," Kevin said, filling Wiley in on what he had taken away from the conversation with Stan.

"Did he mention suspects?" Wiley probed.

"He said they don't have any," Kevin answered. "He wanted to be double sure we hadn't seen anybody else up there, so I think he figures we are in the dark, too."

"Good. They have nothing but suspicions then," Wiley said, smiling deviously.

"Well yes–but they have the footprints and rope scar," Kevin reminded Wiley.

"That's not enough to go anywhere with," Wiley suggested.

"I guess not, not without knowing who else was there," agreed Kevin.

Kevin had been saving the critical question for last. He was trying desperately to figure out just the right way to phrase it. He didn't want to let Wiley know that he had any doubts about his honesty with him, but he needed to hear Wiley's explanation for what the deputy had told him.

"There is one thing though, Wiley, that Deputy Phillips said. I can't make sense of it, is all," Kevin began.

"What's that?" Wiley asked.

"He said the snow had melted up there, back to about the depth it was last November. He said that the rope scar on the tree was only about a foot above the snow. Like the rope was intended to trip Bryce up, *not* hit him in the neck," Kevin stated, glad to have it out.

Wiley's face was expressionless. He looked straight at Kevin for about five seconds and then shook his head.

"I don't know. I don't know where he's getting that. I saw the rope. I untied it for Christ's sake. It was neck high, just like I said it was!" Wiley paused. "He's probably wrong about the snow. It's probably deeper now, than then."

"Four feet deeper?" Kevin interjected. "How could he be that far off?"

Kevin hadn't wanted to go here, but he wanted to put this issue to rest. After all, it meant the difference between a foolish trick and murder.

"Are you doubting what I saw up there?" Wiley asked, demanding an answer. "Are you calling me a liar?"

"No.–Just tell me how he could have it that wrong, that's all," Kevin retaliated, firmly.

"What difference does it make? What possible difference could it make? Mary put the rope there and Bryce is dead because of it!" Wiley hissed in Kevin's face. "So what the hell difference does it make? Tell me! What difference?" Wiley was livid.

"It makes a big difference, Wiley. It's the difference between murder and an accident."

"No! Wrong! An accident would be what we *said* happened to Bryce. The difference you're talking about is the difference between murder and manslaughter! Those are *both* crimes, and either way, Bryce is dead!" Wiley yelled, just loud enough to make his point, but not enough to be overheard by someone who might be in the hallway.

Kevin looked Wiley square in the eyes and said, "There is a difference, Wiley. If the girls murdered Bryce, they deserve to be left in the cave–forever. But if they killed him because they screwed up, they don't. They deserve to be punished, but not killed," Kevin tried to reason with Wiley.

"If we *don't* leave them there, we'll go to jail. Are you willing to go to jail, Kevin?" Wiley asked.

"Look, Wiley, you just level with me. You tell me the truth about what you saw up there, or I walk. Tell me the truth and we can discuss how to handle it," Kevin demanded.

Wiley thought about that, weighing his options.

"Okay–It's like the deputy said. Satisfied? The rope *was* only a foot high, but they still killed Bryce! They did!" Wiley implored, hoping Kevin would see that.

"Why'd you tell me different, Wiley? Why'd you lie to me?" asked Kevin, wanting to understand.

"Because you're too easy. You'd let it slide. Eventually you'd find a way to understand, just like a jury would. *'Poor girls, they didn't mean to do that. It was all a terrible accident.'* That's why I told you what I did. I need you to help pull this off. Those bitches need to pay for killing Bryce. It doesn't matter where they tied the rope," Wiley said, pleading his case.

"It matters, Wiley, but you're wrong about one thing. I'm not as forgiving as you think, and you're also wrong about another thing. I do think they should pay, but not with their lives, not if they didn't set out to murder Bryce," Kevin stated, with finality.

Wiley's stare remained fixed on Kevin. He was thinking about what Kevin had said.

That's good, Kevin thought. *He's giving it some consideration.*

"Look, Kev. I know you don't want to go to jail and neither do I. If we go through with this, and then let the girls go after scaring the crap out of their parents and them, we *will* go to jail. That's a fact. But–what if we leave it up to them?" Wiley suggested.

"What are you talking about? Leave it up to them, *how?*" asked Kevin, leaning forward, looking for an answer in Wiley's eyes.

"We do what we planned to do, but instead of leaving and never coming back, leaving them trapped in the cave to die in the dark, we give them a way out," he suggested.

"How?" Kevin asked.

"When we leave–we leave them tied up, loosely, so they can get free. We leave the ladders in place so they can find their way out of the cave. If they can find their way back to civilization, fine. If not, they perish up there, lost in Short Pines. Hell–we'll even leave the rope hold up so they can use it, if they get that far," Wiley told him, laying out his *new* plan.

Wiley paused and waited while Kevin thought it through. He could see that Kevin was at least giving it some thought.

"Well? What about that? Are you willing to take *that* much of a chance for Bryce? If they don't make it back, they'll never be found, for years, anyway–maybe never. We're home free and their fate is in their own hands. Now that's justice, right?" Wiley asked.

Kevin thought about it hard. That did seem just. Maybe even something that Sam Elliott would approve of.

Baker's dead because of you. I know you only meant to give him a lickin', but you killed him just the same. So I'm givin' you a chance to save yourself. I'm leaving you here, barefoot and unarmed. If you make it back to rendezvous, fine. I'll be there waitin'. By then, if you make it, you'll either see the justice in this or you'll try to kill me. It'll be your choice.

"Yes–that's justice," was Kevin's only response.

"Then you're still *in?*" Wiley asked.

"Still *in,*" Kevin confirmed.

Kevin said good night to Wiley, promising to return the next day, and drove himself, and his doubts, home to Birch Lane.

When he awoke, Thursday morning, Kevin still had misgivings. He was *in,* as he had told Wiley, but his mind swam with uncertainties. He thought the shack might be the best place to find the answers he needed.

He had not been back there since Bryce's death, or in fact, since the last time the three of them had fixed it up together. The last visit the boys had made there together, had been six months ago, but it seemed so much longer, nearly a lifetime ago. That one last visit had seemed to mark a turning point in all their lives. They had fixed the shack up nicely, but for whom? Perhaps it was to become their legacy, found one day, renovated and cleaned, by the next generation of mountain men.

Kevin rarely ventured to the shack without the others unless he was seeking solace from some particularly disturbing injustice perpetrated on him at school. He had discussed those times with Bryce, but he had never shared them with Wiley. Truthfully, he feared Wiley's reaction.

"That's our place, Kevin, not just yours! It's for the three of us! None of us should go alone! It ruins it! It ruins the magic!"

So he had kept his solitary visits to himself, or had sometimes shared the experiences with Bryce, but he had *always* avoided telling Wiley.

But today was one of those days he simply *had* to go. He needed to be there, in that dimension of his world. School could wait. He went out the patio door and into the woods. It was still cold. He moved on toward the large outcrops and the passage between them. Kneeling before the portal he removed his key from his pocket and inserted it into the lock, giving it a twist. He removed the lock from its hasp, pushed the door inward, and crawled into the dark room. Standing, he lit the lantern, illuminating their private world. He waited an appropriate amount of time, and began:

"Oh great ghost of Jim Bridger and friends. We have arrived at rendezvous. We ask only for the warmth of your fire and the pleasure of your company. If you've a mind to share, your coffee smells inviting and your stew, delicious. Are we welcome at your fire?"

Kevin waited, but no reply was forthcoming. He took one last look around and blew out the lantern. Having crawled out the small door, he looked back once more, closing the little door and locking behind it, the good times of his youth.

CHAPTER 42

❀

Over the next few weeks Kevin spent a lot of time with Wiley at Carver Mercy. The school year was drawing to a close and graduation was only weeks away. Wiley, being trapped in his traction device and confined to the hospital, had to finish his high school career in bed.

"One of the benefits of a broken leg," as he had put it.

He would certainly miss the graduation ceremony, but that didn't seem to bother Wiley in the least.

Kevin could empathize with him on that count. He had considered skipping the ceremony himself, and if it weren't for his parent's excitement over the whole affair, he most certainly would skip it. He had no friends at school with whom he wished to share graduation with, anyway.

Kevin had elected to serve as Wiley's envoy, bringing him his lessons and assignments each afternoon and returning his completed work to each teacher. The teachers were very cooperative in seeing to it that each day's work was carefully spelled out for him and in the main office before the end of the day. Kevin had merely to stop by the office and pick it all up before leaving school each afternoon.

Kevin also served as Wiley's tutor, explaining what the teachers had said in class, and helping him with the work at hand. When not doing schoolwork, they spent time talking about hunting, fishing, hiking, camping and a myriad of other topics as well. They did not, however, speak much about the plan.

Kevin had done the math, as had Wiley, and it would be months before they could even consider embarking upon it. What had been planned as a summer event was now postponed until at least September, when Wiley would be back to full strength. Kevin had thought about that with some concern. They were seniors, as were Mary and Alicia. There would be no new school year at Carver High for any of them. By September, there was no knowing where Mary and Alicia might be. Mary had seen to it that *everyone* knew she was going to Evans, on academic scholarship, but she hadn't talked much about it since she was busted for cheating.

Evans was a prestigious college in the eastern part of the state. Although some traveling would be required, it was not out of reach. That would not be so bad if indeed she ended up there. The big concern was that she could go somewhere totally out of their striking range, like Harvard or Yale. She had the grades and her dad had the money.

Alicia, on the other hand, was not a brilliant student and her family had no money to speak of. If she went away to college, it would likely be to the community college in Bennett, a mere three–hour drive away.

Whatever their plan for abducting the girls was to be, it could not be conceived until they knew where to find them in September. But there was nothing to be done about that now, so the boys spent their time together talking about what boys generally do. They were content with each other's company and their dreams of adventure in the mountains.

The school year came to an end in early June. The seniors, Kevin excluded, threw a big party at the Mount Crane Lodge, and finally did burn it down. The volunteer fire department swore that it had been done intentionally, but they really couldn't tell. They were just a collection of good–hearted carpenters, mill workers, and whatever, that had combined to form the Carver Volunteer Fire Department. They knew how to put out a fire, but that was pretty much the extent of it.

The few kids that could be placed at the scene of the fire swore that it was just a cook fire that had not been fully extinguished upon their departure. That was probably the case, as determined by Sheriff Dramico.

With school over for the year, Kevin began work at the lumber mill, working alongside his father. He had attended the graduation ceremony, without putting up much resistance, because he realized that it was important to his parents to see him on that stage, diploma in hand.

Work at the lumber mill was rough. It was hard, bone tiring work, and he found himself spending much less time visiting Wiley at Mercy. He preferred coming straight home after a day at the mill, and plopping down on his bed for a nap. He still made it to the hospital on weekends though, where Wiley and he would wile away the hours talking of hunting trips to come and explorations not yet made.

In early July Wiley was sent home in a body cast. He was wrapped in plaster from mid–chest to the bottom of his mending leg, and halfway down the good leg. The plaster suit was conveniently cut out in the crotch area for the necessity of doing his bodily businesses.

He was mobile through the use of a special wheelchair; a table on wheels actually, that he could push about the house. It took him a while to get the hang of navigating through the doorways, and during this learning period, his father was none to happy about the dents and dings to the woodwork. But when it became too much for him to handle, Mr. Coates would find his bottle and it all became all right again.

That didn't surprise Kevin at all, for in the six weeks that Wiley had been confined to Carver Mercy, he had never once crossed paths with Wiley's dad. Mrs. Coates had been there on several occasions, but to Kevin's knowledge, not his father. Kevin had asked Wiley about it once, and was shrugged off in short order. In all fairness to Mr. Coates, he may have come upon occasion, when Kevin hadn't been there, but Wiley hadn't wanted to discuss it.

With Wiley back home and closer at hand, Kevin's visits became more frequent again. He would take an hour or so to drop by and chat in the evenings after returning home from the mill. He did this almost daily, and continued to spend most of his weekend time with his buddy.

Wiley was cut from of his plaster prison early in August and freed from the bedpans, which had become the bane of his daily existence. Kevin had become acclimated to the hard work at the mill and was much less tired at the end of a day's work. He was now spending more time with Wiley than ever before. They had become fast and true friends in every sense of the word.

Although on crutches, Wiley could now get out of the house and go for rides in Kevin's car. Wiley's inability to walk without aid of his supports limited their activity to cruising the mountain roads and taking in new sights, all the while searching for interesting places to explore, when Wiley would be able.

While at work Kevin kept his ears open for word of the girl's plans for the future. He could not bring up the subject, but he could listen. Carver, like any small town, had a grapevine that was well established. You could find out just about anything you wanted to find out, just by listening intently. Kevin would hover near where groups of workers were on break, eavesdropping on their conversations. He knew if he was patient, and kept applying these covert skills, he would soon learn what he wanted to know.

He learned of Alicia's plans first, while shoveling sawdust and listening to a small gathering discuss their kid's plans. One of the workmen said that he was driving his son and Alicia Koppe up to Bennett Community College to pre–register for the fall quarter. He told the others that he was a friend of her dad's, but that her dad, Lucas, was stuck at the store on the Saturday of pre–registration. He said that he had told Lucas not to worry about it, that he'd be glad to drive Alicia up there when he and his boy went.

Kevin learned of Mary's plans later, during the same conversation. One of the men was a neighbor of the Koppes and had asked Lucas' friend, *"What about Alicia's friend, Mary? Is she going to go to BCC with Alicia, or does she have bigger plans?"*

It was apparent to Kevin, from the sarcastic tone in his voice, that this neighbor of Alicia's knew Mary pretty well. The response from Lucas' friend had been, *"Hell yes she has bigger plans. She's going off to Evans come fall. She lost her scholarship and they killed her acceptance, but somehow her daddy got her back in."*

One of the other men had said, *"He probably offered to build them a new library or gym or something!"* They all had enjoyed a good laugh over that comment.

Kevin was anxious to get back to Wiley with this new information. Armed with this new knowledge they could start working out the logistics of their operation. They still needed to come up with a fool-proof plan for the abduction. Now, it seemed as though it was going to be even harder, because they actually needed two plans. It was starting to look very complicated to Kevin. This would require a lot of traveling, both before the abductions, and for the abductions.

He had always considered that they may have to do some serious driving to collect the girls, but now it was becoming clear that the preparation would require the same. They would have to scout out where the girls were living and their daily routines if they were to have even a chance at success. This was definitely going to require a few weekends of study and planning.

Wiley, on the other hand, had already foreseen this coming. Ever since he first regained his feet, he had been absorbed with thoughts of the plan. Even before Kevin informed him of what he had learned at the mill, he had figured that out. It was just what he expected would happen. Alicia would go where she could afford to go, BCC, and Mary would go to *wherever* she wanted to go. He knew her dad would make it happen, somehow. She had never been deprived of anything and daddy wasn't going to let the first time be with the college of her choice. No, Wiley *knew* she'd end up at Evans.

Wiley could also appreciate the logistical problems they were going to have with the girls separated and so far apart. He didn't like it, and he had a solution. It was quite simple actually. They would take the girls *before* they leave for college. He even had the 'Where of It' figured out. Kevin and he would take advantage of the Annual Bon Voyage Party and Dance, at the high school.

The Annual Bon Voyage Party and Dance, was a tradition at Carver High. It was an affair, thrown by the incoming senior class, for the outgoing senior class. A farewell party, which had occurred on the third Saturday in September, every year since 1927, when Wiley's grandfather had thought it up and presented the idea to the school board. The "43rd Annual Bon Voyage Party and Dance, for the Class of 1969" would be the most memorable in its forty–three year history.

Wiley had two of the three pieces of the puzzle already in place. The 'Where of It' and the 'When of It' were decided. The third, and still undecided piece, the 'How of It', was still in question.

CHAPTER 43

On Sunday, June the eighth, following graduation Saturday night, Mary embarked on a group trip to Europe, complements of her father. It was his graduation present to his college bound daughter whom he was so very proud of. Dr. Clemmons was a very busy man, but had always found time for Mary. She was his only daughter and she was his special little lady. Nothing was too much, or too expensive, when it came to pleasing Mary.

The trip called for visiting England, Scotland, and Wales in the British Isles, before crossing the Channel to mainland Europe. There, she would visit Germany, France, Spain, Belgium, and Switzerland, before returning home in late August. It was the trip of a lifetime and the perfect diversion before beginning her college career.

Although Alicia was very happy and excited for Mary, this did leave her very much alone for the entire summer. She had taken a summer job at Morgan's Center Street Market, but she dearly wished for Mary's company during her off days and evenings. The truth of the matter was that she had no other friends beyond Mary. Her association with Mary had left her so completely occupied with Mary, that there had been practically no time for cultivating other friendships. She knew that was how Mary had wanted it to be, and she was okay with that, then. But, now, it left her very much alone in Carver.

Work was okay, consisting of checking out customers in the grocery store and stocking the shelves in the produce department. It wasn't very challenging work, but it was a way to earn the money she would need in the fall, when she left for Bennett, and college.

Wednesday, June eighteenth, started off much as any other day at Morgan's. She was assigned to the produce department in the morning and was stocking a new shipment of lettuce, when she noticed someone standing to her side, watching her. She turned to see if she could be of assistance to them and nearly passed out when she saw who it was.

"Karl?"

"Hi, Alicia. How are you? Long time no see," Karl said, smiling at her, warmly.

"What–What are you doing here, Karl? I though you were in Arizona," she said, trying desperately to find the right words to say.

"I was, Alicia, but I came home for a short visit with my folks. I got home yesterday."

"Short visit? How short, Karl?" she asked.

"Two weeks, but I'd like to spend some time with you, if–if that's okay with you?"

"Sure–*What do I say now?*—That sounds good, Karl. How did you know to find me here?" she asked, still trying to find the right words.

"Oh, I stopped by your dad's store, to pick up something for Pop, and your dad told me you were working here. Actually, I asked him, he didn't just tell me," Karl explained, also seeking just the right words to say, and finding it rather difficult.

"So–you'll be in town for two weeks?"

"Yea, right, two weeks, but like I said, I'd really like to spend some time with you–if you have the time."

"Yea, I think that would be nice, Karl. I have the time. In fact, I'm off tomorrow, if you don't have plans for tomorrow already."

"No, none at all. How about if I pick you up at, say, ten o'clock and we'll go riding? How does that sound to you?"

"Horseback riding?"

"Yes, horseback riding. We can use my cousin's horses, and ride up through Horse Tooth Canyon. His ranch borders on the Horse Tooth National Forest up that way. It's really beautiful country. Have you ever been up through Horse Tooth Canyon before?"

"No, I haven't, but I'd like to. Ten o'clock sounds fine. Thanks, Karl."

"Sure, thank you. I'll see you at ten, then. I better let you get back to work now. I'll see you tomorrow."

Karl smiled at her with that wonderful smile she remembered so well, and disappeared around the shelving. Alicia stood there for a moment, not knowing what to do next. She stared at the crate of lettuce, looked back at where Karl had vanished around the gondola, and let out a soft "Whoop!" This couldn't be happening. She thought Karl had forgotten all about her, that he had gone off to Arizona and had not looked back. Summer wasn't looking so bad after all.

By eleven thirty the next morning, she and Karl were pulling into the drive of his cousin's ranch. They drove beneath the large wooden sign, which read, "Circle Bar Z", and had a brand beneath the wording depicting the description. The driveway was nearly a mile long, leaving the highway and going straight back to the base of Horse Tooth Mountain. There, the ranch buildings were all laid out along the last level ground at the foot of the mountain.

James was awaiting their arrival, with two good–looking horses, saddled and ready to go. Alicia was given the palomino, and Karl, the dun. James' wife, Carolyn, had prepared them a nice picnic lunch, which James handed to Karl in a small rucksack, and then bid them farewell and a good time. Karl filled James in on their plans, in case they didn't return by nightfall, and he and Alicia rode off toward Horse Tooth Mountain and the canyon within.

The day itself was gorgeous, with not a cloud in the sky and the temperature hovering around eighty degrees. There was a light breeze, which helped cool both them and their steeds, and brought the smell of juniper wafting about them. They rode up into the forest of juniper and scrub pine on a course Karl had determined would bring them to Horse Tooth Canyon by two p.m. There, they would visit Karl's favorite spot and have lunch—and talk about the future and what it held for the both of them.

Along the way, Karl pointed out things of interest, which he hoped would be interesting to Alicia, also, and it seemed to him she *had* found them interesting. At least, she seemed to be as excited about seeing them, as did he. The first thing he had pointed out was a Clark's Nutcracker, sitting high on a bare limb of a dead piñon pine. The beautiful, gray, black, and white bird was doing just what its name described, cracking some sort of nut, probably a piñon nut, high up in the tree.

They stopped along the way, twice, to watch the marmots and ground squirrels dashing about the rock talus slope of the east canyon wall. Alicia really got a kick out of the cute little varmints scampering about, doing their daily chores of gathering food and munching on whatever it was they had found to eat.

They rode on, deeper into the canyon, until they finally arrived at the spot Karl had planned on stopping for lunch. He had been here many times before, and this was one of his favorite spots on Earth. It was a depression in the ground, perhaps thirty feet deep, and looking down into it all one saw was lush green, like a garden in the midst of this otherwise rather dry and colorless canyon. The depression was "L" shaped and probably about fifty feet wide by one hundred feet long, growing greener the farther into the base of the "L" one looked.

They rode down into the small valley at the top of the "L" and turned toward its base. Alicia noticed a small stream running along beside them, which explained the greenery, and the further in they rode, the larger the stream became and the greener and denser the foliage became. As they turned the bend into the base of the valley, she saw a small pond and the spring, which fed it. This was truly a neat and very beautiful place. As they proceeded, Alicia noticed that they had ridden beneath a ledge, which provided shade over half of this unique spot.

"This is it," Karl said to her. "This is *my* favorite spot. I wanted to share it with you."

"It's beautiful, Karl. Thank you. How did you ever find this place?" she asked.

"Just riding around one day, a few years ago. I just stumbled across it. It's cool isn't it?" he said.

"Yes, very cool!" Alicia answered.

"Well, let's dismount and spread out our vittles. I'm famished! What about you?" he asked.

"I'm more than ready to eat," she replied.

Karl opened the rucksack and took out the blanket, spreading it on the ground by the pond. He then laid out their lunch of chicken sandwiches, macaroni salad, and a couple of bottles of Coke.

"Sorry, but the Coke will be warm, I'm afraid," Karl warned Alicia.

"Who cares," she said. "Nothing could spoil this picnic. This is too cool!"

They spent the next hour, sitting on their blanket, eating their lunch, and talking about old times, and new. Karl taught Alicia how to skip rocks on the pond; something she had never seen done before, and after several tries, had become quite proficient at it. They removed their socks and shoes and waded in the cool water, and tried desperately to catch a bullfrog they saw lazing on the shore. The frog escaped their efforts, but they had laughed and laughed as they tried, to the point they collapsed in each other's arms on the sandy bank. They gazed into each other's eyes and felt that this moment should last forever. It was so quiet and peaceful here, the only sound, the soft gurgle of the spring, cascading gently into the pond. It was the perfect place for two kids in love to pass a summer afternoon.

"Alicia," Karl said. "I want to tell you how sorry I am for not continuing to write. I got all tied up in my new life down there and so busy with school and work, that I simply neglected to write."

"Was that all it was, Karl? I mean, you were just too busy to write, nothing else?" she asked.

No, not too busy, that's a lame excuse. I had the time; I simply didn't take the opportunities when I had them. And, to be perfectly honest with you–well–there was another girl." He admitted.

"Was she pretty, Karl? Prettier than me? Alicia asked.

"She was pretty, yes, but not prettier than you, Alicia. And–it didn't take me long to discover that she wasn't you–I mean–She couldn't take your place in a million years, Alicia."

"Did you kiss her, Karl? Like you kissed me when we first met?"

"No, not the same as I kissed you, Alicia. That could never happen. I just want you to know that I am sorry for dropping things like I did. I won't ever do it again, I promise. You're the most important thing in the world to me, and I mean that."

"And you, me, Karl. I missed you while you were gone. I really missed you. I got involved with Mary Clemmons after you left. Do you remember her?" Alicia asked him.

"Yes, I do. The doctor's daughter from Pill Hill, right?"

"Yes, that's her," Alicia said, showing a little distaste through her expression.

"If I remember her correctly, she was a bit of a bitch, Alicia. How did you come to hook up with her?"

"We were always friends, even when I was seeing you before you graduated. I sort of kept the two of you separate in my life because she hates Kevin Reynolds and you are a friend of his," she explained. "It was after you left that I got fully involved with her. I sort of let her begin running my life for me."

"I see. Well, I think you should start running it from now on, and I'll help where I can, what do you think of that?" he asked.

"I think that's fine. It's good, actually. Mary and I did something very bad last November, Karl," she finally admitted, wanting to be up–front with him.

"Bad? What did you do that was so bad, Alicia?" Karl asked, sort of flitting away the idea that Alicia could do anything that was actually bad.

"Did you hear about Bryce Spencer?" she asked.

"Yea, my folks sent me the newspaper article. He was killed in a skiing accident, right?"

"Not actually, Karl. Mary and I caused that *accident*," she confessed.

"How? How did *you* cause it?"

"It was Mary's idea, but I went along with it. Bryce busted her for cheating on an exam and she got grounded and lost her scholarship to Evans. She wanted to get even with him, so she thought up a plan to trip him up on the ski slope, using a rope tied to a tree. But–the rope hit him in the throat and–he died. It wasn't meant to happen that way, but it did."

"Wow! Are you serious, Alicia? That's heavy! What about the sheriff? Didn't he catch on?"

"We don't know what happened. We thought we were going to be in a lot of trouble and we were scared, but nothing ever came of it. We were questioned, but nothing ever came of the whole thing. They just said it was an accident, and that, was that."

"Well, you didn't mean for it to end the way it did. I guess that's what's important, but still…"

"I know. But, still, it happened and Bryce is dead. He's dead and it's my fault. I mean I hated him, too. He was such a little snitch and a real jerk, but I didn't want him to get killed. Honest to God I didn't!"

"The important thing, Alicia, is that it *was* an accident. You didn't mean to do it and there is nothing you can do to fix it now. I guess you just leave it where it is."

"But–what about us? Can you still love me–after what I just told you?" she asked, and then held her breath awaiting Karl's reply.

"Yes, Alicia. That changes nothing between you and I. I've done some foolish things in my life, too, that could have gotten one of my friends killed. It was an accident, nothing more. It's too bad it happened, but you didn't mean for it to. That's what's important."

"Thank you, Karl. I had to tell you, I had to. I'm sorry," she said, and began to cry, uncontrollably.

Karl put his arm around her and held her tight. *God, what a burden to carry around with her,* he thought. And he wanted so much to help her through this and make it right for her. He didn't know if he knew how, but he would certainly try, and he *would* stick by her, of that he was certain.

Eventually, Alicia regained her composure, and they shared their second kiss ever. Like the first one had been, it was just a gentle meeting of the lips, and it felt so right to them both. They talked a while longer before Karl decided that they had better be heading back.

"It gets awful black out here when the sun goes down. We don't want to let it go down on us before we get back to the ranch," Karl said. "That could become a problem."

They did make it back to the ranch before dark, and they thanked James and Carolyn for the wonderful time and opportunity. They climbed back into Karl's Jeep and started down the long drive back to the highway, and from there, back to Carver and Greenville. They arrived at Alicia's house at around nine p.m. and she thanked Karl for a wonderful time, hoping that he would mention a next time to her. He did, and she was the happiest girl in Carver at the moment.

Over the next two weeks, they made three more trips back to their private little valley and pond, where they cemented their relationship and promised each other never to get out of touch again. No further mention of Bryce was made by either of them, and at the end of the two weeks, Karl returned to Arizona and his job and school. Alicia contented herself with her work at the market and reading Karl's letters, which started arriving within a week of his departure.

The letters kept coming and Alicia kept responding, right through the rest of the summer. Mary returned from her travels on August the twenty–eighth, and had so much to tell Alicia about Europe and the trip, that Alicia thought she would never hear the end of it. When Mary finally asked how her summer had gone, Alicia had replied, "It was okay. I kept busy at the market and watched a lot of TV in the evenings."

Her relationship with Karl was one thing that she felt no need to share with Mary. Not only was it private, but also, she knew the disapproving response she would receive from her. It was better left unsaid.

CHAPTER 44

❀

*A*ugust gave way to September and on the first day of the month, Wiley called Kevin over to his house for a planning meeting. Throughout the past week they had turned their attention to the problem at hand, the *'How of It'*. They had gone over various scenarios with little success. Their class had planned and executed the previous year's affair, so they had some insight into how it would be played out in the school gym. They tried visualizing the party and dance looking for some answer to their dilemma.

Kevin's approach to the plan was one of treachery and guile. His methodology was to *Trick* the girls into their hands, but every scheme he thought up had too many variables in it. There were simply too many uncontrollable uncertainties and pitfalls involved.

Wiley, on the other hand, favored brute force. Overpower them and take them, but how and when. The gym would be full of kids so that seemed an unlikely place for the abduction. Perhaps in the parking lot, before or after the dance, would be better? The same problem existed there also; too many kids, arriving and leaving.

Wiley decided that they needed to compare notes, taking a think tank approach to the problem. With just three weeks remaining before the dance, time was running short, and they needed a plan for the *'How of It'*.

Kevin arrived at seven o'clock and they began their meeting in closed session in Wiley's bedroom. The door was locked and Wiley's ten–point buck stood watch over them.

"We have less than three weeks to iron this out," Wiley began. "We need to decide exactly how we are going to do this before the dance on the twentieth. It's either that, or we're back to running all over the state to collect them. You know that's unacceptable, so the dance is our last chance to get this done right."

"I know, Wiley, but I haven't come up with anything I'm comfortable with," replied Kevin. "What about you?"

"Me neither. Look, let's start with 'where'. The gym itself is out. Too crowded and totally out of the question. So think, where else? The parking lot seems better, but again, too many kids either coming or going," Wiley stated.

"What about the girl's bathroom?" Kevin suggested. "Girls always go to the bathroom together. When Alicia needs to go, she'll drag Mary along with her, and visa versa."

"Won't work," Wiley stated. "We can't be sure there won't already be girls in there, or that some won't come in while we're in there. What else? Think," Wiley insisted.

"There is nowhere else, unless you want to try to snag them on the way to or from the dance," Kevin suggested, not really believing Wiley would take that suggestion seriously.

No, that won't work either. There's too big a chance of being seen by a passing car. Then there is also the problem of trying to stop them in route. Think again."

Kevin thought for a minute and then stated, "Then it has to be the parking lot. But, during the dance, when everybody is already in there, but early enough so that no one has decided to leave yet. We'll park at the far end of the lot away from the building."

"How…"

"Let me finish, Wiley," Kevin insisted. "Friday night, the nineteenth, we'll drive out to the school with your pellet rifle and we'll pick the spot we will park my car in on Saturday. You'll shoot out the parking lot lights closest to it. Nobody from the school will notice they're out before the dance, because when they all arrive it will still be daylight," Kevin began, laying out the first part of his plan.

"That's good, Kevin, and it would be perfect if we had a way to get the bitches out to your car, from the gym, in the middle of the dance," Wiley replied, sarcastically.

"We do, Wiley! We do have a way," Kevin assured him.

"And how is that?" Wiley asked, with skepticism.

"We let them come to us," Kevin said, smiling slyly.

"Right–Like they are going to walk out into the parking lot to see us. Do we send them an invitation, or what? *'Dear Mary and Alicia, Please meet us in the parking lot. Love, Wiley and Kevin.'* Get real, Kevin!"

"Are you finished?" asked Kevin.

"Yea, I'm done," Wiley answered.

"Good, because that is exactly what we do. We send them an invitation they won't possibly turn down."

"Like what, Kevin? What could we possibly say in an invitation that would get them out there to your car?" Wiley asked.

"We use what we have learned about them from past experience. We use against them, what we have put up with our entire lives. We send them an invitation to make a fool of you *one more time.* We offer them a chance to embarrass you *one last time* before they leave for college. *That's* how we get them out there. *That's* how we do it!" Kevin informed him.

Wiley was silent. What Kevin had said, was profound. That was the one sure thing upon which he and Kevin could depend. Throughout two years of middle school and four years of high school, Mary had never missed an opportunity to humiliate him. She had never passed on a chance to embarrass him and had never overlooked a single opening in his defenses.

"That's brilliant, Kev! You are absolutely right. That is the one thing we can count on from Mary. Do you have a plan for the *invitation*, too?" he asked.

"Yes, I do. And if she doesn't take the bait, no big deal, no one's the wiser. We bide our time and wait until next summer. They'll both be home again for summer break. The weather will be right for the plan, and we'll have another ten months to come up with another idea. Bryce would understand. There's nothing to lose," Kevin stated, confident that he was right about all this.

Kevin *was* right and Wiley knew it. There was nothing to lose but a little time, and Bryce would understand if he had to wait another ten months for the justice he was due. If the girls took the bait, the game was on and there would be no turning back. If they didn't, then no one would be the wiser. It wasn't over at that point, just postponed. He could wait. He'd already waited ten months, what was another ten in the overall scheme of things?

In all reality, perhaps it would be better if they didn't take the bait. The sheriff was on to the fact that they weren't alone on Cougar the morning Bryce was killed. What if he figured it out? What if he did figure out that it was Mary and Alicia who had been up there, with the rope, trying to get even with Bryce? He had no proof, so he would sit on the idea until the bitches disappeared. Then the light would come on, and putting two and two together he would be on Wiley's doorstep when Kevin and he returned from Short Pines on Tuesday evening.

Perhaps the more time that passed between the accident and the girls' disappearance, the better. The more time that passed between cause and effect, the less suspicion would fall their way. Perhaps longer was better. It would be highly unlikely that the disappearance of the girls would be associated in any way with an event that occurred twenty months ago.

Still, Wiley wanted them to take the bait. The plan had its risks, but if it went as Kevin had laid it out for him, they would be under no suspicion. They would have an alibi and the girls would be the victims of another terrible tragedy to befall Carver. Ten months was long enough to wait. They had to take the bait.

CHAPTER 45

"**O**kay, students, please quiet down and we'll get down to business. This is Monday, September 15, and this is Geology 402. I–am Professor Edwards. You may call me Professor or sir, it's your choice, but don't call me late for supper."

Professor Stiles Edwards had always received a laugh out of his new students with his opening introduction to his senior Geology class. It was no different this time, but he always wondered if it was really funny to them, or if they were just being polite with their measured laughter.

He had been teaching this geology class at Reedmore College in Reedmore for the past seven years, and the faces appeared younger and younger to him, with each successive year. He studied them again, noting the class consisted of six male students and one female. They were all seniors, so their ages would be around same, about twenty–one years—*Pups*, he thought to himself.

"Students, this class is labeled Geology 402, but its principal thrust is volcanology, the study of volcanoes and volcanic phenomena. The course will be graded on the results of a midterm and final exam, each providing one third of your grade. The other third will result from your participation in, and term paper on, our field trip to a volcanic caldera on Oriel Peak. This caldera, known as Blind Valley, is very out of the way and extremely hard to gain access to. It is two miles of uphill hiking and then a serious climb into the caldera. We will leave on Friday and return on Sunday. You will be required to camp out there overnight, two nights, exploring and studying the caldera on the Saturday in between. The Science Department will provide all the equipment and provisions, so all you will need is a sense of adventure and hiking boots. Are there any questions, or complaints, thus far?"

"Sir?" One of the boys spoke out, raising his hand in the air.

"Yes, and your name please?" Stiles asked.

"Joseph, sir, and I have a question about the field trip."

"Yes, what about it, Joseph?"

"Well–Why are we taking a field trip to a hard to reach area that requires serious hiking and climbing?"

"Because Joseph, that is where the caldera is, and if you plan to be a geologist, going to remote areas to study natural phenomena is simply part of the job," Stiles explained.

"But what if we can't make the trip?" Joseph questioned, holding out his leg where the professor could see it. "I can't hike two miles on *flat land*, let alone up steep grades."

Stiles studied the boys leg brace and replied, "Joseph, the school can't afford a helicopter to fly us in, as you will undoubtedly be able to do when working for a corporation who wishes to send you to someplace like Blind Valley. Therefore, for cases such as yours I have provided an alternate term paper, which you, or anyone else in your situation, may write for me and obtain half your final one third. That means that you can still achieve an eighty–three percent, and a 'B' for this course, without participating in the field trip. I will also offer you extra credit work that if taken advantage of, can bring you up to a possible one hundred percent. This option, however, is open only to students with genuine disabilities. If you simply do not want to participate, then the best grade you can achieve in this class is a sixty–six percent, or in other words, a 'D'. Anyone else?" Stiles asked, again.

There were no responses.

"Good–Then we will have six people going along on the trip. I'll make those arrangements with the department for your equipment and provisions. The field trip is something we get out of the way, before the bad weather sets in, so we will be leaving next weekend, Friday morning, at six o'clock sharp. That would be the nineteenth of September for those of you without a calendar," Stiles quipped.

The young lady in the class stood and said, "Mr. Edwards."

"Yes, young lady, and you would be, who?"

"Gayle Parker, sir, and I think you had better make arrangements for only five, sir. I'll be dropping this class. No offense, sir, but I am not a geology major. I just needed four more credit hours on my schedule, so I'll get them elsewhere. That trip doesn't sound very good to me."

"Okay, Miss Parker. I'm sorry you won't be joining us, but if you aren't into geology, this trip would be a drag for you, I'm sure. Anybody else?—Good. Okay then, that's five who will be joining me."

Stiles looked around the class, studying the faces once again.

"Let me just say, for the five of you who will be going along, that this trip will be memorable. Blind Valley is a unique place and quite beautiful. I have taken two classes up there each year for the past seven years, one each spring and one each fall. I haven't lost anybody yet, and I don't plan to start now. You will learn a lot and you will have a good time."

He looked at each student to be sure they were all paying close attention, and then continued.

"For those of you who don't know the story, Blind Valley is purported to be the home of the Blind Valley Hermit! Who the heck is that, you ask? Well, he is a one hundred and twenty year old ancient mountain man who is purported to have chosen our valley for his home back in 1878!"

"Excuse me, sir. Jason Whitley. Have you ever seen this hermit, sir?" interrupted the student.

"No, Jason, unfortunately I have not, but there is always the first time. Maybe we'll get lucky this year and find him. Who knows?"

"Yea, *who knows* what he'll do to us if we do find him!" Jason remarked. "I think we'd be better off not looking, and leave him to doing whatever it is he does up there!"

"Jason, where's your sense of adventure?" Stiles asked.

"My sense of adventure is limited to watching horror flicks alone at night, that's where," Jason kidded.

"Oh boy! I can see this is going to be an interesting trip," Stiles remarked.

"Okay, let's get down to business. Joseph, if you'll see me after class I'll give you your term paper assignment. As for you, Miss Parker, you're excused to go see your counselor. Good luck with whatever you decide to take. As for the rest of you, the text we will be studying is *Volcanology*, by Christopher Cromwell, and it is available through the school bookstore. Obtain it today and read chapters one through three for our next class. If any of you who are going on this trip is under eighteen years of age, please stop by my desk and obtain a permission slip for your parents to sign. Are there any child prodigies among you? No. Good. Class dismissed!"

CHAPTER 46

Stiles Edwards and his entourage of five students had left Reedmore College at six fifteen Friday morning en route to Oriel Peak. It had been a long drive of nearly three hundred miles, but Stiles assured his students that the Blind Valley caldera would be well worth the drive.

Stiles was a volcanologist at heart, a geology professor by trade, and an historian by hobby. He had read the accounts of the Blind Valley Hermit and had heard the stories told of his existence. That there may have been such a person living in that caldera totally fascinated him, but his curiosity went far beyond the normal curiosity that might be associated with such a story.

These biannual trips to the caldera were dual–purpose trips, serving as a great educational tool for his students of volcanology, and also helping satisfy his dream of finding evidence of the hermit.

He had traced the evidence back through the mythology and legends to 1878, when the story had begun. What he learned from his research matched closely what his grandmother had told him, up to a point. The original legend started in the lumber camps of that period, with tales of a mountain man named Sam Elliott who had beat three lumberjacks to near death in a fight over trees they were cutting, which he claimed were in his care.

The original legend claimed that the mountain man had said to the loggers, as they lay groveling on the ground, *"God made these trees and He put them in my care. 'Sam Elliott', God said to me, 'protect the forests from their blades.' And gentlemen, that is what I intend to do."*

With that having been spoken, Sam Elliott had disappeared into the forest.

When the men recovered from their thrashing they returned to their camp and told of this huge mountain man who had beat them over the trees they were cutting. The entire camp went immediately in search of Sam Elliott, and much to their displeasure, they found him standing nearly two hundred yards away on a large outcropping above them. They opened fire upon him with their Winchesters but his .45–70 answered back, roaring through the canyons, as one man, and then another, fell dead to the ground.

The lumbermen stopped their firing upon Sam as he turned and vanished from sight. They put the word out to all the other lumber camps in the area about Sam Elliott the mountain man and what he had done. But, Sam Elliott was never seen, nor heard from again. When he disappeared in 1878, he did so completely, leaving behind a young wife and infant daughter.

This much of the legend matched perfectly with what Stiles' grandmother had told him, but the legend went on to say that Sam came back for his wife and daughter and spirited them away with him to wherever. *That* part of the legend was *absolutely false.*

Sam's wife had actually pulled up stakes and moved back east to the Philadelphia area where she and her daughter had lived out their lives. The young daughter had married Mr. Harrison Edwards and raised her family in Philadelphia, as did her children to follow, and their children as well.

This was the story of Sam Elliott, which Stiles Edwards knew to be true, but in all his trips to Blind Valley he had never been able to prove that Sam Elliott and the hermit were one in the same person.

He was probably the only living person who knew the entire story and was more than likely the only person who cared. That did not matter though, for this was a personal matter to him.

He had originally heard the legend from his grandmother, who had heard it from her mother, who had first hand knowledge of the events leading up to Sam's disappearance. But *no one* knew where Sam had gone after the shooting of the loggers.

When Sam Elliott had disappeared in 1878, he had left behind a wife and an infant daughter. That daughter was Stiles' great grandmother.

Speculation had put Sam Elliott in Blind Valley around the turn of the century, but by then, some twenty years later; nobody remembered the mountain man's name. He had simply become the Blind Valley Hermit as scattered reports of a man in furs arose from sightings there. The reported sightings had never been confirmed, and the alleged man's identity, never proven.

This was Stiles' big dream and this was why he had come to Montana to teach. It was his dream to prove that the Blind Valley Hermit was indeed his great–great grandfather, Sam Elliott, the mountain man. Why this was important to him, he had no idea, but suffice it to say *it was*. This would be the fifteenth trip to the valley for Stiles and maybe this time he would come back with his proof.

On his first two trips he had used a marked access road off of Highway 77 to gain entry to the valley, but that had necessitated an eight–mile hike that he wanted very much to shorten if possible. He had done some scouting after the second trip and had come across this unmarked logging road built in the 1920's and abandoned within the same decade. He had been forced to cut a few trees of his own, which had grown up in the path, but with his Suburban in four–wheel drive it was now passable.

It was almost eleven thirty in the morning as Stiles pulled his Suburban to the end of the abandoned logging road, two miles below the Blind Valley escarpment. He and his students unloaded their gear, organized their equipment and set forth into the forest. By two o'clock that afternoon they should reach the base of the escarpment.

Stiles had done some scouting here also, discovering that the extreme east side of the cliff was far more negotiable than any other area of the escarpment. It was still as steep as any other part of it, but the footing was much more solid and more handholds were available for aiding the climber in the ascent.

By three o'clock Stiles and his students were well on their way down the saddle into the caldera. At the top of the escarpment he had explained to his students, as they looked out over the panorama, approximately when it had been formed and how the valley had been created. He explained how the roof of a great magma chamber had collapsed after the magma had erupted from it to the surface, forming the great depression. He further explained that when the magma vented, it did so with such force that ash from this eruption had been found in six–meter thick layers, as far away as Nebraska. *"This, students, is what is known as a super volcano!"* he had told them. He went on to tell them that of the thousands of known volcanoes around the globe, less than twenty super volcanoes were known to exist. He also put forth his theory that Yellowstone National Park sat in an ancient caldera, but that, unfortunately, had yet to be proven.

The group traveled across the floor of the caldera, studying various rocks and minerals that they came upon. At dusk, they had reached the site in the northwest corner of the valley that Stiles had always used on these excursions. They gathered wood, built a fire, and pitched their tents in the clearing that had been awaiting them. Stiles gathered the students around the fire and laid out his plans for the upcoming day.

"We'll be getting up at daybreak tomorrow and we'll have a nice breakfast of whatever you brought along, plus the bacon and eggs provided by the school. If you didn't think to bring anything along to complement you breakfast, like hash browns or grits, then you'll have to settle for what Reedmore contributed," Stiles informed them, smiling and winking.

"After breakfast we will journey to some of the volcanic features which, over the years, I have located here. Take notes and pay attention, because you do have a paper to write on this experience. That is how we will spend the morning, but the afternoon will be a combination of volcanology and treasure hunting," Stiles said, and waited for a response.

"Treasure hunting?" asked one of the students named Joel.

"Yes, Joel–treasure hunting," Stiles repeated. "Let me explain further."

"We will all fan out and travel separately through the valley, your assignment being to locate two items. The first item is to be some sort of proof of former volcanic activity in this caldera. That could be an ash deposit, or loose volcanic rock or an outcropping of volcanic material. Use your eyes and your imagination. The second item of interest to me is any sign of a former dwelling, be it a cabin, a hogan, a kiva or whatever. Again, use your eyes and your imagination. It may be nothing more than a remnant of its former self, but that is all I expect," he said, and then continued.

"Finding the first item is mandatory and is worth ten points extra credit toward your final term paper grade. Finding the second item has nothing to do with this course whatsoever, but will earn you dinner for two at the restaurant of your choosing. Keep your eyes open!"

"Why are we looking for an old dwelling, sir?" Jason asked.

"It's a hobby of mine, trying to prove the one–time existence of the Blind Valley Hermit. Remember my mentioning him in class? So keep your eyes peeled and win that dinner!" Stiles exclaimed. "For now though, I suggest we all get some sleep. Daybreak comes pretty early around here."

CHAPTER 47

Saturday, September twentieth, nineteen hundred and sixty–nine was a clear and balmy day in Carver, Montana. The sky was filled with cumulous clouds, giant puffs of white cotton on an endless field of unimaginably lakeshore blue. The weather could not have cooperated more. If the bait was not taken, it would not be because it was too cold to bother or raining so hard that their perms might get ruined.

Kevin drove down Western Row with Wiley riding shotgun. They crossed the Saline River Upper Bridge, which formed one of two connections between the Greenville section of town and Carver proper. It was the shorter of the two routes from the school to Greenville and the one Mary would most likely use to take Alicia home after the dance.

Alicia had never owned a car of her own and depended upon Mary for most of her transportation. It had been that way ever since Mary had turned sixteen and her father had bought her the green Gremlin she had wanted. There was no doubt that Mary would be driving this evening.

The Upper Bridge route was also the more desolate with nothing more than two baseball fields located near it. Over the years the town had not developed out in this direction as had been expected, probably due to the development of the Jessup Mountain area. It all fit in nicely with Kevin's plan.

"This is the spot, Wiley," Kevin remarked, nodding to the side of the road.

Wiley confirmed Kevin's comment with a nod of his own. It wasn't like this was the first time Wiley had been here, they had gone over this part of the plan almost daily, and had driven by the spot upon several occasions. This was just a final affirmation of what was to occur along this lonely section of Western Row Road.

Kevin steered his '60 Chevy Biscayne toward Carver's retail area. He had been struggling with one aspect of the operation, which he had not previously been able to solve until this afternoon. It had been pure dumb luck that had given him the answer. His next–door neighbor, Ron, had been outside using some sort of aerosol can, and Kevin had noticed the odor right away. He had recognized it immediately, having been subjected to it in the fifth grade when he had undergone a tonsillectomy. He had then gone next door to see what Ron was using and his problem had been solved. A demonic grin had spread across his face as the answer to his dilemma materialized

Kevin pulled into the store lot and found a place to park. Wiley hopped out of the Chevy and ran inside with a mission, to come back with the missing piece of the plot. He was gone only minutes when Kevin saw him burst from the store and approach the car at a pacer's clip. Wiley jumped in the car and without warning, tossed the can to Kevin, who grabbed at it in fumbling fashion, recovered, and began reading the label.

"Awesome!" he said, as he read the name on the front of the can. He rotated the aerosol can to read the back label.

CAUTION: CONTENTS—ETHER

KEEP AWAY FROM SPARKS OR OPEN FLAME!

Kevin smiled that same demonic smile, tucked the can under his seat and said to Wiley, "That's it, the last item we need. Let's go dancing!"

They had planned to arrive late so their parking at the far end of the lot would not look peculiar. By the time they arrived the lot had filled up nicely, it was growing dark, and there was no activity in the parking lot. Kevin backed the car into their darkened space and parked.

Kevin had been right. The lights they had popped the night before, with deadly accuracy, had not been replaced with new bulbs. There was concealment in this darkness, and comfort.

"Okay, Wiley, you know what to do. Remember to pop the trunk but leave it closed. Then scout around and find where Mary parked her car," Kevin reminded him.

"Got it. Go on in and lay the bait. I'll be ready," Wiley confirmed.

Kevin departed for the gym entrance, while Wiley unlocked the trunk, closing it loosely so it would not latch again. He then began walking through the parking lot toward the gym. He looked left and right seeking out Mary's car. It didn't take him long to locate her green Gremlin sporting the license tag, "MARY 16". There was no doubt it was hers. Wiley returned to Kevin's Biscayne and began his preparations.

He went over the plan, one step at a time.

"*Trunk unlatched, check—Engine running, check.* He reached under Kevin's seat and retrieved the aerosol can and the two hand towels, which they had previously folded and stitched into six–inch square pads. He placed the three items on the ground behind the car and knelt down, nestling between the unlatched trunk and the parking lot's brick wall. He waited. The heat from the Chevy's muffler was welcomed, for the evening air had turned quite chilly. "*Anesthesia, check—*"

Kevin studied the crowded gym. The seniors to be and the seniors that were, were all mingling around talking. The Stingers had not come on stage yet, so the dancing had not yet begun. He studied the faces, methodically scanning the room for Casey Cooper. She was Kevin's first choice for the baited hook, but her presence at the dance would force him to move on to his second choice. He didn't think there was much chance that she would be present though, as she was one of the nerds who was probably glad to be free of this school. When it came to abuse, she was the recipient of the worst that was handed out on the girl's side of the geek population of Carver High.

Kevin had singled her out for his hook for that very reason. Mary would get two for the price of one, if she took the bait. Casey Cooper was Kevin's guarantee that Mary would. He continued to peruse the gym, which was decorated with bunting and crepe paper. The committee had ordered a mirrored ball, which was hung in the rafters overhead, turning slowly, casting its spots of bright light about the floor. A record was playing through the PA system as the opening act for the band.

When Kevin had finished his survey of the attendants, he was positive that Casey was not among them. It was as he had both hoped and figured. He was free to use her name without fear of her standing somewhere in sight when he dropped it to Mary.

His next objective was to locate Mary. His eyes had fallen on her briefly as he was placing Casey on the list of no shows. She had been by the snack table, drinking punch in her lacy, low–cut pink dress. He had also noticed her shoes were pointed at the toe and bore high, spiked heels.

He was happy for his forethought on that matter, having thought to bring hiking clothes for the girls, one set of clothing and boots from his wardrobe and one from Wiley's. They wouldn't fit very well, but they were a far sight better than what the girls were wearing to the dance.

He returned his gaze to the refreshments table and Mary was still there, running her mouth and sipping punch. She was undoubtedly telling any who would listen about her acceptance to Evans. Kevin moved in her direction, being careful not to look directly at her, as he wanted to be "surprised" by her presence next to him. He put on his forlorn look and lowered his head, and sidling along the table, moved to where he was standing just to her right.

"Spider" was casting his web, and the pretty butterfly was about to become entangled in its sticky grasp. Kevin reached for the ladle and began dipping himself a punch.

"Well–Kevin. Kevin Reynolds. I didn't think I would see you here tonight," Mary began. "I thought that you and your *lover boy*, Wiley, would have the *decency* to stay away from a gathering of future college students. You know it's really *not* appropriate for you to be here, don't you?"

She hasn't changed a bit, Kevin thought, before responding.

"We just came to see the Stingers, that's all. We heard they are a pretty good rock band," Kevin replied, lowering his eyes to the floor.

"Well, they are. The lead singer, Ricky, is my cousin, you know. I arranged for them to be here. Those juniors couldn't come up with anybody decent," Mary snipped, as she primped at her hair.

"That's nice, Mary. I hear they're good," Kevin answered, in a very low voice.

"Speaking of *we*, where is your queer buddy, Dumbo?" Mary asked. "Did he have second thoughts about mingling with college students, or is he just off somewhere beating his meat?" Mary jabbed.

She's gonna take the bait, Kevin confirmed to himself. *She's gonna take it for sure!*

"He's still out in my car," Kevin answered, lower still. "He just used the dance as an excuse to get out with Casey and do some necking. He's probably all the way to second base by now!"

"Casey who? Cooper? GOD! That's a joke! It's 'Creep Night at Carver High!' Ha!" she laughed.

Kevin saw that look come over her face. That look that said, *I've got to see this! Where's Alicia?*

"Well–they were made for each other, like ugly on a toad," Mary quipped. "I've got to run along, *Spider*. Tell Dumbo to have a good life with his frog princess."

She disappeared into the gathering audience. The Stingers had taken the stage and were tuning up. Kevin turned and inconspicuously meandered through the other kids to the gym door and the parking lot beyond. As he approached the double doors he thought a pleasant thought, *Nope, not another ten months. Tonight! She took the bait...I know she did!*

Wiley was waiting behind Kevin's car when he returned. He took his place beside Wiley and they soaked their homemade anesthesia pads with the contents of the aerosol can.

"If it starts to evaporate away before they get here, rewet it. We have to knock them out fast. As little struggle as possible," Kevin reminded Wiley.

"Then she took the bait? You think she did?" Wiley asked, so excitedly that Kevin thought he would piss his pants.

"Yes, I'm almost one hundred percent sure she did. I used Casey Cooper as your *lover*. That lit her up!" Kevin whispered. "Then she went away quickly, probably to find Alicia. Keep your eyes peeled now. We have to move like cats when they get here."

They were true to form, or at least that could be said of Mary. She was leading the way, working her way through the parking lot, Alicia, tagging along behind.

"Do you see his car yet?" Mary asked. "It's a big black Chevrolet, with wings on the back, you know, fins, but sideways," she explained.

"Yea, I've seen it," replied Alicia. "But I don't see it here. Let's go back inside, Mary. I don't really care if Wiley is out here with Casey or not. Why don't we just leave them be?"

"Leave them be? What's wrong with you, girl? This is going to be great!"

"So what do we do when we find them?" Alicia asked.

"We start banging on the hood and screaming. Scare the crap out of them. Dumbo will probably crap his pants. Busted! Then we run, back to the gym, after they see it's me–*but I want them to see it's me!* I need to get his ass one more time!" Mary proclaimed.

The summer had changed Alicia, and she was feeling that what they were doing was not only stupid, but also, *cruel.* It was a rather novel experience in her life, but the feeling was definitely there. It simply did not feel right.

From Kevin's side of the car he saw the girls change direction and head their way.

"Here they come, Wiley. How's your pad. Still good and wet?"

"Yes, I just rewet it," he replied.

"Good, me too. Get ready."

The girls slowly approached the car, trying to peek through the windshield at the sight within. They stopped short, about ten feet away and Mary pointed toward the car. They proceeded at their creeping gate in the boys' direction.

Kevin was pleased, and relieved, to see Mary's purse dangling from her shoulder. Another variable no longer to be concerned with, but it was a big one, perhaps the biggest. He breathed a silent sigh of relief. The girls finally reached the front of the car, still peering through the windshield, when, suddenly, Alicia turned and began walking away. She looked back over her shoulder and spoke to Mary.

"That's it, Mary. I'm going back inside. This isn't right and I'm through with your stupid games."

Mary stood there, aghast. *What the hell got into her?*

"Wiley," Kevin whispered. "What the hell is going on? Where the hell is Alicia going? That's it–*move!*"

The boys *were* cats! They sprang from behind the car and traveled to the front in a flash. Kevin chased down Alicia and placed his pad over her mouth and nose before she could take two steps. Wiley was offered more resistance by Mary, but got the job accomplished just the same. Both girls struggled against the superior strength of the boys, but to no avail. Slowly, ever so slowly, their struggles ceased and they went limp in the arms of their attackers.

Kevin carried Alicia to the back of the car and nudged the trunk lid up with his knee. He carefully placed Alicia at the back of the trunk and administered the pad to her face for several seconds. He knew what he was doing was dangerous and he wasn't sure how much ether was too much, but he needed her to sleep for a while longer, at least through the rest of the dance. His big concern was that this wasn't pure anesthetic ether, but rather, a generic product, and who knew what else might be contained in it? He could only hope for the best at this point and with luck, she'd wake up, eventually.

Wiley was right behind Kevin, waiting his turn to deposit his prey in the same manner. He followed Kevin's lead, placing Mary in the front of the trunk and applying his pad once again.

"Do you have her purse?" Kevin asked.

"Yep, and here are her keys," he replied, smiling broadly.

"Good, throw the purse in the trunk. You know what to do next," Kevin instructed.

Kevin threw the pads in the trunk and lowered the trunk lid. He made a quick survey of the area to be sure the girls hadn't dropped anything in the struggle, and found Alicia's purse under one of the front tires of a nearby car. He walked to the back of his car and deposited her purse in the trunk and pushed down until the lid latched. Kevin took one more look around, tucked the can back under his seat, and assumed his position behind the steering wheel. He waited for Wiley.

A few minutes later he saw Mary's Gremlin heading for the parking lot exit. *"Phase–Two,"* he said to himself, pulling out of his space and following Wiley onto Carver School Road. Three blocks later they turned onto Western Row and headed for the Upper Bridge over the Saline River, a half–mile away.

As Wiley approached the bridge, he gave the Gremlin some gas and accelerated up to fifty miles per hour. He had already rolled down the windows on both the driver's side and the passenger's. When he had drawn to within about a hundred feet of the bridge, he turned the wheel slightly, and locked up the brakes, sending the little Gremlin skidding off the road and through the flimsy wooden rail. The Gremlin continued past the end of the bridge and onto the grassy ball field, sliding ever closer to the Saline River.

Wiley had no idea how fast to go on his approach and if he found himself in the frigid river, his bad, he'd get out somehow. He hoped he wouldn't travel quite that far, and as luck would have it, he didn't. The Gremlin finally skidded to a stop, fifty feet short of the river.

Wiley jumped out immediately, leaving the car in gear, and it started slowly forward again. He ran to the back and gave it some help gaining speed and momentum, until it chugged off on its own at a pretty good clip. He watched over his shoulder as he walked back toward the road, until he saw the little green car dive into the river.

He stopped to watch as the swift current swung the car around and began taking it downstream. It moved steadily down its course until the last vestige of Mary's Gremlin sank beneath the swirling surface of the Saline River.

"Where to now?" Wiley asked Kevin, as he got into the waiting car.

"Phase–Three! Back to the dance," Kevin answered. He chuckled, turning the car in a u–turn. "Back to the dance!" he repeated.

"I thought I was a goner back there," Wiley commented, sighing with relief. "I wasn't sure if I'd stop short of the river or not."

A tingle went all through his body, like an electrical shock.

"I didn't figure on the grass being all dewy like it was," he added.

Kevin looked at Wiley and smiled.

"Can't figure on everything, buddy. That would take all the *adventure* out of it, now wouldn't it?" Kevin replied, poking a little fun at Wiley.

Wiley smiled back at Kevin and nodded his head.

"Yes–it would at that," he agreed.

With their precious cargo fast asleep in the trunk, the boys continued down Western Row and turned onto School Road. Kevin backed his Biscayne into the same parking space it had occupied during the abduction, and turned off the engine.

"Ready?" Kevin asked Wiley.

"Ready," Wiley replied.

"Let's go dancing!"

It was the boys' intention to go back in and stay until the end of the dance. They would do a little dancing, which would amuse their former classmates, and congratulate as many as would talk to them about their college plans. They would discuss with those who would listen, what their plans for the future were. By midnight, when the dance would wind down, everyone in attendance would be able to clearly remember their presence.

As for Mary and Alicia, they would spend this time fast asleep in the trunk of Kevin's Chevy, dreaming their last *sweet dreams* of their lives. From here on out, until they either saved themselves or perished in the bowl, all their dreams would be nightmares.

CHAPTER 48

❀

*A*l was stirred from his dream of fishing on the Saline, by the irritating ring of his phone. He reached for the alarm clock, flipped the switch, and rolled back over. The bed felt so warm and comfortable.

It couldn't be time to get up already?

The phone rang again.

Damn, it's the phone, he realized, and picked up the receiver.

"Hello, Sheriff Dramico," he managed through a yawn as he brushed his dark hair back from his face.

"Sheriff, this is Stan. Sorry to wake you, but I've got a situation here," he explained, apologetically.

Al looked at his alarm clock. It read two a.m.

"What's the problem, Stan? Kid's burn down the rest of that lodge?" he answered, laughing softly.

"No, sir–I just got a call from Dr. Clemmons. His daughter, Mary, was due home from the high school dance at twelve thirty. Well–she hasn't made it home yet. It's two a.m. now and her daddy is getting very worried," Stan explained, obviously concerned himself.

Al thought for a moment and then spoke.

"Did he check with any of her friends? Maybe she went to a friend's house and just forgot to call home," Al suggested.

"Yes, sir, he did. She went to the dance with Alicia Koppe. Rather, she drove Alicia there. Dr. Clemmons called Lucas just before he called me, and Alicia isn't home yet either, Sheriff," Stan said, emphasizing that *both* girls were missing.

"Any place else they might go?" Al questioned.

"Her daddy doesn't think so. Nothing's open this time of night and if she didn't go to Alicia's house he doesn't know where to begin looking," Stan told him.

Al rubbed his head and threw back the covers.

"Okay, Stan. I'll meet you in the school parking lot in about twenty minutes. We'll try to trace their possible routes home and take it from there. See you shortly."

Al hung up the phone and turned to sit on the edge of the bed. He lowered his head into the palms of his hands, and sat there in the dark for several minutes, thinking, and rubbing his forehead.

Those two, he thought. *Of all the kids at that party, why does it come back around to those two?*

He started to get up from the bed realizing that this was probably as good as he was going to feel for the rest of the day, maybe even longer. He stood up anyway and walked to the bathroom, giving the light switch a flick as he passed it. He splashed some cold water on his face, combed his thick hair, and went back to his bedroom.

Al was a confirmed bachelor, and as was typical, he put on his wrinkled uniform of the previous two days use, and picked up the phone. He dialed Becky at home and asked her to go to the office and stand by the radio. He was afraid they might have need of her services once they were out looking for the girls.

He was sincerely hoping that by the time he arrived at Carver High the girls would have turned up. Maybe they had a flat tire, or their car broke down and they were forced to walk home. That's what Al hoped, but not what he feared.

Stan was waiting in the parking lot when Al arrived. He pulled his Scout up alongside Stan's cruiser and rolled down his window.

"Morning, Stan," Al greeted. "Why don't you park you cruiser and hop in with me. Your eyes are better than mine. I'll drive and you keep your eyes open for anything that might give us a clue to where those girls went," Al suggested.

"Sure, Sheriff. What are we looking for?" Stan asked.

"I don't know for sure. Just park that thing and hop in," Al ordered, his patience thin at this time of the morning.

Stan did as he asked, and climbed into the passenger seat of Al's Scout.

"You told me once before that the Koppe girl lives in Greenville, is that right, Stan?"

"Yes, sir, it is," Stan answered.

"You said the Clemmons girl drove. Did her dad say what kind of car she drives?" Al asked.

"Yes, sir, it's a Gremlin, green, he said," Stan answered.

"The way I see it she would have dropped the Koppe girl off before going home herself. The most direct route to Greenville from here is Western Row. Let's drive out that way and see what we see. First though, reach down there and grab that microphone. Radio Becky and have her call Dr. Clemmons and see if he's heard anything from his daughter yet," Al directed.

He pulled out on Carver School Road and then onto Western Row. Al proceeded slowly up the deserted street so that Stan would not miss anything that may be pertinent. Stan radioed Becky and asked her to place the call. He put the microphone back in its hanger and stared at the road ahead.

This is going to be a long night, he thought. *But that's okay if we find those girls safe and sound.*

Stan also had his doubts.

They had traveled nearly all the way to the river without seeing a single thing of interest when Al suddenly pulled his Scout over to the side of the road, just short of the Upper Bridge.

"Why are we stopping?" Stan asked.

He hadn't seen anything but blackness.

"Look up ahead, Stan. Skid marks leading off the road and through the rail," Al pointed out.

"Yea, I see them, now. I mean I saw them before, but..."

"That's okay, Stan. I was thinking this might turn out to be the case. The girls might have been sneaking some booze into their punch, driving too fast along here, I don't know, but–well, let's go have a look," Al said.

The sheriff and Stan turned on their flashlights and began following the skid marks from off the blacktop, across the dirt shoulder, through the smashed railing, and into the grassy ball field.

The ground sloped down to the river at this point, and they began following the grooves in the grass until the grooves changed to mere depressions. Al stopped and studied the ground. Then he motioned for Stan to follow him further, following the depressions in the grass to the river's edge.

"Looks like they went in here," Al said, solemnly, shining his light out across the swift moving water. "I can't see a thing out there. She must have gone under. The question is how far downstream did she get? Better get Larry out here with his wrecker and some lights. Wake up Lester Brown and see if we can borrow one of his generators. I'm afraid we have a car to fish out of here, and sadly, perhaps a couple of young ladies."

Al lowered his head and wiped away, what looked to Stan, to be a tear.

They stood for a short time looking out over the water. Neither man wanted to say what they were both thinking. If those girls were in that car, in that frigid water, there would be no hurry to find them now. Finally, Stan turned away and began walking back to Al's Scout.

"I'll get on the radio and start waking folks up. Get some help out here," he said.

Stan stopped, suddenly, and turned back to Al.

"Should I have Becky call the Clemmons and the Koppes?"

Al turned his head to look at Stan and replied, "No. Have her make those calls to Larry and Lester. Then have her call the Clemmons and patch them through to me. I'll let them know what's going on here myself, and then I'll talk with the Koppes."

Stan turned again and slowly proceeded toward the Scout. He raised Becky on the radio and set things in motion.

Al came back shortly to await the call from the Clemmons, while Stan went back to the river's edge and began walking downstream, looking for any telltale sign of the Gremlin. He wanted to find it in the grim hope than the girls might still be alive, trapped in an air pocket or something like that. He knelt down by the water's edge and dipped his hand in the froth. He pulled it back and all hope faded from his heart.

Too cold, he realized. *They wouldn't last twenty minutes in there.*

He looked at his watch. The dance had ended over three hours ago. He slumped to the grass, crossing his legs before him, then lowered his head and wept.

By four thirty Lester had his generator running and Larry had his work lights hooked in, shining on the Saline River. Al had them start the operation forty yards downstream from where the Gremlin had entered the water. It wasn't very scientific, but it was something to go by. He had estimated how long it would take for the car to sink to the river bottom, which wasn't that deep, and simply visualized the car's movement through the water as it sank. The answer was that the car had traveled forty yards. Scientific or not, as it would eventually be discovered, Al was only off by a few yards.

While waiting for the call from the Koppes, Al had realized that he was going to need some divers. He had radioed the state trooper post between Bennett and Reedmore and had requested that several experienced divers be sent over to them. The divers arrived at six o'clock, and went straight to work.

Tethered to the shore, so they wouldn't be swept downstream, they entered the water ten yards above where Al suspected they would find the car. They were slowly allowed to move down with the current, their tethers acting as restraint against the force of the river. Eventually, they surfaced, forty–five yards from the car's entry point. They had found the little green Gremlin, resting on its side, on the river bottom in twenty feet of water.

One of the divers made a downward pointing gesture into the river, indicating it was down there, and signaled for the tether tenders to reel him in. The other divers remained in the water, signaling for the tow hook.

It was a moment of relief and anticipation, but most of all; it was a moment of anxiety. The lead diver emerged from the water removing his mask and mouthpiece, and began walking toward Al.

"She's down there, Sheriff, but she's empty," he reported. "Both windows are open, like they might have tried to get out and swim for it. Cold as that water is I don't think they would have made it to shore. Sorry, but that's the long and short of it."

Al lowered his head and stood frozen in place. The other divers had successfully fed the cable through the car and had hooked the tow hook to the cable, forming a loop around the roof of the car. Larry pulled the little Gremlin from the icy river, letting the water slowly drain out, to reduce the weight as he pulled it on to dry land. He finally managed to bring it all the way up on the shore. Mrs. Clemmons screamed and clutched Mrs. Koppe, holding her close. The girls' fathers stood side by side, on weakened knees, staring at the car and supporting each other.

Al walked over to the little car and looked inside. Stan had followed him and watched as his boss climbed into the Gremlin and looked in the back seat, then on the floors, and finally, under the seats. He backed back out and stood, rubbing his chin and looking out across the river.

"Car's empty, Sheriff," Stan said, interrupting Al's thoughts. "I guess we'll have to drag the river downstream," he added.

Al turned, without saying a word, and walked over to the girls' mothers. He talked with them a moment, both comforting them and asking them a question. He then returned to where Stan was waiting.

"We'll have the river dragged, just to be sure, but I don't think we will find them in there," Al stated.

"But, Sheriff, where else…"

"Stan," Al said, cutting him off. "Let me ask you something. If you were a girl who had just drove her car into a freezing cold river, and your car was sinking into that cold water, what would you do?"

"Well—I'd roll down my window and swim out, trying to reach shore, just like it seems they tried to do," he answered, not sure of Al's point in asking.

"That's right, Stan. And that's *all* you'd do. You wouldn't try to find your purse, losing valuable time, trying to take it with you. That would be the *last* thing on your mind. No, we're not just missing two girls here; we're also missing two purses. Their mothers say they both left with purses. Now, they're gone, the girls and their purses. Those girls weren't in this car when it went in the river, Stan. No way in Hell they were in there."

"So where?" Stan asked. "If they weren't in the car, where'd they go?"

"The car didn't skid into the river," Al explained. "It stopped, then rolled into the river."

I think something spooked the Clemmons girl, causing her to hit the brakes. Maybe a deer ran in front of her. She slid off the road and came to a stop short of the riverbank. She was stuck down that slope on the wet grass, or the car stalled out. The girls walked back up to the road to get help, or maybe they were going to walk to the Koppe girl's house. It's not too far into Greenville from here. Someone came along Western Row about then, someone with bad intentions. Opportunity, Stan. Maybe there were two or three of them. They took the girls and rolled the car in the river."

"Why bother to do that, Sheriff?" Stan wanted to know. "Why roll it in the river?"

"To do just exactly what happened. To tie up the law for hours trying to retrieve the girls' bodies, while they put miles between here and wherever the hell they are now," Al explained.

What Al was saying did make sense. Stan could see that now, and right now, he was pretty impressed with his boss.

"So is that what you believe happened, Sheriff?" Stan asked. "I mean is that the theory we are going to act on?"

"There's always more than one possible explanation, Stan. That's my first theory, that someone has kidnapped them for reason's we'd both rather not think about. They were pretty girls, out here on this lonely stretch of road. That's motive and opportunity, Stan. Right now I'm thinking those girls are in serious trouble, or dead," Al said, shaking his head slightly and rubbing his brow.

Stan thought for a moment about what Al had said.

"So we go talk to some of their friends that were at the dance?" Stan suggested, half asking more so than sure.

"That's exactly what we do. We need to find out when they left the dance and if they left with anyone. Someone they knew may be at the bottom of this, but right now my money's on opportunity. I think they just ran into some bad folks out on this road that took the opportunity to do some bad things. That's the way it looks to me."

CHAPTER 49

Daylight finally arrived Sunday morning and helped confirm Al's theory about the car rolling, rather skidding into the river. In the morning light the tracks left in the grass by the little Gremlin were clear enough. Al pointed it out for Stan, showing him the change over from torn and displaced blades of grass; to simple, well defined tire tracks on the wet sod.

Al radioed the state police, issuing an APB for the missing girls. He called it a possible kidnapping and was informed that the FBI would be notified, as was the case in all kidnappings. That was fine with him, he would welcome the help, but in the mean time he wasn't going to waste any time waiting for them.

"Let's get a bite to eat at Laura's, Stan. Then we'll go to church," he said, as he replaced the microphone on its hook.

"Church?" Stan questioned.

"That's where we'll find the most kids in one place on a Sunday morning. The Methodist Church has the largest congregation, so we'll start there," Al decided.

There was no point in running all over town trying to track down and interview individual kids when the majority of them would be at church in just a few hours. It was hard to sit back and wait, doing seemingly nothing, but it seemed the most efficient way to proceed. In the mean time, they'd go to Laura's, get some breakfast and discuss their plans for locating the missing girls. Al called it, "*a time for restoration and reflection*", and Stan understood what he meant by that.

Laura's was a busy place at seven thirty on Sunday mornings. When Al and Stan arrived, the Murphy's were just leaving, so they took their booth in the corner of the diner. They sat down across from one another and began talking over the remnants of the Murphy's breakfast. Lyle, Laura's fourteen–year–old son, came and cleared the table giving Al room to lie out his legal pad and begin diagramming the Upper Bridge area.

As he drew his map he explained to Stan that it would be helpful to explore all the possible routes out of the area. Perhaps they could get an idea of the most likely way the culprits might have chosen to leave the Carver area. The presumption here was that they were not locals, and would not stay in town for long, if at all.

Laura came by their booth and took their breakfast order, bacon, eggs and hash browns for each. Al preferred his eggs sunny side up, and Stan ordered scrambled. They continued to discuss their options and plan their next steps, while Lloyd prepared their breakfast at the grill behind the counter. About ten minutes later, Lyle came around with their steaming plates of "Laura's Finest Dining", and they ate in silence, each lawman thinking through what needed to be done and hoping for a happy ending to this mess. They both realized that whatever the outcome, it probably would not be happy for the girl's or their parents. But some scenarios were better than others, and they hoped at least to find them alive.

Al finished his last morsel of bacon and looked across the table at Stan, who was about to finish with the last bit of egg on his plate.

"Ready, Stan?" he asked, more telling him he was, than asking.

"Sure, Sheriff, ready," he replied, hurrying one last bite of egg into his mouth.

"I want to get over to the church and talk with Reverend Miller before services begin. Explain to him what we have here and get his cooperation. I'll need to talk to the congregation before he gets started with his sermon. I wouldn't want to interrupt him, once he gets going," Al kidded.

Stan nodded in agreement.

They each wiped their mouths on paper napkins pulled from the tabletop dispenser, and headed for the cash register. Moments later they were back in the Scout and in route to the Carver Methodist Church. It was going to be a long day. Al reflected on that, and thought to himself, *or… a long week.*

Reverend Miller was going over his notes for his sermon on "Trust and Faith", when they arrived. Although the Methodist church had the largest congregation in Carver, it was not a physically large building. It was a simple, white clapboard structure, with a steep pitched black roof and a tall pointed steeple above the front portal.

Inside it had hardwood floors, and pews that looked equally as hard, fashioned out of plainly carved oak. The ceiling was plaster, vaulted and adorned with decorative wooden beams. The Reverend Miller was seated in the choir loft, his notes in his lap, practicing his delivery of today's message.

Al was Baptist and not a frequent visitor to this chapel, so Reverend Miller was initially surprised at his appearance before him. After the usual amenities were dispensed with, Al explained to him the purpose for his visit. Needless to say, the Reverend was quite concerned, and agreed to introduce Al to the congregation before he started the service. He pointed to his office and told Al he could meet in there with any of the kids who had attended the dance, and any parents who might have chaperoned it the night before. Not having any children of his own at Carver High, Reverend Miller had not been asked to chaperone himself, so he could be of no help to Al in that respect.

Al thanked the Reverend for his cooperation and he and Stan left him alone to rehearse his sermon. They took a seat in the front row of pews and awaited the good people of Carver to arrive. Al went over in his mind what he was going to say to them and how he would present it to them. There would undoubtedly be folks in the gathering that knew the girls, perhaps even relatives that had not learned of their disappearance yet. He wanted to break it to them in the gentlest way he could find. It was certainly not an announcement he was looking forward to making.

By nine–thirty the little white church had filled with its faithful and Reverend Miller took his place at the altar. He announced to the congregation that the sheriff had an announcement of importance to make to them, and that services would begin thereafter. He also informed them that he would be available for counseling, immediately following the service, for anyone who felt the need of his comfort and advice. With that said, he motioned for Al to come forward.

"I'm sorry to have to delay your service like this, but I have a serious matter I need your help with. What I need is information. Those who can be the most help to me right now are the students and chaperones that attended the high school dance last night. The Reverend has offered me the use of his office for a conference. So I'd like to meet with any students or parents who attended the dance last night. If you would just follow me to the Reverend's office, I'll make it as short as possible. Thank you."

Al had decided not to break the actual bad news in the public forum. It would get back to them all, as soon as his conference was over. That way, the news would come from friends and family, rather than from an official. It seemed to him the kindest way to handle it.

Al closed the door and turned to face the small room Reverend Miller had offered for his meeting. There were seven students each wearing concerned looks and whispering among themselves, as he began.

"I want to thank each of you for agreeing to meet with Deputy Phillips and myself," he began. "I would like to begin by finding out if any of you know when Mary and Alicia left the dance last night. I am sorry to say they never returned home after the dance and they are still missing. Secondly, and more importantly, did anyone see who they might have left with?"

A buzz filled the small room as the kids began talking among themselves. Shortly, a young lady raised her hand as if in class at school, and Al acknowledged her.

"Sir, I saw Mary and Alicia leave around nine thirty or so," she stated.

"That's pretty early, ah…"

"Sally, Sally Carter, sir."

"That's pretty early to leave a dance, Sally. Are you sure of the time?" Al asked.

"Pretty sure. The band was just beginning to play their first or second song. I thought it was strange, too. That's why I noticed, I guess," Sally said.

"And you saw them leave the building–alone?" Al asked.

"Yes, sir."

"Did you see them come back at all during the evening?—Anyone?" Al inquired.

They all shook their heads, indicating that they hadn't.

"Sir," another girl said, raising her hand in the air also, as Sally had done.

"Yes, Miss. Your name is?" Al responded.

"Kayla Phelps, sir."

"Yes, Kayla, go ahead please," Al encouraged.

"I heard Mary telling Alicia something in the lady's room. I don't think they knew I was there. I was in the–the stall," Kayla continued, a little embarrassed at the picture she was painting for the sheriff.

"What did you hear, Kayla?" Al asked, leaning forward, his interest apparent.

"Mary was saying something about going out to the parking lot. She was saying something about Wiley Coates being out there neck–ah, outside parking with Casey Cooper. Then they left the bathroom," Kayla informed him.

"What time was this, Kayla?"

"Around nine thirty, like Sally said. I remember because the band was just starting to play when I came back from the lady's room."

Wiley Coates, Al thought. The name grated on him. *And why does it always come back around to him?*

"Tell me, Kayla. Did you see Wiley Coates at the dance? Was he there?" Al questioned.

"Yes, sir, he was. He stayed until the dance was over. Rose and I walked to my car with them."

Rose nodded her affirmation.

"Them?" the sheriff asked.

"Wiley and Kevin," Rose replied. "They were there all night."

One of the boys chimed in, "Not *all* night. Wiley must have had Kevin take Casey home when he was finished with her. Probably didn't want to be seen in public with her," the boy said laughing and cheering himself on.

Al looked sternly at him and the boy ceased to be amused.

"Why would you say that?" Al asked him, his face drawing even more stern.

"Well–you know. She's a–a dog, kinda," the boy replied.

Al hadn't asked his name yet, and he didn't really want to know. He had little use for a wise ass. He looked at the boy harshly and said, "Why did you say he must have taken her home? *That's* what I want to know about," Al pressed.

"Yes, sir. I said it because she wasn't at the dance. At least I never saw her," he stammered.

"Any of you other kids see Casey at the dance?" Al asked.

The general consensus, as displayed by the negative shakes of their heads, was no, she hadn't been there.

"Okay, thanks, kids. Can anyone think of anything else that may be helpful before we break up here?" Al asked, hoping for something concrete to grab onto.

"Sir," another boy spoke up.

"Yes, son, your name is?"

"Hank, sir. None of this makes any sense to me. Casey is my neighbor from across my street, and her folks and mine are good friends. Casey is going to Boston College this fall and she already left four days ago, last Wednesday. She couldn't have been with Wiley last night."

Al dismissed the kids, thanking them again, and looked at Stan with a blank stare. He was completely up a tree. He had two missing girls who had left the dance early to go to the parking lot to embarrass Wiley Coates and a girl who was, at the time, in Boston. They never came back to the dance, but Wiley, whom she had gone out to pester, was there all night with Kevin. Nothing was adding up for him and he was leaning back toward his original theory of opportunity, when one of the girls popped her head in the door.

"Sheriff," she started. "I was just thinking about something I didn't think about before."

"You're Karen Jones, right? Artie's daughter," Al commented.

She smiled and said, "Yes, sir. Do you know my dad?"

"Sure, we used to bowl together. You used to tag along sometimes when you were just a little bit," Al said, showing Karen a sweet smile. "You were probably too young to remember I suppose."

"No, sir, sorry. Anyway, I remembered that I saw Kevin talking to Mary by the punch bowl. It surprised me at the time, because they hate each other and all."

"When was this, Karen? About what time would you say?" asked Al.

"It was before the band started playing, maybe around nine or nine fifteen," she said.

"Okay, thank you, Karen. Tell your dad I said hello and we'll have to get together and roll a few frames sometime soon."

"Sure, Sheriff. I will."

Al started adding it all up in his head and then turned to Stan, who had been paying close attention to Al's questioning of the kids.

"That cements it for me, Stan. I don't know what's going on, but those boys are mixed up in it to their eyebrows somehow."

Stan looked a little puzzled and replied, "Wiley and Kevin? But the two girls, Rose and her friend, said those two were at the dance until after midnight, Sheriff. That other girl said that Mary and Alicia left at nine thirty or so, alone."

"I know all that, Stan, and I know it doesn't add up, but somehow those two boys are mixed up in all this. Come on, there's something I want to check out," Al ordered, as he was already going through the door into the chapel.

"Are we going to go talk to Wiley, Sheriff?" Stan asked, trying to figure out the next move on his own and trying to keep up with Al, as he jogged toward the exit.

Al was already climbing into the Scout as he answered, "Yes, we are, but there's one other thing I want to take a look at before we do."

Five minutes later they were pulling into Larry's Conoco station. Al jumped out of the Scout and motioned for Larry to come over. Larry read the urgency on Al's face and trotted over immediately, leaving the pump handle in his customer's tank.

"Larry. Where'd you tow Mary Clemmons' Gremlin to?" Al demanded.

"It's around back, Sheriff. Why?" asked Larry, but Al was already headed that way and didn't benefit him with an answer.

He turned the corner around to the back of the station and saw the Gremlin by the back fence. His pace quickened and upon reaching the car, he threw open the door and peered in at the dashboard.

"Ten o'clock." he said, watching the second hand, "—and it's *not* running!"

Larry got wind of what was going on and offered, "It wouldn't be, Sheriff. The electrical system shorted out when the car went into the river."

"Good, that's what I was hoping. Larry, get a battery and hook it up to this clock. I want to see if it works at all," Al ordered.

Larry did as instructed, and after finding the right wires, "Okay, Sheriff, she's wired," he said.

Al watched as the second hand jerked forward and then smoothly made one circuit, then two, and the minute hand followed at its own creeping pace. They all watched to be sure it would continue in that fashion, and after five minutes, Al was convinced that it was functioning accurately. He turned to Stan and began laying it all out for him.

"Mary is seen talking to Kevin at nine fifteen. At nine thirty, Mary and Alicia are overheard talking about going out to the parking lot to razz Wiley and a girl, who as it turns out, was in Boston at the time. At about that same time Mary and Alicia are seen leaving the dance; say around nine thirty. At ten o'clock Mary's car goes into the Saline River, but the girls are not in it. They never return to the dance. Stan, who do you suppose put the bug in Mary's ear about Casey Cooper?" he asked.

"Kevin?" Stan answered.

"Kevin. Kevin Reynolds, who would no more strike up a conversation with Mary, than a badger would a woodchuck. But there they were, talking at the punch bowl just forty–five minutes before that little Gremlin went into the river."

"But the boys were at the party *all night*, Sheriff. Rose said so," Stan questioned, trying to get an explanation for that.

"They were *perceived* to have been there all night because they were among the last to leave. Nobody was keeping tabs on them. They could have been gone an hour or more without being missed."

Stan reflected on that and responded, "Yea, you're right. Who *was* keeping tabs on them?"

"Come on, Stan. Now, I think it's about time we have a word with Mr. Wiley Coates."

CHAPTER 50

*M*ary was the first to stir, feeling about the blackness until she located an arm.

"Alicia, is that you?" she asked, into the darkness.

"Mary? Mary, is that you? Where are we? What's happening?" she wept, her voice, vibrato.

They had awakened in a dark and confined space, sensing motion, but feeling only the cold, splitting headaches and intense nausea. Reality, for the girls right now, was confusion and extreme discomfort.

"I'm not sure, a car trunk, I think," Mary replied; as she listened to the even hum filling their space.

"I think I hear tires, on a road, don't you think so?" Mary asked.

"I don't know! I just want to know what's going on. Why are we in here?" she bellowed.

Beginning to shake off the effects of the ether, Mary was starting to understand the situation and its implications.

"Because we've been kidnapped, that's why!"

The events in the parking lot were beginning to come back to her. At first, she remembered the smell of ether, that horrible, nasty smell. The whole movie was playing slowly in her mind, coming in pieces, a little at a time. She remembered a rag being put over her face. She saw someone rushing her from behind a black car. It was dark and she could not see a face in the slim moment it was all taking place. All she could see was a black silhouette, a black cutout in the dark night. Those ears sticking…"

"My God, Alicia, it was Wiley!" Mary screamed, coming to this realization. "It was that prick, Wiley, who gassed me!"

"Then it must have been Kevin who grabbed me," Alicia suggested.

"Sure it was—Casey Cooper my ass! They tricked us into that lot!" Mary said, realizing what must have happened.

"But why? Why would they do that? What did we do to them that was so bad?" Alicia sobbed, shaking Mary's invisible arm.

"Not them–Alicia–Bryce. Wiley did see me up there, and that's what this is all about."

"But why didn't he just go to the sheriff and tell him?" Alicia stuttered, between sobs.

"I'm not sure, Alicia, but I'm beginning to think we are going to wish he had," Mary speculated.

She started to say something else, but noticed her body shifting hard to the right, and the even hum of tires on pavement changed to the sound of crunching gravel.

❧   ❧   ❧

"Change!" Wiley screamed at her, his face distorted with hatred. "Change now, or I'll do it for you!"

Mary looked up at him from the ground, terrified and sobbing huge tears. Her makeup was streaked and her mascara was running down her cheeks in meandering black rivulets.

"Why? Why are you doing this, Wiley?" she pleaded.

She had thought she was in control of herself before the trunk was opened, but seeing the moonlit forest all around, and feeling totally isolated and alone, she had lost it all over again.

Kevin was with Alicia, a few feet away. She was too terrified to question what was taking place, obediently changing from her party clothes into the hiking outfit Kevin had brought along for her. Tears ran down her face, too, but she was silent in her sorrow and fear.

"All right, I'll change," Mary, said. "Turn around, please," she pleaded.

He could not recall having ever heard Mary say the word please before, not to him, of course, and not to any of her friends, either. This had to be a first!

"Turn around and get clobbered with a chunk of rock–I don't think so. Change! Now!" Wiley demanded. Mary surveyed the area as she began slipping out of her party clothes and into the fatigues and boots that had been thrown on the ground beside her. It was dark and it was scary.

They had walked uphill a short distance before they were stopped and ordered to sit on the forest floor. Kevin had opened a large duffel bag and had removed his and Wiley's hiking clothes, placing their own dress clothes back in the bag. Kevin had secured a gun holster around his waste and had hoisted a pack onto his back. Wiley had changed his clothes also and put on a similar backpack, and had slung a rifle over his shoulder.

Kevin had also opened a second duffle and had pulled out the clothes that she and Alicia were to wear, and had distributed each article to the ground beside them. He had already stuffed Alicia's dress clothes into the bag and had set it on the ground next to a large hole with a mound of loose dirt beside it.

They dug that hole, she had thought. *My God! They have this all planned out!*

As Mary finished changing, Kevin stuffed her clothes into the duffel and laid it in the hole, covering it with the mounded loose soil. He then retrieved a few pine boughs and draped them over the freshly dug soil.

Wiley ordered the girls to stand, and grabbing Mary's shoulders, physically pointed her up the hill.

"March!" he demanded. "We've got a long way to go!"

They climbed single file, Kevin leading the way, followed by Alicia, then Mary, with Wiley bringing up the rear. Every time Mary faltered along the way, she would feel the cold steel of Wiley's rifle barrel across her back, and then a shove.

They trudged on through the forest, ever upward, their path visible only by the light of the moon. They hiked in silence, as Mary had learned the penalty for trying to talk to Alicia, early on. To stumble or linger was to find Wiley's rifle across her back and a solid shove, but to talk to Alicia brought much worse. The one time she had tried she had found herself sprawled in the pine needles, a boot squarely between her shoulders.

Alicia had stopped her sobbing, probably for lack of air. Mary offered no further protests, as she had felt Wiley's conviction across her back, once too often. The hours passed, as the grade grew steeper. The trees fell away behind them, giving way to small scrubs, then to nothing but tundra, alabaster and lichen. And still, they continued up.

Neither girl could even begin to imagine what to expect. If it was rape on their minds, the boys could have had them several times every mile of the way. Why keep climbing? Murder? They were miles into the middle of what seemed to be nowhere. What was wrong with right here? Get it over with, for Christ's sake. The thoughts, fears and possibilities darted through their minds like the strikes of rattlesnakes; swift and painful they came, seeking their prey.

It was chilly, but it was the fear that kept them frozen. Run—and you get shot in the back. Attack—and you get beaten down to the ground. Delay—and they push you harder. Plead—and they laugh. There was no out, but to keep climbing, keep pace, and keep praying.

At one point, Mary looked up and noticed the sky was growing a deep blue and wondered what daylight would bring. It was nearly daybreak, Sunday morning; surely they had been missed by now. She knew her father would already be in contact with the sheriff, and they were out of the trees now, so maybe a helicopter would spot them soon. It was almost daylight; surely the helicopters would come soon.

But then, the verity of her situation became apparent, realizing that no one would have a clue where to look for them. The sheriff would have roadblocks set up and would be searching the highways and sleazy motels, but no one would be looking on an isolated mountaintop! She fell back into despair, passing helplessness on her short journey to hopelessness.

Mary watched the ground as her feet fell upon it, step by step, and mile by mile. When she had the feeling that they could not possibly go higher, she looked up from the ground, and there, before her rose the escarpment. For the first time in nearly eight miles, she felt compelled to speak.

"Wiley, we're not going up there–are we?" she panted, as she pointed a finger to the massive cliff.

"Yes, my dear Mary, that is exactly where we are going," he answered, laughing a bitter laugh. "But don't worry, we prepared a rope hold, just for you, to make your journey more pleasant. You simply hold on tight—and pull. If you let go—you die. It's really very simple," he said, coldly. He did not laugh, and any vestige of a smile had vanished. His face was as stern and hard as a stone statue. His gruesome countenance terrified Mary, but that is exactly what it was intended to do.

Reaching the base of the escarpment, they rested, taking a short breather of ten minutes. Kevin then began showing the girls the knotted rope and explaining its purpose. He demonstrated the proper way to use it, hand over hand, and keeping the body at a right angle to the cliff. He let each of them practice several times, the girls applying his instructions as he continued to coach them.

As for Wiley, he would have none of it, but was glad that Kevin was teaching them to make it to the top. After all, he wasn't done with them yet. They hadn't suffered enough to get off so easy as to fall to their deaths here. But he could not personally bring himself to participate in the training. His hatred for Mary was too deep to communicate anything but that which would make her cower in fear and submission. He would let Kevin handle this necessary delay and exchange of conversation. He had nothing to say at this time.

Kevin had convinced the girls that there was no turning back. They should pay attention and learn what he had to teach them. To do otherwise was to perish right here, at the foot of the cliff, the only question being how far they would fall. They seemed to understand what he was saying and got the hang of it rather quickly. When he was satisfied that they knew enough to make it, he signaled to Wiley and they started up in the same procession as they had traveled the last eight miles.

The climb had grown no easier since the last time the boys were here. If it was tough on them, they knew it was torture for the girls. But the girls did well. There were some close calls, some very close calls, but they hung in there, and kept climbing.

Wiley wondered if curiosity had replaced some of their trepidation, as they actually seemed to be enjoying the climb—*Had they found it to be an adventure, as he and Kevin had on their first ascent? Why not? It was exhilarating. If so,* he thought, *let them enjoy it. It will only make the blackness of the cave a more bitter pill to swallow.*

Kevin climbed to the top, scrambling over the secured end of the rope, and stood, looking out over the bowl below. Alicia and Mary followed his lead and stood beside him.

"Welcome to Short Pines," he announced, sweeping his open hand across the panorama before them. "Welcome to the domain of Sam Elliott!"

The girls were amazed at the sight below them, each even managing a smile. Their smiles were measured, as if they were not sure they should, but couldn't help it for some unknown reason. Mary thought to herself, that in all her life she had never imagined a place such as this could exist. This near perfectly round bowl nestled with exacting symmetry into the side of this geometrically acute mountain peak. It put her in mind of fitting a circle inside a triangle and then rotating the circle forward until it appeared an ellipse. It was that perfect. Why she was thinking in such abstract terms, she hadn't a clue. Perhaps her mind didn't want to believe what her eyes perceived as real. But, reducing it to geometry wasn't helping; it wasn't making it all go away.

The congeniality and tranquility of the moment ended as Wiley appeared over the crest of the escarpment. He looked at the girls standing by Kevin and literally saw red. Blood red.

"What the hell do you think this is, Kevin? A fricking scenic tour? Shove off! We have ground to cover before nightfall! You two bitches, fall in line!" he screamed.

Kevin had seen the look on Wiley's face before. It was frightening to him, and had totally erased any slight ease the girls might have been feeling. Their faces showed fear again, deathly fear.

Kevin had momentarily diverted his attention from the mission. The sight of Short Pines lying before him once again had temporarily distracted him from the purpose for being there. He knew it, and he forced himself to picture Bryce lying limp against the tree. That was the only tool at his disposal with which he could focus hate on the girls who had laid his friend in his grave. It worked, as it had before, and he smiled at Wiley and started down the long saddle into the valley.

Mary and Alicia were glad to be going down hill for the first time since this hellacious day had started. Their legs were tired and rubbery, and their feet were blistered from the rubbing of the oversize boots. What they were not thankful for was Wiley's ever–increasing animosity toward them. He was getting worse with every mile traveled. He had become more belligerent and nasty, less tolerant of their slowing pace, and totally intolerant of any communication among themselves. Mary felt that if she were able to talk with Kevin, perhaps reason with him, the outcome of this journey into a nightmare might come to an equitable ending. Wiley, if left to his chosen path, would surely see them dead.

The unlikely foursome had made their way down to the floor of Short Pines by noon. The girls were requiring more stops, which only served to fuel Wiley's anger and wrath. Kevin was growing uneasy with Wiley's temperament, and with each verbal outburst or physical abuse aimed at Mary, he grew all the more fearful.

His principal fear was that Wiley would try to alter the agreed upon plan, not affording the girls their chance at freedom. They both understood that the girls' successful journey back to civilization would mean jail for them and Kevin was willing to live with that, to take the chance that Sam's justice dictated.

The girls' crime was a crime of stupidity and childlike foolishness. They had not meant to kill Bryce, but their direct action had led to his death. Under those circumstances, they deserved the chance to save themselves, as was agreed upon, and as Sam Elliott would have agreed. Kevin was not sure, however, if Wiley was still of the same mind, or in truth, had ever been. They needed to talk.

As they approached their original campsite, Kevin stopped, turning back to face the others. He looked past the girls to Wiley and suggested that they take a short break.

"The bitches don't need a break! They're fine!" Wiley shouted, grimacing and spitting out the words like venom.

"I need the break, Wiley," Kevin retaliated. "We're stopping!"

Wiley stared straight into Kevin's eyes, fixed on them, like a hawk bearing down on a rabbit. Then, as if the exchange had not taken place at all, his face relaxed and he broke a faint smile.

"Sure, Kev–I didn't know you meant you needed a rest. We'll take five and rest, but only five, we still have a long way to go."

Kevin responded, "Okay," and motioned for the girls to sit. He walked back to Wiley and sat down beside him.

"Wiley–We've got to talk–Now," he began.

"About what?" Wiley asked, pulling a Baby Ruth from his pocket.

"Wiley, I know your tired, hell we're both tired. We've been up over twenty–four hours, but you've got to ease up on the girls a little," Kevin suggested, actually testing the waters.

"Ease up? Why? We didn't bring them up here for a picnic. Scaring the crap out of them is the whole idea, remember?" Wiley replied, seeming quite rational now.

"I know that, but it's the cave and the dark, the fear of being left there that is supposed to do that for us. We're supposed to be cool about it, methodical and deliberate, not showing any emotion. That will keep them off guard. It will keep them guessing about what's on our minds. We discussed all this, remember?"

Kevin paused and awaited a reaction from Wiley.

"I don't know. They're pretty scared now, and I like it. I like watching that bitch squirm," Wiley replied, nodding toward Mary.

"You haven't changed your mind have you?" Kevin probed, addressing his real concern.

"About what?" Wiley questioned.

"About keeping them in the cave for a couple of days and then giving them their chance at freedom. The chance they deserve under Sam's Law," Kevin reminded him.

"Sam's Law? That crap's just in your head, Kev. You don't have a clue what Sam's Law was. You dreamed it all up in your head. Sam probably would have blown them away the first chance he got. That's what Sam's Law would have been!" Wiley said, coldly denouncing Kevin's beliefs.

"Is that what you're planning to do? Blow them away?" Kevin accused, staring directly into Wiley's narrowed eyes. "You're gonna change the rules now that we're up here?"

Wiley stared at Kevin for a moment, saying nothing, then answered.

"No, I like the plan exactly the way it is. They'll never make it out of here on their own. They'll die a slow death up here, wandering around until they die of thirst or exposure. No, Kev, I like the plan just fine, except that I'd like to be able to watch as they realize that they are going to die up here in this forest. I'd like to see it happen," Wiley said, deliberately, but still his face appeared rational. It was relaxed, not twisted and contorted as it sometimes had been.

"So we're okay with the plan then? Nothing's changed?" Kevin probed.

"One thing," Wiley started. "Maybe we could stay up here, out of sight, and watch them. We could trail along parallel their movement, without them knowing we're here, and watch as they whither and die. What about that?" Wiley asked, his face drawing taught again.

"Can't do it, Wiley. We have to stick to our schedule. We have to be back home by Tuesday evening, like we told our folks. We don't know what's going on back in Carver. They know the girls are missing by now. They've probably found Mary's car, too. When they don't come up with their bodies in the river, they'll be questioning everybody who was at the dance. We have our alibi, but we need to be back home when we said we'd be. If the sheriff comes round to question us, our folks are going to tell them about our camping trip and that we'll be back Tuesday night. So that's when we have to be back. That's it," Kevin explained.

Wiley's face relaxed again, and he said, "Yea, you're right. I just wish I could watch, that's all."

"So we're okay with the plan? The whole plan?" Kevin asked, again.

"Yes, we're okay with the whole plan," Wiley answered, mussing Kevin's hair, in a friendly gesture. "I'll ease up a bit, too. I'll play it like you said, and keep them guessing. But let's get going now; I want to be in the cave before dark. I really do need some frickin' sleep."

Kevin couldn't have agreed with Wiley more. He was far past the normal definition of exhausted. He thought back to how Karl used to say—"I'm ten o'clock tired at two." For the first time since hearing that expression, he felt like he truly understood it. The lack of sleep, the tension created by what they were doing, the altitude, and the extreme exertion had all combined to drain him completely. The thought of sleeping sounded so good right now, that he'd welcome a porcupine for a pillow, if he were only allowed to lie down for five minutes.

Kevin reluctantly came to his feet, motioning for Alicia and Mary to stand also, and resumed the lead. The girls fell in behind and they proceeded deeper into the pine forest, Wiley assuming his position at the rear.

The plan called for cutting through the woods to the cave rather than following the curvature of the cliff. The girls would have their chance at survival, but the boys had decided not to make it too easy for them. Following the cliff would give them landmarks to easily retrace their steps, providing them bearings with which they could navigate their way out. They would get their chance, but they would have to be smart to emerge to their freedom, not simply dumb rats following a maze.

The afternoon wore on as they wove their way through the forest of short pines. The boys were numbed by fatigue, drained from the tension. The girls were silent, placing foot before foot in a mechanical march to uncertainty.

Wiley had been true to his word, backing off the girls, neither abusing them verbally, nor butting Mary with his rifle when she stumbled or faltered. Perhaps he had truly come round to Kevin's reasoning, or perhaps he was simply too tired to bother.

Suddenly, Kevin stopped abruptly, craning his neck and sniffing the air. He turned and began jogging back, past Alicia and Mary, toward Wiley, and grabbed Wiley by the arm.

"Do you smell that, Wiley?" he asked.

"Smell what? I don't smell anything," Wiley answered.

Kevin sniffed the air again, but the odor was gone.

"Nothing, I guess. Probably my imagination, but I thought I smelled smoke, that's all."

That comment brought Wiley to full attention. He looked about, trying to fix his position in the valley. He spun around abruptly, facing the northwest, and inhaled deeply through his nose. Nothing. He moved in that direction.

"Kevin, watch the bitches. I'll be right back," he ordered.

He moved off to the northwest, hunched as if stalking prey, stopping occasionally to smell the air. Finally, he disappeared from sight.

"You can sit down for a while until Wiley gets back," Kevin informed girls. "But rest quick, he may not be gone long."

They did not hesitate for a minute, collapsing on the bed of pine needles beneath them. Mary looked up at Kevin through pitiful, reddened eyes, and asked, "Is it okay if we talk to each other, Kevin?"

"I guess so," he answered. "But keep it low and stop as soon as you see Wiley returning. You don't want him going off on you again."

Kevin could smell the odor again now, and it was definitely wood smoke that he smelled. He began to realize what Wiley had picked up on immediately, that they were very near the campsite they had found while searching for Sam's home on their first trip here.

Who the hell could they be—and what the hell were they doing here?

Several minutes passed before he spotted Wiley creeping back from the forest, stopping from time to time to look back over his shoulder. As he approached he put his finger up across his pursed lips, and whispered to Kevin, "That camp's in use–four people–six one–man tents."

"Who are they? Can you tell?" asked Kevin.

"An older guy, maybe thirty or so, and three boys, about our age. Their tents are stenciled 'Reedmore College', wherever that is. Ever heard of it?"

"Yea, it's in Reedmore, about six hours from here," Kevin answered.

"Well, what the hell are they doing here?" Wiley asked, his face growing taught.

"Sounds like a field trip to me. They didn't see you did they?" Kevin asked.

"Hell no! I was careful. They don't know we're here."

"Then maybe we should just head to the cave and bypass them. They'll probably be gone by the time we leave. They're probably just here for today and will be leaving tomorrow."

"Yea–probably, but how the hell did they get here? Where was their car? I didn't see it anywhere along the access road," Wiley questioned. "And I didn't see any signs that anyone had used our rope to climb up here, not a single track or abrasion in the soil anywhere near or around it. Six people would have messed up the ground a lot; I'd have noticed." Wiley said.

"We'll worry about that later, Wiley. For now, let's just bypass them and go to the cave. Once we're in there they will never know we have been here," Kevin suggested.

"We can't worry about it later, Kevin. We have to worry about it, now. Didn't you hear what I said? Six one–man tents, but only four people in camp! There are two more somewhere, whose where-abouts we have no idea of!"

"So what are we supposed to do about that?" Kevin asked. "We can't just sit here and wait for dark to close in on us. We found our way to the cave once in the dark, but we might not be so lucky a second time. I say we move on, quietly, and draw a big circle around them. We can still make it to the cave before dark."

"But what about the other two?" Wiley asked.

"We have to take our chances and hope we don't run into them along the way. That's all we can do," Kevin insisted.

"Okay," Wiley agreed. "Swing to the right a few degrees and we'll give them a wide berth," Wiley instructed.

Kevin went back to where the girls were sitting and instructed them to get to their feet. He then took the lead, heading out in a northeasterly direction to provide plenty of space between them and the Reedmore party.

They had traveled no more than a hundred yards when suddenly; a very large young man appeared before Kevin, not ten yards away.

"Hey! Hello! Who are you guys?" he asked, waving to Kevin.

Kevin was frozen in his tracks and in his ability to respond. The sudden appearance of this young man totally shocked him into complete inaction.

"I'm Joel, from Reedmore College," he greeted, trying to elicit a response from Kevin. "Are you guys up here on some sort of field trip, too?"

Wiley was moving to the front now as Joel spoke. It was obvious that Kevin was dumbfounded and someone had to do some fast-talking. But just as Wiley had reached Kevin and was about to greet Joel, Mary let out a scream, pleading for help.

"We've been kidnapped!" she screamed. "Please help us!"

Joel didn't know what to think. There was total surprise in his face and his first reaction was to back off a step or two. He looked at Mary's tear stained, terrified face, and then at Alicia, who had fallen into a ball on the ground, and he rushed Wiley as the reality of the situation struck home.

He grabbed Wiley before he could even begin to react, and threw him to the ground with incredible force. Joel was big and extremely fast, turning on Kevin all in the same move, and picking Kevin up, dashed him forcefully to the ground. Kevin was stunned and Joel turned back toward Wiley, who was just beginning to regain his feet. Joel swung his booted foot catching Wiley square in the jaw, sending him somersaulting backwards into a tree. As Joel turned back to deal again with Kevin, he found himself staring down the barrel of Kevin's Ruger.

"That's far enough, Joel!" Kevin yelled. "Wiley! Are you all right?"

Joel had frozen in place. He was bigger than the two of these boys put together, but not foolish enough to rush Kevin's gun. He wasn't afraid, but he was not stupid, either. He decided to test Kevin's resolve by feigning a move toward him.

"Click"

Kevin had cocked back the hammer of his .357 magnum and Joel halted again putting his hands up as he backed away a step. It was the classic standoff, Joel not willing to be shot and Kevin not wanting to pull the trigger.

Wiley resolved the situation as Kevin watched Joel's face explode and then heard the sharp crack of Wiley's Winchester. Joel melted to the ground, a pool of blood forming around his head.

"Christ, Wiley! What the hell did you do that for?" he screamed, his screams being nearly drowned out by Mary's wailing.

"What the hell else was I going to do? He would have beat us to a pulp!" Wiley yelled back at Kevin.

Mary's hysteric screaming was cut short as Wiley gave her a swift boot to her stomach. Alicia was still curled up in a ball on the ground, her face buried in her chest.

"What the hell are we going to do now, Wiley? The others will have heard that shot. They'll come to check it out. We've got to move out of here, now!"

Before Kevin could say another word, Craig Moffit, who had been returning to camp also, and had heard the commotion near by, came bounding out of the woods. He tackled Wiley, knocking him to the ground and getting a chokehold on him. Mary began to scream again and Kevin lost it. This was too much.

This is out of control!

As Wiley managed to wriggle free of Craig's chokehold, Craig now preventing his escape by holding onto Wiley's boot, Kevin drew and leveled his Ruger.

"Hey!" Kevin yelled, and Craig looked his way.

The distinct boom of the .357 echoed throughout the valley and Craig twitched once, and then lay motionless.

Mary stopped screaming and fainted on the forest floor. Alicia remained in her cocoon.

"Are you okay, Wiley?" Kevin asked his buddy.

"Yea–okay, but now we attack!" he stated through his twisted gaze. "Neither of these assholes were at the camp, so there are four more of the bastards still there! We aren't going to be surprised again, we attack now!"

Wiley spun on one heel and started in the direction of the campsite and Kevin began to follow him. The bloodletting had begun and there seemed no alternative now but to finish the job.

"It's them or us!" Kevin was thinking.

"Wiley–what about the girls?" he asked.

"They're not going anywhere, and if they wander off we'll track them down soon enough," he answered.

The boys began making their way through the forest toward the camp. They stalked silently, keeping their eyes open for movement and their ears tuned to the forest before them. They each realized that they might be met along the way by the rest of the party coming to investigate the shots they had undoubtedly heard.

As they approached the camp from the concealment of the forest, they were surprised to see all four people still sitting around the campfire. They crept in closer and listened to the conversation. They were discussing the shots they had heard, but seemed to be drawing the conclusion that it had been hunters.

Apparently they aren't too familiar with this valley, Wiley thought when he heard their conclusions. *Nobody hunts up here*—But that was fine with him if that was what they wanted to believe.

Wiley motioned for Kevin to advance on three, holding up three fingers and motioning toward the camp. He then folded his fingers back into his fist and raised just one–then two–and finally–three!

The boys were out of the woods and into the camp before the group had any idea what was happening. Jason Whitley was the first to fall, a casualty of Wiley's Winchester. Kevin took out the other two students with three shots from his Ruger. It was over in just seconds, the only survivor being Stiles Edwards, who lay on the ground staring up into the cold steel of Kevin's pistol. His eyes were filled with terror and he was visibly shaking.

Kevin stared down his barrel at the man's eyes and said, in a cold and calculated voice, "This–is from Sam Elliott."

Kevin thought he noticed some form of recognition in the man's eyes as he had spoken the name. He wanted to ask him if he had known that name, but his hammer had already fallen, and Stiles Edwards, the great–great grandson of Sam Elliott lay dead in his ancestor's forest. Kevin had no way of knowing, but if Sam's ghost had been watching, he may have just fallen from his graces. That could be a serious problem up here in Sam's kingdom.

The two boys stood amidst the destruction they had caused and looked at each other. They were feral.

Kevin looked down at the man he had so callously blown away, and felt nothing. He moved to the next body and studied the young man's face with the same indifference. He didn't even bother to look at his other victim, but walked over to where Wiley was studying his one trophy.

Kevin stared upon the partially covered profile of Jason Whitley and at first there was no recognition. As he continued to look he sensed some familiarity in the line of the boy's jaw and knelt down, taking the boy's chin in his hand and turning his face toward him. Suddenly, he snatched away the boy's sock cap, and trying to stand and jump back simultaneously, fell on his ass and continued scooting back as fast as he could manage. He finally stopped and still sitting, looked up at Wiley with a look of total despair.

"Crap, Wiley!" Kevin screamed, through choking sobs and staring through stinging tears. "I know him!"

"What? What do you mean you know him? Who—How—Kevin?"

"You don't remember him from school?" Kevin asked. "He was a senior when we were freshmen. You don't remember him?"

"No, Kevin, I don't. How do you know him? We never hung out with seniors when we were freshmen."

"He's my dad's best friend's son, Jason Whitley is his name. His dad works with mine at the mill and they are best friends. Crap! How in the hell did we get here, Wiley? How did we do this?"

"We didn't know, Kevin. We just knew that they were going to get us caught, that's all. We had to do it. We did."

Kevin was silent. There was just too much going through his mind right now to think clearly about anything. He stared at Jason and then looked around the camp.

"Wiley, we've got to find a shovel. We've got to bury Jason. We can't just leave him here like this, it's not right."

"Look, Kev. You do what you have to do and I'll go back and watch the bitches. But don't be too long. We're running out of daylight and we still have a ways to go to the cave. Okay?"

Without uttering another word, Wiley left the campsite and went back to retrieve the girls. They were, as they had left them. Mary had regained consciousness, but lay on the pine needles in a fetal position, shaking and whimpering. Alicia showed no change at all from her regression to the cocoon.

Kevin rejoined them within the half hour.

"I couldn't find a shovel, Wiley. I just covered him with pine boughs and said a little prayer."

"That's good, Kev. That's all you could do," Wiley assured him. "You okay now?"

"Yea, I'll be all right. It's just that Jason was a good guy, Wiley, almost a mountain man himself. He knew the names of more trees than even you or I do. He was pretty cool, that's all."

"Sorry, Kev. Just remember, you didn't kill him, I did. That'll be on me for a while because it sounds to me like I'd have liked him. He was just in the wrong place–well, you know."

"Yea, I know," Kevin answered.

Kevin took a minute to reload his Ruger while Wiley got the girls to their feet. Without speaking any other words between them they continued their journey to the cave.

The captors, their prisoners in tow, emerged from the forest. They crossed the open expanse between the forest's edge and the towering mountain above. Wiley stopped to roll over a large log, and from beneath where it had lain, he lifted a ladder and proceeded toward the cliff. The girls watched as he carried it beneath one arm. Kevin could only guess what they might be thinking.

They moved on, over a small rise, and the coal black slit in the gray granite wall, came into view.

CHAPTER 51

There were no cars parked in the Coates' drive when Al and Stan arrived around noon. Al pulled his Scout into the drive, and he and Stan walked up the front walk. Stan rang the doorbell several times, with no response from within, and Al finally stepped in front of Stan and banged on the door with his fist.

"Coates! Coates, are you in there?" Al yelled.

Calvin Coates' drinking had brought him to familiarity with Al, and on more than one occasion. It was never a serious matter. He didn't drive when drinking, and he didn't drink at the bars, where he might have found trouble. Calvin simply liked to go out for a walk when he had polished off a bottle of Mescal. Generally, this would be late in the evening, and Al would receive a call from a neighbor informing him that Calvin was sleeping it off again in their front yard. Al would swing by, or Stan, and escort him back home and through his front door. That was the extent of it. There was never any trouble, or another call–until the next time.

"Calvin Coates! If you're in there, open up!" Al barked.

"Not home, Al," Stan offered. "There're no cars in the drive, either."

"Looks like, but with Calvin you can never be sure if he's home, or just 'sleepin'. Let's try the Reynolds boy's house. We can talk with him in the mean time, and maybe Wiley is over there and we can catch them together."

They boarded the Scout and backed out of the drive onto Mill Street. They covered the two–block drive in no time, and as they approached Kevin's house they saw Buck, climbing into his Bronco.

"Hey, Buck!" Al called out his window, pulling up to the curb. "Kevin home?"

Buck backed down out of his truck and sauntered over to Al's Scout.

"No, Al, he's not. What's up?" Buck asked.

"Buck, we've got a problem. Mary Clemmons and her friend, Alicia Koppe, never made it home from the dance last night. Stan and I are questioning any kids that were at the dance to see if they can help out. Maybe give us an idea or two."

"Gee, Al, that's awful, but maybe they're just off on a lark. You know, before going off to college and all," Buck speculated.

"We found Mary's car in the Saline, Buck. The girls weren't in it and I've a hunch the divers aren't going to find them downstream either."

Al's face became even more serious.

"I need to talk with Kevin and Wiley about what they might know about this."

Buck looked at Al with a look of astonishment, and then said, "You don't think the boys are mixed up in their disappearance do you? Hell, Al, they wouldn't have anything to do with those girls. They never got along. Why would they get involved with them in some crazy scheme?"

"Buck–I think you're missing the point here. We don't believe the girls are off on a lark. We think they are in some serious trouble, and Kevin was seen talking with Mary less than an hour before her car went into the river. Now, we don't pretend to know what's going on, but we are hoping that Kevin can shed some light on the matter. Do you see where I'm coming from, Buck?" Al asked.

Buck didn't say a word. He stood there looking at Al, rubbing the side of his face. After a few seconds he revealed, "They went camping. They were going to leave right after the dance and go camping. They were going to go straight there to save time. Kevin had all his gear and a change of clothes in the car when he left here to pick up Wiley," Buck explained.

"They were going to go camping, at midnight, in the dark. Did I hear you right, Buck?"

"There's a good moon right now, and the boys know that area like the back of their hand. Sure, why not? They're good in the forest."

"What area, Buck? What area did they go to?"

"The west side of Horse Tooth, over by Liddelman. They go there a lot," Buck relinquished, looking confused and worried.

"Say when they'd be back"? Al asked, abruptly.

"Yea, Tuesday night. I gave Kevin Monday and Tuesday off from work. They wanted to have one last good campout before Wiley leaves for Casper," he explained.

"Thanks, Buck, I'll keep you informed," Al yelled back, as he pulled from the curb.

"Where to now?" Stan asked, still trying to keep pace with Al's thinking.

"Liddelman," Al answered. "Get on that radio and call Becky. Ask her to phone the forest service and get the radio frequency for the Liddelman fire tower. I want to talk to whoever's in that tower. Then radio the state boys and ask them to meet us..."

Al pulled abruptly over to the side of the road.

"Hand me that map in the glove box," he said.

Al studied the map and continued.

"Ask them to meet us at the junction of Highway 20 and Forest Access Road 4. Tell them we are going to need four or five men and to bring their hiking boots."

He handed the map back to Stan and pulled back onto the road.

The west side of Horse Tooth was on the opposite side, in relation to Carver, and it took Stan and Al nearly an hour to circumnavigate the mountain and reach Forest Access Road 4. The state troopers were awaiting their arrival by the time they pulled from the highway onto four. Al climbed down from his Scout, followed by Stan, and approached the six troopers, who, judging from the apparel they were wearing, were ready to go.

"What we have here men are two boys out on a camping trip. They are potential witnesses in a missing persons case. They are *not* suspects. The boys don't know we are up here trying to find them, and they are *not* hiding out from us. I want to make this all clear, because I don't want them getting hurt through some misunderstanding. They are *not* dangerous. They will be armed, because they are doing some hunting while up here also, but I repeat, I do not consider them dangerous. Now just bare with me for a minute while I go radio the fire tower and see if we can get a starting point for this search. I'll be right back and then we'll get started."

He turned and started back for the Scout.

"Stan, get Becky on the radio and see if she has that frequency yet."

A few minutes later, Al was in contact with the fire tower, but the ranger on duty had not seen any smoke rising from anywhere on his side of Horse Tooth. Al had hoped that the boys would have a campfire going, but if they did, it wasn't putting off any smoke. He requested that the ranger keep an eye out and radio him on his walkie–talkie band frequency if he saw any sign of a campfire.

Al returned to the waiting troopers and they discussed their plan for the search, fanned out in their prearranged search pattern and began up the west side of Horse Tooth.

It was an exhaustive four–hour search up and down the slopes of Horse Tooth, which yielded not one sign of the boys. The eight men, all experienced in search techniques, were ninety–nine percent sure those boys were nowhere on this side of Horse Tooth. If they had another two hours of daylight, they could be completely sure, but they didn't have it.

Al decided to try to locate Kevin's car. Finding two boys on the side of a very large mountain was one thing, but finding their car should be a lot easier, if it was anywhere around here. Finding the car wouldn't yield the boys, not until they returned to it Tuesday, but if they did locate it they would know that at least they were in the right place. They could than escalate the search operation with hope of positive results.

There were only a few accesses into this area along which to park a car. The troopers had made the drive here in three cars, so counting Al's Scout they had four vehicles with which to search the access roads. This search yielded the same results, no black Biscayne could be found.

By now it had grown completely dark and Al was one hundred percent certain that Wiley and Kevin were not in this area. He thanked the troopers for their assistance, and they departed for other duties. Al radioed the fire tower ranger for one last check, but the ranger informed him that he still had seen nothing. No smoke before dark, and no campfire glow now. Al thanked him for his help, also.

"Stan," Al started. "If those boys are not up here, which I am certain they are not, then they lied to their parents about where they were going. Why would they do that?"

"Because they were really going somewhere they weren't allowed to go?" Stan stated, in question form, not sure if that was the answer Al wanted.

"Yes, that could be one reason. Or, if they are somehow involved with, or responsible for the girls disappearance, they wouldn't want anybody to know where to look for them."

"Just in case it came round to you or I asking their folks where they might be?" Stan stated, again posing his thought as a question.

"That's right, Stan, just in case we did."

"What's our next step then?" Stan asked.

"We get some sleep, that's what. You've been up well over twenty–four hours, and it's been about seventeen for me, and that was on three hours sleep. If I know those boys like I think I do, they're deep in the woods somewhere. The question is where, and we'll never find that out in the dead of night. We'll go home for now and get some shuteye and first thing in the morning we'll visit Judge Jackson. We'll also add Kevin's Biscayne to the all points we issued for the girls, just in case they are moving by night, but I don't think so. If they've got those girls, Stan, they'll be in the woods where they are comfortable, and feel safe."

"Trouble is, Sheriff, there's nothing *but* woods around here."

Stan had hit the nail square on the head.

Monday morning arrived too soon. Al awoke, feeling like he had just laid his head on the pillow. He dressed, ate a quick breakfast of toaster waffles and jam, and stepped outside. He was greeted by a blast of bitter cold air and densely falling snow.

What the hell—He had just watched the weather forecast on the television before retiring last night. There had been no mention of a change in the weather, certainly not this drastic a change—*Where the hell did this come from?* He cleared the snow from the windshield of his Scout and headed for the station house.

Stan was waiting in the parking lot when Al arrived. He motioned for Stan to come get in the Scout.

"Where'd this weather come from?" he asked Al.

"Damned if I know, but we better take my Scout. If it keeps coming down like this we are going to need it, and then some."

"Are we still going by to see Judge Jackson?" Stan asked.

"Yes, we are," Al, answered.

"Are we going by there to get a search warrant for Wiley's room?"

"Yes, and for Kevin's. I'm hoping they may have left something that might give us an idea of where to look for them. I think the judge will issue the warrant after we tell him what we know so far," Al explained.

"Why not just ask their parents if we can have a look? They might agree to it if we explain what's going on."

"Those boys are eighteen now; adults. I'm not clear on their legal rights in a matter like this. It's their folks' homes we are talking about, but it's the boys' rooms we need to search. I don't want any technicalities getting in the way, down the road."

Judge Jackson listened closely while Al laid out the case before him. Judge Jackson agreed that Al's reasoning was sound, but complained that everything he had was very circumstantial. Kevin could have been talking to Mary about anything. Nobody had heard what he or she had said to one another. The girls' car went into the river at ten o'clock, but the boys were at the dance until midnight. Where were the girls for those two hours, obviously not with those boys? They may have lied to their parents, or simply changed their minds about where they would camp. They were boys, after all, prone to doing boyish things.

When it was all said and done, the judge simply couldn't see his way to issuing the warrants. Stan and Al were back to square one.

"Now what, Sheriff?" Stan asked.

Al gave it some more thought and replied, "I don't know for sure, Stan. I just don't know."

"What about a helicopter? Do an aerial search for the car?" Stan suggested.

"I thought about that Stan, and it would be like looking for a needle in a haystack. Even if we got lucky, and flew right over it, I doubt we'd see it. If the boys are up to no good, they'll have it well hidden in the trees, or covered with brush. Think about it, Stan. If we're right about all we put together so far, and Wiley and Kevin have those girls someplace, they did a lot of planning for this. That car won't be sitting out in an open field for the world to see. You can bet your mama's boots on that."

Al suggested they go back to the station and look over a map of the entire area. Try to put themselves in the boys' shoes and try to determine where they might have chosen to go.

"If we can narrow it down to a few locations, maybe we can do some good," he said. "At least that's worth a try."

Stan agreed that it was about all they could do for the moment. That, and check back in with the state boys to see if they had any ideas. What was nagging at Stan, and the sheriff too, was *why* the boys would do this. Sure, they didn't get along with Mary or Alicia, but why go to this extent, kidnapping and who knows what else, to get at them. It just didn't make sense.

What finally turned the light on for Stan was when he retrieved something that was rattling around the back of his head, and brought it forward. He was trying to think of any friends the boys might have that they may have confided in, or hinted to about all this. The only name that kept coming to mind was Bryce, and he was dead.

He pictured Bryce all crumpled against that fir tree. Then he thought about the circumstances of his death. He pictured the pine tree with the rope scars on it. His mind's eye turned to look across the slope and he saw the tracks in the snow. Two sets of tracks...

"Two sets of tracks, Al!" he said excitedly, looking up from the map spread on the desk. "Two sets!"

"What?" Al asked, looking totally bewildered.

"Two sets, Al, Mary and Alicia! Wiley and Kevin saw them up there with the rope. That's what this is all about! It was Mary and Alicia up there that day, and the boys saw them. They lied about the fox, they lied about the rope fence, and they lied about not seeing anyone up there! They probably even got rid of the rope!"

Al looked at Stan with his mouth agape. He was thinking about what Stan was saying, and it was getting clearer by the second.

"They decided–right up on that mountain–that morning–before we ever talked with them—that they were going to handle those girls themselves," Al said. "Is that what you're thinking, Stan?"

"Sure," Stan responded. "They had just seen their best friend killed and they saw who did it. Word is those girls gave them hell their whole lives. What they saw happen to Bryce was like the last straw. They decided, right then and there, that *they* were going to get even. That's why this was so thoroughly planned out. They've been planning it for ten months."

Al thought for a minute, and then asked, "What was that, Stan? What was that last thing you said?"

"They've been planning it for ten months? You mean that?" Stan asked.

"Too long, Stan. That's too long to wait, and they didn't need ten months to come up with this plan. I think they'd have wanted to get even much more quickly. Ten months is a long time to hold all that hate together, and not have second thoughts about it. They'd have planned it much sooner. What stopped them?" Al asked, as much of himself as Stan.

"Maybe winter," Stan suggested. "It was a bad winter. If their plan called for going up in the mountains with the girls, this past winter would likely have stopped them."

"So winter wasn't practical for their plans. What was wrong with June or July? That would have been perfect for them. Why the hell wait until late September?" Al asked.

"Wiley was laid up all summer, Al. I heard talk of it down at Laura's one day. He took a bad fall up in the mountains and nearly died, you know."

"Damn. That's right! I did hear about that. Did they say where it happened?" Al asked.

"No, sir. They just said it was up in the mountains. Didn't say where."

"You know, Stan. It's a long shot, but it's all we've got right now. Maybe Wiley's fall happened while they were up in the mountains making preparations for taking the girls, or scouting a place to hide them out. Maybe we need to find out where this fall took place. I think we need to have another word with Buck Reynolds!"

CHAPTER 52

*M*ary closed her eyes, and then opened them. It made no difference. This cave they had entered was the blackest place she
had ever been, and she couldn't even see Alicia in front of her. She
reached out to touch her. Her hand found Alicia's back and although
she had known she was there, the confirmation was comforting.

Wiley had gone in first carrying his ladder and Kevin was now in
the rear. She had thoughts of turning back to him and pleading with
him for their release, but she knew Wiley would hear and that
thought terrified her. She could hear clearly, what she had come to
realize, was the ladder bumping the walls of this place. She in turn
knew Wiley would hear any attempt she made at seeking Kevin's
compassion. She walked on in silence, stooping to avoid contact with
whatever she could not see above her.

Mary had noticed, before entering the cave that Alicia had
changed completely over the course of their trek. She had been
whimpering and crying at the outset, but as they traveled the last few
miles to this spot, she had fallen deathly silent, and expressionless.

She had smiled at Alicia in an attempt to reassure her, but her gesture had elicited no response. Alicia's visage had remained blank. She
had not even blinked, but had stared right past Mary as if transfixed
on some distant object or specter. Mary remembered fearing that
Alicia had withdrawn into some sheltered world of her own. Her

concern had been, and was currently, that if they emerged safe from this reality, would Alicia be able to return from hers. It was a question Mary had no answer for.

It was funny, Mary thought, that she should take comfort in the increasing warmth of this darkness. She had noticed, as they proceeded from outside to within, that the temperature had risen to an almost comfortable level. Outside, although not freezing, it was quite chilly. In here, on the other hand, it was warm by comparison, yet dank and stuffy. What little comfort this new warmth provided however, was simultaneously expelled by their passage into the unknown blackness of the mountain.

Mary's progress was abruptly stopped as she collided into the back of Alicia, who had stopped her forward movement completely. Mary listened and could hear the ladder knocking and clunking on the walls with far more activity than before.

The boys had flashlights, she had seen them, but they had not used them as they had worked their way into this place. She found that peculiar, and surmised that they knew exactly where they were going, probably from previous experience. She listened and heard what sounded like someone climbing the ladder.

Wiley's going up, she thought—*Or down?*

Kevin must have read the audible sound, too, for he spoke for the first time since entering this hole.

"Mary, tell Alicia to move forward, locate the ladder and climb. You follow her."

Mary did as she was told and Alicia responded. She could hear Alicia scaling the ladder, then indiscernible sounds moving away and fading to nothing. She started climbing herself, and upon reaching the top she felt out in front of her, but her hand found nothing. She froze there, not knowing what to do.

Kevin's voice rose up from below.

"Just wait there, Mary, and Wiley will be back in a minute. He's helping Alicia over the other side now."

That, in itself, sounded ominous to Mary.

The other side of what, she wondered?

She didn't like the sound of it, although she had no idea of what Kevin was talking about. "The other side" had connotations that she'd rather not think about, and she wasn't sure why she had. She hoped only that it wasn't a premonition. She stood there, perched on the top of the ladder and staring into pure blackness, and for the first time her own mind visited another reality.

It was the reality of what had happened along the trail to this place. She had no idea of what had happened when the boys had left them for that short while, but she did know what she had seen with her own eyes, and it terrified her. This misadventure had turned a new page in its seriousness. She had imagined all sorts of things the boys might to do Alicia and her, but now she had a visual to consider. She had witnessed the brutal murders of two boys at the hands of Kevin and Wiley, and this petrified her.

She hadn't much time to consider this though, as Wiley's voice brought her back to the here and now.

"Mary, your turn," he said sternly.

My turn for what? And then following Wiley's instructions, entered yet another passage; one in which crawling was the only way to negotiate the length of it. Finally, after feeling that the space was about to close in around her, Wiley helped her onto another ladder.

This time, they went down, and "down" had another connotation that worried her, but then again, *We're already in Hell, aren't we?*

Mary heard Kevin come down the ladder behind her. They were all down here now, but where? There was nothing but deep ebony blackness all around. She put her arms out, slowly, and they found no barrier. She had the impression they were in a larger area than they had previously been. That was of little comfort to her, but then a little was better than none at all. She heard a faint "click" and saw light for the first time since entering this subterranean world. Wiley had turned on his flashlight and was walking away from them. The light from the beam was not sufficient to tell her much about their surroundings, but it was light, blessed light.

Kevin indicated that the girls should follow, and they all moved off in the direction Wiley had gone. When he came back into view in Kevin's light beam, he was filling a lantern from an old metal can, his flashlight lying nearby to illuminate the procedure. Kevin stepped up and raised the glass globe, as Wiley had finished the filling and was now striking a match.

Yellow light began filling the massive room; so large that the light melted away before reaching any boundary she could detect before her. Mary turned and looked to her rear. The light did reach the end of the room in that direction, and she could now see where they had come from. She saw the ladder she had just descended rising up to a black hole, high on the wall. Although she was as far from comfortable as she could ever imagine being, actually *seeing* where she was, and had been, was of some small measure of comfort. It was at least something to anchor her fears to.

She remembered, as a child, she had never been afraid of the dark. It was what might be lurking in the darkness that had terrified her so. Now, at least, she could see what demons might approach her in this most terrible of places. She sat in the gray powder of the floor, without being instructed to do so and began to weep. Alicia, responsive for the first time in hours, sat down alongside her, placing her arm around Mary's shoulders. She smiled at Mary and gently rubbed her arm.

Wiley walked back and retrieved the ladder from the opening. Without speaking a word, he stooped and picked up the oilcan and began moving deeper into the room, the ladder under one arm and the oilcan hanging from the other.

Kevin told the girls to stand and follow Wiley, which they did, deeper into this mysterious and awful place they had been spirited away to. After they had traveled a short distance, Mary watched as

Kevin and Wiley lit another lantern illuminating still more of this expanding cavern.

Kevin then told the girls to have a seat and walked over to Wiley, who seemed to be engaged in deep thought.

"Hey, Wiley, I'm beat! I mean I am *really* beat! We've got to get some sleep. We've been up since Saturday morning!"

"I know. I don't think I've *ever* been up for thirty–six straight hours before in my entire life! I'm bushed too," Wiley finished, stretching his arms and yawning at the thought.

"The girls are wiped out, too. Do you think if we tell them to get some sleep now, that they'll stay down while we do?" Kevin asked Wiley.

"Probably. If we wait 'til they're out they probably would, but it's too risky. The way I see it, the only safe thing to do is put them down with Sam and pull up the ladder. That way *we* can rest in peace, so to speak."

Wiley waited for the argument to begin.

"Wiley–You know how I feel about that, but right now I am too damn tired to argue about it. I just want some sleep," Kevin replied, much to Wiley's surprise.

Wiley had expected an all out fight, but it didn't come. He understood though, because he was so damn tired that if Kevin had argued, he would have agreed to try it his way.

The truth though, which Kevin wasn't willing to share, was that it wasn't exhaustion that kept him from fighting on this point. It was disillusionment. This valley, which he had come to consider sacred over the time since they had first discovered it, had now turned into an Armageddon of their own creation.

"Wiley–What are we going to do about those people we killed back there?" Kevin asked, as a tear ran down his cheek.

"There's nothing to do, Kevin, except hide their bodies and possessions on our way out," Wiley stated, bluntly.

"I don't think I can go back there, Wiley, I really don't think I can."

"I'll need your help, Kev. I can't do it alone," Wiley pointed out.

"But we killed them. They were just up here–on a field trip–that one big guy, Joel, said, and we killed them!"

"Kevin, it was them or us. Kidnapping is a capital offense. That means that if we had let them rescue the bitches, we go to the gas chamber! It was them or us!" Wiley said, trying to convince Kevin that they had been left with no other alternative.

"Gas chamber? You *knew* that before we started this? I thought you said we would go to jail if the girls make it back, not the gas chamber! You knew that? You never mentioned that before!" Kevin rambled, quite worried over this new development.

I didn't mention it because I just thought of it, a little while ago, after we left their camp. I really never gave it any thought before, because I don't believe the bitches will find their way back. I don't now, and I never did. You're the one who seems to think they have a chance, not me," Wiley explained.

"But–the gas chamber, Wiley. I don't know about that," Kevin said.

"Well, it's too late to worry about that now, Kev. What's done is done. If the bitches don't make it back, and they won't, we'll still be okay. When they finally find that group from Reedmore, there will be no way to connect them to us. Nobody will ever know we were ever up here," Wiley said, trying to alleviate Kevin's fears, and truthfully, his own.

Okay, Wiley, we'll talk about it more in the morning. Right now, I just want to sleep. Go ahead and put the girls down with Sam. I don't care anymore, anyway," Kevin admitted.

Wiley smiled at Kevin and patted him on the arm, and then picked up the ladder and the oilcan and walked toward Sam's home. Kevin herded the girls toward Sam's dwelling, following in Wiley's wake. When they reached the opening, Wiley put the ladder in place and climbed down with the oilcan, emerging a few minutes later. Darkness still emanated from the hole. He looked at Mary and smiled, something she had never seen on Wiley's face since this whole ordeal had begun.

He tossed her a tin of matches and said, "You girls will be spending the night with our friend Sam. He's a mountain man and a buffalo hunter, so treat him with respect. There's a lantern down there if you're afraid of the dark."

Mary was totally confused, and couldn't put reason to what Wiley was saying.

What the hell is he talking about? Mountain man and buffalo hunter? Sam?

Wiley motioned for the girls to start descending the ladder, Mary first, then Alicia. When they were free of the ladder, Wiley pulled it up.

"Come on, Kev, let's roll out our bags," he said.

The boys spread out their bags and slipped into them. They lay down on their sides; heads perched on the palms of their hands, elbow to ground, and facing the entrance to Sam's home. A few moments later they saw the glow of the lantern shine from the portal. Then they heard the screams.

"Meet Sam, ladies," Wiley snickered, as the screams slowly subsided.

"Good night, Kevin."

"You, too, Wiley," Kevin replied.

CHAPTER 53

$\mathcal{M}$onday, *Day Two* was wasting away, and Al knew it. He had no more idea of what Wiley and Kevin had planned, than he knew where to look for them. What he did know was that time was precious, and it might be running out for Mary and her friend. Deep down, he hoped that the boys planned to do nothing more than give the girls a good scare. But if that were the case, why get a kidnapping charge thrown at them? He felt their plans went beyond simply frightening them and going to the chamber for having done it. If they had planned this as well as it appeared they had, the plan would include a way to get away with it. Al could see that happening, only if the girls were to disappear—forever, with no apparent or *provable* link to the boys!

He pulled the Scout into the front lot at Cutter's Mill, exited the vehicle and began looking around.

"Stan, do you know where Buck works here?" he asked.

Cutter's Mill was a big place, perhaps ten acres, with multiple buildings, mountains of cut timber, stacks of finished lumber, and roadways running every which a way. It was hard to know where to begin looking for Buck.

"No, Sheriff, I have no idea, except that he's a foreman, I believe."

Al spotted a lumberman crossing the main parking lot and hailed him.

"Looking for Buck Reynolds. Any idea where we might find him?" Al called from a distance. The worker looked at his watch and then addressed Al.

"Probably on lunch break about now," was his reply. "Building 'C', it's marked plain enough. It's the third building down the main lane in, on the right. Can't miss it," he finished.

Al was already on his way, followed by Stan, as he yelled back, "Thanks!"

The rough hewn wooden structure was clearly marked with a large letter "C", painted black on a white sign board and nailed to the end wall.

The lawmen entered the building to find rows of wooden tables, filled with lumbermen enjoying their noon break and discussing every topic from the upcoming World Series to the weather.

Al perused the faces of the workers, and finally located Buck, who in turn had apparently just seen Stan and him. Buck rose and began toward them as they walked toward Buck. Meeting somewhere in between, they sat on a vacant bench and talked.

"Hi, Buck. Sorry to bother you at work and all, but we need some additional information," Al started.

"Sure, Sheriff, is there anything new on the missing girls? Did you find Kevin up on Horse Tooth? What did he have to say?" Buck rambled.

Al cut him off before he could get in another question.

"Nothing new on the girls, but Kevin and Wiley were not up on Horse Tooth, of that we're certain," Al replied.

Buck looked dumbfounded.

"Well—Where could they be then?" he asked, genuinely surprised at Al's comment and becoming somewhat confused by this revelation.

"We don't know, Buck, and that's what we need your help with. Wiley had a bad fall last spring, which laid him up all summer. Stan and I were wondering if you knew where that fall occurred?"

"Yea, Kevin said it happened on Oriel Peak, just below the escarpment into Blind Valley. Why?"

"We're just working on a theory, Buck, trying to play out a hunch is all. I'll get back to you on it when I know more. Thanks again for your help," Al said, as he rose from the bench.

Buck stood also and said, "Sure, Sheriff–please do. If I hear from Kevin I'll let you know."

On the way back to the station, Al discussed the Oriel Peak area with Stan. That was some rugged country up there, and very seldom visited by anyone. Oriel Peak was centrally located in a thirty mile square area, about nine hundred square miles of nothing. There were no roads through it, no fire towers, no fishing lakes, absolutely nothing but forest and mountains. It was about as much a wilderness as was left in these parts.

"Stan, get on the phone and call the state. Get as many troopers as they can spare. I don't want to try to search that area with just a handful of us this time. Call the county also, and see if they can help out with a few men. I also want our life squad personnel up there and a couple of ambulances. See if you can pull a second unit from somewhere, maybe Liddelman."

Al went back to looking at his area map. The Oriel Peak area was huge, but Buck having pinpointed the area of Wiley's accident as below the climb into Blind Valley, at least narrowed it down to which side of the peak. Al was studying that side of the mountain on his map with intense scrutiny.

"Stan, look at this. Highway 77 takes you right near the base of Oriel. There's a little unpaved road off of it that goes right up near the foot of Oriel, and it's below the escarpment."

"What's the road number," Stan asked.

"It doesn't seem to have one," Al replied. "But, it's the only one in that area."

Al checked the scale on the map's legend, and reached for his ruler.

"From the end of that road, to the base of the escarpment, is seven point five miles, as the crow flies. That's as close as you get on wheels. From there, it's a pretty steep hike up to the base of the cliff."

Al looked up at Stan, who had come over to see what he was referring to.

"It does look like that would be the logical jumping off point," Stan said. "Is that where you want me to tell everybody to assemble?"

"Yes, and I want them there as soon as possible. We won't be able to get this all put together before dark, but I want them there so we can get started at first light, tomorrow morning. And tell everybody to dress warm, bring tents, and their gas heaters. It's gotten pretty darn bitter out there, and I imagine it will get a lot colder tonight."

Stan looked at the map again and pointed to something that caught his eye.

What's this little marking mean? Is that a road, or just a trail? It looks like it goes much closer to the escarpment than does that access road," Stan pointed out.

"Hold on, I'll check the legend," Al said, moving his finger to that area of the map and locating the matching key. "Ah–here it is. That indicates four–wheel drive access only."

"It sure gets us closer to where we want to be," Stan remarked.

"It gets my Scout closer, but the ambulances and police cruisers won't be able to use it, especially in all this new snow we've gotten. I also doubt that Kevin could have gotten his Biscayne up there. You and I can check it out on our way up, but let's have everyone meet us at the end of that graded access road," Al decided.

Stan turned and started to walk away to make the calls.

"One more thing, Stan," Al stopped him.

"Yes, sir?"

"If the snow lets up enough, I want a helicopter hovering over us at sunrise. We're going to need every advantage we can get. See if you can arrange that, too."

About an hour later, Stan reported back to Al. He had good news and not so good news, but nothing really bad.

"Sheriff, I've got it all arranged. The state is sending sixteen men, but we have to pay their overtime. I told Masters that if they found Mary Clemmons safe and alive, her daddy would probably pay them triple time. He liked that idea. Got hold of Simkins at the county and he is sending six of his men. I've got our ambulance and life squad coming, and the one from Liddelman. I told them all to think like Eskimos and dress accordingly, and to try to be there before nightfall today."

"And what about the whirlybird?" Al asked.

"I talked with the chopper pilot at Bennett and he checked his weather reports. He says he can't fly in this mess, but the front is supposed to move out of that area by about eleven a.m., and he'll be there right behind it."

"Good, Stan. Give him a call back and ask him to start searching up high on the peak, then work his way down our side, to the tree line. There's no sense in having him search over the trees, we can take care of that from the ground."

Al looked at his watch. He wondered why an hour could go by so fast, at a time like this, and could go so slow when you had nothing to do.

Time—We are either running out of it, running short on it, or never had enough in the first place, he thought.

"After you make that call, Stan, we'll swing by your place and pick up your winter gear. Mine's already in the back of the Scout," Al continued.

"Then are we going up to Oriel?" Stan asked.

"Then we are going up to Oriel. We should be able to make it there well before dark ourselves, and have a look around. We'll check out that four–wheel drive road first and then move on to the access road. Maybe we can find something that will tell us that tomorrow isn't going to be another big waste of time and manpower. I have a feeling it won't be, but it would be nice to know ahead of time that we are finally looking in the right place."

The drive out 77 was tricky, as apparently this unpredicted storm had caught the county road crews by surprise also. Al located the small four–wheel drive road, after passing it by once, and nearly passing it by a second time on the return. He pulled his Scout off Highway 77 and onto the small road, which with all the new snow was only visible as a cut through the trees. The road immediately went up ahead of them at an angle that would have been a good test of his vehicle on dry ground.

"There's no way we're going up there, Stan," Al commented, shaking his head and studying the incline before him. "The boys came up here before all this snow, but still, there is no way Kevin got his Biscayne up that road even then. Let's back out of here and go meet up with the others."

They backed out onto the highway and drove to the snow covered dirt and gravel road that had been indicated on Al's map. There was still enough daylight for at least an hour's search, which Al intended to use to try to locate Kevin's black Biscayne. The one thing he knew for sure was that the Chevy would not be able to get too far a field. It would be somewhere near the road, and probably at the end of the road, as that would get them the closest to Oriel as you could get before being forced to hike.

They continued to follow the road, up and up, into the forest. Al was glad for his four–wheel drive, and hoped the others would not have too much trouble joining them. The snow was pretty deep, even for this side of the range, and it was still coming down.

Upon reaching the end of the road, he pulled his Scout to the side, and he and Stan climbed down into the snow and looked around the area. Al seemed to stop and make a mental note of something a few times, then, he said to Stan, "I see only three places where the trees are far enough apart to get a Biscayne off the road."

Stan agreed and they hiked into the woods as far as they could go, walking between the widest spaced trees, until there was no further a car could have gone. The woods had closed in around them on all sides.

"Dead end," Stan said.

They returned to the road, backtracking their leg holes in the snow.

They selected a second point to try, but this time, they would wear their snowshoes. The snow had turned out to be deeper, and less firm, than they had initially thought.

If it had not snowed though, it may have blended in with the background colors of the forest, and may have never been noticed. As they crested a small rise and looked downward, Stan spotted what appeared to be a dark green tent sitting on the snow. They turned directly for it and drawing closer it became apparent that it was not a tent, but pine tree boughs forming a tent–like structure. They began removing the boughs, one by one, and there, neatly tucked away was a 1960 black Chevrolet Biscayne.

Stan let out a "Whooop!" and Al patted him on the back and said, "Good find!"

Al studied the gray stems of the cut boughs.

"Stan, those boys sure did do some preparation for this."

"How's that, Al?" he asked.

"These cuts were made at least two weeks ago, maybe longer. They must have made more than one trip up here, preparing for Saturday night. But why here? Where in sam hill are they going to go up here? There's no shelter, no water, no nothing! It just makes no sense!"

Stan picked up one of the branches and studied it. The sheriff was right again. The cuts were definitely not fresh, having turned gray and beginning to crack. He gave the branch a good shake and needles covered the snow at his feet, as they fell from the limb.

"You're right, Al. They're not fresh cut at all."

On their way back to the road, they were relieved that they now knew they would not be wasting their time, or that of the help they had coming. Perhaps tomorrow would prove to be the end of all this. Each man made a silent prayer to himself, asking that the outcome be favorable. It was a moment of hope and uplifting for them both, but one of melancholy, too.

When they reached the road, they saw that the first of their search and rescue team had arrived. They explained to them what they had found, and to each in succession as they arrived. Everyone went about pitching tents, cutting firewood, and preparing for the morning, and nightfall slid in as they were nearing the completion of their tasks.

The tents were pitched in a circle, with a large campfire blazing in the center. The men formed a circle around the fire, sitting on their campstools, or packs, and discussed the strategy for Tuesday's search. When the decisions were all made, and the plan understood by all, they retired to their tents for a good night's sleep. To every man, they agreed that they would need it.

CHAPTER 54

$\mathcal{A}$s always seemed to be the case, Kevin awakened first, and just as before, all concept of time was lost. He looked at his Timex to get a handle on it and discovered that he had slept over twelve hours. Although he rarely ever slept that long, it didn't surprise him upon this occasion at all, remembering *well* how he had felt before retiring. He rolled over in his bag and saw Wiley, still fast asleep, and the ladder beyond him. The sight of the ladder brought to mind, for the first time this morning, the girls, down in Sam's house. His second thought was of their screams when they had lighted the lantern and become acquainted with Sam Elliott.

This was not supposed to happen, he thought to himself. *I should never have let Wiley talk me into that.*

But, things had changed and what was done was done. He didn't feel like dwelling on it. Their safety and the need to secure the girls, warranted Wiley's decision to confine them someplace, he rationalized, and Sam's home was the only place where that could be accomplished. Besides, this place, this whole valley, no longer held the magic it had before. He couldn't help but see the look in the man's eyes as he spoke the name Sam Elliott. His eyes had momentarily, for the briefest of moments, lost their look of fear and had changed to a look of recognition, yet bewilderment. *What had that been all about,* he wondered? Was it just his imagination, or had the name meant something to him? Kevin was sorry now that he would never know the answer to that question.

Kevin was trying to enjoy the solitude of the cave and the time it afforded him to try to sort things out. He was in no hurry to awaken Wiley. He lay there, snuggled in his mummy bag, thinking about what the day might bring. It was Monday morning, and he wondered what plans Wiley had for the torment of the girls today.

The plan called for making them fetch and tote water from the stream and making references to the fact that they had enough food to last for several days. Then they would drop their first bomb, making reference to having to go hunting in order to stay longer. The idea was to make the girls believe that they were stuck here with them, for an indeterminate period of time, toting water and doing their cooking. Then they would start with the conversations, intended to be overheard, discussing which boy wanted which girl, for *himself*. The dialogue had been prearranged, as if in a play, and was laced with sexual innuendo. The goal here, of course, was to lead them to believe they would become sex slaves to the two men they despised most in their lives. They would play out the charade for the entire day, leading the girls to believe that this had become their lives for as long as the boys wanted them, perhaps forever. The final conversation would reveal the reason why all this was happening to them.

"*They never should have messed with Bryce,*" would be the coup de grace. Perhaps they will have figured that out by then anyway, but it didn't really matter. They would go to bed Monday night, with Sam Elliott's bones, believing that they were trapped for all time in a terrible nightmare, and all because they just had to mess with Bryce.

When they would awake Tuesday morning, they would awake to pitch blackness, their lantern having run dry, alone and with no hope for escape. They would fumble in the dark and discover the ladder, back in place for their exit from Sam's home. They would climb it, only to find more blackness. They would call out our names, "Wiley!"—"Kevin!" but there would be no response. They would come to realize slowly, that they had been abandoned in the black of the cave.

Panic would set in at first, but then they would eventually get their wits about them and pull up the ladder. They would decide which way they should go to find the passage by which they had entered. If they chose the right direction, and didn't waste too much time, they would eventually spot Wiley's flashlight, lit and pointing the way to the hole in the wall. If they took too long, going in the wrong direction, too many times, the fresh batteries they had put in the light would eventually die out. If that happened, they may never leave the cavern, becoming permanent residents and sleeping with Sam Elliott for eternity.

But, if they made the right choices, and found the light burning, they would see the opening and put their ladder to it. They would climb to the passage and through it, finding the other ladder still in place where he and Wiley had left it. They would climb down that ladder and follow the slit to daylight.

Emerging from the opening, they would head for the woods from which they had come, not knowing that the sure way home was to follow the cliff around to the saddle. If they were very lucky they would find their way through the forest of Short Pines. It wasn't likely they would though. They would probably become disoriented and walk in circles until they became dehydrated and dropped.

If they did make it to the saddle and managed to climb to the top, the escarpment awaited them. In their weakened and exhausted state, they would probably fall to their deaths or serious injury, as Wiley had done. Unable to travel they would perish there, at the foot of the cliff.

Kevin rolled to his side and something jabbed him in the hip. He reached down and realized that he had been so tired before retiring, that he had forgotten to remove his gun belt. He rolled back and reached out to touch Wiley. Several pokes later, Wiley yawned and said, "Morning, Kev. What time is it?"

"Eight o'clock. Time to get started," Kevin answered.

"Can I have five more minutes? Just five? I never slept so good in my life."

"Sure, but then we get started. We have only today to set their frame of mind, to make them begin paying for Bryce. We have to squeeze as much torment into the next ten or twelve hours as we can," Kevin replied, getting into the part of the plan he liked best. For Kevin, the plan had lost some of its appeal with the events of yesterday fresh in his mind, but once again he pictured Bryce's body lying lifeless in the snow.

"We have to deliver Bryce's justice, then go to bed, and awake to deliver Sam's," Kevin, said, through a shallow grin.

Wiley finally squirmed out of his sack, and stood. He stretched and yawned, declaring, "It's going to be a good day!"

He walked over to the entrance to Sam's house and lowered the ladder. Bending forward, he yelled down the hole, "Rise and shine, bitches!"

He turned to Kevin and smiled. There was no reply from the hole.

He leaned forward again and yelled, "Get the hell up here bitches! *Don't* make me come down there and get you!"

Again, he smiled at Kevin, this time raising the palms of his hands at his sides, as if to say, "*Who knows?*"

"One last chance bitches! Get up here!"

A long, silent moment passed.

"I guess I'll have to go down and get the bitches. Now, I'm getting pissed!" he said to Kevin, his face starting to twist. He turned and stepped onto the ladder, descending.

Kevin watched as Wiley disappeared into the hole.

Boy, they're gonna get it now, he thought. *Wiley's pissed!*

Kevin barely had time to complete that thought before he heard the loud roaring explosion erupt from below. His mind swam. He had recognized it for what it was.

"The Sharps!" he screamed.

He bolted for the ladder, and leaped onto it, climbing down as fast as he could. At the bottom he saw Wiley, sliding down the wall, his chest torn open and painting a crimson stripe on the dark granite as he slumped slowly to the ground. Through the clearing blue smoke he saw Mary, not Bryce, as he had in his dream, sitting on the floor next to Sam's bed and pointing the still smoking Sharps straight at him.

Kevin slowly reached down and removed the thong from his Ruger's hammer, and then drawing the pistol from its holster, he leveled it before him. Looking down the barrel, Mary's eyes came into focus. The only sound he heard was the sound of Mary cocking back the hammer of the Sharps.

"It only holds one cartridge," he said to Mary, in a dry and emotionless voice.

He cocked back his own hammer, and looking down the barrel at Mary's terrified blue eyes, one last time, he squeezed the trigger.

The Ruger leapt in his hand, and when it settled back he saw Mary, lifeless on the floor, the Sharps across her chest. He slowly panned to Alicia, who was cowering in the entrance to the lower level. He looked down the barrel once again; placing it between her closed brown eyes and cocked back the hammer once again.

As he slowly applied pressure to the trigger, he heard a voice. He was confused and relaxed his finger, for it wasn't Alicia, nor Wiley or Mary that he had heard speak. It was a man's voice and it had said, *"Enough"*. He lowered the pistol, ever so slightly and turned to Sam Elliott's corpse.

"Enough, mountain man. You've eked out your revenge and it is enough. In doing so you have laid waste to my seed. Leave this place while you are still able, for I have sent you a storm to test your metal."

Kevin lowered the hammer and dropped his Ruger to the ground. He was numb. Had Sam just spoken to him? The image of the man's eyes in the camp flashed before him, like a movie. It wasn't simply in his mind, like a mere thought! He was actually seeing it all over again, the recognition in the man's eyes as he spoke Sam's name. His lifeless body sprawled on the ground in a growing pool of blood. As he watched, terrified and in shock, snow began to cover the man's body, heavy snow. And then, through some strange and inexplicable phenomenon, he *knew* what it all meant!

He felt as though a heavy weight had been lifted from him, but another weight of immense proportions had replaced it. Bryce was gone and now Wiley lay dead in this God forsaken place. He had just done what he had never imagined he could ever do; murder a girl. And there sat Alicia, terrified beyond all possible belief, guilty of no more than following Mary around like a stupid puppy.

The voice, whomever or wherever it had come from, was right. It was *enough*. It was too much. He looked at Alicia, trembling on the floor and knelt down in front of her. He reached out to her and she withdrew quickly, scooting back and away from him.

"Alicia," he spoke, softly and gently. "It's over. We're getting out of here. I'll take you home now. Please, try not to be afraid."

He reached out to her again. This time she did not retreat, but she would not take his hand. Kevin understood, and couldn't really blame her. What she had been through the past thirty–four hours was more than anyone could be expected to endure and not be at, or beyond, their breaking point.

"Alicia, listen. I'm going to go up that ladder. I'll wait for you up there. When you are ready, come up and we'll go home, I promise. I truly mean you no more harm."

He smiled at her, and took the folded blanket from Sam's bed, placing it over Mary's body, hiding her from Alicia's view. He then turned to Wiley, who was sitting against the wall, and laid him gently on his back.

"Take care, Wiley," he spoke, through swelling tears. "*Geronimo,* buddy."

Kevin walked slowly past Alicia, and down into Sam's storage area. He came back shortly with another blanket, and covered Wiley. Still stooping by Wiley's side, he turned to face Alicia and smiled once again. He then climbed the ladder, not looking upon Sam again, and waited in the cavern for Alicia to collect herself.

Kevin sat on the ground a few feet from the opening, and patiently awaited Alicia. He knew she had some serious issues to come to terms with before she would emerge, and it was a good twenty minutes before she climbed out over the top of the ladder and stood erect before him. Kevin smiled at her, but she did not return the favor. She simply looked at him with no expression at all, as two tears formed and ran down over her cheeks, falling to the dust below. In her sorrow, her brown eyes looked twice the size he had remembered.

Kevin walked toward the ladder, Alicia stepping away, and pulled it from the hole. He turned to Alicia and said, "Come on, Alicia, let's go home." He began walking toward the front of the cavern. He listened, and heard Alicia's footsteps falling behind him. He smiled and slightly picked up the pace.

By the time they reached the exit tunnel, Alicia seemed to believe that he intended to help, rather than harm her. She still didn't speak, but she seemed to have relaxed a little, and when he attempted to help her up the ladder, she did not refuse his help. They traversed the tunnel and he helped her descend the ladder into the slit, and they proceeded single file through the course of the slit and saw daylight ahead.

When they reached a point where there was enough light to see each other, Kevin turned about and smiled at Alicia. "Daylight!" he said, jubilantly. Alicia looked past him at the light coming through the opening to the outside world. She looked back at Kevin, and she smiled back at him. It was a small wisp of a smile, and unsure, but it was a smile. Kevin felt part of that new weight lifted from him.

Kevin faced the opening, once again, and walked toward Alicia's freedom. Freedom for him was no longer a reality. He would be free, he hoped, to help Alicia out of this valley, but having accomplished that he knew what lay ahead for him was anything *but* freedom. He accepted that as the justice that was now due Sam and the group from Reedmore, led by a man on more than a mere field trip. He *knew* that now.

How ironic, he thought, as he approached the daylight, *that two people could set out to avenge a friend and in trying to preserve their own freedom, had became the architects of the same injustices they had sought to rectify.*

They exited the slit and their smiles quickly faded as a blast of arctic cold air greeted them. There was snow everywhere, and it was deep. Kevin guided Alicia back into the slit and back to where the air warmed once again. "Damn! Where the hell did that come from!" he yelled. But he *knew* where it had come from. He had just refused to believe it until he actually saw it for himself. It was Sam's justice, and what he and Wiley had set in motion could not now be stopped. Alicia would now pay for being Mary's shadow, just as surely as he would now pay for being Wiley's. He understood that now, and he was powerless to change it.

At Kevin's outburst, Alicia had drawn away from him again.

"I'm sorry, Alicia, I'm sorry. I didn't mean to scare you," he pleaded.

Alicia nodded as if she understood.

"It's just that we can't stay here and starve, and getting home through that storm is going to be extremely hard, maybe even impossible."

Alicia opened her mouth, but nothing came out. Then on second try, "I want to go home, Kevin. That's all I want to do; go home," she said, in a pathetically small voice.

"Do you realize how cold it is out there, and how hard it will be walking in that snow?" he asked her.

"I don't care, Kevin. I don't want to stay here. I can't. I want to go home," she replied, with a little more force than before. "I want to go home and see my mom and dad and Billy–and Karl."

"Okay, Alicia, if we are going—Ah–Who's Karl, Alicia?" he asked, realizing that she had no brother named Karl.

Karl Deutsch, your friend, Karl," she answered.

"Karl Deutsch? You know Karl? How?" he asked, confused over her bringing Karl up.

"He's my boyfriend, Kevin," she answered, sheepishly.

"Since when?"

"Since June, but we've known each other a lot longer," she replied, smiling at that thought.

"Karl was home in June? I didn't know that, and I didn't know you knew him at all."

"He was here for two weeks, Kevin, but he spent all his time with me, except for his time with his parents," she explained.

"Damn!" Kevin shouted. "Sorry, Alicia, but damned if I knew that."

Kevin began thinking about his friend and what he had now done to him. *"God, if I don't get her out of here okay, that's another person's life I have screwed up! Damn–it to Hell!"* Kevin looked at the ground, and then at Alicia, smiling at her and wiping a tear from her cheek.

"Okay, like I started to say before, if we are going to try to get out of here, we have to give ourselves every chance. You wait here, in the warmth of the tunnel, while I go back for some things we'll need," Kevin instructed.

He could tell she didn't like the idea of staying there alone, but he believed she understood the importance of what he was saying, and she agreed. Kevin went back into the cave, and once in the main chamber he ran back to where he and Wiley had slept and began cutting on their mummy bags with his hunting knife. When he had finished he had created two pullover coats by cutting off the ends and fashioning armholes in the bags. He and Wiley each had a sock hat in their pack, which they had used for sleeping on chilly nights, so he retrieved them.

There was nothing else of use for the problem that faced Alicia and him, so he put on his "coat", drawing the tie strings tightly around his neck, and rolling Alicia's tightly under his arm, started back to join her.

On his way back, Kevin wrestled with the choice of cutting straight across the forest to the saddle, the shorter route, or following the curvature of the cliff to their destination. There were pros and cons to either choice.

The cliff route provided sure guidance, and no chance of getting lost, but it was longer. The forest route was shorter and would mean less time in this bitter cold, if they didn't get lost. The forest route would also have shallower snow; much of what fell being still in the boughs of the trees, and less drifts, the trees acting as windbreaks. That would mean less fatigue as well as less time in the cold.

When he returned to the opening, he found that Alicia had already made his decision for him. He had been away from Alicia for nearly thirty minutes, but he had no idea how long she had been gone. Kevin ran from the cave and saw the line of Alicia's boot prints headed straight into the forest.

God! Why didn't she wait! She can't last an hour out here in what she's wearing!

Immediately, he began following her tracks across the open expanse between the forest and the cliffs, and then into the forest. She was drawing a fairly straight line in the snow and her prints were evenly spaced; so far she was okay. Kevin continued in the trail left for him by Alicia. A half hour passed before he began to notice her steps had grown smaller, and each planting of her foot was now preceded by a drag mark in the snow. She was weakening, succumbing to the cold. He plowed on, trying to pick up his speed.

Another fifteen minutes had passed and Alicia's trail was now curving to the east, the drag marks more pronounced. She was starting a *death circle*, her orientation lost to the frigid air. He tried to run, but it was pointless as the snow was far too deep. Then, as he looked up from her tracks, he saw her delicate form lying twenty yards ahead, on the snow.

Kevin rushed to her side as fast as the deepening snow would allow, and dropped to his knees beside her. He tried desperately to revive her, but she lay there completely unresponsive. He felt for a pulse and felt the gentle beat of her weakening heart beneath his fingertips.

Thank God! he thought, and began pulling her makeshift coat over her stiffening body, and fitted Wiley's sock cap over her head. He scrambled about like a man gone mad, digging into the snow, collecting firewood and tinder and hoping for a fire starter as well. He felt blessed as he came up with the sappy pine knot he was hoping for.

He wasted no time in constructing and lighting his fire, and when the blaze had materialized and had taken hold, he went to bring Alicia to it, placing her as close to the blaze as he could. He sat down on the snow beside her and rubbed her hands, trying to restore the circulation to them. They were so cold and blue.

He began to weep, and the tears froze to his cheeks before ever finishing their course. It was then that he realized just how cold it really was. He sat there rubbing Alicia's frozen fingers until the fire began to die down.

More wood, I need more wood, he realized, and he started to stand. As he tried to rise he noticed that Alicia's body had become rigid, her arm fairly refusing to move. He felt again for a pulse as more tears started, then froze on his face. He came to his feet and kicked snow over the dying fire, screaming, *"God damn you Sam Elliott! God damn you to Hell!"*

He slowly gained control of himself and picked Alicia up from the snow, placing her lifeless body across his shoulders. He looked around the forest, which looked different than it had on the way in, and he began to walk. With its blanket of new fallen snow the forest had changed and Kevin had to try very hard not to become disoriented. There were no stars or moon or sun to navigate by. There was just snow, falling randomly from a dark gray sky.

He had traveled perhaps only a half–mile, when he began to notice the cold seeping through the openings in his contrived coat. His face already stung with the cold and frozen tears, and his ungloved hands were stiff. His peach fuzz mustache was crusted with frost from his breath, and each inhalation stung like sucking up bees.

The hours passed and the snow fell. If there could be a blessing in it all, it was that the temperature seemed to have risen slightly. Kevin thought about that, and realized that his body was just numbing to it. It was no warmer, just more deceivingly cold. He plodded on, Alicia's weight, the snow, and the cold slowly wearing him down.

When he thought he could not possibly take another step, he broke from the forest and saw the saddle before him. He turned his face to Alicia's, and pointed to it, but she did not respond.

"Alicia, are you doing all right?" he questioned.

Alicia did not answer and Kevin did not notice.

"Alicia, listen carefully. This is the saddle. We make it to the top of this and over the other side, and we're home free. It's easy going after that, down hill all the way. Okay?"

While he awaited her response he reflected on what still needed to be accomplished.

It was a long way up to the top, and then there was the escarpment to go down, in all this snow. If somehow they made it, it was no warmer over on the other side, and there were still eight miles to go, to reach his car. He knew his car would be hopelessly stuck in the snow, but if it started, there would be warmth, eventually, and for as long as the gas held out.

"Okay then, let's go home," he whispered.

The climb up the saddle was grueling. It had been hard before, but in this snow and cold, carrying Alicia, it was nearly unbearable. He was now close enough to the top to actually believe that he might make it. His mind was playing tricks on him though, as he found himself doing ridiculous things like counting his steps, backwards to the top—49, 48, 47, 46—and so on. It had to be the cold; there was no other explanation, but he wasn't looking for one. It all seemed perfectly normal to him as the cold slowed his mind and chilled his brain.

As he came to within fifty feet of the top, he slipped and fell forward, dropping Alicia behind him as he let go to break his fall. As he struggled to regain his feet he saw that Alicia had begun sliding down the steep grade, back into the bowl.

"Alicia!" he yelled. "Alicia!"

"Alicia," he whispered, and started back down to help her.

CHAPTER 55

*A*l was missing from his sleeping bag when Stan awoke in their tent Tuesday morning. It was still dark. He looked at his watch to discover it *was* morning, just a little before six. He pulled on his boots, lacing them snugly and crawled outside to find Al standing and staring at the star strewn sky above.

Still damn cold out here, he thought to himself, trying to shake it off.

"Morning, Al," he said, through a stifled yawn.

"Morning, Stan. Looks like we'll have our chopper earlier than expected. The front's already moved through."

Stan looked up to the Milky Way, glimmering in a sparkling band across the black morning sky.

"Cleared up nicely. Do you think it will warm up any though?" Stan asked, hoping for an affirmative reply.

"Already has, Stan. According to my thermometer, it was eighteen below when we went to bed last night I just checked again, and it's warmed up all the way to five below now. The weather shifted back to westerly early after we bedded down. See–there's very little new snow on the campstools and equipment. It should turn out to be a good day for our search."

The rest of the men were beginning to stir, and the encampment came to life with activity. Everyone to a man was checking gear and preparing for the efforts that lay ahead. Daybreak was upon them and at sunrise they would fan out and begin combing the Oriel Peak area.

The radio frequency that Stan and the chopper pilot had agreed upon was dialed into each two–man group's walkie–talkie, as they gathered for a last minute consultation. It was Al's party, so he addressed the gathered men.

"Gentlemen. We have two innocent girls up there that are in need of our help. We believe they were abducted by two boys, Kevin Reynolds and Wiley Coates, who were acting out of revenge for the unfortunate death of a friend of theirs. They believe the two girls, Mary and Alicia, are responsible for that death. That's what this is all about. I'd like not to have to hurt the boys, but our primary mission is to save the girls. Is that clear to everyone?"

Everyone nodded, or spoke, implying that it was.

"Sheriff, are these boys armed?" asked one trooper.

"Yes, they are armed. Whether or not they would fire upon any of us is not known. Two days ago I would have bet not, but who knows how desperate they will feel if confronted? Just be careful and avoid, if you can, putting those little girls in any further jeopardy. Are there any other questions or concerns before we get started?" Al asked, receiving no further replies.

"Okay then–let's break up into our search groups and get started. Let's find those little girls!" Al implored, rooting them on.

The group split up into twelve pairs, and spread out into the forest. The plan was to work upward from a wide base, with each of the groups ascending toward and converging upon the base of the escarpment. The two life squad units would go straight up to the base, with their stretchers and equipment, by the most direct route. They would rendezvous there, and if they needed to go higher, would climb the escarpment, splitting into six groups of four men each. Four groups would descend into Blind Valley and fan out, while the other two would circumvent it on either side, following the lip of the bowl to the upper portion of Oriel Peak, then, go up again. The life squad units would wait at the top of the escarpment, ready to move in any of the three directions, if the need arose.

So the search was laid out, and scarcely an hour into it Al stopped and listened to the sound of an approaching helicopter.

"That's our boy!" he exclaimed to Stan, thankful that the weather report had been wrong. "That will give us three extra hours of his time, if we need it."

The chopper circled overhead and Al put his walkie–talkie to his mouth.

"Ground One to Air One," he broadcast. "Good to see you here so bright and early. Over."

"Air One to Ground One," came the reply. "Good to be here, Sheriff. I'll get up to the top now and have a look around. Over and out."

With that, the chopper made a sweeping banked turn and flew toward the summit of Oriel Peak.

The search continued throughout the morning, the groups slowly working their way toward the escarpment. Al and Stan could hear the steady drone of the helicopter in the distance above them, as they followed the central route directly to the top, the medics following along behind them. The going was rough and tedious, taking three quarters of an hour to cover each mile. The weather pattern had definitely changed from the polar exposure to a warmer, more westerly pattern. The temperature had risen throughout the day to merely freezing, warm by comparison to the previous night.

Stan and Al were the first to reach the base of the escarpment, arriving at three thirty in the afternoon. They had not seen any tracks, or other signs of the boys, since finding Kevin's car. Al hadn't really expected to with all the new snow that had fallen. This blanket of white would undoubtedly have covered up any trace of their passing. What he had hoped for, of course, was to have come across them camped out on the mountainside, but that had not happened.

The chopper had returned to its base for refueling a short time ago and would return soon, but for now there was an eerie silence on the mountain. Al thought about his search plan as he looked up the escarpment. Perhaps, now that he had seen it first hand, that part of the plan had been too hastily decided upon.

How in the heck would the boys get Mary and Alicia up there, he wondered?—*Even without all this snow it would be extremely difficult, if not impossible!*

He shared this thought with Stan, who agreed that it looked doubtful.

The life squad medics arrived five minutes behind Al and Stan and sat down on snow–covered rocks to await the rest of the group. It was a rest they all needed, badly.

The deep snow had not only slowed their progress more than Al had anticipated, but he had not even considered the additional fatigue it would cause among them. He thought about their later–than–expected arrival to this point, and what to do about it. Their progress had been slowed greatly as the mountain had grown steeper and they had become more fatigued. There was little time left before nightfall, certainly not enough to press onward or up the escarpment.

His biggest fear was that they would have to return to their encampment for shelter and start again in the morning, making this same climb all over again. They could start earlier tomorrow, before dawn, and they could all come up the direct central route to save as much time as possible. They could then fan out around the valley, searching the side slopes of Oriel Peak, saving the escarpment as their last resort.

Whatever he decided to do he needed to decide quickly, as there was not even enough daylight remaining to get all the way back to camp.

What a damn waste of precious time!

As Al sat thinking about his limited choices, he heard the engine of the chopper in the distance. He listened for a moment, and his face brightened.

"Ground One to Air One, come in, Air One," he signaled. "Over."

"This is Air One, go ahead. Over."

"Welcome back, Air One. We are right below the escarpment leading into Blind Valley. Can you come over this way and see if you can find a place to put down? Over."

"I'll take a look, Sheriff. I'll be there in two. Over and out."

Al heard the chopper coming closer, and then it appeared in the sky to his left. It circled the area, hovering for a moment before Al's radio crackled.

"Air One to Ground One, come in. Over."

"Go ahead, Air One," Al responded. "Over."

"I'm coming in, Sheriff. There's a nice little flat spot about one hundred yards to your west. What's on your mind? Over."

"Two things, Air One. First, can you pick up one of the men and fly down to the access road and find a place to land down there? Over."

"Roger that. What's the other thing? Over."

"Would the two of you be able to pick up our tents and sleeping gear and fly it back up here to us? Can you carry that much? Over."

Al was praying he could.

"I think so, Sheriff. We'll sure give it a try. Over and out."

The pilot brought his bird down gently on the snow, the runners sinking in until it was resting neatly on it belly. Al had already started in that direction and arrived shortly after touchdown.

"Thanks, Air—What's your real name, anyway?" Al asked.

"Al, sir. Just like yours. Al Quatrain," he answered, showing a large, toothy smile. He was a handsome kid of about twenty–five years.

"Well, Al Quatrain. I'm sending Stan along with you to help load it all up. I sure do thank you."

"No problem. We'll be back before you know it."

Stan boarded the whirlybird and Al Quatrain lifted her gently out of the snow. The chopper rotated once, dipped its nose and flew off toward the encampment. When Al returned to the base of the cliff the other search groups were beginning to arrive. He waited until they had all come in and then gathered them for an announcement.

"Gentlemen. Now that we are all here I'd like to fill you in on something. We are fast running out of daylight and rather than return to base camp I am having the chopper pilot fly our equipment up here. The idea is to save valuable time. My though is to camp up here tonight and get an early start around both sides of the mountain, in the morning. If there is anyone here who wants to call it quits right now, you are free to return home. You've done your part and it's greatly appreciated. That's all I have for now," Al finished.

The men looked among themselves, discussing it a bit, and became silent. One of the troopers addressed Al, saying, "We're all staying, Sheriff. It sounds like a good move and we aren't ready to give up on those little girls just yet."

Al smiled broadly and thanked them all. They settled into the snow and relaxed, awaiting the chopper's return.

Al's thoughts went back to the planning for Wednesday morning. The escarpment looked forbidding, too forbidding. He simply could not imagine the boys getting those girls up there. Perhaps climbing that escarpment in the morning would be like barking up the wrong tree. Maybe they should split into two large groups and fan out, one group going east and the other west, circumnavigating the valley and the crest of Oriel Peak.

But where in sam hill were those boys heading in going around this mountain? There's nothing up here!

Al pulled out his map. He studied it carefully, concentrating on their current elevation and circling the peak with his finger. He wondered what kind of shelter might be had for four people for any length of time.

Perhaps a cave? But there are none marked on here. Perhaps the boys knew of a mine? But there have never been any mining operations back here, although a prospector might have dug a shaft out at some time in the past. Look for crossed 'picks and shovels', he thought. But there were none.

Al was stumped. The boys were up here someplace, their car bore that out, but where in the hell could they be? He literally, hadn't a clue.

Al Quatrain was true to his word, settling down nearby in under an hour. Al and several of the men went to meet him and began unloading their gear.

"Sheriff, I'm going to make use of what little light I have left and have another look around up there. Then I'll head back to base and return bright and early. I'd stay up here with you boys, but if I leave this bird parked on the snow all night, and she lists, I'll be in a world of hurt," he explained.

"Understood, Al said. We'll see you in the morning then, and once again, thanks for all you're doing. Have a safe trip home."

The chopper lifted from the snow as Al, Stan, and the rest of the men carried the gear back to where they would set up camp at the base of the escarpment. Al looked up and waved at the chopper as it disappeared over the top.

Everybody went to work setting up camp, cutting wood, talking about their trip up here, and what tomorrow might hold. None of the troopers or county deputies had ever been up in this part of the mountains and they found it quite fascinating, comparing it to this place and that, they had been before. They were happy and glad to be there, but in the backs of their minds, they couldn't forget *why* they were there.

Al began helping Stan lay out their tent, but just as they got started, his radio began to crackle. He picked it up, answering, "This is Ground One, go ahead. Over."

He heard nothing but static.

"This is Ground One–Sheriff Al Dramico, go ahead. Over."

"Sheriff, is that you?" a voice asked, so distorted that Al could barely make it out.

"Yes, this is Sheriff Dramico. Who am I talking to? Over."

"Sheriff, it's me, Becky!" the voice said, still quite garbled.

"Becky? Did you say, Becky?" Over.

This time the response was nothing but static, completely indiscernible.

"Becky. If that's you and you can hear me, switch to channel 'B'. I repeat, switch to channel 'B'. Over."

Al immediately switched his radio to channel "B" and listened anxiously. Becky would not be calling him up here unless there was something very important she had to tell him.

"Sheriff? Can you hear me now?" Becky's voice came through, loud and clear.

"Yes, Becky, go ahead. I hear you fine now. Over."

"Sheriff. I've been trying to reach you all afternoon! I received word from the Reedmore PD that they are missing a college professor and five students. They were due back Sunday night but they never returned. Uh–Over."

"What's that got to do with us, Becky?" Al asked. "Over."

"Ordinarily nothing, but since they were on a geology field trip to Blind Valley, the Reedmore PD wanted to give you a heads up to be on the lookout for them. When they called the state police for assistance, they were told all of their available men were already up in that area. They suggested that Reedmore call you since you were in charge of the operation up there. Over."

"We've got six more people up here? Missing? Over."

"That's right, Sheriff. Six more! Over."

"Why the hell did they wait until Tuesday to report them missing? Over."

"I don't know, Sheriff, they didn't say, but they have a map of where the professor always camps when he goes there. They are driving it over to you. Over."

"They'll take hours getting it up here! Call them back and ask them to radio me with some details from their map. Tell them to use this frequency. Over and out."

Al turned to Stan who had been listening, his jaw on his chest, and said, "Can you believe this? Now we've got six more people to find up here! Somewhere! Do you believe this?"

Stan just stared at Al and shrugged his shoulders.

"Come on, Stan, let's get this tent pitched," Al said, shaking his head.

They were just putting the first pole in when the radio blared again.

"This is Reedmore Police Vehicle Three, calling Sheriff Dramico. Come in, Sheriff. This is Patrolman Simpson. Over."

"Yes, Simpson, this is Al Dramico. What can you tell me from that map you have? Over."

"Well, it's a pretty well drawn map, to scale and all. Professor Harrison's campsite should be located in Blind Valley, in the northwest quadrant, so to speak. It appears to be about five hundred yards in from the middle of the bend in the northwest wall of the canyon, on a forty–five degree angle into the forest. Does that help? Over."

"Hold on."

Al quickly took a look at his map and saw immediately what Simpson was referring to.

"Yes, that helps a lot. I see exactly where you are talking about on my map. We'll have a look. You can continue with that map to our base camp. If we need it, I'll have the chopper pilot fly down and get it from you. Over and out."

"Stan, there's no way in hell we can get into there before dark," Al said. That's clear over on the other side of the valley—Unless, Al could fly a few of the men over there and drop them in somehow, maybe on ropes or something like that. Hell, maybe he's even got room to land over there."

"Air One, come in. Over."

"Go ahead, Sheriff."

"Al, is there any place for you to land that bird over in the northwest section of the valley? Over."

"Hold on," Al said, as he swung the chopper in that direction, and dropped back down into the valley.

"Sheriff?"

"Go ahead, Air One, I'm here. Over."

"There's plenty of room over here between the cliff and the forest. Over."

"How many men can you carry? Over."

"Three."

"Then can you come back over here and pick up three of the men and put them down in that northwest curve of the valley wall? Over."

"On my way. Over and out."

Al asked for volunteers for this new search, because it probably meant sleeping in Blind Valley for the night. There was light enough for them to begin their search over there, but probably not enough time left to bring them back out before dark.

There was no lack of volunteers, so Al picked three men and briefed them on what Patrolman Simpson had told him over the radio. Al Quatrain had returned and had set his helicopter down in the same spot in the snow as before. The three volunteers gathered their sleeping bags and tents and boarded the awaiting chopper.

Al and Stan went back to erecting their tent for the third time and finally completed the task. Al asked Stan to come in and help him study the map for anything he may have overlooked in the way of shelter for the kids to use. They spread the map out on the floor and began going over it, inch by inch, looking for anything that might be a likely, or not so likely place for the kids to hide out.

Al's radio began to crackle again.

"Hello, this is Ground One. Is anybody there?" he queried. "Over."
The radio continued to crackle and a voice came through the static.

"Ground One, do you read me? This is Air One. Over."

"Yes, Air One, go ahead. You're all broken up. Over."

"I think that's because I'm below you on the other side of the escarpment, down in the valley. I dropped your boys off in the northwest corner and decided to circle the perimeter of the valley one last time. Good thing I did, because I've got two bodies below me here. Over."

"Two bodies? Repeat Air One. Over."

"Roger that. Two bodies. Can't tell much from here. I can't put down between the trees and the slope, not enough room, and the slope is too steep to land on. They are near the bottom of the hill directly over the top from your location, lying in the snow. No movement. Over."

"Can you make out anything about them, male or female? Over."

"No, sir. All bundled up with hats. I can't tell. I'll hover here as long as I can to spot them for you. Suggest you hurry. Over."

"We are on our way, Air One. Good job, Al! Over and out."

The others heard the conversation and were already preparing to ascend the escarpment. There was a hubbub of activity, with men darting here and darting there, gathering what they would need.

Al barked out some commands.

"Stan and I are going up first. I want the medics right behind us, followed by the rest of you!"

There was only one route up, that looked feasible, and Al started climbing, followed closely by Stan. They had climbed only ten or fifteen feet before they realized just how difficult and treacherous this was going to be. One of the medics, who had started up just to their left, suddenly fell. As he slid back down the cliff, grappling for a handhold, he suddenly stopped sliding and screamed to Al, "A rope! Sheriff, a rope!"

He was holding in his hand, a knotted piece of rope, about three feet long, the other end of which disappeared into the snow. He pulled himself to his feet and gave the rope a swift snap, like whipping a bullwhip, and fifteen more feet erupted from the snow.

Al moved laterally toward the exposed rope and picked it up some fifteen feet above the medic, giving it another snap. More footage exploded from the snow and Al tugged on it hard. It held. He looked down and yelled, "Everybody! This way!" and began making good progress up the cliff, hand over hand, step by step.

As Al neared the crest he began to hear the chopper engine, distant and muffled. Negotiating the last few feet he stood atop the escarpment looking down into Blind Valley. He was aghast. He had never been here before and it was breathtaking. He heard the chopper *below* him and looked toward the sound. It was hovering near the bottom of the long slope down into the valley.

"Air One, this is Ground One. We have your location. Over."

"Hello, Sheriff. I am right above the bodies. There has been no movement, sir." Over."

"Is there *anywhere* over here for you to put down? Over."

"No, sir, I checked. Not here. Best I can do is go back over and put down where I did before. If you can get them over there, I can fly them out—but it doesn't look to me like there's going to be any hurry. Over."

"Roger that, Air One. We have your ground location marked. You can go on over and take a breather. I'll let you know if we'll be coming over in a hurry, or not. Over and out."

The chopper rose straight up until it had climbed above their heads then dipped its nose and disappeared over the top of the saddle.

During their conversation, Al and the rest of the party had not stopped walking down the slope. Going down was a whole lot easier than coming up had been and they were making good time. It still took over half an hour to reach the bodies near the bottom. As Al approached them he noticed the sleeping bag coats.

They hadn't figured on this weather either, he thought, studying their improvised outerwear. He circled around to where he could get a look at their faces.

"Damn, Stan. It's Kevin and Alicia," he said, in a low, almost disappointed tone.

They were huddled together, locked in each other's arms, looking into each other's faces. Al motioned for the medics to move in, as he stepped away and turned to Stan.

"Damn shame. It almost looks like they were friends trying to help each other stay warm. Damn shame, Stan," Al said, lowering his head and staring at the snow at his feet.

"Yes, sir, it sure is," replied Stan.

The medics went to work checking the bodies. Their somber silence was broken when one of the attending medics yelled to Al, "Sheriff! I've got a pulse on the boy! It's weak, almost nothing, but it's a pulse!"

Al turned so fast he nearly fell down.

"A pulse? On the boy? What about the girl?" he asked, impatiently.

"No, sir, she's been gone for hours. Frozen solid, I'm afraid."

Al stared at Kevin and thought, *And he stayed with her anyway? It looks like he was trying to take her home. But if she died hours ago, why didn't he keep going?*

Al could read sign and he noticed the sliding marks in the snow leading to Alicia's body, *and* he also noticed Kevin's tracks coming *down* the saddle to her. He'd follow Kevin's tracks back up on the way out and try to determine what had happened.

"Air One, this is Ground One. Come in. Over."

"This is Air One, go ahead, Sheriff. Over."

"Air One–keep those engines warm! We will, I repeat–we will be coming over the top in a hurry! Over and out."

CHAPTER 56

The rescue party managed to get Kevin over the top and back down to the awaiting chopper. Al Quatrain flew Kevin out, Stan accompanying him, to Bennett Memorial Hospital. The rest of the search party stayed behind to follow the original plan, in hope of locating Wiley and Mary on Wednesday.

Stan was instructed to stay with Kevin at the hospital in the event Kevin regained consciousness and could be of help with locating them. Kevin was suffering with severe hypothermia, and he was comatose. The attending specialist at the ER gave him barely a 20–80 chance at survival. He did not think he would regain consciousness, before passing away.

Al and his search team bedded down for the night at the foot of the escarpment. There had been no word from the three–man team Al Quatrain had deployed in the northwest corner of the bowl, and Al assumed that they, too, had bedded down for the night and would also resume their search in the morning.

Finding Kevin and Alicia *in the valley* had changed Al's planning once again. He was now going to concentrate all efforts in Blind Valley. He had backtracked Kevin's solitary tracks to within fifty feet of the crest of the saddle. He had seen where Kevin fell, dropping Alicia, who had slid back down the steep grade to the bottom of the saddle. What amazed him completely was that Kevin had gone back down for her and then *stayed with her*. Knowing what he knew of the relationship between the two, it just didn't make any sense at all.

As Tuesday night broke into Wednesday morning, Al's team was scaling the escarpment once more. They used the rope hold provided them by either the professor or the boys, Al wasn't sure which, but was glad to have it either way. He was puzzled by the fact that they had not seen the professor's vehicle anywhere along the access road, and was wondering if perhaps the group from Reedmore had already left by the time they had arrived Monday afternoon.

Maybe they aren't even up here anymore, he thought as he climbed. *Maybe they left Sunday, as planned, ahead of the storm and ran into trouble on their way home.*

He could only hope. He never gave a thought to the small logging road, marked four–wheel drive only, he and Stan had found on his map and checked out earlier.

Al crested the summit of the escarpment and looked down into Blind Valley, thinking, *That's a lot of valley to search!* He gathered the men around him, as they each arrived at the top, and held a meeting. He laid out his plan to them for searching the valley.

"Okay, men. We have three men already in the northwest corner of the valley now. They have their particular goal of finding the professor's campsite and checking it out. Our principal goal is to locate Wiley Coates and Mary Clemmons, but we will also keep a sharp eye out for the Reedmore group as well. I have my doubts that they are still up here, but we won't discount that possibility. My initial plan is to try to backtrack Kevin Reynolds through the forest to wherever he came from. Maybe that will lead us to the other two. Any questions?"

"Let's divide up into three groups. I'll lead one group down following Kevin's tracks and the other two groups will go east and west of us. The destination of the two lateral groups will be the north wall of the valley. My group will go wherever the tracks lead us. Watch the time and gauge your progress. We want to all meet back here in time to get back down to camp by dark. If there are no questions, let's move out."

Al had thought about moving their new base camp to within the valley to avoid having to scale the escarpment each day, but if the weather took another turn for the worse, he reasoned, they didn't want to become trapped in there.

The three groups began the long descent into Blind Valley and eventually disappeared from each other's view in the forest. Once again, the medical personnel followed along behind Al and his group.

Kevin's tracks were quite clear and easily followed. There was just the one set of tracks, indicating that Kevin had been carrying Alicia for quite some distance. They followed the staggered tracks through the forest of short pines for quite some time; still there was just the one set of tracks.

Al was growing more impressed and amazed at Kevin's apparent determination to carry Alicia out of this place. He couldn't help but wonder, given the past history of the two, what could have happened to cause Kevin to be so driven in such an unlikely endeavor. Maybe Kevin's tracks would lead him to the answer. He listened and heard the faint sound of Al Quatrain's helicopter, off to the west.

Good, he thought! *Al's back.*

They had traveled for nearly two hours, slowly following Kevin's tracks deeper and deeper into the forest, until they came upon the remnants of a campfire. Al studied the scene laid out in the snow before him. He could see where two people had arrived, one following along behind the other. One person had dropped to the snow, the other kneeling beside the fallen one. Kevin, he assumed had been the active one, then going about gathering the ingredients for a fire. Al could see where Kevin had picked up Alicia and carried her to the fire in an attempt to revive her. Apparently it hadn't been enough, as he saw that Kevin had carried here away from there to where they had found them.

Al could only imagine what had led to this point, but perhaps he would find his answers at the beginning of Kevin's trail. He led the men in the direction from whence Kevin and Alicia had come. The radio began to crackle.

"This is Ground One, go ahead. Over."

"Sheriff, this is Ground Two. Over."

"Yes, Ground two, how was your night in the woods? Over."

"Fine, Sheriff. We have located your professor's camp and, I believe, your professor. Over."

"Well, what the hell has he got to say for himself? Over."

"Not much, Sheriff, he's dead, murdered by gunshot! Him and three of his students! They've been dead for quite some time, sir, frozen solid and completely buried in the snow! Over."

"*Three* students! What about the other two? Over."

"No sign of anybody else. We've been digging around for them throughout the whole camp. I'm pretty sure they're not here, sir. One more thing, Sheriff. One of the students had been covered with pine limbs before the snow came, almost as if he had been buried. None of the others were done that way. Over."

"Okay, Ground Two keep looking and prepare the ones you've found for removal. Over and out."

"Damn!" Al yelled into the emptiness of the forest.

"*Damn...*" echoed back at him.

He thought about what he was now presented with.

Now, I've got five dead, four of them murdered, four missing, two of which I can probably assume are also dead, a captive girl and a murderer, or two murderers, one of which is still on the loose, or dead! On top of all that, one of the killers takes the time to cover up one of the bodies, but not all of them! Damn! What a frickin' mess!

The men had all heard the conversation and completely understood the frustration Al was feeling. Al called them all together and told them that they would continue to backtrack Kevin and Alicia and with any luck, the trail would lead them to Wiley and Mary.

Everyone shook their heads in agreement and the Ground One party moved out into the tracks left for them and heading in the direction of the west by northwest wall of the canyon. The radio crackled again as Al had taken his fifth step in that direction.

"Ground One, go ahead. Over"

"Sheriff, this is Air One. We've got a problem, Al! Over."

"Go ahead, Air One, what's the problem? Over."

"We've got a northwester moving in fast! Heavy snows predicted for the higher elevations. I'm going in to pick up Ground Two right now, I've already radioed them and they are in route to our rendezvous point. I've got to get them out of there and get this rig down before it hits. I suggest you get moving out as quickly as possible. The weather service says this is going to be a bad one! Over."

Al looked at the trail of tracks ahead of him and shook his head. That narrow ribbon in the snow was his only link to Mary's salvation and the capture of a probable murderer, Mr. Wiley Coates. He started to move forward, following the tracks as the light in the valley suddenly grew dim. He looked up to a boiling gray sky moving across the bowl to the southeast and recognized it for what it was.

He ordered the men to turn–about and they headed back the way they had come. Within minutes he saw the first snowflakes drifting down through the treetops and settling to the ground. He looked back over his shoulder to the trail that would be obscured within a few hours, and his heart sank within his chest.

"*I'm so sorry, Mary,*" he mumbled under his breath, which he could now see again for the first time today.

The search parties had made it back to their encampment before the worst of the storm hit, and hunkered in for the duration. When the storm had passed they spent five more days in Blind Valley, looking for any sign of Wiley or Mary. The thin thread of hope, which Al had been following in the snow the day before, was gone. They found no sign of Mary or Wiley. They found no sign of the other two students who were also somewhere within this Hell of a valley.

Al Quatrain had flown fresh provisions in daily to sustain them in their efforts, but all efforts had been in vain.

As the weather service was predicting even more abnormal winter weather for their area, the search was postponed until more normal conditions became available. They would probably have to wait until spring to retrieve the Reedmore Parties' bodies and look again for Mary and Wiley.

At the hospital in Bennett, Kevin hung in there, improving slightly, ever so slightly, with each passing day but remained unconscious and unable to help in their efforts. Finally, after two weeks in the hospital, the doctors declared Kevin out of danger, with stable vitals and a normal core temperature, but still he lay in a coma. That, the doctors had no way of knowing, would last how long. The only prediction they could make was, *"Maybe tomorrow, maybe next week, or perhaps he would remain this way forever!"* In short, it was in God's hands now; they had done all they could do.

Alicia's body, which had been retrieved before the last storm, was brought down from the mountain, and taken to Doc's for preparation. The family held a nice funeral for her and buried her at Glen Laurel in Mrs. Koppe's plot, something they had never dreamed would ever happen, when they had purchased it several years before. Her parents bought another plot to her side, so that one–day, she would rest permanently between her mother and father.

Karl came for Alicia's funeral, all the way from Arizona. He laid the first rose upon Alicia's casket and whispered a short prayer. He thought back to when they had first met, Alicia standing beneath a locust tree, and he on his new motorcycle. He had just turned seventeen and Alicia was thirteen. A group of young girls in the front yard of one of the girl's houses had flagged him down as he had passed them. They had all wanted a ride and he had been quick to gratify their requests.

One at a time he had driven them around the neighborhood until finally, all but one had ridden. She had been standing behind the rest of the girls under a locust tree, pretty and petite. He had informed her that it was her turn to ride and she had replied, "*No thanks. My mother wouldn't approve.*" He hadn't even learned her name when he had driven away, wondering if he would ever see her again, and if so, when? For some strange reason, he had not been able to stop thinking about her, and it had been that way ever since.

He thought about their private spot, their little valley, and the promises they had made one another there. He began to cry and had to turn away from her casket. He'd come visit again, he promised her. But it would be later, after the pain had subsided what little it might. It was a promise he would keep for the rest of his life. Twice a year, in June and September, there would always be a dozen fresh roses on her grave, signifying the *physical* duration of their new-found love. The emotional duration was perpetual.

Karl didn't bother to visit Kevin upon his arrival, his first inclination being to go to the hospital and finish the job that Oriel Peak had failed to do. His one–time friend had stolen his life–long dream, and all that was important to him. The urge to go snuff out what little life remained in Kevin had been great, but in the end he had thought better of it. After the funeral and a short visit with his parents, Karl had left for his deserts of Arizona, leaving behind a broken dream and a worthless one–time friend.

Eventually life returned to normal around Carver, except for the Reynolds, who made weekend trips to Bennett to visit Kevin at the Drake Convalescent Home.

Life remained unsettled for the Clemmons family also, not knowing what had become of their Mary. They assumed she was dead, but held out hope that she might be found alive, one day. "*Perhaps she wasn't even up there with Kevin and Alicia. Maybe they had split up and gone in different directions,*" they prayed. They grasped at any explanation that might bring them a slight ray of hope, or provide them with a reason to go on.

Calvin Coates took to hitting the bottle even harder than he had before. Mrs. Coates eventually left him for unknown parts, and Calvin was found the following February, on his sofa, his .44 Colt beside him, shot dead by his own hand.

Al Dramico finally retired and Stan was elected Carver City Sheriff. The community felt he had gained the experience needed to protect them in their daily lives, and besides, they all knew and liked him. He won several awards over the years that followed for his community service and police duties. His major accomplishment was the creation of the Carver/Greenville Youth Foundation; dedicated to helping the children of his valley understand and gain their full potential in life.

Al Quatrain went off to Viet Nam to help with the war effort. His services were sought after and highly appreciated. He served nearly a full tour before being shot down over Cambodia. He never came home to Montana.

Carson Whitley never spoke again to Buck Reynolds, nor did their wives ever speak again.

And Kevin Reynolds slept through it all. Months had turned into years and years into a decade. But in the eleventh year after his near death experience, he awoke.

The doctors agreed in unanimity that it was a medical impossibility. They agreed that it had to be something more than the damage he had received at the hands of the cold, which had kept him away so long. They had known since the end of the first year that he was no longer comatose, yet nothing that could be said or done ever achieved any response from Kevin. Their conclusion was that he had awakened from his coma into a catatonic state, a condition sometimes characterized as suspended animation. He was one hundred percent non–responsive to any stimuli.

He would eat, when spoon fed, and had held his body weight, which had surprised them all along. Upon becoming communicative, he was sharp and clear and seemed to be in possession of all his faculties. The consensus of opinion was that his catatonic state had been produced by something "horrible and beyond human endurance". That *was* what was written in the official record.

Stan was notified of Kevin's *resurrection* immediately and he paid Kevin a visit at Drake the next day. When he entered the room Kevin knew him right away and greeted him warmly.

"Put on a little weight, Stan?" he asked, smiling.

Stan looked down at his expanded middle and replied, "Guess so, Kevin. You know how it is. I got married a few years back and she feeds me well."

"Anybody I know?" Kevin asked.

"No, I doubt it. Her name is Karen and she's not from Carver."

They chatted for a short time and Stan eventually got around to the purpose of his visit, the whereabouts of Wiley Coates and Mary Clemmons. Kevin's reply took Stan completely by surprise. He had expected perhaps anything but what he heard.

"Wiley and Mary? How the heck should I know? The doctors tell me that I've been asleep for over ten years. They could be anywhere by now."

Putting it mildly, Stan was totally confused and pressed Kevin a little further.

"Weren't they up in Blind Valley with you and Alicia?" Stan probed, asking the question as casually as he knew how.

"Alicia Koppe? Why would I be up in Blind Valley with her? Come on, Stan, get real."

"But–*that is* where we found the two of you. That's why you are in here. *That* is why she is dead," Stan told him, his voice growing stern.

"Alicia, dead? How, Stan?" Kevin asked, seeming truly surprised.

"She froze to death in Blind Valley. We found her in *your* arms. Don't get cute with me, Kevin! I want to know what happened to Mary Clemmons! Her folks want to know what happened to her! What I need to know–from you–is whether or not Wiley and Mary were there, too? And either way, if you have any idea where we might look for them?"

Stan had grown quite angry at Kevin's charade, and it was showing.

"Stan!" Kevin shouted, "I have no idea what you are talking about! I went to bed one night in 1969 and woke up here in 1980! That's all I know! I lost ten years of my life," Kevin murmured, quieting down with his last statement. "And I have no idea why. Catatonia? What the *hell* is catatonia? Whatever the hell it is, it's sure no explanation for ten years gone, that's what I *do* know!"

It was obvious to Stan that Kevin was becoming very agitated, or at least he wanted Stan to think so. He wasn't really sure if Kevin was on the level with all this or whether he was just a damn good actor.

"Tell you what, Kevin. I'll give you some time to think about what I've said and I'll be back to see you in a few days. How's that sound?" Stan asked.

"That sounds fine to me Stan, but before you *come back* see if you can get a better explanation for *catatonia* than they gave me, okay?"

Stan stood and walked out of Kevin's room, turning down the hall toward the main entrance.

Mr. Kevin Reynolds, he thought. *I think we are just going to let a jury sort all this out.*

Sheriff Stan Phillips passed through the main entry doors of Drake and into the parking lot beyond.

Epilogue

"So that's it, Father. The jury didn't buy my amnesia act, so here I am. I've exhausted all of my appeals and I've received two stays. The new governor has already denied my request for another stay, so here I am. I've had twenty–one years to think about it since I woke up at Drake."

"Do you have any regrets, my Son?"

"Sure, Father. I've got regrets. I regret letting the girls go down into Sam's house. I regret being too tired to think about the Sharps being down there and I regret what happened to that group from Reedmore, especially Jason. I also regret shooting that professor before I found out what he meant to Sam. *That's* what set him against us! I've had time to think about it and I think it was Sam who showed Mary how to use that damn Sharps! She didn't know anything about guns. Do you think that's possible, Father?"

"Anything is possible, my Son, even that I suppose, although I don't believe the Church would agree to that reasoning."

Kevin didn't reply at first, but sat on his cot thinking about something distant before coming back to the conversation.

"I also wanted to get Alicia out of there alive. That really is the truth. Not just because of Karl, but because she deserved to live. Mary was one thing, but Alicia was just a puppet at the end of Mary's strings, a dumb puppy following along behind her, wagging her tail.

I realized that at the end and I tried, Father, I honestly tried to save her."

"Why did you stay with her on that mountain after you realized she had died?" the priest asked.

"I couldn't leave her there alone. I couldn't do it. She wasn't dead at first so I tried to keep her warm. I built her that fire, but it didn't help. I tried to get her out, but I was too exhausted and cold to carry her any further and it would have done no good. I could never have carried her down that escarpment alone. So I lay down beside her and tried to keep her warm. That's all I could do Father. She didn't die alone."

"But she was already gone at that point. What made you stay with her then knowing you would freeze as she had done?" he asked.

Kevin didn't know what the priest wanted to hear, so he decided to be honest in his reply.

"I don't know, Father. I just couldn't leave her alone up there. No other reason than that, I guess."

"That did show great compassion. Is there anything else you'd like to tell me?"

"Yes, Father. I'd like to be forgiven, but I can't be absolved, because I haven't repented for what I did to Mary. I can't. She killed my best friend; despite the circumstances, she killed Bryce. Then she killed Wiley, which I can understand, but I can't forgive her even that. The best I can do is to help her parents a little."

Kevin paused again as he took something from his pocket.

"Are her parents still living?" the priest asked.

"Her father is, maybe her mother, I'm not sure. One of the guards told me her dad is on the *guest* list, you know, a spectator for when they drop the pellets. I want you to give this to him, or have someone give it to him. It doesn't matter who."

Kevin held the folded paper out toward the priest.

"It's a map Father–to the cave. But you tell whoever goes in there to leave Sam and Wiley be. Wiley's folks are both gone anyway. And also ask them to put Sam's Sharps back in his arms. I didn't think to do that at the time. I wouldn't be giving you this map at all except that I thought Mary's dad might want to give her a Christian burial, that's all."

"Why now, my Son? Why now, after so many years, would you want her father to have this peace of mind? Is it in an effort to repent for having killed her?" the priest coached, hoping for an answer that would allow Kevin absolution.

"No, Father—It's because there's no time left…"

Kevin heard the electronic lock clack open and looked up through the bars to see Jesse. His uniform, usually all rumpled and a mess was clean and pressed. His hair, combed neatly, was quite a change from its usual scruff.

"Supper's here, Kevin," he said, smiling a small, self-conscious smile.

"What do you have there, Jesse?" Kevin asked, returning his smile.

"Two bacon cheeseburgers and a large fry—just like you ordered."

Kevin's smile sagged a little as he stared at Jesse with a disappointed look.

"Oh yea—I almost forgot," Jesse added. "And—a Chunky bar."

Jesse reached into his shirt pocket and tossed the Chunky to Kevin.

"Thanks, Jesse," Kevin said, smiling. "I'll save it for the governor's phone call—to celebrate."

About the Author

C.H. FOERTMEYER was born in Cincinnati, Ohio in 1949 and again lives there, where he divides his time between web authoring, writing, and a full–time job.

Formally educated at New Mexico State University, Mr. Foertmeyer had the opportunity to travel the Rocky Mountains and the New Mexico deserts extensively, gaining insight into these areas he writes about.

0-595-21686-2